GW00374706

Published by magnificent!
www.desburkinshaw.com

Paperback version ISBN 978-1-9160664-0-3
E-book version ISBN   978-1-9160664-1-0

Dedicated to the memory of Philip Kerr.
Bernie Gunther will live with me always.

Also, to the memory of my cousin, David Yea.

Chapter 1

Porter Norton's flat, Sylvester Path, Hackney
Sunday, 19th March 2017: 5.30pm

The girl he had killed followed him around the kitchen with yellow, accusing eyes. As usual. Stare all you want, Janine. Today I die too. Time for music, food and wine.

Porter Norton tidied a pile of 78rpm records, opened his final bottle of St Émilion, and pulled the filet from the fridge. "The condemned man always gets a final meal, eh?" He looked up, half expecting an answer from the girl in the framed newspaper cutting. *Foster Girl dies in House Fire.*

He trimmed the steak, tapping his knife to Artie Shaw's *Prosschai* crackling in the background. A quick slurp of wine. "My sister could wind up the Dalai Lama, but I'm glad I saw her today. I bought her a bun. She didn't eat it." Still. It was a time of goodbyes and goodbye tokens, so he toasted the girl in the photo. "Prost. Sorry for everything, Janine."

Earlier, Porter had bumped into his sister at the Gloucestershire Royal. Their gran was in week three of her coma. At 99, truthfully, there was little hope of Ida ever coming around. The siblings had agreed to a DNR, but had disagreed over whether to turn off life support. The default was to keep it on until nature or medicine resolved the issue for them.

So they staggered their visits. No-one, sick or otherwise, would benefit from hearing Porter and Cherry argue. Practiced since childhood, they were like rival tom cats staking their claim on an alley full of fishmonger bins.

Today, Porter had arrived first and sat at Ida's bedside. Safe in her silence, he spoke of his plan to die. "I'll never understand how you kept it together, Ida," he said, stroking her hand. "I don't have that kind of strength. When you first took us in, I hated you. Trying to replace my mum. Selfish little sod. Too late to call you 'mum' now."

His thumb stroked her hand in slow, circular motions. "Sorry I failed you. I killed that little girl. Tania left. I've been sacked. The press are out to get me. I'm gonna get struck off...it's so...physical, the pain."

He brushed fluff from his jacket. "We should swap places. Cherry would switch me off in a flash. Sorry, I can't quite bring myself to end your life support. I know - you'd think that was weak of me too." He squeezed, because he felt it was the right thing to do, but his eyes only moistened, not teared as he hoped.

Porter fumbled for a bedside tissue and found his fingers exploring a tub of sputum. Disgusted, he wiped his fingers on his trousers and shook his head. "I guess I've always known I was going the way of Dad and Granddad,"

He glanced at the heart-rate monitor. It was ticking along at 65bpm. He felt a yowl of protest and frustration coming on. He let go of her hand, linked his fingers together, pounded them against his heart and bayed. "Aaaaaawooh!"

"Have you gone nuts again?" Cherry demanded, batting the door open.

"Again?"

"How is she?"

"How is the comatose 99-year-old? Comatose. How do you think she is?"

Cherry shrugged. "I didn't think you were coming today."

"Goodbye-ee wipe the tear baby dear, from your eye-ee. I am allowed to say goodby-ee?"

Cherry grimaced tighter than an un-shucked oyster. "Are you ok? Sure?"

Porter stood and offered the chair. "I know this has been coming," he said, gesturing at the bed, "but it doesn't really help, does it?"

"Porter, are we trying to set a record for the number of unanswered questions in one conversation?"

"I don't know. Are we?"

Cherry sat without acknowledging the gift of the seat. She gave Ida a perfunctory once-over. Straightening an invisible kink in the sheets, she said, "Are you still coming over to see the kids on Wednesday?"

"Maybe. I'm in a funny mood."

"So help me... You'd better not mention that curse again."

"Cherry…"

"Make sure you do come over. The kids are asking after you. Just cos you're going through shit, don't wallow. I'll do a roast."

Porter sighed. "You make your meal sound remarkably unappetising." He checked his iPhone XS Max. "I've got to get home. You staying for a bit? You'll call me if there are any problems?"

Cherry pulled out her own phone and fake-dialled. "Hi, Porter. It's Cherry. I'm calling you. There's a problem: You've gone nuts again."

"Cherry. *Goodbye-ee.*" And he continued to sing as he walked away, ignoring Cherry's headshakes of pity and disappointment.

Five hours later, rolling his steak about in garlic butter, Porter was ready.

Poor Cherry. As much comfort as a pair of nettle knickers. They had been fighting over the Norton Curse since they were teenagers. Porter had evaluated the evidence for and against it. Cherry had dismissed it with snorts and expletives. Once she had a son of her own, simple dismissal was no longer good enough. The curse had been tied up with duct tape, slaughtered and buried under the patio.

She was happy to regularly point out that Porter's life was a mess – a bunch of self-inflicted failures. "You're about as much use as a sniper with Parkinson's," she had once screamed. The other customers in Pizza Hut had looked on in embarrassment.

He threw his steak in the pan and enjoyed the sizzle. Giving it a hefty prod with the knife, he momentarily pictured his sister's face.

Family legend had the curse begin in the 1800s when Mortimer Norton was killed in a brewery accident. It was the first in a series of disasters to strike the male line. Mortimer's son, Harry, was shot as a deserter in World War 1. Harry's own son, Geraint, committed suicide. Geraint's son Owen - Porter's father - hanged himself the day his wife died.

Orphaned overnight, Porter and Cherry were brought up by Ida, who had otherwise lost her entire family. The quarrelling siblings would forget Ida's tragedy on far too many occasions.

Porter always felt pre-destined to be next. Now that he was being attacked from all sides, now that Ida was as good as gone, he knew his time had come. After a good meal anyway.

6

Porter pulled out his treasured copy of the *High Society* soundtrack, signed by Frank Sinatra. He slipped the vinyl from its sleeve and placed it on his 1950s gramophone. It crackled and spat through the lead-in groove, and his namesake's famous overture began.

In most ways, a thoroughly modern man who wore his technology as obviously as a gunslinger wore pistols, Porter still enjoyed the sound of vintage music above all else. He had developed a sideline restoring old 78s, de-clicking them, enhancing frequency ranges, and creating faux stereo mixes. The results came out as short-run CDs via a boutique label in Portugal. Behind the exquisitely maintained 50s gramophone, was his Mac Pro-driven audio workstation. The defiantly-old and the definitively-new, happy together in this uncommon sanctuary.

The walls of his flat, the bottom floor of a Georgian property in the oldest street in Hackney, were lined with musical film and theatre posters from the golden age of Hollywood. Some were signed. Pride of place went to an annotated George Gershwin manuscript. As he happily prepared his death, he desired a happy soundtrack. None was happier than *High Society*. He sang along to *Who Wants to be a Millionaire?* - only breaking off to talk to the photo of the girl. "I hope my dying helps your parents feel avenged. Even if they are bastards." The final meal was ready.

He popped the first two of a planned 60 diazepam tablets. Ease into it. He glugged the last of the wine, washing down the final mouthful of the steak. Flipping the vinyl, he sat down to deal with three letters.

The first was to Cherry. He told her how much he loved her and the kids, spelt out all his reasons and confirmed everything was left to her. "Don't throw away the Gershwin manuscript. It's worth a bob or two." Bar a few similar stage directions, it was a short letter. He sealed it and wrote *To Cherry* on the envelope.

His will was long since written and witnessed, but he gave it the once over, adding a short note explaining his decision to die to a small, but slightly wider audience. He apologised again for causing Janine Crane's death and sealed that too.

The third letter was to his ex, Tania Muriskava.

A toughie. He opened a bottle of 15-year-old Glenfiddich, slugged a large glass of neat whisky and popped two more pills. He was starting to feel sleepy.

Dear Tania,

I'm so sorry it came to this. Don't blame yourself. I'm leaving today because of a dozen things - not just because you don't want me anymore. I know you're more David Guetta than Jules Styne, but for me, you were always my perfect fit.

Remember that night at The Ivy when I sang to you on the way home? "That certain night..."

That's no good. She hates *A Nightingale Sang in Berkeley Square*. No point bringing that up. He screwed up the paper and threw it in the bin. *True Love* played in the background. And where is *my* guardian angel tonight? Actually, where the hell has it been all my damn life?

Did you ever read that poem by Shelley - Music, When Soft Voices Die? It sums up beautifully how I feel right now.
Rose leaves, when the rose is dead,
Are heaped for the beloved's bed;
And so thy thoughts, when thou art gone,
Love itself shall slumber on.

He crossed that out too. He was aiming high-brow, with a dash of mad romanticism, but instead, found he had Whitney Houston singing *I Will Always Love You* in his head.

It's not your fault Tania. Love you. Porter. X.

He glanced at the paper in disappointment. "Great. The worst suicide note in history. So tired." He sealed the envelope and propped it against the teapot with the others. The phone rang. He let it go to answer machine.

"Hey, Porter, it's Dave. You in? Five-a-side tomorrow at 7pm, Finsbury Park. Fancy it? Call me." Dave hung up.

Porter waved at the phone but lost his balance and fell to the floor, mumbling in pain. It's Porter Norton – come and get your clown nose. With the grace of an octopus trapped in the spin cycle, he hoisted himself back up and flipped the vinyl. Side A again. "A new start for the end," he toasted no-one in particular. He winced as he jogged the stylus, causing a criminally loud scratch.

He began to take the pills in earnest, five at a time, each batch washed down with a large swig of whisky. Fifty. Fifty-five. Sixty. One last swig. Done. Shoes off. He lay on the battered Chesterfield like a medieval potentate awaiting his conjugals. Porter closed his eyes and listened. "What an elegant, swellegant party this has been," he lied through his slurry mumble, before sinking back into the cushions.

Thirty seconds later he sat bolt upright. "Ow! Christ on a bike – what's that?" Ninja with sharpened blades slashed at his feet in a frenzy. He looked down in fuzzy disbelief. His socks were on fire. Small flames jumped and danced across the ridges of his toes.

An unfamiliar voice said, "Porter, you need to put that out and puke, please. We've got work to do. You're no good to anyone hobbling. Or dead."

Chapter 2

Sylvester Path, Hackney
Sunday, 19th March 2017: 7.45pm

After a few seconds of jumping up and down and slapping at the flames, the fires were out. Singed cotton hung from his blackened toes like seaweed from a rock.

"Puke. Puke or you'll die," re-iterated the sourceless voice. A needless instruction. Porter was already stumbling towards the bathroom. He was feeling terrifically ill. Tottering like a Weeble, a door handle caught his funny bone, adding to his nausea. Sinking to his knees, he bounced his chin off the toilet bowl in time to bring up a torrent of burning, whisky vomit. Sweating and straining, he heaved again. "Fingers down your throat," said the voice.

Through a broken calliope of inhuman noises, Porter continued to an empty stomach, finally resting his head on his arms encircling the toilet rim. Drool and spittle fronds dangled from his lips. He retched again but came up empty.

"That's it. Better out than in."

He wanted to lie there, like a teenager home from their first real party. His chin was on the porcelain, but the burning intruded. Pulling off what was left of his socks, he flung them away and staggered to the bath. He tried to drape in his feet but fell and slid. He cracked his head and finished, on his back; a small puddle of that morning's bathwater soaking his shirt. Using his toes, he fumbled open the cold tap and did his best to alleviate the pain in his feet.

"Messy," said the voice.

For the first time, Porter tried to see who was talking. His high-sided Victorian bath got in the way. Slipping and sliding he eventually found purchase and peered over the edge.

There, in the middle of the room, he saw the head and shoulders of a white plastic robot hovering mid-air. What the…? Robot? No. A ghost? Porter could see the towel rack through it.

"What the hell's going on?" he squawked, scrambling to sit up, but only managing to slide backwards, banging his head again.

"I was going to do the introductions later," the disembodied head said, "In brief? I'm a messenger. We need to talk. I can't do that if you're dead, so we need to get you cleaned up." It pointed. A white hand appeared, cropped at the bottom as though its owner was speaking from behind a frame.

"Great. I never felt mad until now," said Porter, massaging his toes.

"Really? I saw you talking to a newspaper clipping earlier. Have a shower or something. You reek. Back soon." The thing disappeared.

There's no doubt that Porter had wanted to die tonight. He had approached his suicide scientifically, pre-ordering the Valium months ago. But now, 30 minutes later, sitting in a bath, his feet stinging, he had the germ of life back in him. You nearly died, you nearly died. For the first time since he was a boy, Porter began to cry.

Leaving the bathroom in a robe, his head was awash with pain, alcohol and the effects of diazepam digested before the clear-out. Unable to bend, he kicked the burnt socks under the sofa. They stank. The record player hadn't ejected. Annoying rumble and click from the playout groove filled the room. Porter was too wobbly and disorientated to turn it off. There was no sign of the messenger thing. He began spooning ground coffee into a cafetiere.

"Feeling better?" said the voice.

Porter spun, flinging coffee everywhere.

"Stop doing that. What the hell are you?"

"I'm a messenger."

"Consider *that* message delivered. Who from? Spit it out!"

"From whom. Don't know. Can't tell you that. I would, but I don't know. I just know that I have to deliver a message." Between sentences, it hung still and lifeless, eye-to-eye with Porter. He liked his ghosts with Victorian moustaches, craggy faces and a whiff of Dickens. This...thing...looked like it had been designed by CAD.

"Do you have a name? Are you a ghost? Why don't you blink? God, listen to me."

"No. You can call me The Gliss."

"The Gliss? What does that mean?"

"What does *Porter* mean? *The Gliss* is what I am. Simple."

Porter rubbed his feet. He wasn't going anywhere yet without doing a passable impersonation of the Little Mermaid. "Ok, Gliss. I'm game. What's your message?"

"*The* Gliss. Get yourself comfy first."

Porter poured his coffee and plonked himself down on the Chesterfield. In Porter's bruised and fragile state, it had morphed into a bed of nails, he, the novice fakir.

The Gliss re-appeared. "Are you ready?"

"I feel like the cast of *Geordie Shore* are living in my head, but, yes. What's going on? Am I imagining you - *this*?"

"You're nowhere near creative enough to imagine me."

"Ah, insults. Nice. Please get on with it. I still appear to be dying."

The Gliss hovered, a floating white ceramic death-mask. "I'm here to save you. And give you a mission."

"Ok, Clarence. I'll buy. Why the hell me? There are no petals in my pocket. Can't you pick on someone else?"

"I'm here not *for* you Porter, but *because* of you. Five suicides in five generations. Uh-uh. Can't happen. You've triggered something rare indeed, a Quincunx. You and your ancestors have offended the natural order of things. Now you have to put things right."

"Wait...A what?"

"Quincunx. Sorry, I have the spiel, but I'm not clear on the details."

Tutting, Porter picked up his phone and Googled a definition. "It doesn't mean anything. It's a pattern of five dots - like the number five on dice."

"So, what's an apple got to do with computing? Are you always this literal?"

"No, but I'm not taking classes on symbolism either. Help a drunk, drugged man out here: What on earth are you talking about?"

The Gliss sighed. "Ok. Nature can't tolerate that many suicides in one family. Every death causes pain and misery for those left behind. The cumulative debt must be atoned for. You, the fifth, have to put it right."

Porter laughed. "You've got the wrong man then. I'd have been the third, not the fifth," said Porter. "Am I really arguing with a ghost?"

"I'm not a ghost. I'm The Gliss."

"Yes, yes, yes. But that doesn't change anything. I'd have been the third, not the fifth. My great-grandfather was shot for desertion in WW1. His father died in an accident. True - my father and grandfather killed themselves. But that's only two out of five."

"You tried. The Quincunx is only triggered by the *attempted* fifth. I assure you, I couldn't be here if there weren't *four* suicides before your attempted *one*."

Porter sipped the coffee. After the drink and drugs, it was like getting a snog from Aphrodite. "Ok. Putting the disputed suicides to one side…what do you mean *atone*? Walk-naked-down-Mare-Street-flogging-my-bare-back-with-a-whip or donate-a-fiver-to-The-Samaritans type of atone?"

"Neither. You've got to put right some historical injustice. Maybe two. Maybe a dozen. We won't know till it's done."

"And then what - you go away again?"

"Yes, but who knows when. Five is a lot to make-up for. It's not a simple equation of saving five lives to cover the five suicides. Each suicide caused many levels of suffering. When you've done enough, the Quincunx will end."

"Suppose I said I believed you, which - guess what? I don't - how does this bad movie play-out? Is it one of those Faustian things where I'm tricked into thinking I saved myself? Then the Devil pulls a fast one, and I'm back on my deathbed where my suicide left off?"

"I think you probably get to live. But I don't have answers. Just the message."

"Which is?"

"Do you mind turning that record off? The clicking's driving me mad."

"You're touchy for a ghost. Sure." Porter obliged, took another sip of the heavenly coffee and sighed. "Let me hear it."

Before The Gliss could answer, the phone rang. Instinctively, Porter picked up, never taking his eyes off The Gliss. He still wasn't sure that this Clarence wouldn't morph into a Damian or a Xenomorph.

"Porter, it's Cherry. How are you?"

Without thinking, without sarcasm, and without filtering, Porter data-dumped his sister. "Me? I tried to kill myself earlier but then a ghost saved me by setting fire to my socks and ordered me to throw up, but only now tells me that, to say thanks, I have to atone for generations of Norton family sin and solve some historical crimes. Just another Sunday. How are *you,* Cherry?"

"Be serious. You had me worried earlier. Are you ill again? Look what happened last time."

"You love bringing that up, don't you? Well, there really is a ghost, and he's about to give me some kind of mind-bending message. Could we talk later?"

"You're drunk. Don't do anything stupid. I'm on my way."

"No! Don't! Sorry - I didn't mean to be so emphatic about that. But you know, what with the ghost here and everything...I'm kinda busy."

"Hmmm. See you on Wednesday."

"Ok, Cherry, if I can get rid of the ghost, I'll be there."

"You're weird, Porter Norton. You know that, right?"

Charlotte Street, London
Sunday, 19th March 2017: 8.05pm

Cherry took her phone off-speaker as the call was ending. Her psychiatrist friend, Orit Neave, whistled. "I see what you mean. He sounds crazed. What the hell was he talking about?"

Cherry, signalling to the waitress, said, "It's happened before. When he was 21, a girl left him. He took it badly, got pissed and tried to kill himself. Ida found and saved him. Earlier, I caught him howling like a wolf over Ida's comatose body. And that phone call.... I've never heard him hallucinating like that before. Ghost, my arse."

Orit sensed a potential client. "He sounds in crisis to me. Want me to speak to my mentor, Justin? Porter's showing obvious signs of disturbance. Cherry, he started that conversation by saying that he'd just tried to kill himself. *Tried*, not, *was going to try.*"

"He's alive now. But you're right. I've no idea what's going on in his head. I'd better let Tania know."

"His ex?"

"We're still mates, though I'm not allowed to tell him that. She cares for him - I think - but she's moved on. Don't wish to be harsh on my brother, but you can see why?" Cherry shooed away Orit's attempt to put a tenner towards the bill. "Leave it for now. I'll speak to him when he's not pissed. He's always been obsessed by the suicide thing - nothing new there." She told her friend about the Norton family curse.

"Do you believe in it?"

"Me? Don't be daft. It's still affected us all though because of the idiots who have. My Dad had three sisters - triplets. None of them had kids in case they had a boy. And yes, every man going back four generations, has met a sticky end but that's proof of nothing. I don't like superstition. It's the 21st century."

Cherry dropped precisely 12.5% in coins on the plate as a tip.

Sylvester Path, Hackney
Sunday, 19th March 2017: 8.12pm

"Your sister?"

"She means well, but she always treats me like I'm about to do something stupid," replied Porter.

"Like, kill yourself and talk to ghosts?"

"Touché."

The Gliss continued his explanation without further judgement. Porter appreciated that. "So, the Quincunx demands you atone for the pain caused by the suicides in your family. You have to look into some historical injustices and put them right."

"From my own family history?"

"Not necessarily. But by the sounds of it, you could do worse than take a look at some point."

"I'm a failed solicitor, not a detective. I don't have the skills or resources."

"Not failed - suspended. You'll have more resources than you think. Me for a start. And…a bit of a superpower."

"Of course I will. And what superpower would that be?"

"If you get close enough…"

"Go on…"

"To the remains of a dead person…"

"Yes…"

"You'll see and hear them speak. Should be interesting. DeadWords we call them."

Chapter 3

2nd Army HQ, Flanders
Tuesday, 12th December 1916

"And that gentleman," said General Hubert Plumer, "is how we are going to cause chaos and heap destruction on the enemy frontline."

The former Boer War commander, now in charge of the British Expeditionary Forces' 2nd Army, waited for the baying to die down. "It goes without saying, this is absolutely Top Secret. Some of you will be ordering men to dig. It's essential they don't know why. We run spot checks, but The Bosche may still occasionally tap into our comms lines. We do it to them; they probably do it to us.

"I can't emphasise enough. Tell no-one, discuss this with no-one. HQ will deliver specific instructions to each of you. Make queries face-to-face at HQ only. Under pain of court-martial, do not discuss with the rank and file. Am I clear? Good. Dismissed." The assembled officers stood to salute, scraping back their chairs in a cacophonous scramble.

Capt. Farleigh Featherstone turned to his table and whistled.

"The Aussies have been digging for a year already," said Capt. Cecil Braxted, closing his briefcase.

"I did wonder what they were up to," said Capt. Georges Pelenot. "How much explosive is going down there?"

"One million pounds," said Capt. Alex Wootton.

"I hope we don't end up arse in the trees with Fritz when they set that lot off."

"Aww. Diddums. Want me to buy you some ear-muffs?" said Braxted, bringing an arm down on Pelenot's back, harder than was necessary.

Laughing, the group straightened their uniforms. The four officers looked as carefree as anyone could in the perversity of Flanders in 1916. None registered the on-going boom of distant heavy artillery fire. Yet, so up-ended was their world, simple birdsong might have halted any of them in their tracks.

"It's a good plan," said Wootton. "When we throw that switch, Fritz'll be so punch drunk…in we'll go…jelly under our boots."

"Make sure you keep it to yourself Wootton, or Plumer will tear you up for arse-paper," said Pelenot.

"Yes. It'd be bad news for blabbers," said Braxted.

"Corkscrew down your pecker bad," said Featherstone.

Sitting in a trench, three miles away, was an unassuming private, Maximilian Cartwright. He had no idea fate was sharpening its corkscrew just for him.

Chapter 4

Porter's flat, Sylvester Path, Hackney
Sunday, 19th March 2017: 10.45pm

Porter felt rougher than a sandpaper hanky. He sipped his fourth coffee and quizzed The Gliss. "This superpower: Can I turn it on and off? Or am I just stuck with it? It sounds horrible."

The Gliss glided mid-air. He stopped in the general area of a framed manuscript. "Ah, Gershwin. My favourite."

"£1,900 at auction in LA. You're facing me though. How can you see it?"

"My face is for your comfort - to help you acclimatise. Nobody ever owned this face. I'm not a ghost. I'm a bit more multi-dimensional than that," said The Gliss.

"You have eyes in the back of your head then?"

"And my ears, nose and scalp."

"I can hear the dead then?" said Porter, rubbing an aching temple. "That's nice."

"Not all the dead, no. Just those that died in, let's call it, unhappy ways. Providing you're touching - or near - their remains, of course."

"Of course. Am I likely to be near a lot of remains then? I'm a bit squeamish, to be honest."

"We'll see."

Porter thought for a second. "Assuming I'm not mad, and that you're not an unlisted side effect of mixing diazepam and Glenfiddich, that could be a handy skill. Does it include famous people? Could I speak to Gershwin at his grave? He died young and unhappy. And his sweat must be all over that manuscript? Does touching DNA count? Or," Porter shuddered, "are we talking squelchy stuff?"

"You can't *speak* to anyone – famous or not. You can only hear. They won't know you're there."

Porter looked disappointed and noted the squelchy-stuff question had gone unanswered.

"You can hear a CD, but you can't have a conversation with it," The Gliss elaborated. "Not unless you've gone bobo, anyway. The older the remains, the weaker the signal. There's no use sitting on Shakespeare's grave, hoping he'll tell you how many plays he wrote. It's quite a privilege you know. Lots of people have the potential. Only a few ever go on to become Sensitives."

Porter got up and paced about with a limp. The pain took his mind off the tsunami nausea battering him from all sides.

"How many have the potential? Why haven't I heard of this before?"

"At what point in history, in which culture, would it have been ok to say you could hear the dead speak?"

"Mediums do it all the time," Porter countered, before admitting, "You're right though, most mediums are thought of as one currant short of a muffin."

"Sensitives *see* the Dead too. How would you describe it without sounding mad? Stick an old lady in front of a crystal ball with bangles for earrings and people go along with the entertainment. But, put a lawyer on *The Graham Norton Show*, stroking a bit of bone, claiming she can see its former owner talking… That would be her last day in practice."

"Hmmm. How do you know if someone has potential?"

The Gliss nodded. "You've heard of tinnitus I presume? All tinnitus sufferers are potential Sensitives. Imagine the sound of an un-tuned radio signal carrying encoded dead voices. Woooooo. Sensitives can tune in and decode that signal. It's why tinnitus is so hard to treat - it's often not an illness at all."

Porter chewed this over. "So, Pete Townshend of The Who and Lemmy, God rest him, were potentially Sensitives? They both had tinnitus. Amazing thought."

"No, Porter, they were idiots who stood in front of large amplifiers without earplugs for 50 years and diddled their ears. Tinnitus is a telling sign but only the heavily traumatised actually become a Sensitive. People like you."

"You make me sound unusual. I'm not. Suicide is commonplace, attempted suicide even more."

"But not many people are the latest in a line of five suicides. That's your trauma. It extends past the span of a single lifetime."

"Ah. So how will this superpower help me to solve ancient mysteries then?"

"Not ancient. I've already told you; the more time goes by, the harder it is to hear anything. 'Recent past' would be more accurate. Would you like to hear about the man you're supposed to help?"

"I couldn't give a rat's arse, to be honest. Plenty on my plate already, ta," said Porter.

"You don't have a choice," said The Gliss. "You really do have to atone for the pain the Nortons have caused."

"I don't get it. I'm not a detective."

"Every case you solve will ease your pain a bit."

"My existential pain has been my constant companion for 41 years, my friend. I tried to end it all, remember? That's not much of a threat."

"I meant the physical pain."

"What physical pain?"

"This gift comes at a price. You feel rough now? Wait till you hear your first dead person talk. Headaches, nausea on a biblical scale. Pro-action is the only relief."

"A Maleficent gift," said Porter.

"Not all gifts are pleasant."

"True. Someone bought me a Michael Bublé CD for Christmas. Ok, so if I don't co-operate, I'm going to be in agony for the rest of my life? Speaking as a solicitor, that sounds an awful lot like blackmail."

To Porter's surprise, The Gliss began to sing. Porter recognised the tune instantly. "Hey, that's *Wouldn't it be Fun* from Cole Porter's *Aladdin*. Who the hell knows that one?"

"You do."

"Are you poking around in my brain?"

"I've seen the memory palace where you try to remember all the major Hollywood musical songs and composers, yes."

Porter folded, head in hands. "Me and whisky are through."

"Want to hear or not? It's a case you might like actually. Your great-grandfather was shot for desertion in Flanders in World War I - correct?"

Porter nodded in spite of himself. The Gliss looked like he was about to deliver a lecture. "Sometime before your relative was shot, a British private called Max Cartwright was falsely executed as a spy in Flanders. You have to right that wrong."

"Go on. I'm listening."

"That's it really. It's not like I have a bunch of paperwork for you to peruse."

Porter slammed his hands down on the table. "That's the stupidest thing I ever heard. Just a name? Some guy's been dead 100 years? And I'm the one supposed to put that right? How? Why? He's dead!"

"It's been a difficult night for you," said The Gliss. "Let's talk in the morning."

"Let's not," shouted Porter. But the apparition had vanished. "I'm not taking this BS, do you hear?" The Gliss hadn't, but the banging from upstairs showed his elderly neighbours definitely had. Then, as an afterthought, Porter said, "And how am I supposed to sleep with eight cups of coffee in me anyway?"

More bangs. "Alright. Alright." Porter cursed all ghosts and all elderly neighbours.

He picked up the *High Society* sleeve. He admired how Cole had managed to slide in sex and drugs references without upsetting vanilla America. *Bottoms and Tops*? Every time he heard it, Porter thought of his promiscuous namesake and sniggered. Another of those references came to mind now: Crosby and Sinatra's banter in *Well Did You Evah?* Bing urges Sinatra to grab a line. Porter and Ida had argued about it.

"He meant sing the next line," said Ida.

"No. He meant grab a line of cocaine," said Porter.

"Sing."

"Cocaine."

"Sing."

"Cocaine."

"You're a rotter, Porter Norton. Stop ruining things for me."

Smiling now, he said out loud, "Grab a line. Yes, please. I need some clarity." Only joking. The cocaine dabble-days were long gone – like one-night stands, hoodies and Adidas 3-stripe.

He saw the prized Gershwin manuscript. Taking down the frame, he held the glass to his cheek. Nothing. Grabbing a knife from the drawer, he prized open the back and removed the precious sheet, covered in handwritten scrawl. Nothing.

He reasoned the hottest spot must be where Gershwin's palm had rested on the right while writing. Porter pushed the page against his cheek. Nothing.

"Now look at it. It's got a rumple in it." Furious, he put the display back together, the knife in its drawer and cursed The Gliss. "You owe me 1900 quid, you bastard."

Someone with a cane banged on his ceiling again.

Chapter 5

Ypres. Charles Gilpin's bunk.
Sunday, 4th March 1917: 2am

Grizzling, the Reverend Charles Gilpin woke up and turned off his Zenith timepiece alarm. It was time to prepare for Private Cartwright's execution. Gilpin was too exhausted to even resent the obligation. He climbed from his bunk as weary as a mid-career pit-pony.

Gilpin had joined the Church in 1901 because he hankered for the quiet, uneventful life. This wasn't it. "A vicarage, a subsidised cellar and a garden. Not exactly redefining avarice, was I? he cursed, pulling his breeches down.

His dreams were destroyed by his Western Front call-up. At the start of the war, Anglican clergy were purposely kept from the frontline. Maybe the top brass wanted to boost morale, perhaps they belatedly recognised the godlessness of war, but in January 1916 they changed tack. There were now more than 20,000 chaplains serving in France and Belgium. Gilpin was furious, depressed and frightened to be one of them. He had never expected or wanted to dole out comfort to the sick and mutilated - and, sweet Jesus, some of those wounds were straight from Bruegel. Even staring at suppurating wounds was preferable to dealing with spies, traitors and malingerers.

Squatting over a pot, he pissed and farted himself fully awake. No paper. He used a handful of water to clean his arse. Wiping his soiled hand on his flannel nightshirt, he stripped in the bitter cold and slapped on his dog collar and jacket. His socks were still wet from yesterday. He must remember to ask his mother to knit some new ones. The army was running a campaign to get the women of Britain knitting socks for the troops, but he had been stuck with the same pair for a year. He heard a rat gnawing wood somewhere nearby.

He picked up a beaten leather satchel, popped in his penknife, an apple, a small wooden pill box and a hip flask of brandy. Suppose the fellow could write? With a sigh, he added a pen, paper and envelope. And a Bible - for all the good that would do Cartwright now.

Emerging into the cold night air, he thanked the Lord for the blissful quiet. Not a shell to be heard. He passed a few sentries along the way, gave the password and eventually arrived at the block where Cartwright was being held.

He was surprised to see two captains he knew, bent over Cartwright, haranguing him. The condemned man was backed into a corner, holding his arms up to defend himself. Gilpin assumed the officers had beaten him. They were only shouting now. He didn't care either way. Cartwright's crimes were despicable. Gilpin's own charity had disappeared with most of his faith (and his breakfast) the first time he witnessed a head explode. In any case, he officially need feel no guilt. The Church of England supported capital punishment in both civilian and military life. Privately, many of his colleagues didn't. Gilpin wasn't one of them. Like it or not, this was his job.

"Ahem, gentlemen."

Both officers stood and turned as Gilpin wafted into the cell.

"Sorry, Reverend. Just having a quiet word. This bastard - sorry Reverend - said some vile shit – apologies again - in court earlier. Trying to get an apology before justice is served," said the bigger of the two.

"I understand. Good night, gentlemen," Gilpin said, with a shoo-ing gesture, dismissing them.

There was an awkward silence, punctuated only by grunts from the private. It was now clear he was indeed recovering from a winding.

"Didn't do it, Reverend. Spying. Never would," said Cartwright, breathlessly.

"I'm here to pray with you, not take confession. Here."

He handed Cartwright the hipflask. Later he would dish out morphine from the pillbox - partly to ease the pain of dying, but also to ensure docility during the transfer to execution pole.

Cartwright said he didn't drink.

"Drink tonight, man. It'll help," said Gilpin, twisting open the hip flask.

Cartwright spluttered and offered it back.

Gilpin took out the Bible, his apple and penknife. He began peeling the apple, letting the skin fall carelessly to the floor.

"Do you want to make your peace with God?" he asked.

Cartwright took no notice. "I didn't do it."

Dung and acid violated the air. Gilpin held his nose.

"Sorry, sir. Messed my trousers. My guts are more frightened than my head."

Gilpin pushed his stool back a few feet.

"You may deny the spying charge Cartwright, but the court-martial had no doubt you did it? And they had evidence. They said you took the tunnel plans for the Messines Ridge mines and were caught with them in No-Man's Land. They say you tried to give them to the enemy."

"Not true. Yes, I did have the plans with me, but I was set up. I didn't take them."

This was a new one.

"Set up, you say? By whom? Why?"

Cartwright was silent.

"Come on, man, you're claiming conspiracy. Tell me about it. Did you say this at the court-martial?"

"I tried. At the end. I could see I was a goner. But I couldn't tell the whole story. Nothing could have saved me anyway. The truth would have killed my mother. I tried to tell as much as I could." Cartwright shrugged. "You saw for yourself: all it got me was a beating."

"It's your last chance to repent. Did you defame those officers in court?"

"Not *officers*, plural, no." Cartwright stared at the floor. He didn't appear particularly ashamed. I would be. No, he's resigned. Strange.

Gilpin took a bite from his apple. He held it under his nose to mask the smell of faeces.

"Come, private. Speak up." It wasn't that Gilpin wanted to take confession. He wanted to get away from the smell. But he was nosy, in spite of himself. "Perhaps you should confess before it is too late."

Cartwright paused and lifted his head to look directly at Gilpin, assessing his trustworthiness.

Gilpin mistook this thinking time for continued reticence.

"Speak, for Heaven's sake man. What could have happened that was so bad?"

Cartwright stared Charles Gilpin in the face.

And told him.

Chapter 6

Hackney Central Library, Mare Street
Monday, 20th March 2017: 9am

Porter was shaky on his pins the next morning. The pills and
alcohol had been in his system long enough to sap and disrupt him.
He closed his front door and turned right, into the short passage that
led to Mare Street. He liked to compare the brief solitude of that
walk to an LP's lead-in groove: a few seconds of almost-silence
before the music begins.

The musics of Mare Street spanned centuries. There were the old
notes of recorder, flageolet and harpsichord from Hackney Central's
time as a rural village outside London. There were the playground
songs of Victorian ragamuffins, cheerily miming executions to *Here
comes a chopper to chop off your head*. There was the sound of
Louis Armstrong jazzing it at the Hackney Empire. And still there
was more: the echo of Vera Lynn records playing in the vanished
working men's clubs; the sub-bass of reggae and ska throughout the
60s and 70s; easy-listening cheese coming from pop-ups selling old
vinyl to hipsters; the current mélange of Adele, Little Mix and
Stormzy. Mumford and Sons launched their last album in the Oslo
bar. Porter could imagine their smug faux-folk faces gurning away.

Porter may have been the only Hackney-ite humming Jerome
Kern to himself today, but he belonged. This was home.

He had a theory about hangovers. They could go one of two
ways: Way One was the wrong 'un. The one that left you in slow-
motion agony, unable to keep down food, get rest or deal with the
world. Way Two left you hungry and shaky, but with the gift of an
illuminating shifted lens. Today, he was on the second path. He felt
empathy and love for his fellow citizens. Strange. Yesterday he
couldn't have given two hoots for any of them.

He grabbed a takeout coffee next to the Empire and eyed his
destination - Hackney Central Library. Maybe a little research would
turn up a mention of this Cartwright bloke.

"Worth a go," he reasoned. "If I find nothing, at least it'll prove yesterday was a bad dream." He had been doubting his sanity all morning.

His iPhone rang. It was his solicitor, Namita Menon.

"How are you, Porter?" she asked, without waiting for a reply, "I'm reviewing your case. I need you to come over."

Porter groaned. "I'm feeling a bit dicky. Can it wait?"

"Not really. I'm already thinking of pushing for a delay with Runyon's team so we can shore up your case."

"Namita - do we have to?" said Porter, in alarm. "I'm broke. I've got two month's money left for the mortgage. I really need to wrap this up as soon as possible. I can't get work anywhere till I clear my name."

"Exactly. To do that we have to prepare properly. Come on. You know this."

"I really am feeling rough today. Can I get back to you?"

"Don't leave it long. Speak later." And she rang off, with frost.

Porter needed to win. Runyon's gross misconduct charge had neutered him professionally. The Daily Mail and the red tops had torn him to shreds. *Solicitor's Error Caused Girl's Death.* He wore every headline like an embarrassing teenage tattoo that had outlived its use. For the first time since Janine's death, he felt *angry* at the way he was being treated. Not just sorry for himself, which had been his default state for the best part of a year.

"You utter bastards!" he couldn't help saying out loud in front of Hackney Town Hall.

"Yeah, you tell 'em mate," a teenager shouted, tapping his head, causing his girlfriend to giggle.

As he crossed in front of the Town Hall steps, The Gliss appeared from nowhere and said, "Off to the library then?"

"Flip," exclaimed Porter, jerking spastically, spilling coffee.

A large woman with 2 bags of shopping, stared at him like he was an extra from The Walking Dead. She shifted two steps to the right.

"You frightened the bejeezus out of me," Porter berated The Gliss.

Now it was the turn of a suited and booted man, reading the sports pages, to look up. He saw Porter was nothing to worry about and went back to the odds.

"Porter. No-one else can see or hear me. You might do well to remember that."

"You're a figment of my booze-addled imagination. How would they see you?" whispered Porter.

"Yet here you are - heading to the library – on the say-so of a figment."

"Because I'm going to prove that there's no-one called Max Cartwright and therefore no you," said Porter.

"May I make a suggestion? If you're going to talk to me in public, hold your iPhone to your ear. Then you can talk freely without being ogled by all and sundry."

"You're tech savvy for a ghost."

"I'm not the ghost of a medieval monk. I'm a messenger from across the ages. I've seen it all: from the wheel to the spingle."

"What's a spingle?"

"You'll see. If you hang around till about 2027."

"You can see into the future?"

"Vaguely?"

"What's mine look like?"

"Vague."

With a shrug of impatience, Porter took his advice and acted the stage direction of *man-taking-phone-call*: pacing in tight aimless circles, swivelling his head like a disco-dancing Dalek, looking into the distance, nodding occasionally.

"Let's cut to it, Porter. I guarantee you will find mentions of Max Cartwright, but it will all be bare-bones stuff. There's only one way you can find out the truth of all this."

"And that is?"

"Cartwright is buried in Swansea. Go visit his grave. Let his remains speak to you."

"Swansea? Are you out of your mind? Forget it."

"Let's make a deal. If you find a record of Cartwright - which you could only have known about through me - we go to Swansea."

"No way."

"Remember that pain I warned you about."

"This is a library. No talking," said Porter in a bid to head-off this latest nonsense. He stuffed the phone away and shuffled through revolving doors that Twiggy would have found claustrophobic. The Gliss shadowed. Porter ignored him, as convincingly as a postman ignores a low-growling dog.

The reference library was one of Porter's favourite Hackney haunts. It was home to a curious mix of groups: multi-ethnic schoolchildren working on their homework; writer-types pulling up research, and the lost and lonely. The latter sometimes comprising the first two groups as well.

He pulled up a chair, yanked out his scuffed and cracked MacBook Pro, set up a personal hotspot on his iPhone, and googled. Basic research first, detailed library archive search later.

Private Max Cartwright. WW1. Enter.

Not for the first time in his life, Porter was frustrated by Google's schtick - to give you hundreds of pages of responses, even though it had found nothing germane.

Maximilian Cartwright. Wales. Soldier. Enter.

Nothing.

List of soldiers executed for spying. WW1. Enter.

Top of the search engine results was a BBC article about 11 people shot in the Tower of London for spying. Further down the list was a website ***www.theywereshotatdawn.co.uk***.

He clicked.

What a dog of a website. Illegible brown Cochin font against green. It had been homemade by a prominent Pardon campaigner. If you could get past the design flaws, it was full of nerdy detail. It commemorated all 306 British soldiers executed during the Great War. Most were executed for breaches of military discipline - throwing away arms, desertion, striking an officer. Most had, in fact, been pardoned by the Labour government via The Armed Forces Act 2006. Only 40 convictions still stood because of the nature of the crimes: murder, mutiny and spying.

Porter scrolled down the list looking for Max and received the first of three big shocks heading his way.

The entry read:

92635 Private Harry Norton. 3rd Bn, Worcestershire Regiment. Shot for desertion. Aged 24, August 16th, 1917. Plot 63. Aeroplane Cemetery. West Vlaanderen. Ieper. Belgium.

Porter knew this piece of family history, of course, but had never looked it up, never taken an interest in the details of it. Growing up, it was a taboo subject with Ida. She had borne the worst of the execution's long-term consequences. He felt his heart beating faster.

"Keep looking, Porter," said The Gliss.

Porter found a small sub-section of the list. Executed for Spying. And there it was. Shock number two.

24324. Private Max. Cartwright. 3rd Bn, Worcestershire Regiment. Shot for spying. Aged 23, March 4th, 1917. Buried St Dyfnog, Llangenneth, Wales.

Porter pushed back his chair, dumbfounded.

"You couldn't possibly have guessed that. You see, I am real. And so is your mission," said The Gliss.

"Harry Norton and Max Cartwright were in the same battalion and killed a few months apart. That can't be a coincidence?" whispered Porter.

"I honestly don't know," boomed The Gliss, immune from the library's *Silence Please* signage. "It looks like we're going to Swansea though. If you visit Cartwright's grave, all should become clearer."

"I'm not going to Swansea. What do you want me to do? Dig the poor lad up? Hug his bones?"

"Standing on his grave should be enough."

"Forget it."

Porter packed away his laptop. He had been in the library for 15 minutes. He had expected to pull dusty old books and interrogate dusty old librarians. But, no, five minutes on Google had been enough. You could have stayed at home.

He squeezed through the revolving doors into Mare Street and took his iPhone out to make another pretend phone call.

"Listen to me, whatever you are. Yes, I'm officially freaked…owwww."

The phone rang for real with the third shock of the morning.

"Hello?" said Porter, rubbing his ear.

"Mr Norton? I'm calling from the Gloucestershire Royal Hospital? We thought you'd like to know your grandmother has come out of her coma and is asking after you."

"What? That's great. Wow. Thank you. Have you spoken to my sister, Cherry?"

"No, just you."

"Thanks, don't worry, I'll call her."

As Porter dialled Cherry, The Gliss said, "I do love a road trip. Gloucester is only 100 miles from Swansea."

Porter tried one last time: "Let me tell you this: I'm *not* going to Swansea. I *am*, however, going to ring my doctor and tell her I'm going mad."

"That's not what's going to happen," said The Gliss.

Chapter 7

Gloucestershire Royal Hospital, Gloucester
Monday, 20th March 2017: 4pm

The M4 was a nightmare. It took five hours to reach Gloucester. Porter stepped through the hospital doors, and iron hammers immediately began pounding his head.

"It's a hospital," offered The Gliss. "Bit of a hotspot for the dead and dying. Like cemeteries and Westfield."

"It's frickin' sore," said Porter, massaging a temple and pressing the Tower Block lift. "This the pain you warned me about?"

"No. That's background noise. Have you ever read about Nelson's crew having limbs sawn off without anaesthetic?"

"Yes."

"That's the sort of pain I was warning you about."

"Oh great. I look forward to that." Porter's stomach knotted.

Rubbing his hands with antiseptic gel, he entered the Critical Care Department and was directed to Ida's room.

"Porter," said Ida matter-of-factly. "I'm so glad you came. Is it Christmas yet? I feel like I've been away for months."

"No, it's March. Three weeks out cold though – you old Sleeping Beauty, you."

He kissed her forehead, feeling guilty that a few days before he had promised to commit suicide over her unconscious form. "Cherry and I have both been here."

"They said. Thank you. Did I snore?"

"No. But you farted a lot."

"Don't be disgusting."

"How you feeling now?" he said, taking her hand.

"Like you look. I'm old and dying. What's your excuse?"

"I went to a party last night. I've got a bit of a head-on today."

"Still drinking at your age."

The Gliss was gesturing like an emoticon on acid. Porter interpreted the flailing arms and encouraging winks to mean, "Ask Ida about your mum and Dad." Porter understood but wasn't keen. Ida had spent 40 years dodging as deftly as a downhill slalom Olympian.

"She's your last source," said The Gliss. "She's not stupid. She'll talk."

With a sigh, Porter groped for a way in. "Ida. We thought we'd lost you."

"I'm still here. For now."

Porter took a deep breath. "It made me think, there are some things I should've asked you by now."

"Your mum and dad?" Her face temporarily darkened. "I don't suppose it will do any harm now. Go on, open up the sores. Don't feel guilty." But she pressed his hand, giving him permission.

Porter had no questions prepared for a conversation based on secrets the CIA would have concluded were in "deep cover." Unsure of his ground, he talked about himself. "It's that bloody curse, Ida. Things haven't been going great for me recently. It's honestly like it was out to get me."

Her face changed the second he mentioned the C word. Her frailty was the only thing that gave him time to finish his thought and protected him from a punch. "Bloody curse. You know there's no such thing. How can someone as intelligent as you even think that?" But her illness tamed the latent Cockney bruiser in her. More from exhaustion than compassion, her face softened. "You want to know what your dad thought about the curse, I suppose?"

"Yes."

"Get me some water. I'm drier than an Arab's roof. Has someone been stuffing my gob full of crackers?" She shifted her position, tilted her motorised bed up a few degrees and took a few sips. It was all prep-work, psyching herself up to talk. With a shake of the head, she began.

"When I married your grandfather, that stupid curse was all he talked about. He changed over the years. First, it was 'if there's a curse.' But that morphed into 'when will the curse strike?' Geraint became obsessed." Ida took another sip. "I loved that man, but it wasn't easy living with him towards the end, let me tell you."

Porter listened in amazement. She had never volunteered much of anything before. Her preferred form of communication had always been The Bark: short, sharp exclamations, delivered in a dynamic range that went from lion tamer to town crier. Whole paragraphs without a loud-hailer was a revelation.

"One day I came home and found Geraint hanging from his own braces. I never thought life could get worse. And I'd already seen our baby die during The Blitz."

Porter looked up. "Air raid?" Ida shook her head.

"Cot death probably. Poor little sod was only two months old." She paused.

"I'm sorry, Ida. I didn't actually know that."

"Times were different. Thanks to the bloody Germans, death was everywhere. It might sound cold now, but I put that one behind me pretty quick. A terrible, terrible day though."

Porter sensed something else was coming.

"But there was one more day, even more terrible. Your mother died and then…" Her voice faltered slightly. "Your father, Owen…my lovely boy…he'd been a changed man since his dad died. Then he met your mum, they had you two. Everything was getting better. But, as you know, your mum, the love of his life, died of cancer. And that was that. He killed himself the same night."

Porter looked for tears, but Ida's face remained dry. He wasn't crying either. Weren't they both the definition of resilience? Or repression. One of the two.

"I feel so guilty now that I let Geraint and Owen have the conversations they did. They'd sit at the kitchen table and talk about Harry Norton and that damned curse all the time. Both of them, completely obsessed."

Porter stroked her hand as if to say, "I'm sorry for putting you through this." Ida pushed his hand away. She had started, and she was going to finish.

"We had Harry's effects - his diaries, an old hip-flask and his spectacles. Geraint and Owen would get them out and study them like they were maps to the Holy Grail. Do you know the story of how Harry took a hip-flask and cigar tube with him to Flanders? He'd pretend to drink from the flask and take a cigar from the tube. Both had been empty for years. Harry said in his diary that they were his most prized possessions.

Geraint would argue, 'How could a man who spent all his time trying to gee up his mates suddenly desert them?' They were both so proud of Harry's service. Geraint could never accept his father's desertion."

Ida sighed, and Porter could easily imagine her in an apron, cooking a tough Sunday roast, tutting at her husband and son's silliness, as they pored over documents at the kitchen table.

"All that reading ever did was to confirm to them that the curse was real." She shook her head and shrugged.

Porter nodded in understanding. "You think Dad thought the curse had come to get him too?"

Ida nodded. "Definitely. He became paranoid. He was well primed by the time your mum got the cancer. I did love Lis." Ida took time out from her own grief to pat Porter's hand.

"Owen was inconsolable towards the end. He'd rant all day about the bloody curse. We didn't understand mental illness then. I should've seen." She stopped for a second, struggling with the memory.

"When your mum passed, Owen didn't cry. He…crumpled. I was looking after you two, but I should've looked after my own boy – even if he was a grown up. You two were alright. Kids can take anything."

Porter, remembering his own childhood pain, wasn't so sure about that. He nodded for her to continue.

"I'll never forget. Owen came upstairs with the doctor and told us Lis was gone. He hugged you both, and we all cried together. Later that night, he went back downstairs to where Lis was laid out. He took off his belt and hanged himself from the door, bless him. Just like his dad had done. I found him in the same room as Lis at breakfast. *That* was the worst day of my life."

There was silence as both paid brief, silent tribute.

"I wonder how it all started?" said Porter, interrupting the quiet.

Ida snorted. "Stupid cow. Geraint's mother, Alice. She told Geraint about Harry's execution and the accident that killed his grandfather, Mortimer. She said it was a curse. I doubt she meant it literally – more like, a run of bad luck. It was Geraint who became obsessed with the idea of an actual curse."

Porter thought for a minute. "I guess Harry's death as a deserter would've had a terrible impact on his family?"

Ida said: "Geraint talked about the injustice of it all the time. Harry signed up without telling Alice and left her with four children to look after. Because he deserted, she lost her army widow's pension. People abused them in the street. It was terrible really."

"What do you think, Ida? Is there a curse?"

She took Porter's hand urgently. "You forget it, do you hear me? I'm not stupid. I know what you're asking. I don't give you permission, do you hear? Fight, you little bastard. Fight back. And you make up for my lost baby, son and husband. Do you hear? I'm not losing you too."

Porter couldn't speak. He scrunched his face up, hoping the constricted muscles would hold back tears. He put his head on her chest. She enfolded it with her arms, and both dimly remembered the last time she had done so - the night his mother died. "There, there. Shh. There, there, my brave little boy. It'll be alright."

I wonder how different life would have been if the silly old cow had given me a cuddle every now and again? Ten minutes is better than nothing.

Ida pushed him away and said, "There's something I want you to have."

Porter sat up.

"I'm 100 next year. I want my telegram. But this has given me a bit of a scare. Go to my house. In the attic, you'll find a King Edwards' cigar box. Inside, you'll find what I have left of Harry's belongings. There's the hip flask, the diaries and a letter from one of his friends.

"Geraint and Owen always said the man who wrote those words could never have deserted. Time to pass it all on to you. But remember: it's your family history, not a curse. I know you act like a wet fish and haven't done a proper day's work in your life, but I honestly think you're stronger than either my son or my husband. I'd die happy knowing you'd put an end to all this rubbish."

Porter said he would drive over and get the box later.

"Porter? I haven't said it often, but I love you, son. I'm proud of you. I'm so pleased you came. Now toddle off will you, I'm absolutely knackered."

Porter laughed, said "I love you too…*Mum*."

"Shut up, you idiot," said Ida, her face flushing for a second.

The Gliss was delighted. "You see. It's a bit like professional networking. You gotta get out there, face-to-face, to progress."

"You sound like a TED lecturer," said Porter, but then graciously admitted, "It was good - easily the most open conversation I've ever had with her. Thanks." They rounded a corner to the exit. "I'll drive over now and pick up...Jesus!" Porter exploded into a ball of white light and pain as two porters wheeled a cloth-covered trolley past him.

"You alright, mate?" said one of the alarmed porters. His seen-it-all colleague strolled on, undisturbed.

"My head! What's happening?" screamed Porter on his knees.

"Mate?" the porter asked again. The trolley was now six metres away, and the pain was receding as fast as it had arrived.

In shock, in pain, in denial, Porter accepted the porter's arm. "Yes, yes, I'm ok," said Porter. "Migraine."

"You should get that looked at," said the porter, moving on.

It was The Gliss' turn to speak. "Dead body. Told you it would hurt."

"Hurt?! Is that a joke?"

"Lucky they kept moving. The pain was bad because the signal was strong. I guess whoever was on the trolley has just died."

"I thought *I* was going to die."

"Did you hear anything?"

"Screams and a thunderstorm bouncing between my ears."

"The porters were too quick for DeadWords to form. Let's get out of here," said The Gliss, "before we bump into anything else. It looks like we're going to Swansea after all."

"Alright," Porter finally conceded. "It's not that far from Ida's house. I owe you that. I can't drive now. We'll overnight at the Ibis next door, head to Swansea and stop off at Ida's on the way home. Where's the hospital shop? I need some paracetamol."

Chapter 8

St Dyfnog Church, Llangenneth, Swansea
Tuesday, 21st March 2017: 12pm

The Reverend Richard Gossamer was not a happy bunny as he put down the phone. April Stebbings. No! One person with movie star looks in the whole parish, and he was bailing on tea and muffins with her? Because some eejit from London wants to trace a grave? Bastard.

And he knew the type: earnest, crusty bores with a degree in *Time Team* who thought everyone was as interested in their family history as they were. But no point risking a complaint to the diocese either. Your CV needs all the help it can get.

Gossamer's was a temporary posting which he was hoping would become permanent.

"Whoever this effing chump is, let's get him outta here double-quick," said Gossamer. Looking up at the altar, conscious he might want to also consider his celestial CV, he added, "Amen."

Ten minutes later the church door swung open with a creak. A nervous forty-something snuck into the church. He looked like a boy chosen to ask a grumpy neighbour if they could have their ball back.

"Good afternoon," said Gossamer.

"Reverend Gossamer? Porter Norton? We spoke on the phone?"

"Richard will do. Nice to meet you." Gossamer skipped the niceties. "Your grave - I have the documents. But it won't be easy to find, I'm afraid, as it's unmarked." Registering Porter's look of disappointment, he added, "But we have the plot map, so who knows?"

Gossamer scanned the map as he walked, trying to keep the wind from tearing the paper from his hands. "According to the registrar, this man Cartwright was shot as a spy in the First World War, correct? Somehow his body made its way home. I thought they buried all the cowards where they shot them?"

"I'm not too clear on the details," said Porter. "Maybe the charge was so serious they didn't want to bury him with the good soldiers?"

"Maybe, maybe," said Gossamer, ignoring the sarcasm.

They entered the cemetery. The be-robed Gossamer sashayed through the tombstones like Montserrat Caballé arriving at her retirement party. "The vicar at the time must have been very tolerant, allowing a spy to be buried on consecrated ground. Then again, there's no gravestone, so it wasn't exactly red carpet. Maybe he knew the family. What's your interest?"

Porter, having spent precisely 23 minutes on Google and Wikipedia boning up on the executions, had no ready answer.

"Oh. I. Err."

"Say you're paying respects or something," said The Gliss. "You represent people in court. You know how to lie."

"Shsssh," said Porter.

Gossamer looked up. "Excuse me?"

"Not you," stammered Porter. "I was thinking how, er…still it is here."

"Yes, very," said the vicar, realising anew how desolate his churchyard could be. "The grave should be around here somewhere. Look for a depression in the earth." Gossamer cross-referenced his chart. After a bit of weed pulling, it turned out there was only one disturbance without a gravestone.

"This is most likely it," said Gossamer.

"What do I do now?" said Porter to The Gliss.

Gossamer, assuming the question was aimed at him, shrugged as if to say, "How the hell would I know?"

"Stop talking," said The Gliss. "Go and stand on it and be ready for a jolt."

"I'll do that," said Porter. "And I can't stop talking, can I? You're giving me instructions."

The vicar checked to see if someone new had snuck up behind him. Porter approached the edge of the plot, pinched his nose like a virgin swimmer preparing for the deep end, and hopped in.

"Are you ok?" said the astonished vicar, surveying Porter in a crouch in the middle of the depression.

"Nothing," reported Porter.

"Lay down," said The Gliss.

"Are you mad? It's damp."

"Do it."

He did. His back got wet but nothing else. "Now look what you've done. Nothing." He looked up to see the Reverend bending over and staring down at him.

"Of course, it's hard to be *exact* with an unmarked grave," said the shaking vicar. "It's supposed to be forgotten. Look, seriously, are you ok, Mr Norton?"

Before Porter could answer, The Gliss surprised him by singing *Pick Yourself Up,* ordering Porter to jig around a bit.

"Jig? You mean dance? Are you mad? He'll think I'm nuts." A quick glance at Gossamer, however, confirmed this process was well underway.

"Dance, Porter. It'll help."

Porter's dancing experience consisted of one best-forgotten school disco, a slow dance with Tania that ended with her big toenail hanging off, and a Runyon's awayday in which he and various colleagues had line-danced like broken marionettes.

"Copy Fred," said The Gliss. "As long as you generate some energy and move around a bit."

With a sigh, Porter started to dance. He had the movement and agility of A Stair, not Astaire. Gossamer moved backwards, looking around hopelessly for help. Porter stopped, took a step back and with some justifiable annoyance, said, "Nothing. Absolut...."

Three equally disagreeable things happened at once. First, someone tried to drown him by rapidly dunking him face down in a bath of viscous, white gloss paint. Second, the same malefactor attached his eyes and ears to the mains, quickly flicking the on-off switch. Thirdly, this someone or something, which quite definitely had it in for him he now realised, filleted his brain into thin slices, squeezed Naga chilli and grit onto each layer before grinding everything back together: A blinding vortex of pain and light, all to a cymbals and timpani accompaniment Hans Zimmer would have thought OTT. Yet, through the cacophony, Porter became aware of another sound. It was a voice.

Max Cartwright. He didn't know how or why he knew that for sure, he just did. Max said: "I'm scared. Mum. I didn't do it. God help me. I'm scared. Mum. I didn't do it. God help me. I'm scared. Mum. I didn't do it. God help me."

The ferocious lights began to clear, and Porter started to adjust. The pain remained, but the balance had see-sawed back in favour of Porter's senses. He was ready to focus, allowing the pictures to come.

He had a faint vision of a soldier tied to a post. The image was foggy, so he concentrated on the voice, letting its message dissolve into his consciousness like butter on crumpet. Once it was in, Porter allowed himself to think. These are his last thoughts. He's about to die. Flip.

The picture was beginning to come into focus when the spell suddenly broke. Porter found himself lying in the gravel, a dirty stick jammed between his teeth, the vicar sitting on his chest.

"Don't struggle there's a good man," said Gossamer.

The Gliss deadpanned, "He thinks you're having a fit."

Porter struggled back. The vicar finally got the message. They stood up, Porter clasping his temples and spitting out bits of bark.

"You probably got a mouthful of squirrel piss from that," said The Gliss.

Porter pointed at his own head and said, "Migraine."

"Migraine? You were in spasm, gibbering," said Gossamer.

"I get it pretty bad."

"Very. Are we done? Unless you want a photograph?"

"No, thanks. I've seen what I need to."

They walked back to the church, both in discomfort.

A new sensation. White lights nibbled at Porter in waves. He caught fleeting words from some of the church's graves. It made him feel like his ears were being tickled with nettles, and he flinched every few feet. Gossamer now looked positively panicked.

"You've been properly activated," said The Gliss. "You can hear *all* those who died now. Just the ones who had big problems luckily, or you'd drown in it. Walk past and through it. Pretend you're an aloof movie star at a premiere. Let the flashbulbs bounce off you."

Dazed, Porter said goodbye to Gossamer and returned to his car, filling The Gliss in as he went.

"I heard him. I actually heard Cartwright speak. He said he didn't do it."

"We knew that, or we wouldn't be here in the first place. This was to prove to you that I'm real, the Quincunx is real, your mission is real."

Porter found some old aspirin in his glove compartment. The dregs of a two-day-old cup of Costa coffee sat in his cup-holder. He grabbed it and, with a wince of disgust, swigged down the aspirin with the cold and bitter remains.

"My head. It's killing me. I really have to do this? I'd rather kill myself than go through that again," said Porter.

"You might get killed in action in an investigation, but I think you'd only get more burnt socks if you tried to top yourself again," said The Gliss.

"What do you mean 'killed in action?'"

"Like it or not, you have to help Cartwright out."

"What? And then I'm free?"

"I don't know."

"Fat lot of good you are."

Porter leaned back against his old green Volvo estate. "Why did you make me dance? Was that true about my dance creating energy?"

"No, but I thought it would help if you moved around a bit while we found our hotspot. It worked, didn't it?"

Porter buckled up as the Right Reverend Richard Gossamer looked out from behind the safety of his church door. "What an effing madman…er…Amen."

Flanders - Officers' Mess
Wednesday, February 28th 1917: 9.37pm

Capt. Alex Wootton came back to the piano and put down a pint glass for Capt. Georges Pelenot. He took a big gulp from his own.

"No luck with that nurse then?" asked Pelenot.

"No. Her friend said she'd already had too many suitors tonight and she wasn't going to dance with anyone else," said Wootton.

"She'd have to be puggled to dance with you anyway," said Capt. Featherstone.

"The older Sisters have got their beadies on us," complained Wootton. "We've got no chance."

All three stood in silence, ogling the prettiest nurses.

"I wonder where Braxted is tonight? Not like him to miss a dance," said Pelenot.

"He said he was coming, but there was some trouble today," said Featherstone. "A desertion. He's trying to sort that out I think."

The trio fell silent again. No-one wanted to deal with deserters or the consequences.

Two nurses, dancing with each other, twirled past and smiled at the captains. But none of the men felt like dancing now.

"I've had too many," said Pelenot, eventually.

"Drinks?" said Wootton.

"Desertions."

"Any of the fellows get executed?" asked Wootton.

"Two. I had to finish them off myself. Damned friends in the firing squad refusing to do the British Army's dirty work."

"Good Lord."

"Worst two days of my war," said Pelenot.

Since 1915's General Routine Order 585, the army had effectively reversed the guiding principle of British justice - a man is innocent until proven guilty. Now a deserter was considered guilty until proven innocent. As court-martials often only took a day and were carried out according to the principles of Roman military law, to be accused was, more often than not, to be found guilty. A deserter's best hope was to be one of the many thousands whose death sentence was commuted.

"To be honest, I'm not convinced executions maintain discipline or morale," said Wootton.

"What to do though? If we didn't punish the malingerers...," said Featherstone.

"Maybe," said Pelenot, "but some of these men are just broken. Yet, we're not able to take their health into account."

The music continued to play, the nurses continued to dance, the captains continued to stay silent.

"What's the matter with you chaps," said Capt. Braxted, rushing into the mess hall, detecting the sombre mood.

"Where have you been? What happened to you? You've got mud all over your uniform," challenged Wootton.

"Knocked myself out, banging my head on a trench in the dark," said Braxted. "I'm ok now."

"You sure you didn't bump into one of the nurses and find a quiet spot?" said Pelenot.

"I wish. Come on cheer up - the damn dance will be over in a second. It's what? 11pm?"

Braxted's effervescence lifted the others. Featherstone stepped onto the dance floor, cutting in on the two nurses dancing. Pelenot and Wootton headed over to push their suit with two others. After some banter and a polite bow, Featherstone triumphantly began waltzing with the prettiest one. The wallflower nurse sniffed at Braxted as she passed back to the safety of her colleagues watching on.

"Suck my manhood, you whore," said Braxted under his breath, as he smiled and saluted her playfully with his glass.

Chapter 9

St Briavels, Ross-on-Wye
Tuesday, 21st March 2017: 3.30pm

Porter and The Gliss pulled up a few yards from St Briavels Castle, once King John's hunting lodge on the Welsh border. It was a tiny village for a castle this impressive. Ida's cottage was more or less opposite the modern entrance.

The young Porter had found the village oppressive and suffocating. He and Cherry were free to roam, but you could stroll the village twice in the time it took to suck all the flavour out of a homemade ice-lolly. The castle had thrown shadows over Porter's childhood. Literally. The towers' morphing penumbra grew like wraiths on Porter's bedroom wall every night, until his room was consumed with darkness.

Now, he stood between the castle and the ancient church directly opposite and stared at Ida's house. Where tourists saw beauty, he, a former inmate, saw San Quentin. When his mum and dad died, the thatch had become a crown of thorns, the fastidiously maintained rose-beds, quicksand. Ida said children were resilient, but salted razors of grief had sliced at Porter for years, without mercy. When respite came, it was too late. The orphan pain had merged with the troubles of puberty. He emerged molten and melted, a vile distortion of the perfect candle his mother had hoped to light and set off into the world.

Yesterday's conversation with Ida was still nipping at him, but he grudgingly acknowledged that he had been lucky. Fostering and adoption had lain in an alternate universe had it not been for her sacrifice and intervention. This could be the last time you come here. You would miss it. Admit it. He pulled out the keys he had never given up, though had rarely used.

"Aren't you excited this time though?" asked The Gliss. "A little treasure hunt always does a man good."

"It's not much of a hunt, is it? She told me where the box is."

"You're so literal - the contents, not the container."

Porter paused at the front door. Over the years he had developed a fascination with the distortions in its leaded glass as Ida had shuffled to answer his knock on his rare visits. Today, there was nothing but a marbled reflection of himself. The house was as silent as a packed elevator.

"You grew up here? Doesn't that explain everything," said The Gliss, looking around.

"It wasn't so bad. There were good times too," said Porter.

They moved to the kitchen, The Gliss bobbing behind like a child's party balloon, wobbling on its ribbon. The milk in the fridge had turned to cheese, but there were boxes of herbal tea. Porter brewed some nettle and peppermint. He picked up a blurry Polaroid of himself and Cherry bathing in the early 70s. Skegness was it? Or Yarmouth? The two children had their arms around each other.

"We'll never be that close again," he said. "Funny how people bang on about the benefits of family. But what if it's your family that makes you feel the loneliest?" He put the photo down, kissed two fingers and transferred a kiss to Cherry.

He opened a kitchen drawer. "Look at this. Same as it was 30 years ago." Inside was a violent, dusty hash of life's detritus: keys, strings, marbles, caked-dry blu-tack, hoops, screws, buttons, paper - and a large piece of rolled lead. "I used to play with that when I was a kid," said Porter, shaking his head. "It's a wonder I didn't get poisoned."

"Why'd she keep it?"

"Wait till you get upstairs - you'll see," said Porter. "This woman throws away *nothing*. That damn attic gives me the heebie-jeebies. This'll help." He pulled his phone out and pressed play on the original cast recording of *Gypsy*. To its tinny accompaniment, he pulled down the loft ladder, switched on the lights and headed up into the Attic of Ultimate Dread. The Gliss hummed along to *Dainty June and Her Farmboys*. However, as soon as he peeked inside the attic, he suggested that Carl Orff's *Carmina Burana* might have been a more appropriate soundtrack.

The attic still smelled of mildew and rat's piss. Porter had hidden up here as a teenager when privacy was only ever snatched, never given. The inverted V of the roof and its troll spiders gave him the willies then, and it gave him the willies now. Ida's hoarding mania was evidenced everywhere; old dresses, glass jars of rotten fruit that looked like evidence seized from the lair of a Victorian serial killer, bundles of *Woman's Own* magazines from the 50s featuring chubby women in girdles, one half of a pair of tan-leather shoes. You name it, there was a sad specimen somewhere in this museum of chaos.

"If this place were a book, it would be *Jack the Ripper's Diary*," said The Gliss.

"I always thought it was haunted," said Porter. "Seems a bit silly now I'm up here talking to an actual ghost."

"I'm not a ghost. I'm a messenger."

"Really? Transparent, white blobby thing. Suspended mid-air. Not of this world? Have you looked in the mirror? Do you have dictionaries where you come from?"

Porter stooped to avoid the cobwebs and glanced around in trepidation. This would be a long 10 minutes. But they found the cigar box almost immediately. It sat on an old dresser, iridescent thanks to a spear of light coming through a hole in the thatch.

Porter sensed a vibe.

"It's your powers. Harry had a bad death. It's got his stuff inside. You're tuning in," said The Gliss.

Porter took a breath and opened the box. He saw two well-thumbed, yellowing notebooks, a pair of spectacles, a hip flask, a crumbling leather wallet and two buttons. He couldn't see in the gloom and decided to bolt, knowing childhood spiders lurked eternal. As he scuttled down the ladder, clutching the box, he felt the old familiar shudder and the same relief when the door slammed shut without smoky black fingers hauling him back in.

He didn't want to stay at Ida's for long, but curiosity meant he had to skim the notebooks. "Can you do anything with those Mickey Mouse gloved hands of yours? Make tea? That sort of thing? Anything useful?" asked Porter.

"I don't have a physical dimension so, no, my silver service skills aren't what they could be."

Tutting, Porter held up the hip flask Harry Norton had carried till his death. He tried to unscrew it, but the cap was rusted shut. He imagined himself in the trenches, clutching the flask to his chest. "This represented home for Harry," concluded Porter. "It stood for better days and something to aspire to."

Choked, he examined the rest of the contents and found the wallet empty, the spectacle lenses scratched and foggy. He got nothing from them. Opening the first notebook, he saw faded ink and handwriting, bunched-up and tiny. Harry was either trying to save paper or protect his privacy. The first entry was dated July 1914 and was clearly aimed at Harry's wife.

I'm on the train, heading to the front. I'm a bit frightened if I'm honest. We always joked one day we would visit Paris, didn't we Alice? Now I just want to be back home in England. God, I miss London.

A one-inch square, sepia print fell out. Was this Alice - his own great-grandmother? The unwitting originator of the curse? Whoever she was, she didn't look like a party girl. She wore a black dress that Queen Victoria would have dismissed as dowdy. A doily veil draped overhead completed the look.

"Was it a comfort or a torment to have this with you in the trenches, Harry?" said Porter, turning the photo over. The back was foxed but bare.

"A bit of both," said The Gliss. "Might have helped him satisfy any urges he had."

"Don't be so vulgar. You talk like a teenage boy in a bikini shop."

"You think all those young men stopped having urges because they were in the trenches?"

"Didn't they give them bromide? Ok. I get your point, but it's irrelevant here - and tasteless. I want to get a feel for Harry. Don't ruin it."

"How did several million soldiers deal with their urges, I wonder?" said The Gliss, ignoring Porter.

"Give it a rest. Couldn't you be all doomly-silent, like the Ghost of Christmas Future?"

"If I *was* a ghost…"

The first notebook was half diary/half letter, written in the trenches and was chock full. The second book was lighter. About a quarter of the pages had been torn from the end – probably used as emergency toilet paper. The writing continued to the final extant page. The second journal's first entry was dated June 1917. Its first line was stark.

I've been in Flanders for two weeks, and it's even worse than France.

Porter flipped to the end and was able to make out the last few sentences in the dim light. It was Harry's final goodbye to his wife, dated 14th August 1917. Hours before his execution.

Alice, so much for being patriotic. What a mess.

You'd think I'd be scared? No. It'll be quick. I've seen so many people die horrible, slow deaths. Hundreds. Young men, from both sides, screaming with terrible, untreatable injuries. You'd think I'd hate the Bosche, but they look like us in death. Only then do you see the peace in their faces. That will be me soon - at peace, asleep. Try to think of me that way. Be happy I avoided the thousand other worse ways it could've ended for me here. Be grateful and pray for me.

There's no time to say anything but how much I love you and the children. I try not to think about them growing up without me. But I know they're in the best hands. It isn't fair what's happening - never let anyone tell you otherwise - but this is justice in the British Army, and I signed up to it. I love the children. I love you. Your husband, Harry.

Porter wiped his sleeve across his eyes. He'd seen many films, read several books, absorbed the poetry and been shocked at the end of *Blackadder Goes Forth,* but this reaction was new. This was his ancestor. Porter realised he was sniffling for himself too. He was lucky to be alive. If it hadn't been for The Gliss setting fire to his feet…

Time to go. He snapped out of it, squeezed his nose between thumb and forefinger, and put everything back. He wrapped the cigar box in one of the 2,000 plastic bags he'd known Ida kept under the sink. "No-one does this much shopping," he cursed, as the squashed bags ballooned from the open door, like wasps exiting a nest in search of revenge.

Closing the front door, he looked up at the house and whispered goodbye. He sensed Ida probably wasn't coming home.

"It was good to see this," Porter said, waving the packed diary. "Harry and Max aren't obviously connected, but Harry's words really got to me. Cartwright's voice on the grave hurt physically - a lot - but Harry's voice in the diary felt like mine from a different time. It really hit me in the gut."

"It's why we came." On the drive over, The Gliss had annoyed Porter by asking about hip-hop. Consequently, he had been banished to the back seat for the return journey."Are we sure Harry and Max aren't connected?" he said. "I'm here to pass on messages and don't have insider info, but it does seem a bit of a coincidence you should hear both these men's last words today. They were from the same battalion and regiment, both were executed by the British Army in the same war, in the same area."

Porter agreed. "I think whatever sent you is forcing me to identify with Cartwright by dragging my family connection in. It's worked by the way. I'm intrigued enough to go and research a bit more on Max and Harry. Maybe they knew each other?"

"I doubt it," said The Gliss. "The dates? Max was executed in March 1917, Harry, August 1917?"

"Right. Ah I see," said Porter, glancing over his shoulder at The Gliss. "Harry's diary said he'd been in Flanders two weeks…May/June 1917? Cartwright had been dead months by then. Still, you're right. It is a big coincidence. I guess when we get back…"

He turned back to the front as The Gliss shouted, "Watch out!"

Porter slammed on his brakes and ran straight into a startled man, who managed a quick "Uh Oh" expression before disappearing to the ground.

Porter's car swerved, a book and lit cigarette bounced off the windscreen and bonnet. A panicked spin of the wheel and a dent-making stop against a bench.

"Damn."

Porter jumped from the car and ran over to see how the Death by Dangerous Driving charge was shaping up.

"Goff almighty," said the man. "I thought I was a goner. Off to Le Mans, are we?"

"I'm so sorry. You stepped in front of me. I did brake. Are you ok?"

"They always said smoking would kill me," the man smiled. "I'm fine. No harm done - apart from the grazed knee and smack on the bonce."

"You wanna sit down? I'm so sorry, I'm a good driver, normally."

"I'm fine. Where's my book?"

Porter picked it up for him. *The Most Haunted Building in the World? A History of St Briavels Castle.* It was wet and torn, the spine broken.

"I'll get you a new one. Sorry," said Porter, handing it back.

"I've got a spare," said the man, lobbing it into a bin like a schoolgirl cricketer giving underarm a go. He lit a cigarette.

"Most haunted building in the world? I don't know about that. I grew up here," said Porter. "Creepy, sure, but never heard a reliable report of a ghost. Porter, by the way, Porter Norton."

"Nice to meet you. Feng - Feng Tiān." They shook hands. "I don't believe that rubbish either. That's why I'm here hunting ghosts actually - part of my quest to prove they don't exist."

"You hunt ghosts to prove they *don't* exist?"

"Me and The Doves. I'm here to prove they're wasting their time. They're the ones hunting actual ghosts. I'm the unbeliever."

"The Doves?"

"Ah, sorry. A little group of ghost nuts…named after a pub in Hackney."

"Hackney? I'm from Hackney. Do you mean The Dove in Broadway Market?"

"You know it? How funny."

Feng crushed his fag packet and threw it away, delved into a pocket and pulled out a fresh pack.

"Be prepared. Ex-boy scout Tiān at your service. Dib Dib Dib. Dob Dob Dob."

Porter looked at the smokes. "It's been three years, but I'm having a strange day. May I?"

Feng offered, and Porter lit up, savouring his first drag since David Cameron was Prime Minister. The pair stood in respectful silence for a few seconds, toking away.

Porter rotated the fag in his fingers. "Why do you waste time looking for something you don't believe in?"

"Proper scientific method - test the proposition. A belief in the supernatural - ghosts, Goff - is a way for humans to defer taking responsibility for life as it is - free will and all that jazz."

"You've said 'Goff' twice now. I hope you don't mind me asking, but do you have a speech impediment?"

"I never use the G Word," said Feng without malice. "Monkey superstition."

"Your English is good," said Porter.

"You expect every Chinaman to sound like Jackie Chan?"

"I didn't finish...I was going to say, it sounds like you're second generation."

"Sort of. Been here since 10. My father fled the Cultural Revolution, we followed. I feel English, British anyway."

"How you getting on with your quest?"

"Never seen a ghost so far. Doesn't prove anything of course."

"Not even here?"

"It's supposed to be infested with them. There's one room here, the Oubliette, where a ghost strokes you in the night. Not in a nice way either."

"Is there a nice way to be stroked by a ghost in the night?"

"Probably not, but then I've been single for a while," said Feng.

They were interrupted by a large man in jeans and a loud jumper waddling down the ramp. "You ok, Feng? I saw what happened from the window." Turning on Porter, the man barked, "You should be more careful, you bloody idiot."

"I'm fine, Carson," Feng interceded. "Half my fault. No harm done."

"Oh. Sure. Ok. Great. Be more careful next time," said Carson. Embarrassed, he gestured at the castle. "They've got broccoli soup for dinner." Unsure of how to proceed, Carson loped back up the castle ramp, muttering to himself.

"Good man, Carson," said Feng.

Porter hesitated. "You've heard a few strange ghost stories then?"

"Are you joking? Of course. They're all nuts. Lovely, but nuts. Susie is a medium who sees ghosts once a week. Every week! Funnily enough, it coincides with her séance evenings. Every Tuesday. £20 admission upstairs at some dodgy Dalston boozer. Dolan's as cheery as Dracula with toothache but harmless enough. As soon as we turn up at any investigation site, he'll say he's seen something. Mad and gullible, but he's got a van."

"You don't have a car? You're a spiffy dresser. I'm sure you can afford a car."

"I'm loaded. Ex-investment banker. Trouble is, behind the wheel, I'm a terror to puppies, street furniture and grannies alike. After my third instructor took early retirement rather than give me another lesson, I realised I should probably leave it to others. Ironic that I finally get knocked on my arse by someone who claims he *can* drive."

Porter and Feng burst into laughter. It was Porter's first big laugh for more than a year. Rubbing tears from his eyes, he looked at his new acquaintance.

The Gliss spotted the look in Porter's eye. "Hey. I know what you're thinking. Don't do it. This is between you and me."

Porter ignored him. "Feng, how would you react if I told you that I woke up from trying to kill myself this week - please don't ask – only to find myself permanently haunted by something ghost-like calling itself The Gliss ever since? It's here right now, hovering next to you."

Porter assumed Feng might back away. He didn't. He pulled a device out of his pocket, turned it on and waved it about. It clicked.

"I'm not getting a reading," said Feng, disappointed.

"The Gliss says I'm honour-bound to save dead people," said Porter, who let the Geiger counter pass without comment. "I'd say I was going mad if I hadn't heard a dead soldier speak to me this morning when I stood on his grave. Madness. Clearly. What do you think?"

"You're clearly disturbed," said Feng. "On the other hand, so am I. And chill. You have a long way to go before you're competing with The Doves. In fact, you look and sound boringly sane.

"You're baiting me, I know, but I can't ignore what you're claiming, can I? As long as you don't mind me eventually exposing your fraud, it looks like I'm buying you a pint." Pointing to a pub down the road, Feng asked, "Is that one any good?"

Porter, for the first time in three days, with some relief, was able to answer a question with basic, certifiable fact. "Yep. It's great."

Chapter 10

The George Inn. St Briavels, Ross-on-Wye
Tuesday, 21st March 2017: 5pm

"Those crazies believe anything - fairies, ghosts, elves. Drives me nuts," said Feng, quaffing vigorously, his eyes bulging.

"Never thought I'd become one of them," said Porter.

"What do you do?" asked Feng.

"Nothing," said Porter, with edgy bitterness, causing Feng to raise an eyebrow. Porter elaborated off Feng's look. "I'm a solicitor but haven't worked for 6 months. A little girl - Janine Crane - died. I'm partly to blame. Tribunals, civil cases, regulatory hearings… you name it."

"A minister without portfolio," said Feng. "Me too in a way - living off ill-gotten City gains. No wonder you're depressed. Ghosts are probably a healthy distraction."

"I'm not happy about it. Who wants to diagnose themselves as hearing voices? Talking with dead people? Next stop, a padded cell."

The Gliss said, "You're not talking *with*, you're listening *to*. All you've heard are tape recordings - echoes taking a long time to decay. There's no sentience. Manmade recordings have been around since Edison. It's not that far-fetched, is it? Humans and tape recorders both run off electrical energy."

Porter repeated this for Feng.

"The Gliss - he's not a ghost then?"

"Says he's a messenger. Doesn't know where, or who from. Annoyingly omnipresent. Like a postman who squats your house after dropping off a parcel. You don't work either?"

"City trader in the 80s. Million quid bonuses, all that Gordon Gecko jazz. Had a few million in the bank and thought - why the hell am I still screwing over the Third World?"

"Is there a Mrs Tiān?"

"Goff no. It'd be a Mr Tiān - if there were one."

"Er. That's nice."

"Don't be uncomfortable. You're not my type," said Feng, before asking, a tad too quickly, "Is there a Mrs Porter?"

Feng had 50 minutes to regret asking, as Porter gave chapter and verse on the Muriskava saga.

The Gliss stopped the fight in Round Seven. "The man is dying, Porter. Give it a rest."

Embarrassed, Porter whipped out Harry's hip flask. "Enough of me. Look at this."

Feng was impressed and relieved. He listened to the history and flashed his Geiger counter over the flask. "Nothing. Beautiful story though. A symbol of one man's dream of home in a world at war."

"He could've kept his dream of home alive a lot longer by not signing up in the first bloody place," said Porter. "It caused a lot of problems."

"I think it was noble. A quality in short supply today."

Two pints and a skim of the notebooks later and Feng was up to speed.

"It's obviously no coincidence that Harry and this Cartwright both met sticky ends and fought together. You realise that of course?"

"We've discussed it. There's no evidence they fought together. In fact, they almost certainly never met," said Porter.

"Maybe. It means no evidence of a *direct* connection. But same battalion, same war, same end, brought to your attention at the same time? Of course, they're *indirectly* connected. You don't know how, that's all," said Feng. He dissected a soggy beermat, building up the courage to speak. "Can I see you do your grave trick? How about we go to that church over the road, and you give me a quick demo?" Clearing his fingers of wet card with a flick and a rub, he grabbed his machine and waved it.

"Geiger counter, right?" asked Porter.

"Similar. It's a custom-made EMF meter."

"Which is what?"

"Measures electromagnetic fields. The Nuts think ghosts are detectable. Never had so much as a blip in 100-plus 'haunted' houses," said Feng, air-quoting.

Porter fiddled with his own beermat. "Your logic is based on the assumption the Nuts are right - that ghosts generate electromagnetic fields. If ghosts exist but don't emit anything, you could test for a million years and still get no positive."

"You're right, but even the so-called experts say they do. It's another lie I aim to disprove. How about that demo?"

"No thanks. I'd never do it again if I had my way. It was like being drowned, electrocuted and stabbed all at once."

"You said Cartwright's signal was weak - a few words, foggy image? Yet, a brand-new corpse on the trolley stunned you? Does suggest some kind of sliding scale?"

"It's called the Recession," said The Gliss. Porter translated.

"But what would happen if you were near a fresh but not immediately-dead body?"

"I doubt I'd live to tell the tale. It felt like my eyelids were being spot-welded shut and my ears drilled clean."

The Gliss tutted. "Watch him, Porter. His face suggests he's about to suggest something idiotic. I can hear the broken clockwork from here."

"Let's see how stupid his plan is then," said Porter.

"You know, if you are lying, you're a bloody good actor," said Feng, marvelling at the one-sided conversation.

Porter translated The Gliss' caution.

"He's right, actually. I've had a bit of a brainwave," said Feng. "I know how we can get our hands on a fresh corpse."

Conscious of a few home-town looks, Porter said, "Keep it down. What do you mean *fresh corpse*? It's not 1800. I'm neither Burke nor Hare."

"1828. Of course not," said Feng. "All we have to do is go to a funeral parlour and pay our respects to whoever they've got in."

"What? That's the most morally dubious thing I've ever heard!"

"I worked in The City. I've heard worse."

"No way. Not only is it dodgy but it hurts like hell. Ended up on my knees. Can you imagine that in a funeral home…and who said anything about '*we*'?"

"You don't get away that easy. Private viewing. No-one'd see how you react, except me."

Porter studied his new acquaintance. Fifty-ish? Enviably youthful skin. Expensive suit - Paul Smith? Look at the hole in his knee. My fault. All those years dealing with muppets coming off the streets with dubious and half-arsed claims and cases. Now? Porter looked up at Feng's face.

Embarrassing. He thinks I'm the muppet.

The Gliss said, "Porter, pay attention. Maybe this isn't such a stupid idea. We don't know for sure how strong your powers are. Testing them out could be useful."

Feng wouldn't take no for an answer. "I know the perfect place. I'll find out who they've got in and organise it. It's not illegal to pay respects."

"But we won't be paying respects, will we? We'll be using someone as a prop."

"Embrace The Strange, Porter. You are nuts, but if you want my help, I need to see what you've got."

"I don't know…sounds dangerous and I'm not keen to have my head spot-welded and drilled regularly."

"Tish and pish. You going back to Hackney tonight?" asked Feng.

"Yes. Can't wait to get out of here."

"Perfect, the funeral parlour's in Stoke Newington. Leave it to me. I'll sort out a visit for Thursday morning."

With some surprise, egged on by The Gliss, Porter agreed. Your life is going seriously wrong. But, when you think about it, what could go wrong, really?

Porter's flat, Sylvester Path, Hackney
Tuesday, 21st March 2017: 11.30pm

Porter opened his door and was greeted by wafts of burnt sock. Wine. Now.

He rummaged through his rack. Castillo de Maluenda's *Punto y Coma Viñas Viejas* from Calatayud. A mouthful in more ways than one.

The cork made a satisfying pop. Porter elbowed a ton of crap off the table to make space for the wine and research. He laid Harry's diaries out, next to a Holmesian magnifying glass he would need to decipher them. He usually used it to inspect the condition of record grooves.

Where's The Gliss? Who cares! Ciento y la Madre!

The Gliss was currently persona non-grata after singing all the way home from St Briavels. He sang Ethel Merman's loudest numbers, songs he had presumably picked up during his intrusions into Porter's memory palace. Porter had explained the difference between pure aesthetics and pure cataloguing. Yes, it was true, he had tried to remember as many songs and their musicals as he could, but no, he didn't want to hear most of them.

"If you could stick to Berlin, Kern and Porter's top 200 ditties I would be eternally grateful. Better still, keep out of my head altogether and let me listen to the CDs instead."

Nonetheless, The Gliss had inflicted musical delight after delight all the way home. Porter had turned on Magic FM and sang along to chart hits from the 80s in an uncharacteristic and unsuccessful bid to drown out The Gliss.

But he was gone again for now. Thank the Lord. Thank Goff.

Porter chuckled at the thought of his strange new friend, toasting him out loud. "What a loon you are, Feng. But cheers for listening."

With a sip of wine, Porter picked up the magnifying glass and settled down to see what Harry Norton had to say for himself. When he touched the book, a dull ache lapped over him. Not worth an aspirin, but something was coming off the pages.

London
July 1914

I'm on the train, heading to the front. I'm a bit frightened if I'm honest. We always joked that one day we would visit Paris, didn't we, Alice? Now I want to be back home in England. I know I'm doing the right thing, but it's also the hardest thing. I couldn't stay at home knowing all my friends have signed up. The Germans are bullying us. Do you remember that story about my first job in the brewery before I met you? When I broke Gibbons' jaw for pushing Stansfield around? That's my attitude towards bullies.

I think it's because I saw how my father never stood up to anyone. I hate bullies. When he died, my mother said, "We're destined for the workhouse now." She never said a thing about my poor father, crushed by a pile of beer barrels. She didn't respect him. She saw he'd been pushed around for years. She wasn't surprised he'd let us down again by dying. Please don't think of me like that Alice, even though I know you're angry. I'm doing this for you and the children. Every night before bed I picture you and say all your names out loud as if I'm kissing you all goodnight. You believe in God, but I only believe in family and justice. Let's hope this stupid war is over quickly and painlessly.

I've been travelling with a great group of lads. We're all from London, but we're from every district, so all strangers. Not so the country boys. I've seen groups of 12 from one village alone who signed up together. I hope we all make it home to tell our stories. The talk is, it'll only take a few months. I've made friends with a few. There's a great lad, Bill Beale - what a mouthful that name is - who's from Doncaster. We both joke about the other's accent. There's a Scot from Glasgow, Gordo, whose accent is even worse. You can make out every tenth word. Unfortunately, it always seems to be the same word: whisky. Some chance. We haven't seen ANY booze for a while, let alone whisky. I said I'm not religious and our chaplain is a good reason why not. I don't like him at all. You can tell he's uncomfortable around us. Gilpin always has an apple in his hand. Where on earth does he get them? None of us has seen fresh fruit for a month – all our food comes in tins. What's worse, he uses his penknife to peel the damn things. Who peels apples? Watching it fall to the floor wasted is maddening. There was a right barney one day between two soldiers fighting over his scraps.

Gilpin comes around and says, "Bless you my son" like a comedy vicar at the Music Hall. One of the lads mooned him. Gilpin tried to chasten him: "God sees all." We choked ourselves laughing at the image. Mind you, he didn't report him, and he could have done, so maybe he's alright really.

Porter awoke with a painful start. He had head-butted his wine glass nodding off. He looked in the mirror and saw a red crescent emerging from his right eyebrow. "That's great, what a perfect end to the day," said Porter, sore and annoyed.

The Gliss appeared. "Not sleeping? I should if I were you. We have to research Cartwright tomorrow. It'll be a day when much is discovered. I can feel it in my water."

"Stop nicking Ida's phrases from my head. Goodnight, Gliss."

"*The* Gliss."

"I can't say 'Goodnight *The* Gliss.' It's bad English."

"Think of *The* as a first name, like Eric."

"Eric?"

"Eric Gliss or *The* Gliss as you will continue to say."

"Goodnight Eric."

The Gliss tutted and disappeared.

Chapter 11

Porter's flat, Sylvester Path, Hackney
Wednesday, 22nd March 2017: 6am

Porter loved his sash windows. Until they jammed.
Impersonating The Hulk, he scraped and squeaked the sash open
wide enough to let out the odours of a fried breakfast. Smears of
yolk, ketchup and stringy rind were all that remained. A smiley face
emerged as Porter drew shapes in the sauce with his finger.

Ping. A text from Cherry.

What time you arriving?

A swipe of the iPhone left bean sauce all over his screen. He
cursed but he wasn't in the mood for a fight, so he ignored her. He
hefted his magnifying glass like a blackjack as if warning the world
in general, and his sister in particular, not to mess with him today.

"How's your head?" said The Gliss.

"Sore and now you can add eyestrain to my list of complaints."
Porter waved the notebooks at The Gliss. "Harry had a hell of a
journey to go from the man in these to his execution. He seems
genuinely fired up to do his bit."

"Lots of them did. But that was before they saw everyone being
pounded into smithereens or madness."

"I get that, but it doesn't feel right. And we know for a fact he
definitely didn't commit suicide – whatever you say. In fact, he
seems rational, conscientious and controlled." Porter sat back and
used his fingers to count off the reasons.

"It's his attitude. Firstly, he says how upset his wife Alice and
the children were when he signed up. But even then, he doesn't
regret it. It was voluntary conscription for the first couple of years.

"Two, he fought in The Somme and nearly bought it there - a
shell flattened him to the floor, killing several others around him.
After France you can tell he's definitely in shock, but not shell-
shocked."

"Reality bites and all that," said The Gliss.

"Exactly. Listen to this."

Porter flipped through the book, squinted through the magnifying glass and read.

Alice, do you remember the little pewter hip flask and cigar that old Mr Greenbaum gave me the night before I left? I smoked the cigar and drank the tot a VERY long time ago. Still, every night I get them both out, unscrew and smell them. For one second, I am back home with you and the children. The smell is gradually fading, but they are my most prized possessions. And your photograph, of course. Wish I'd been able to afford one of the children too. But that's my one job now - to fight the good fight and then get home to see you all again.

Porter looked up. "Once again, reading the official explanation and listening to your claim, Harry doesn't sound like either a potential deserter or suicide to me. And I only say suicide to keep you quiet. It's a matter of record he was killed by the firing squad."

The Gliss made a clumsy attempt at a shrug. "You make a good case for his general war, but he was out there a long time. He signed up at the start and was still there in 1917. Many people went mad a lot sooner than that."

Porter pulled the hip flask out, popped it on the desk next to the notebook and studied it. He caressed its curves and dents and re-tried to open it. This time it gave a little and, after much grunting, it came open with a grinding sound as the rust in the grooves separated. He put it to his nose.

"No way! I can smell whisky!"

"A century on? Sure *you've* not been at the whisky?"

"Can you smell?"

"No nose. This one's for show."

"I assure you it does."

"Do you have the cigar tube?"

"No, that probably got thrown out," said Porter. "Harry's effects were sent home but why waste time and money on an empty cigar tube? That would be like sending a cigarette box home."

"Of course. Doesn't change anything though. Whatever the official record says, Harry must have committed suicide, or I wouldn't be here. I come to save the fifth remember?"

Porter tried to rest his case. "So, the records lie about his execution? Are you suggesting someone else was executed in his place?" He absentmindedly brushed the notebook cover.

"These books are sad, but actually, I envy his kids. He keeps saying how much he loves them. That's more than my dad ever said to me."

Losing both parents in 24 hours had devastated both Porter and Cherry. The ways they had dealt with the loss had evolved differently. Cherry thought all suicides were malicious failures. It was a simple equation: if you have children, you don't desert them. Porter was lukewarm about his father but couldn't find it in himself to outright condemn him. The phone pinged. He used his sleeve to clean the screen. Cherry again.

Call me.

Tied up. Speak later.

Unacceptable. Now, please.

Can't. Meeting my solicitor.

BS. You're down in the dumps. Call me.

Ok. I'm not in the mood.

I've bought food.

I'll pay for it. Seriously.

Scott and Ruby want to see you.

Want to see them too, can't today. Next week.

We're away. You promised.

Got to go now. X

Don't you sodding X me. I'm furious.

I can see that. Soz. X

Whatever - MUPPET!

"She'll be standing in the kitchen now doing her Rumpelstiltskin impression," said Porter, shrugging.

"She thinks you're weak, doesn't she?" said The Gliss.

"It's why she's so protective of Scott. She's determined the curse won't touch him."

"She's seen how it's affected you. She's right to be worried."

"You can't make me feel guilty. I'm not my dad. I'm not leaving any children."

"Apart from Scott and Ruby you mean?"

"That's ridic…" And Porter stopped. "Oh."

"As enthralled as I am by your family history, could we get back to the notebooks? It's not just a task you know. Cartwright's case is worth doing for its own sake. Freeing a soul up by solving it will do you good."

"Soul?" said Porter mischievously. "That's a bit of a giveaway isn't it?" Porter leapt on the chance to make The Gliss explain himself.

"I meant *soul* as a synonym for *person*. You know, one of those redundancies that enable conversation to work?"

"You don't deal in souls where you come from?"

"Oh wow! I almost answered and gave myself away. I hope you're better at cross-examination than that piece of clumsiness implies?"

"I'm a solicitor, not a defence lawyer. I don't cross-examine anyone."

"Maybe you should."

"Meaning?"

"If you didn't take people like your sister and Tania on face value, you might have a better relationship with them. They both seem to dictate all the terms."

"You're deflecting. So, there are souls. Does that mean there's an afterlife?"

"So, there are souls? Doesn't mean you can infer the existence of Heaven and/or Hell any more than you could if you just found out for the first time about cats."

"I think souls are more germane to the idea of an afterlife than cats."

"According to your human-centric view maybe. As a non-human, I presume that any afterlife would be full of moggies. But what do I know? I'm a messenger. I only know my message."

"That's crap - you know a lot about history and music too."

"From your head. You have more in common with your sister than you think. You both like to dismiss others when you disagree with them."

"Whatever. I'm going back to the book. Are you sure you can't make coffee?"

"I presume that was rhetorical?" said The Gliss, and for the first time in a while, raised his hands. He was using them to apologise, but, white and disembodied, it merely looked like The Gliss was doing jazz hands.

One cup of espresso later, Porter sat up with a jolt. "He was wounded. Harry was wounded."

"Where?" asked The Gliss.

"In his arm. In Ypres, I mean," said Porter, gripping his magnifying glass hard.

Harry Norton's diary - Ypres
May 21st, 1917

Alice, please don't worry, but I'm recovering at the moment. A mortar fell next to our trench during one of the battles, and my left arm got damaged. It'll be alright the nurses say. Not like some of the poor blighters here. But I'm fine. I'm coming home as soon as we've won this war.

"See. His mind is fixed on home. Getting home. I doubt traitors plan that far ahead. Suicides definitely wouldn't," said Porter.

"Don't most dying soldiers scream for their mum? It proves nothing," said The Gliss.

Before you ask: Yes. It hurt. A lot. A piece of shrapnel sliced down my left arm, damaging the muscle. There was blood, but by a miracle, no arteries were hit.

I came to, thinking I was dead, staring up at a dark black roof with sounds of torment everywhere. "Well Harry, looks like you've gone to the other place after all," I said. But when I moved my head, I saw I was still very much alive, on a stretcher in an old barn.

Eventually, a nurse tells me we are in some place called Ooderdom? Ourdadom? It was a field hospital and the worst place I've been so far. All around me were men in agony - nurses working out who could be saved and who could not. That blasted idiot Gilpin was walking around, peeling his apple as usual. A nurse asked him not to eat out of respect, and he stowed his penknife away in embarrassment. The worst of the worst I have seen so far was a seby next to me. I spent some time trying to comfort the poor devil.

Porter interrupted. "What the hell is a seby? Harry's handwriting is terrible." It took a few minutes of research and deciphering before they deduced Harry meant *sepoy* - one of the many Indian soldiers recruited from the Empire on the promise of money and prestige.

He wore a turban and had a monstrous beard and moustache. The leg closest to me was missing, and I could see his hipbone and muscles. A gash further up had left intestines poking through. He was dying of course. The nurses moved on - there was nothing they could do. He looked at me, blood and spittle flecking his beard. Who knows what language he was speaking? Something from Hindustan, maybe? He wailed and clawed at me like a drowning man. Eventually, compassion led me to take his hand.

I kept asking the man what he was trying to tell me, but he had not one jot of English, nor I one jot of Punjabi. I held his hand and watched him maniacally try to pass a message on to me. But it was no good, and the man died soon after. I soon began to wonder, who was he trying to message? His wife? Mother? Children? I thought of you and the children and almost went mad on the spot. Dying without words away from one's loved ones must be the worst kind of torment.

It's why I keep this book, Alice. If anything happens to me, they'll send it home, and you'll know exactly what I was thinking. For the millionth time, please don't hate me for doing the right thing. If I sinned in your eyes, please believe me: Every man here is paying for their sins.

"I'm glad I got to read this," said Porter. "I've got nothing from my father or grandfather. I never really knew them. But after 50 pages of this stuff, I feel connected to Harry."

"We really need to concentrate on Cartwright though," reminded The Gliss. "Interesting as Harry is, Max is your mission."

"Yes, but there may be a connection – you said so yourself - and it's all good background reading at least."

"There is a metaphorical connection between Max Cartwright and the sepoy," said The Gliss.

"Have I missed something?"

"The importance of last words. You heard Cartwright's last words. He was probably high on morphine, rum and fear. Who heard those last words? No-one. Until you came along, Porter. He's been waiting for someone to hear his claim of innocence. You have the chance to right wrongs. A great gift. Harry had the same experience with the Indian soldier."

Porter exclaimed, "Look at this!" Straining once more to read the cramped and jerky writing, he read aloud an entry from June 1917.

Alice, something terrible happened today. I met a young private from Durham called Al Hobbs. He was crying his heart out. You see this a lot. Not everyone can take the constant bombardment. Some of them need to go home and recover, but the army doesn't tolerate weakness. We've heard some get executed for being ill.

I spoke to Hobbs, but he was like one of those old boys you used to see from Colney Hatch - shouting and wailing in the street until someone knocked them senseless for peace. Hobbs was inconsolable. I dragged him into one of the cubby holes dotted along the trench so none of the officers could see him. Between gulps, the boy told me he wasn't frightened. He'd been mistreated by one of the officers. I told him to not say such things. It could get him killed. He carried on. I couldn't do anything to calm him. Eventually, I had to go. I asked one of the other men to look out for him.

Later we heard an explosion outside the mess. We ran out. Hobbs was dead. He had pulled the pin on a grenade and held it to his face. Two other men were injured in the blast and had to be treated for shrapnel wounds.

I've seen some things, but the sight of Hobbs' headless corpse lying there made me sick to my stomach. What kind of world is this? The worst of it, Alice, was that I kept imagining our Geraint. What if it had been him lying there? He is too young to ever play a part in this war. Pray God there will never be another like it.

"Certainly puts your problems in perspective," said The Gliss.

"I feel guilty enough. Give it a rest."

"Sure."

Porter smelled roast beef coming from the flat upstairs. Damn. He was missing Cherry's roast. "Do you mind if I go out and get some lunch? They do a nice roast at The Clapton Hart," said Porter.

"All you seem to do is sleep, drink espresso and eat," said The Gliss.

"That's the human machine for you. Sorry, we are so fallible compared to your greatness. I also need a pee."

"Another weakness."

Porter had lived with women so long, had become so fed up with their inevitable complaints of drips, he always sat now, even when peeing. He propped his elbows on his knees, cupped his chin and thought about Private Hobbs.

"You can stand up now Tania's gone," said The Gliss.

"Do you mind?" said Porter. "Is nowhere private anymore?"

"Relax. Your todger is of no interest to me. I'm all about the work."

"Clear off. I'll carry on reading over lunch. If you have to follow me, I'll see you at the pub. Let me have 10 minutes to myself for flip's sake." The Gliss disappeared without rejoinder.

It took Porter 20 minutes to walk through St John at Hackney's churchyard and up Lower Clapton Road before arriving at the Hart.

Funny place. Derelict for years but now re-opened. Deliberately only semi-restored. Seats with worn out springs, bare brick and wood gave it a louche and decadent shabby chic feel, mirroring the louche and decadent shabby chic locals who flocked there on Sunday for the impressive roasts.

Settled at an old school desk *sans* varnish, Porter got out his books and glass. He glanced around.

A couple in their 70s, who looked like they were on an uncomfortable weekend down from Leeds, sat with their bearded son and his bearded boyfriend. The dad looked resigned but uneasy, and the mum tried to leaven the mood by showing the boys some photos.

It reminded Porter of the first time Cherry and Ida had met Tania in a pub. As soon as Tania had popped to the loo, Cherry had said, "You're batting above your average there, Porter."

Ida had said, "She's a stuck-up bitch."

"Which is it?" Porter had said in exasperation.

"Whatever makes you happy, love," said Ida, patting him on the thigh.

Bloody women. He turned back to the notebooks. There was a lot of repetition - anecdotal stuff about trench mishaps and characters.

The most consistent character, unnamed but stalking every page, was Harry's guilt. The entries got shorter and more sporadic as time passed. It did look like he was wearing thin a bit, admitted Porter.

There were a few gaps, but at the start of July 1917, there was an unexpected flurry as Harry regained his diary mojo. They were in a completely different style, cryptic and - Porter wasn't sure at first, but soon found the word - *sinister*.

And one significant tonal change: It looked like Harry had stopped writing for Alice and was making notes for himself.

Harry Norton's diary - Ypres
July 2nd 1917
I spoke to the private in question. No answer.

July 4th 1917
Charles Gilpin
Charles Devereaux
Sidney Dellfield
George Blenof
Roger Braintree
Alexander Wooton (sic)
Cecil Braxted
Peter Scanlon
Maurice Feldman

The last two names had been crossed out without explanation.

July 7th 1917
Our captain, Cecil Braxted, is an excellent, brave sort who really does seem to care for us. He is also, in keeping with his position of command, strict. When he got wounded, I heard his first words on coming-to were, "How are the men?" But then there was the night poor Samuel fell asleep on duty. Braxted pistol-whipped him. Even that was an act of mercy. Braxted could have had him court-martialled. Other men have been executed for falling asleep on lookout.

July 9th 1917
Billy (Beale) came to me worried about another of the young privates. He's stopped talking to everyone, cries himself to sleep at night and is very jumpy if anyone approaches him. Billy doesn't want another Hobbs.

July 13th 1917
Devereaux is in the clear.

July 17th 1917
What is the point of going through all this when the worst enemy is within? This is cankerous. How do I cut it out?

"That sounds ominous. Almost suicidal?" teased The Gliss.
"That's not what I'm getting," resisted Porter. But the next line made his heart sink.

July 28th 1917
It's my sad duty to end this, though I suspect it will be at much cost to my dear Alice and the children.

Finally, Harry's last entry. August 14th 1917. He reverts to the Harry of old, writing directly to his wife. Porter had skimmed this at Ida's but now re-read it with care.

Alice, I wanted to do what was right for our country. Look at the mess that has gotten me into? You would think I'd be scared?

Porter repeatedly read the last few lines, in morbid pity and unexpected sadness.

There's no time for me to say anything except I love you and the children. I try not to think about them growing up without me. But I know they are in the best hands. It isn't fair what's happening - never let anyone tell you otherwise - but this is justice in the British Army, and I signed up to it. I love you, your husband, Harry.

The rest of the pages were missing, leaving violently ragged stubs. Porter cross-referenced his notes. Harry was executed on August 16th, 1917. He hated to admit it, but it did sound as if Harry was cracking up towards the end of July. He might indeed have had suicide on his mind. But, there was still no easy way to get around the fact he was killed by firing squad - assuming the paperwork was all-correct and that really was how he died.

Tucked into the flyleaf were two letters, both in fragile envelopes. One was Harry's letter to Alice, officially sanctioned on the eve of his execution. Porter was confused by its brevity. Did you feel you had covered everything in your notebook, Harry?

Dear Alice, Dear children,
As suspected, things haven't gone well. By the time you read this, I will be dead - killed by my own comrades for desertion. Don't grieve for too long.
To have survived this long, knowing in my heart of hearts that I might not make it home, has been a rare punishment. I'm so sorry for the suffering this will cause you all. I've only done my best and tried to be a good man. Please remember me this way whatever else you may hear.
I love you all,
Harry, your husband and father

Porter wondered if this got home before the official notice. What a letter to receive. Were you too frightened to write more Harry? Your handwriting is proper haywire here.

"Your notes to Cherry and Tania weren't much longer," said The Gliss, reappearing in a brick alcove to the left of Porter.

"Aargh! You made me jump. You're right. Don't rub it in." A passing waitress stared at him, eyebrows raised. Porter pulled out his phone, fake dialled and held it to his ear. "Can I read this other letter in peace please?"

Porter took it, gingerly removed it from its envelope and groaned when he saw the state of the writing.

"Harry looks like a medieval illuminator of scripture compared to this," whistled The Gliss.

"It's from Billy Beale - after the war - no censorship. Maybe it's more forthcoming?"

But Beale had been barely literate. He intended to console, not illuminate.

Der Alice,
I am Bill Beale. I was good frend of yor husbnad. Harry was a good man and lookd afer us al. It was not rite wat hapened to him. I was there. Harry was brave to the end. I went to his sell afer and was goin to send his things bak. He kep his flarsk and rote sum nots in a book but the captin was upset too and said he wood do it. Hope you got them.
I think of Harry offen and wood like to come see you won day.
                    Yours
                        Bill

"Harry's death caused a lot of problems for my family. In truth, you can't tell much from these sad notes, can you? I was thinking. Might he have killed himself by deserting, knowing he'd be executed if caught? But even that doesn't feel right."

"Sounds plausible though. Nice diversion though Harry is, you need to think about Cartwright. Are you meeting up with Feng tomorrow?" asked The Gliss.

"It's a bit dodgy, isn't it? Aside from the moral issue, I'm not keen on seeing any more corpses right now either."

"You can't avoid the dead. You live in London. They're everywhere. The little headache you have now will keep getting worse until you end the Quincunx. You don't have to see dead people, you just have to be near their remains."

Porter finished up his meal. "I'll think about it. The idea of dead people throwing psychic tentacles out to grab me isn't giving me the most pleasant of sensations."

"And a man who got Michael Bublé for Christmas knows of what he speaks?"

"You got it."

Chapter 12

Porter's flat, Sylvester Path, Hackney
Thursday, 23rd March 2017: 7am

The postman came early. Porter heard the letterbox flap and took it as his cue for breakfast. Not until he felt the grit and chill of the stairs on his bare feet, did he remember Feng's plan for this morning. He felt the grit and chill on his conscience too. Sneaking around a funeral home had never been high on his list of personal ambitions. Give it a miss. Definitely.

He collected the post and stuck the kettle on. An unwanted catalogue went straight in the bin. In guilt, he immediately retrieved it and put it in the recycling bag. He flipped on Radio 4 and opened the letter. It was from the Solicitor Regulation Authority.

Dear Mr Norton,

We have now set a date for your Solicitors Disciplinary Tribunal. It will be held at our offices on April 10th at 9.30am. This concerning case PHT674/32 on charges of Gross Misconduct. Your solicitor, Namita Menon of Quendell's and Co, has also been advised of this date.

We advise that you arrive in plenty of time for the hearing, which is scheduled to last at least 3 hours…

Porter read no further. The only *news* here was the date and time. As soon as he had told his old boss he was taking them to an industrial tribunal, they had referred him to the SRA, an attempt to have him struck off.

The Gliss asked, "More bad news?"

Porter cursed. "Expected. I wouldn't be surprised if they ask me to drop the tribunal in return for them pulling this," said Porter, flapping the letter about.

"Would you?"

"I'd still be out of a job, and they still wouldn't have shared responsibility, so no."

On cue, the phone rang. It was Porter's old boss Nicholas Runyon.

"Hi, Nick. I guess you're checking I got the letter?"

"Porter. I'm unhappy things have come to this, I really am. I was hoping we could clear this up between us."

"I was just telling The Gl…a friend…you might try that."

"It's such a waste of time, energy and money to go this route."

"But what choice do I have? You fired me, I'm unemployable."

"Even if I give you a good reference, anyone doing due diligence will find out about the Janine Crane case. I can't help that."

"If I hadn't been working 18-20 hour days, if you'd employed other staff, the mistake wouldn't have happened. It was my screw-up, but it only came out of a work culture of bullying and under-resourcing. That's down to you. I think it's a 50/50 case, so I have to fight it."

There was a pause.

"I'm not here to fight, Porter. Drop your case: We'll withdraw ours. You'll still be free to practise. If you lose, you'll be struck off."

"Yes, but when I detail my case at the tribunal – oh, and did I tell you the Daily Mail and The Guardian both want to come? - your clients will see perfectly well how you under-resourced their cases, despite charging premium fees. I'd say - with no pleasure at all - you have as much to lose as I do."

Another pause.

"I doubt the papers would be interested," said Runyon.

"Weekes from the Mail has left messages all month. She's after me, but she'll soon realise she's getting you too. I'd rethink your strategy if I were you."

"Porter, we used to get on pretty good?"

"No, we didn't. You were my boss, and I kissed your arse. You've always been a dick. You're delusional to think anything else."

"This isn't personal, don't make it so."

"Is that a joke? I've been vilified, attacked and deprived of work. It's very personal. We could've put on a united front, but you chose to scapegoat me. I'm cornered, Nick. And that's when animals are dangerous, right?"

"Drop the industrial tribunal: We'll withdraw our complaint," repeated Nicholas.

"I'm sorry, did we go back in time five minutes? I can't and I won't. You're a total bastard Nick Runyon. A stuck-up, only-got-there-with-your-parents'-help, cowardly, sexist, racist, everything else-ist, bastard with a capital B. And I will stand up to you to the last. Understand now, you bag of shite?" But Runyon had hung up on the capital B.

The Gliss coughed. "Interesting choice of phrases there, Porter. Not fond of him then? Sounds like a total…er, pain. Sorry, I'm not in your class re insults."

"It makes me mad. I hate injustice."

"Is that why you became a solicitor?"

"No. I stumbled into it. Injustice? Helping neighbours settle boundary disputes is hardly prosecuting Nuremberg, is it?"

Porter re-tied the knot on his gown belt and poured more coffee.

He left a message for Namita."I've been sent the SRA letter. Can we talk?"

He looked from the window onto ancient Sylvester Path. Until recently, a wall from 1666 had stood opposite his flat before it was flattened to make room for the Hackney Empire's new offices. When he looked out, he always saw the ghost of that wall. Stupid really, but he had identified with it as an object out of time, as well as now missing it aesthetically.

"Stop moping," said The Gliss.

"I'm calming down."

"Go meet the ghost-hunter. It'll take your mind off things."

"What's the point?"

"We need to find out how far your powers extend. This is a safe way to do it."

Porter turned from the window and caught sight of himself in one of the five mirrors Tania had left behind. He looked at his stupid, gullible face.

You idiot. You're going, aren't you?

Cherry's house, Canterbury
Thursday, 23rd March 2017: 8.30am

Orit had a bloody cheek, but who could blame her? Cherry put the phone down on her friend with a latex-thin goodbye, showing her resentment by rough-handling a pile of Ruby's comics.

To be fair to Orit, Porter was showing signs of trouble again. Still. Calling her boss like that was presumptuous. Cherry scooped handfuls of Lego from the carpet and threw them back in the box, clinker-clanker. Orit floating plans for a mental health assessment for Porter was tactless, and probably self-serving, but, ultimately, a good idea. At least she'd confessed.

"I'm worried about him Cherry," Orit had justified. "He's in real danger, so I got a second opinion from Justin. I didn't want to jump right in and cause a fuss."

"Or mess. Look what happened with that actor you tried to section?" said Cherry.

"It's not my fault he missed that call from Spielberg."

"You didn't help."

"He wasn't a terribly good actor, Cherry."

"He persuaded that judge he wasn't nuts?"

"Can we go back to Justin?"

"What did he say?"

"Same as me. You need to keep an eye on him. He mustn't deteriorate. Act now."

"Get him sectioned?"

"He needs assessment," said Orit, choosing her words carefully.

"He's always been a bit strange Orit. Let me think about it."

Bloody curse. Why were all the men in her family so obsessed with this idiocy? Men. Cherry included her husband Rob in this. He was like a wraith morning and evening. At the weekends he materialised into something more substantial and then faded again with the Monday morning alarm.

She had never forgiven her father. Others were touched by his fatal despair for his dead wife, but Cherry hated him for it. She had been softer as a child, missing her dad despite the pain. But then she had children of her own and set about loving them with a ferocity that surprised her.

Throughout her first year of parenthood, she had hardened. What kind of man leaves their kids behind? She had no time for the concept of depression-as-illness. It was a selfish state of mind. Her mother had a real disease. Cancer was tangible, you could see it in photographs. Her Dad was a moron who didn't get his priorities right. He might have even survived if it wasn't for the curse tainting everything. Idiots.

Cherry picked up a photo of Porter and the kids. A heart-shaped Habitat frame. Scott idolised Porter for some reason. Their conversations about the relative merits of Ed Sheeran and Bing Crosby amused her. But she didn't want Scott to be exposed to the toxic curse in any form.

When her brother and son were together, she always worried Porter would bring the damn thing up. She told Porter his testicles were on the line. "I'll have you locked up before I let you pass that crap on to Scott," she had shouted at Porter once. Was that angry promise about to come true? Where are my shears? She put the frame back. No fingertip kisses from her. She tutted and shook her head again.

She plumped a heart-shaped cushion and thought of Porter. What he needed was to get over Tania and take a big dose of common sense - and have some space to sort himself out. He wasn't a danger to himself. Not yet anyway. Just don't do anything mad, Porter. You'll be alright.

Chapter 13

Mustham & Sons, Stoke Newington Church Street, Hackney
Thursday, 23rd March 2017: 10am

"I'm not going in," said Porter staring at the black & gold Victoriana of Mustham & Sons funeral home.

"Relax, Porter. It's not illegal to pay your respects," said Feng, looking svelte in another Paul Smith suit. "I've done this before with the Doves."

"Seriously Feng, I'm not happy about this."

The Gliss appeared. "Your friend's right. There's no real danger here, but maybe there's something useful to be gained?"

Porter wasted a few seconds perusing the street. It retained a lot of its 18th-century charm, including narrow bends and curves no modern road designer would dare contemplate. Porter had walked it a thousand times, eaten in many of the restaurants and cafés. He knew the sights - World War Two camouflage patterns still visible on the Town Hall; Defoe Road named after its former resident, the *Robinson Crusoe* author; *The Auld Shillelagh* where he once magically got off with a model called Deidre. Pulling back to the perilous present, all that cosy history disappeared. Mustham & Sons, which he could swear he'd never seen before, sucked energy like a black hole, leaving him shaking, nervous and besieged by uneasy conscience.

"What's the plan?" he said, coming to some kind of acceptance.

"According to the Hackney Gazette," said Feng, "there's a woman in her 20s in there called Soraya Adair. Overdose. Funeral's next week. The parents talked about her in the article, and I've checked their address. More than enough info to get us in." Nodding at the entrance, he said, "They're expecting us. Well, they're expecting Nick Flavell and Joe Crenshaw anyway."

"And they are?" said Porter.

"You're Nick, I'm Joe."

"Joe Crenshaw? Sounds like a lumberjack from the Mid-West, not a Chinese Brit," said Porter.

"It'll do," said Feng. "It's too late to change it."

Porter slapped his forehead. "For heaven's sake. Let's do it then. Nick Flavell. Sheesh."

"This," said The Gliss, "is going to be interesting." And he made sarcastic noises which, Porter only realised as he opened the door, were meant to sound a little bit like cars crashing.

Despite his panic, as the door closed, with a sweet tinkling bell, Porter prosaically wondered how they managed to keep the place so quiet with old sash windows. It was, appropriately enough, deathly quiet.

A man with an outrageous 19th-century pompadour and coppiced moustache slipped from behind a black velvet curtain.

"Gentlemen. I'm Eric Jeune, director of Mustham & Sons. How may I help you?"

Porter glanced at The Gliss and did a double take. Through his translucent form, he could see a CCTV camera pointing straight at him. A small blinking light confirmed it was on. Great.

"We spoke on the phone? Joe Crenshaw? Nick and I are...were... friends of Miss Adair?"

Porter noticed Jeune's raised eyebrow at the mention of Crenshaw. Jeune had no doubt been anticipating a beefy American.

"A terrible loss," said Jeune. "Her parents and brother came yesterday."

"Yes, she was stonkingly popular," said Feng.

"Stonkingly? Her parents said she was reclusive and isolated?"

"Yes, she went through a bad patch but was virtually a socialite before her illness," said Feng.

"She became reclusive, but we still managed to work together, right up to the end," said Porter, thinking he ought to make a contribution.

"I thought she hadn't worked for over a year?"

"True, but before that, we worked together."

Porter couldn't read Jeune's reactions, but he thought he saw him glance up at the CCTV camera.

"You'd like to pay your respects today?"

"Yes, we can't make the funeral next week, unfortunately," said Feng.

"If it was the week after..." said Porter, "...but you know. Work. And stuff."

"Shut up, Porter. He's not sure about you two," said The Gliss. "Neither of you should take up poker."

Jeune ran a finger through his moustache with a sound like riffled cards. Unsure of what else to do, he put aside his long-cultivated distrust of everyone and invited them to sign the visitors' register.

"If you could wait five minutes, please. We will go prepare Ms Adair for viewing," said Jeune.

"Seriously, that guy is straight from a Frankie Howerd sketch," said Feng.

They sat, side by side, hands on knees, looking like two statues guarding an ancient cave. They moved simultaneously, sitting back and folding their arms identically.

"Me forward, you back?" whispered Feng.

"We look like synchronised swimmers. Relax a bit. Don't look but there's a CCTV camera…I said *'don't* look'."

"So what? We're just seeing our friend."

"The one you both evidently know so much about?" sighed The Gliss.

"I don't like it. My headache's getting worse," whispered Porter.

The Gliss chipped in. "I'm glad you dosed up? This could be intense. Remember, you're a sensitive now. Don't touch the body or you'll find yourself in the room with a tiger."

Porter translated.

"Oh, I can't wait to see this," said Feng. "Lions and tigers and bears!" He patted the device in his pocket.

Eric Jeune returned and ushered them into a room where an open coffin lay ready for their inspection. Porter kept his back to the wall waiting for a reaction. But when it came, it wasn't the one he was expecting. It wasn't even supernatural. With a jolt, Porter realised he hadn't seen a dead body since crying beside his parents' bodies as a child. His legs jellified, but there were no blinding flashes of light or pain, no voices.

"I'll leave you gentlemen for five minutes to pay your respects. Press the buzzer if you need me."

Porter barely heard him. He had been hypnotised by a stage magician once. He remembered feeling blurry and warm, cut-off from the world. It was like that now.

Feng was in the present, however, and getting increasingly annoyed at Porter's non-reaction.

"Getting anything?" Silence. "Come on we haven't got long." Feng stared at his new friend, who looked spaced out and distant. Feng looked as suspicious as a schoolteacher crashing in on a toilet of silent, staring boys.

"Porter. Can you hear me? Follow me."

Feng took Porter by the arm, and they moved to the open casket. Soraya Adair was beautiful and stately. A terrible sight.

"Porter! What's going on? You getting anything?"

The Gliss hovered. Porter remained static, an android on standby.

Feng waved his hand in front of Porter's face to break the trance. He gave up. "Let's go Monsieur Arcati."

Porter dimly registered this. Let's. Go. Lettttttt's Gooooo. LLLL EEEE TTTTT SSSSS GGGGGGG OOOOOO.

The sounds poured noisily into his head like a bag of marbles being tipped into a tin mug. A thought formed: If Feng gives up on you, you're on your own. He looked down at Soraya: Only one thing to do.

The Gliss, springing to life, shouted, "Oh no, you don't!" but was powerless to stop Porter from reaching out and grabbing Soraya Adair's hand.

A thousand flaming pins the size of knitting needles pierced him from every direction, through eye, muscle, heart and brain. Glass shards whirled about him, forming into fists of energy which punched and sanded his skin to blood.

That's how it felt. All Feng saw was Porter crumple to his knees. But Feng was delighted with the Vincent Price melodrama. Porter came across as a small-town evangelist, casting out demons in the Mid-West.

Feng was finally convinced: Yep. No doubt about it. Porter was just another loony. He pulled out his EMF meter expecting silence. But the roomy ambience came alive with fast tock-tock-tocking. The VU meter's needle pinned hard into the red. "What the hell!?" said Feng.

Porter, still on his knees, reached up with both hands for support on the coffin. Feng waved his meter around excitedly. Which was when Eric Jeune came rushing back in.

"What on earth is going on here?" he said in shock. "Is that a Geiger counter? What's happening? Let go of that coffin! I knew something was wrong! I knew it! Stand up!"

"Oh, give it a rest, dear," said Feng.

"Don't call me dear," said Jeune.

"Oh, purr-lease. Look at that haircut Liberace wouldn't be seen dead in. It takes one to know one, darling. You're the dog who called the chien a hund. He's upset - can't you see that? He was in love with her," said Feng. It was off the top of his head but sounded feasible.

"What the hell are you doing with that thing?" said Jeune.

"It went off in my pocket. Meant to put it on silent. Work gadget. Sorry about that."

"I'm not happy, I'm most definitely not happy about this."

Feng ignored the disturbed funeral director and pulled Porter to his feet. "Come now, Joe. It wasn't meant to be. Time to go."

"What? I thought you were Joe?"

"We're very close. Come, Nick, let's go."

"Imposters! Outrageous!"

Jeune protested all the way to the door, but Feng and Porter were outside within seconds.

The pain was subsiding. Shaken and stirred, Porter looked at Feng.

"We've got to find a newsagent. Don't say a word. She gave me a message."

Eric Jeune was livid. Liberace! The cheek! He screen-grabbed a CCTV image with one hand, dialled the phone with the other. Someone picked up. "Is that Stoke Newington police?"

Chapter 14

Stoke Newington Church Street, Hackney
Thursday, March 23rd 2017: 10.45am

Porter grabbed a pen and notepad and immediately began writing. Feng caught up, placated the flustered shopkeeper and paid. The newsagent starcd at Porter, who was frantically scribbling, desperate to get Soraya's message down before he lost it.

Porter's phone rang. It was the *Close Encounters* ringtone attached to Tania. He all but dropped the notebook.

"Tania?"

"Hi, Porter. Don't get excited. I need a favour."

"Anything, you know that."

"Are you in on Monday?"

"Not sure yet. Why?"

"Can you make sure you're not? I need to pick up the last of my stuff."

Porter was crestfallen. "I can be there. What time you coming?"

A silence. "Porter, don't start. I'm not ready. Is that ok?"

"I'd love to see you," said Porter, aware of the grovel in the undertone.

"No. Please. Is Monday ok?"

He caved. "Sure."

"Thanks, Porter." She grudgingly asked how he was doing. "But keep it brief."

The undisguised calculation stung.

"Not so good," he confessed. "Tribunal coming up. Could get struck off."

"Good luck with that."

"Thanks."

"And Porter…?"

"Yes?"

"Don't be in on Monday. Please." She was gone.

Feng jogged his arm. "You've been standing there for a minute now. Bad news?"

Porter snapped back to life. "Shit!" He resumed scribbling, this time in fits and starts.

"I'm struggling. I didn't have enough time to recreate my walk," complained Porter.

"In English?" said Feng.

"I was creating a memory walk. I only got as far as the Hackney Empire."

"That clears that up. What the hell are you talking about? Let me pay for this."

With a raised eyebrow from the man behind the counter, the two stepped out into the street. Feng picked up the conversation. "You were saying? Memory walks, Hackney Empire and all that?"

Porter had been asked many times and knew it was best to show, rather than tell, people how memory walks worked.

"I pick a route that I can't get jumbled up, like that," said Porter, pointing, in sequence, to a bus stop, a draper's and a mosque. "Then merge those markers with what I'm trying to remember. A string of sausages swinging from the bus stop, a suit made of onions in the draper's window and mashed potato smeared over the dome of the mosque. When I get to the shops, I redo the walk, remember the image, and that's my dinner sorted."

"I saw a card shark do something similar memorising a shuffled pack by turning every card into an image," said Feng.

"Trust you to know a card shark but, yes, that's right. Anyway, that's what I did - plonked lines down from Soraya's suicide note on the route from St John at Hackney Church to the Library. But I did it quickly. It's fading."

"How far did you get?"

"Creating? All of it. Remembering? Most of it. I've had no time to rehearse it. Can I have five minutes quiet please while I get it down."

"Take a deep breath. Let's go through it together. What was first on your list?"

"No need to start there. I remember up to the Empire - that was one of my markers. Here's what I've got so far."

He handed Feng the notebook, who read it out loud.

"Dear Mum and Dad. I'm so sorry. It wasn't your fault. You were brilliant, but you couldn't save me. When I was a child Gillson (sic?) next door would come over and make me do things to him. I wanted to tell you but knew you would only blame yourselves. He took photos and threatened to show them to you if I told anyone. I felt sick all the time. Darren has been a great brother too. Such a shame we can't carry on all our adventures together. I really couldn't carry on. I don't want you thinking it's your fault or that I don't love you all. I do. I feel like one of those people who go to a Swiss clinic to die though. It's my choice. I don't think there was anything that could be done."

Feng stopped reading and looked up. "How accurate is this?"

"Verbatim more or less."

"And she told you to write it down?"

"It was odd. Once I got over the pain of seeing her, I saw she was in distress. I could sense the pain wasn't about dying, she wanted to explain herself. Is this another case?" he said, looking up at The Gliss.

"I think it is. But maybe all you have to do is get this note down? And get it to her parents, of course."

"Of course. As if I didn't have enough on my plate."

Feng said, "The Gazette said there was no suicide note. *Open Verdict.* Coroners avoid suicide verdicts to help the families. Unless there's no question about it."

"The Gliss says Soraya is probably another case for me. She was definitely distressed that she didn't leave a note. It was incredible. There she was, as real as you. She was sat at her computer, writing."

"She didn't speak to you?"

"She didn't acknowledge me at all. I could tell what I had to do."

"You're either mad or touched by the hand of Goff."

"But there's more to remember. When I get to the Hackney Empire, my memory walk starts getting fuzzy. Not enough rehearsal before Tania called."

"Tania messed you up."

"Oh, you've no idea."

"What do you remember at the Hackney Empire?"

"I'm in the foyer by the ticket office. Something to do with alcohol and Steve McQueen."

"Alcohol? Steve McQueen?"

"The picture I created. I've got gin in my head for some reason."

"Like in *The Great Escape?*"

Porter clicked his fingers and said, "*Exactly* like *The Great Escape*. I imagined the Es from the Empire logo were huge potatoes. Tubes were coming out of them into a barrel. Steve McQueen was there, holding a ladle - dripping alcohol onto a battery."

"And you can decipher that?"

"The picture is the sentence. Two E's equals E's equals **He's**. They were made of potato and running through tubes in a **still**. The battery had a plus sign. I could confuse that with **positive**. But in this case, I was aiming for **(a) live**. Write it down. That's the next sentence. *He's still alive.*"

"That seems like a lot of work just to remember a sentence."

"Not for me. I can conjure up pictures like that in two or three seconds. The markers on the walk tell me what order to put them in."

"Ok. Where did you go after the Empire then?"

"Nowhere - I looked up. There's a colossal 3D logo on the side of the Empire. Distinctive. I've used the two E's again. Both have giant eyes with Soraya reflecting in them, pointing at herself. Something to do with contact lenses? I remember now. E equals **He** again. Contact lenses equals **contact(ed)**. Soraya pointing at herself equals **me**."

Feng whistled. *He contacted me.* He wrote it down and patted Porter on the arm. "And next?"

"The vision looped again. This time I saw her log on. I missed it the first time. That's the bit I'm really struggling with. I think she wanted me to log in and send the email to her parents."

"Say what?"

"The next place on my walk is the café patio on the corner of Mare Street and Reading Lane. Email was easy, sadair@sadair.com. The password's the problem."

"It always is."

"I remember using chalk to draw objects on a giant blackboard propped up against the café. I must've been desperate. Symbols are never as good as using real objects or people. I'm used to doing this, but it was a bit confusing when I was receiving the visions. Creating images was like trying to tell someone their husband has died in the middle of a rollercoaster ride."

"What did you draw?"

"Matt Smith as Doctor Who, with a giant slash through the middle of him."

"What does that mean?"

"I can't think. I keep picturing Amy Pond, his assistant. No. That's not right. The slash usually means *miss the middle out of something.*"

"So, you have shorthand in these images you create?"

"Lots. Red paint usually means danger, stop, blood etc. Context usually clears up the specific meaning."

The two sat on the floor. Porter looked hopelessly at the book. Feng held out a pen.

"Porter, why don't you try and recreate the drawing? Would it help?"

Porter held it, twiddled the pen, doodled a Tardis, gave up and sat in silence.

"Do you think Matt Smith was a good Doctor?" said Feng.

"The best ever. It helps Matt had the strongest assistant of the lot with Amy Pond. You're a Whovian too, are you?"

"A *Whatian*?"

"Whovian. *Doctor Who* Fan."

"I suppose I am. Tom Baker was my favourite. I liked his scarf."

"Yes, I had one as a kid. As an adult though, I prefer Matt's bowtie."

"Yes, but that stupid fez didn't suit him."

"Fez! That's what I drew. Matt Smith as the Doctor with his stupid Fez on. But with a slash meaning no E. **Fz**.

"Yes. The next picture is simple but… It's Ted Rogers walking backwards with his fingers in the air, doing his trademark, *321* finger-count. But why is part of the third finger floating free like it's been cut off?"

"Ted Rogers?" asked Feng.

"Don't you remember? In the 70s? Dusty Bin? It must mean **321**. Finally, there was a load of old ladies in lace caps, sewing."

"Which means?" asked Feng.

"**SEWING**, in caps," said Porter. "I try to be literal creating the pictures. It's quicker."

"So, let's get this right, the password is **Fz321SEWING**?"

"Think so. I need some aspirin and an internet café right now."

Chapter 15

Bytes Cafe, Dalston Junction, Hackney
Thursday, March 23rd 2017: 11.15am

With the message and log-on details retrieved, an internet café found, and four aspirin swallowed, it was time for coffee.

Feng looked around the shabby café with glee. "It's like the backstreets of New York or Hong Kong," he said. "Kids buy time, whack on a headset and game with other kids, in other internet cafés, half a world away. Silly really - they all have computers at home."

"It's about location as identity, isn't it?" said Porter, picking some dishwasher-eluding scrag from the side of his mug. "Once, it was done through music and fashion. This lot connect to their tribe through gaming in dumps like this."

"What's The Gliss up to?"

"Observing quietly. I think he's trying to learn about human body language. He has the lingo down pat, but his face has the emoting ability of Mr Potato Head."

"I am here you know," said The Gliss.

"It speaks!" said Porter.

Feng stirred his coffee with a pencil and sucked it dry. "You and The Doves, Porter: it's me who's the odd man out. I've never seen anything to make me believe."

"And your EMF freaking out Liberace back there doesn't count?"

The pair grinned, then chuckled, then snorted. Soon, both were belly-laughing. A few gamers gave them zombie-eyes before rotating back to their screens.

The Gliss butted in. "There is a proof for Feng, of course. Get into Soraya's emails. Feng was the one who suggested Soraya. Porter could only know her password through his powers."

Porter passed this onto Feng, who became excited but more business-like. He sped things up and purchased their computer time.

"You couldn't possibly have fixed this, could you?" admitted Feng. "Obviously, if you get into that account, I'm going to have to re-evaluate my entire life."

"We're not in yet. Where's the notebook?"

Feng entered the passcode and their hour began ticking away on a counter: 59:59 descending.

They hit the first hurdle immediately. Soraya had her own domain name.

"She could have been on Hotmail and made it easy for us," said Porter.

"Try webmail.sadair.com," said Feng. It worked. A log-in page appeared.

Porter took a deep breath and placed his cursor in the user field.

57:22. He tapped out Soraya's email address.

57:01. The cursor moved to the password box. Feng read it out. F z 3 2 1 S E W I N G.

56:47. He pressed send. The page refreshed. *Incorrect login. Username or password not recognised.*

Curiously, Feng and Porter had the same simultaneous thought: *Of course. What did you expect? Madness!*

The Gliss said, "Check it. You may have jumbled stuff. What was that about the disjointed finger? It must have stood for something?"

Porter said, "Yes, I guess. I haven't rehearsed it since we wrote it down. It'll be harder to remember now."

Feng got the gist of this. "Are you sure about Fez and Sewing bits? Ok. Then it must be the 321 bit?"

"The Gliss asked me to think about the disjointed finger," said Porter.

Feng drew three fingers, cut the last one free of the hand and held it up. "Make you think of anything?"

"An exclamation mark. 32!" said Porter. "I think you're right."

52:23. They entered the new password. Same error message.

"Describe the image to me again," said Feng.

"Ted Rogers, the TV host, is standing there counting his fingers off at me. 321. But the third finger has separated from him. It's floating."

"No," said Feng. "Something's missing. Is The Gliss listening? What's missing?"

The Gliss said, "I thought the Rogers man was walking backwards? 32! Backwards."

Porter didn't wait. Clumsy, excited fingers eventually typed in the new password.

47:22. F z ! 2 3 S E W I N G. Enter.

The page refreshed again. Soraya Adair's inbox lay before them. "Goff almighty," said Feng.

Feng, The Gliss and Porter, stayed in the café another 10 minutes. Feng reset the computer's clock back a month and restarted the computer. They found an email to Soraya's parents in her inbox, copied the address and sent the message.

"I need another coffee," said Porter. "Let's sit by the canal."

Ten minutes later the trio were staring at joggers, graffiti and aggressive geese heckling the pedestrians.

The Gliss faced Porter. Several oblivious cyclists passed through him.

"How did Soraya compare to your experience at Cartwright's grave?" he asked.

Porter translated the question for Feng and replied to them both.

"In the 80s I had some friends with a VHS machine. Miracle of miracles, their dad was a dirty bastard with tons of poorly hidden porn. Shot on bad cameras to start with, by the time we got to see them they were completely blurred and distorted from being 10th generation copies. The sound was mountains of hiss. We still watched them of course."

"Your right arm has a limp to this day," smirked Feng.

Porter ignored him. "Now, think about a blockbuster at the world's best IMAX cinema with 25-speaker surround sound. That's the difference. I felt like I was in the room with Soraya. With Max, it was like being trapped in an echo chamber. Faint. Ghostly. Thin. All the colours had run and, yes, there was mountains of hiss. Life was still there, still real, but seriously degraded." He rubbed at his sore temples again while Feng took notes.

The Gliss spoke. "That's the Recession again - or Slide, as it's sometimes known. Over time, the messages dissipate along with the person."

Porter shifted. "I don't believe in God or the afterlife, but I could do with knowing how these voices are possible."

The Gliss began his usual defensive spiel. "I'm just a messenger but… don't look at me like that, Porter… but I honestly don't think there is an afterlife. The difference between your experience with Soraya and Cartwright is about the extent of the Slide mostly."

Feng windmilled in excitement as Porter translated. "The voices Porter hears are like footprints being washed away by the ocean? They don't mean anything?"

"More like bruises that fade," said The Gliss. "Energy and emotion create a mark or recording. Time heals, and the bruise fades. Something like that."

"Time heals? Good one. I must remember that," said Feng.

Porter made a face-scrunch. "It's true I could feel the Recession from Cartwright. We were un-bridgeably distanced from each other. But Soraya…It was like she was actually with me – and I felt she knew I was there too. It reminded me of trying to hold a conversation with someone in the shower. You can see and hear them, you're sharing the same room, but nonetheless, you are in very different physical and acoustic spaces within that room. The conversation is compromised."

Feng played up to his inscrutable Chinese credentials, rubbed his chin and said sarcastically, "Interesting. Interesting."

The Gliss said, "I don't think these are *souls* or *people* – not as you know them anyway. They're not in limbo or en route to somewhere celestial. The voices you heard are part of this world – real, actual phenomena. Fading electrical energy, basically – similar to the way radios carry on after you've cut the power."

"Cartwright and Soraya were different experiences," said Porter.

"Yes, but so is chatting with Feng and listening to Soraya. You can place all these voices on a spectrum, from weak to strong. It's nothing more, nothing less."

Porter told Feng and then asked The Gliss, "So what will happen if I get to the truth of Cartwright's story? Or more to the point, what if I don't? He's not coming back to life, and you say he's not in limbo? I'm sorry to repeat myself, but what's the point? In practical terms, I'm not doing anything for him, am I?"

"I don't know," said The Gliss. "Maybe his dissipation will be hastened by you? A kind of palliative?"

"I'm a doctor now?" said Porter.

The Gliss shook his head. "You're overthinking it. The Quincunx must exist for a purpose other than for the mission's sake. Sorry, but I don't know what that purpose is. Maybe dispersal gives a clean ending, and that's what the universe strives for?"

After translation, Feng said, "That's a fantastically unfulfilling answer."

The Gliss rolled his eyes. "OK. Why do things reproduce? Reproduction often leads to the death or deterioration of the host, yet every living thing strives to do it. It's the commonest process in nature. But does it make philosophical sense to ask: *why* do things reproduce? Asking *how* things reproduce is something for science but *why* is only a question for ontology."

"Ontology never provided a definitive answer to anything," said Porter.

"My point exactly," said The Gliss. "But your basic question is an ontological one."

Feng chipped in. "There must be an awful lot of Quincunxes being triggered then. Millions die each year with a sad story. That's what gets me about all these ghost-hunters - they always claim to see the same kind of people - soldiers, anarchic clergy, kings and queens, witches, highwaymen. It's never Bob-who-worked-at-the-pickle-factory."

"You're a ghost-hunter," said Porter.

"Yes, but a ghost-hunter who doesn't believe in them."

"I can't get my head around being given this sort of power if it's all pointless," said Porter.

The Gliss shifted its position and looked Porter in the eye. "I'm not getting through, am I? Not everything in the universe gets a resolution. If you measure *meaning* as something eternal - then nothing ever achieves true meaning because human behaviour and consequences are never eternal. All human problems are local: local to them physically, local to their era. If it can even be said to exist, *meaning* - with or without a moral dimension - is always localised. Who wouldn't argue that Hitler and the Final Solution were bad things? But think of the many Jews who escaped to England because of the Nazi threat, had children and grandchildren, some of whom became doctors and saved many lives in their careers? No Hitler, no doctors. It's a paradox. Outside of social proscriptions, even the most heinous act can have positive moral and physical outcomes. And if you go back to prehistoric times, then it simply doesn't matter anymore whether caveman A battered caveman B to death with an ox bone."

"Ah," countered Feng, "but what if caveman B was the first in a long line of people that would otherwise have already led to a cure for cancer? It's theoretically possible to trace all our lines back to a caveman somewhere."

The Gliss replied, jerking his thumb at Feng to let Porter know to pass his answer on. "Scientists know that one day the Earth won't exist. Humans will die out. Whether a cure for cancer exists or not is only of universal concern while humans exist. On an eternal timeline, it doesn't matter. You see?"

Porter and Feng discussed this and indulged in another bout of collective shrugging.

"Metaphysics won't get us anywhere," said Feng. "I'm not sure what I've seen today, but I do want to see what you two get up to next."

Porter clapped Feng on the shoulder, greeting his initiate. "You're welcome. Tomorrow, I'm going to the Imperial War Museum to do some research on Max Cartwright and, if I have the time, Harry. I'd go today, but I have to see my solicitor this afternoon. I'm about to be struck off unless I get my case sorted."

"Call me then. I'll give you a hand at the museum." Feng handed over a worn-out business card.

"I wonder what will happen when Soraya's parents get that email?" mused Porter.

"They'll either take it on face value and believe it, or they'll call the police to say they've received an impossible email that makes them think she might have been murdered. The police will trace the ISP to the internet cafe, the store owner will show them their CCTV, and then we'll both end up on *Crimewatch* as persons of interest."

"You have a real knack for giving people a touch of the screaming abdabs, you know that, Feng?"

"Glad to help."

Chapter 16

Quendell's & Co, Dalston Junction, Hackney
Thursday, March 23rd 2017: 12.20pm

Namita Menon put down the binder, looked up at Ron and Shirley Rigson and stared. She was a pro-starer. Licensed to kill. Shirley immediately looked down at her own fidgeting hands. Ron defiantly held Namita's eyes. For a full five seconds. Then he broke and gazed at his shoes.

Namita gloated. She was right. Screw the commission. She had too many genuine clients on her books. She tucked one side of her black shoulder-length bob behind an ear – a deliberately "feminine" gesture that some clients later rued for confusing with "weak."

"You still claim the meals on wheels service accidentally poisoned Mrs Rigson's father?"

Ron answered. "He was throwing his guts up. We just want compensation from the council. It's only fair." He looked up but was again forced to look down as the Indian Tiger went back on eye attack and said nothing. She counted slowly to 15 in her head. One, two, three, four, five, six… She had learned the technique from a journalist friend. Stay quiet. Let them do the talking. People hate silence and fill it. Seven, eight, nine…

"Look, Ron, I think we should go. This was a bad idea," said Shirley, trying to stand up. Ron pulled on her arm to sit down and confronted Namita.

"I don't understand the problem, Mrs Menon."

"Ms Menon."

"Sorry, Miss Menon."

"Ms Menon if you don't mind."

"Sorry, Ms Menon," said Ron flustered. "All you have to do is write a letter for us. That'll probably do it."

Namita took a few seconds to examine her desk. Her hair fell back out from behind her ear. She would come up, her bob framing her face like Robocop's helmet. She did so now, slowly and deliberately.

"I can't support you in a case of attempted fraud." She paused for effect. "Or attempted murder."

The Rigsons were both startled. Shirley looked terrified. Ron decided it was worth another shot.

"That's a bit insulting, isn't it? My father-in-law nearly died."

"Then you are lucky he didn't."

Something dawned on Shirley. "What do you mean attempted *murder*?"

Ron said nothing.

Namita looked at the clock. Norton was due in 5 minutes, Washburn after that. She needed to be quick to fit in a solo lunch for once. Time to end this. She threw a folder over to them.

"Your allegation was so serious we did a little investigation ourselves. If we'd taken on your case and won, we'd get a big pay-out. If we'd lost, we'd have wasted a lot of time. It was worth paying for a few tests first. We sent the vomit sample you gave us for testing. It came back positive for cyanide. Small traces but definitely there."

"Cyanide?" said Shirley.

"Naturally occurring cyanide," repeated Namita. "They also found ground apple pips and rose thorns. Think of your garden. Ring any bells?" Shirley was now looking Namita directly in the face while Ron was staring at his hands.

"I have a few special investigators on my books. I got my best one to take clippings of your roses and apples."

"You've been in our garden?" protested Ron.

Namita held up a hand. "We sent those for testing too," she lied. "The lab says the thorns and pips in the vomit are from your trees and bushes."

"I don't understand," said Shirley. "What's that got to do with cyanide?"

Namita pulled a print-out from her folder. It was a Wikipedia page. Shirley devoured it and discovered that apple pips and rose thorns both contain minute traces of cyanide. She turned in fury to her husband, understanding all, at last. "You tried to kill Dad? You said you'd only make him throw up. You bastard."

"Luckily pips and thorns only contain minute amounts. It'd take at least 150 apple pips to kill a man," said Namita. "Happily, your dad's fine and was never in any real danger. I'm bound by client privilege not to report this. However, I'm sure the police would find out if we continued with the case once we start exchanging documents etc. I've presumed you won't proceed, and my bill is waiting for you on your way out." The Rigsons got up. Their next booking will be for a divorce lawyer. Idiots.

Five minutes. Time for a cancer stick. She popped out on to the Juliet balcony and lit up. To her left, the City of London's towers stood greyed out in the gentle haze of London's pollution. To her right, lay the fleshpots of Dalston Kingsland. Once voted the coolest place in Europe by Italian Vogue. Namita thought it was a dump. It had no centre or cohesion: a zoo with the cages open. The City boys might be screwing up the world, but the Dalston mob were just screwy. She blew her smoke towards Dalston, giving it a symbolic finger.

A quick glance at her watch. Two minutes to Norton. Rerun the details. No, enjoy the damn cigarette. It'll be fine.

A buzzer rang. She stubbed the fag out in a small plant pot and returned in time for Norton to enter with Eileen, her PA.

"Mr Norton for your 12.30, Ms Menon," said Eileen confidently before whispering, "And Nora Washburn is here too."

Namita glanced at the clock. Lunchtime sooner if she got her skates on.

Porter updated her on the calls he'd been getting from Tawney Weekes at the Mail, the letter from the Solicitor Regulation Authority and his phone call with Nicholas Runyon.

Namita Menon, the Tigress of Quendell's, was not pleased. "You do realise he could have been taping that call? Can't you control yourself?"

"He deserved it," said Porter, crossing and uncrossing in the lumpen chair Namita had spent many hours selecting.

"Maybe, but I'm here to win your case, not settle scores. Weekes, the journalist - you haven't spoken to her I hope?"

Porter snorted. "Of course not."

"Some restraint then. Please apply the same to your old employer from now on." She flicked through the case notes.

"Here's our problem, Mr Norton. Sorry, you prefer Porter, right?"

Porter, who felt like he was sitting on a Toblerone, fiddled with his lapels. Namita sighed. "It's so unfair. All the blame lies with the parents. If they hadn't abused the kid…"

"It's Janine. Please use her name," said Porter.

"If they hadn't abused Janine, if they hadn't tried to put the blame on each other, she wouldn't have been in care in the first place. Now the poor girl is gone she'll never get the court hearing her case deserved. All that's left is for the legal system to extract its pound of flesh through civil actions, like the one against you. It's the public's anger that puts you in jeopardy."

"I'm guilty though," said Porter, fidgeting with his hair.

"You're guilty - of making an honest mistake. A mistake that was caused by your working conditions."

"I feel like I started the fire that killed her. I can't help that."

"The fire was an accident in her foster home. An electrical fault. It could have happened anytime."

"Yes, but she was only in there that extra night because I made a mistake."

"You made a *mistake*. Exactly. You didn't set fire to the building. Two different things entirely."

"You're right. That's a fact. However, another fact is that I feel guilty. Irrational though it may seem."

"Porter. I'm working your industrial tribunal case, not your conscience. Have you seen a priest lately?"

"I'm no Catholic. I did see a vicar." Porter remembered Gossamer's face. "Didn't do much good for either of us."

"I'm no priest, vicar or therapist," said Namita. "A child is put in care while the courts decide who abused her. They conclude it was the father. The mother's given custody. You're on the tail end of an 80-hour week, forget to sign one page of her release documents. The handover's delayed a day. There's a fire in the house overnight, and the child is one of three who died. You're blamed for her death by a public who no longer believe in *accidents*. They demand a scapegoat. But it mustn't be you, Porter. You're innocent."

Porter crested the high waves of his guilty pain in silence. He hated going over the case history.

Namita flicked through her dossier. "Remind me. The day the mistake was made - what was Runyon's reaction when you heard from social services the custody release form was incorrectly completed?"

"Social Services called me back about 4pm that day. Nick was fine. It was a procedural mistake. They happen. We sent the re-signed papers by courier that same day. Our new receptionist didn't book express, so the courier made a few other drops before he got to the council's offices with our stuff. By that time - you know what the council are like, out at five on the dot - the case-handler had gone home. Nick was supportive and called Janine's mother himself to say the handover would be the next day instead."

"How did Janine's mother react?"

"Kerry? The so-and-so didn't give a damn. Said she was holding a celebratory piss-up with her friends. She didn't cancel."

"What did Runyon say to her?"

"Nick said he was calling on my behalf, to apologise for *our* mistake but the social services team were really to blame for not being there. She told him not to worry." Porter undid and redid the button on his left cuff.

"That's the Achilles heel of their case - Nick blamed someone else, the council. Providing Nick hasn't gotten to Kerry, we can probably work that angle?" said Namita.

"Sure, if we could prove it," admitted Porter. "The telephone call proves no-one blamed me in the beginning. One problem: Nick would lie rather than admit that now and Kerry's too stupid and brainwashed to remember accurately."

"You're not kidding," echoed Namita, who had spoken to the mother several times.

"I knew that call was important as soon as we found out Janine had died," said Porter. "We used to record all our phone calls. I went to get the recording immediately, but Nick was already there and told me, lying obviously, the file had been corrupted and wouldn't play."

"Great minds think alike," said Namita.

"He is a great mind, unfortunately. He lost no time covering his bases. He left nothing to incriminate him or the company. If it went bad, he would be able to pass the blame onto me."

"And it went bad. Quickly."

"Express. Janine's dad was bitter as hell about the physical abuse allegations - even though he was guilty as Hitler. But once the creep actually let the loss of his daughter sink in… It quickly became obvious he'd be going for compensation. Disgusting really."

Namita made a few notes, highlighted a passage, and sat back thinking.

"You know, that recording could still exist," she said. "If things had gone differently and Janine's parents had sued social services instead, that recording would have shown how sympathetic you both were, how seriously Runyon took it and how calm the mother was acknowledging Runyon's wasn't at fault."

"Sure, but once it did go this route, why keep it?"

"When was the last time, as a solicitor, you burned evidence?"

"Never. It's kind of hardwired in not to."

"Exactly. Also, digital files are tricky things. A forensic examination of the system might turn up any number of copies or traces of it. One computer is relatively easy to keep clean, a network less so."

"Yes, but how would we find it? I don't have access, and it's not going to be volunteered?"

"There's a PI we sometimes use called Barry Hammell," said Namita, before remembering that he was an off-book resource and not to be discussed. "And any other number of ways."

Porter knew what she meant but let it go.

"How are you, you know, within yourself?" she asked, signalling the meeting was ending.

"Better than I was a week ago," said Porter, shocking himself with that revelation.

"Someone's got a bit of a thing about a certain beautiful lawyer," said The Gliss as they walked through Quendell's open-plan, second-floor office. "Little fidgets, tiny grooming movements, inability to look her in the eye. Well, well, well."

Porter was desperate to reply but, in so quiet a public space, didn't dare. He fumbled for his phone, mimed an unfeasibly fast dial sequence and began speaking. "Stop it right now. FYI, there's no truth in that whatsoever. She scares the crap out of me."

They cleared the main office space, crashed through two stiff double-doors and emerged alone together at the top of a short staircase. The concrete space was an unpleasant resonating chamber. Porter's voice assumed a metallic echo as, free to put the phone away, he continued their argument. "My relationship with her is purely professional."

"Sure. If you say so."

"I do say so," said Porter as they reached the first floor and stepped into Quendell's showy reception area. "It's uncomfortable knowing that…"

"Duck!" screamed The Gliss.

Purely on reflex, Porter did. As he hit the floor, he heard a crumple of impact as a large bronze bust hit the plasterboard wall where he'd been standing. Unlike Porter, the bust didn't stay down. It began bouncing around the room like a ricocheting bullet. A glass case full of industry awards was the first messy casualty. The supporting column and plinth were next to disintegrate into spiteful pellets of stone. Porter felt several stabs of pain and heard someone nearby scream. He had to double-check it wasn't him.

"Get out!" shouted The Gliss.

Porter didn't need telling twice. He rolled to the doorway across splinters of stone and glass. As he rounded the corner, he was confronted by the screaming receptionist. Her eyelid was torn in a mini-Aladdin Sane stripe. He saw her look past him in terror. He ducked and looked behind, but there was nothing there except the Boom! Boom! Boom! of the bust wreaking havoc. She was scared of him.

"It wasn't me! Are you ok? I've been hurt too," he said pointing at his stinging face.

She gawped in pain and fear. Pierrot teardrops of blood dripped onto her own cheek. Doors clanged on the floor above. Footsteps rang down the stairs.

"What the hell?" said a suited executive, launching himself into a rugby tackle. Porter, back on his feet, was taken straight back down again.

Porter was handcuffed and in the police car, resting his pounding head on a grill between the seats. He had protested his innocence, showed off his cuts and bruises, and demanded to be let free. The more he complained, the more crazed he looked. No-one else had been in the reception ante-room. Who else could have been responsible? He asked to speak to Namita but was told she was in her next client meeting.

"What would you say to her anyway?" asked The Gliss. Porter flopped back in his seat, watching Stoke Newington Road whizz past.

"What I want to know is what the hell caused that? This is one of your dead people breaking all your rules and interacting with me, isn't it?" said Porter.

"They can't. At least, I thought they can't," said The Gliss. "But I can see what it looks like. Sorry, I haven't got an answer for you."

"You didn't say I would be in danger."

"I didn't know you would be," said The Gliss. "Not for sure, anyway."

"That's one hell of a qualification. Am I being punished? Was this an attempted assassination?"

"I don't know. It did feel like that."

"Like what? An assassination?!"

"Maybe."

"By who? By what?"

"Oi you," shouted the copper in front. "Give it a rest, you loony. Wait till you're banged up for the night before you start gibbering. I'm trying to listen to the radio."

Namita Menon opened her door, escorting Nora Washburn out. They were animatedly discussing the rights and wrongs of Nora's neighbour moving his fence an extra inch onto her land every summer. They stopped when they saw the commotion in the office.

"Nathan? What happened to you? You're bleeding?"

Nathan Caiger, who was enjoying having his minor grazes attended to in front of the whole admiring office, said her last client had gone mad and smashed up reception.

"Which client? What are you talking about?"

"That Norton bloke. I had to rugby tackle him. Ruby's gone to hospital for stitches."

"What? That doesn't make sense. Did he get into a fight?"

"No, he went berserk. Smashed up reception. Started throwing the bust of old Ivan Quendell about. Glass everywhere. Ripped Serena's eyelid off. He's been carted off to the nick."

"Are you serious?"

"Shall I come back another time?" said Mrs Washburn.

Chapter 17

Stoke Newington Police Station, Hackney
Thursday, March 23rd 2017: 1.58pm

Porter was processed and stowed in an interrogation room, still handcuffed.

"This must feel very familiar to you," said The Gliss.

"I'm usually here to get someone out, not get booked in," said Porter.

"If the cop does bring a phone back with him, who you gonna call?"

"He'll bring a phone alright. I'm a solicitor. They'll do it by the book. I'll call Feng. *He* can call Namita. I can't ask *her* to call Feng without explaining who he is and why I know him." Porter rolled his eyes. "I'll leave it to him. I'm sure he'll be discreet."

"Your evidence for that particular character trait? His three blogs, Instagram, Twitter and Facebook pages perhaps? He's the opposite of discreet. He's a blurter."

"I need support. I'm still adjusting, ok? Like coming into this station… I've walked past it a million times but thought I was going to be sick when we arrived. My head was squeezed thin as spaghetti. I sensed truly horrible mass suffering. Any idea? Did they have any of the Jack the Ripper victims here? Would be nice to know where I should avoid. I won't last long with headaches like this."

"Sorry, I haven't a clue."

"Fat lot of good you are."

"Sorry."

A young PC came in and said Porter could make his phone call. He sized Porter up, saw he represented no threat and un-cuffed him.

"It's Mr Norton isn't it?" said the PC. "I've seen you before. Defence lawyer?"

"Solicitor. I'm only involved early on before cases get kicked up to the barristers. I remember you. You sat on a client of mine, Rahman Faljani. Got caught nicking e-cigs in Dalston. Said he'd been framed, but who frames someone by shoving e-cig refill boxes down his underpants?"

"I sit on a lot of people. Doesn't ring any bells."

"It does for me. I'm being framed, but I've no idea why. Unlike Faljani however, I've nothing in my underpants."

"The contents of your underpants are your business, sir. This way." The PC escorted Porter to reception. Porter found Feng's tatty business card, dialled, and sighed with relief when he answered.

"A ghost tried to kill you?" gushed Feng.

"Maybe. Can you call my solicitor, please? Write this down. She's in Dalston. Get Namita Menon to check Quendell's CCTV. As soon as they watch it, they'll see I had nothing to do with it. They won't know who *did*, but they'll definitely know that I *didn't*."

Feng agreed and said he'd come to Stokey to bail him out.

"Thanks, Feng. I really appreciate it," said Porter. He nodded to the PC that he was done and ready to go.

As they walked, Porter asked, "Have many people have died in this building?"

"What do you mean? None. A few. Why you asking?"

"Just wondered."

"It's relatively new," said the young PC. "There were a few deaths in the old station. That's a long time back. The original station was Victorian. This one's only been around since the late 80s. People inevitably die around police stations - overdoses, tramps – that sort of thing. Only one suicide during my time…"

"Police brutality?"

"You sure you want to bring that up as I put you back in your cell?"

"Sorry."

"Routine deaths - but I can't even remember the last one."

"Ok. No offence intended."

The PC locked him in. Porter glanced around the one-chair, one-table room. He recalled a client, nick-named Stinky. He had wet himself in this room. It was the same chair. Porter was okay standing.

Detective Sergeant Bob Crawley realised today was going down as a weird one as soon as that funeral parlour called this morning. Two perverts touching up a corpse. On camera. Crawley had seen most things, but this was a new one.

He opened the newly-made case folder and looked at the first CCTV printout. Without the funeral home's allegation, the picture didn't seem particularly suspicious. One of the men was touching the dead woman out of, what looked like, affection.

However, it was the other grabs that set his spider senses tingling. In one, a Chinese man stared at the CCTV. Only crims stared at CCTVs. No-one else noticed them anymore. Another grab showed the Touching Man on his knees. In yet another, the Chinese man was waving some machine about - a camera? If this wasn't criminal, it was indeed abnormal.

And now he had to interview a solicitor brought in for smashing up another solicitor's office. He glanced at his phone screen. Not even 3pm yet.

DS Crawley took the folder and was walking past the front desk when he was *Hey You*'d from reception by a woman. She was strikingly beautiful enough to make him put his brakes on.

"Excuse me?" he said, raising an eyebrow.

"Namita Menon. You have one of my clients. He shouldn't be here."

"They all say that," said DS Crawley, preparing to move on.

"Yes, but I'm also representing the victim. Well, I'm the victim in a corporate sense. The man you have here didn't do it."

He thought for a second. "Are you talking about Mr Norton by any chance?"

"I am. He really didn't do it. I have some footage to show you."

DS Crawley opened the door and invited her inside. Namita moved her Prada bag from one shoulder to the other, bent down and signed in. "We had an explosion at our office. A couple of people got injured. In the confusion, it looked like Mr Norton had vandalised the place. He was cuffed and brought here before anyone checked the cameras."

"You mean, he's actually innocent?"

Namita pulled an iPad from her bag. "Yes. It's quite clear. Norton was lucky not to get more seriously hurt himself."

She set the iPad up. "The main camera wasn't working, but the one in reception was angled so you could see half the room Norton was in. As he walks towards reception, there's an explosion. A brass statue got blown about and caused a bit of damage. You can see Norton fall to the floor when the explosion happens. He was lucky to get out in one piece."

"What caused it?"

"Electrical, possibly."

They watched it together. Crawley turned the iPad on its side to maximise screen size.

"That's odd," said Crawley. "The statue's bouncing all over the shop. Shame we can't see the explosion."

"The main camera streamed black for a few minutes." Crawley shrugged. "There's not much point in holding him then, is there?"

"Not unless you want to give him therapy," said Namita, relaxing a bit now she saw she would not have to fight.

"Therapy?"

"Yeah. Instead of calling me, his actual solicitor, he called a mate of his who then contacted me. Straightaway, this guy introduces himself on the phone as a gay, Chinese, sceptical ghost-hunter."

Crawley smiled. "A gay, Chinese ghost-hunter. Really?"

"Gay, Chinese, *sceptical* ghost-hunter. He wanted to assure me nothing was going on between them. Said Porter wanted me to know he may have been attacked by a poltergeist."

"Did he. And how did you respond to that?"

"I was about to hang up. Like you, we're plagued by loonies... I mean troubled people. I guess I was pretty sharp with him, but he ignored me and told me to check the CCTV anyway."

"And here you are."

"Here I am. No poltergeist obviously but anyone can see Norton did nothing. To be honest, I wouldn't expect him to. He's pleasant enough, if a bit boring."

"I don't know him myself, but some of the boys do. A few of his clients end up here." Crawley tossed a piece of gum into his mouth.

"Excuse me - Mr Sergeant man?"

Crawley and Namita looked up. A flustered and sweaty Chinese man was waving at them from reception.

"Yes, sir?"

"I'm here to see a friend of mine, Porter Norton? I'm Feng. Feng Tiān."

Crawley turned to Namita. "Sceptical ghost-hunter, right?"

She sighed. "Right."

Crawley opened his brown folder. Flicking through the CCTV printouts, Det Sgt Bob Crawley called out, "Dulcie, would you be so good as to escort us all to interview room number two, please?"

Chapter 18

Stoke Newington Police Station, Hackney
Thursday, March 23rd 2017: 3.12pm

Feng and Namita walked side by side, Crawley in front of them, Dulcie behind.

"This is like *The Green Mile* isn't it?" said Feng. No-one replied.

Unaware of the size of the party come to see him, Porter reacted with surprise as Feng, Namita, Dulcie and an older cop entered.

"Hello everyone. Is it my birthday?"

"DS Bob Crawley," said Crawley, introducing himself.

"I'm free to go?"

"Yes," said Namita. "I checked the CCTV, Porter. You're free to go."

"Or not," said DS Crawley with quiet authority.

Namita immediately went up a gear, pulled her iPad out and reminded the DS that Quendell's wasn't pressing charges. The PC shrugged at Porter. Feng tapped his temple. Porter started asking questions. DS Crawley quietly chewed gum and waited for the hubbub to die down.

He opened his folder and threw a picture onto the table. Porter looked at it, put his face in his hands, lowered his head to the desktop and banged it a few times.

"What happened?" asked Namita, who couldn't see the printout.

Head still down, Porter held the picture up for all to see.

Feng said, "Ah."

Porter said, "Yes. Ah."

"Ah indeed, Mr Norton," said DS Crawley. "Or should that be, *Mr Flavell?*"

Namita snatched the printout from Porter's hand, examined it and said, "Is that a coffin?"

"DS Crawley, do you have any paracetamol please?" said Porter.

"I can explain everything," said Feng.

Namita and Porter both looked up in varying degrees of panic and shouted "No!"

Glancing back at his folder, Crawley said, "I'd like to hear from *Joe Crenshaw* here. Not yet though. One at a time. Dulcie, let's get an interview room ready for Mr Tiān. I'll speak to him after I've had a quiet word with Mr Norton here."

Namita nixed that immediately and asked for time alone with her client.

Porter interrupted. "It's an odd story, but I don't think anything illegal was done. Let me explain what happened, please?"

"That's right. We did nothing illegal," said Feng.

"Glad to hear it. No crime has been reported," said Crawley. "I have some questions about your odd behaviour, that's all."

The Gliss appeared and Porter blanked him. He was learning slowly. The Gliss said, "Bit of a pickle, eh?" Porter raised an eyebrow in reply.

Feng said, "It's all my fault. I'm a ghost-hunter. I belong to a group based in Hackney." He waited for a response. Silence. Tugging on the stud in his ear, Feng continued, "I read about the young lady in the Hackney Gazette. So sad that someone her age would kill herself, isn't it? I wanted to pay my respects."

DS Crawley gestured at Porter. "And he's in your club too?"

"No, but he lives in Hackney. We met recently, and he expressed an interest in the paranormal. I told him I was going to visit the funeral home and he asked if he could come along."

"Norton?"

"It's as Feng says," said Porter. "We met at a haunted castle on the Welsh border where I grew up."

Feng added, "We didn't see any ghosts. We didn't expect to. Neither of us believes in ghosts."

DS Crawley said, "If you don't believe in ghosts, why do you describe yourself as a ghost-hunter? Doesn't make much sense."

"I'm a rationalist, DS Crawley. I hate people trying to avoid the real world and all its hard choices by clinging to fabricated distractions like ghosts. I go along to the club as a sceptic. But I'm pretty open-minded, so they don't mind me being there. Also, I buy them muffins."

"I see," said Crawley.

"Well I don't," said Namita. "Porter, why were you using a false name?"

Porter wondered why the most pointedly prosecutor-like question of the session was being asked by the counsel for the defence.

"As he says, I was keeping him company. Was interested to see if anything happened when he got his EMF reader out."

"EMF reader?"

Feng whipped out his gadget. "It's a bit like a Geiger counter. Measures electrical energy. Most believers say ghosts emit lots of it. It would be one way to prove something odd was happening if it went off. Doesn't prove anything if it doesn't, of course."

DS Crawley said, "So you read about Soraya Adair in the paper, made up some names, went to pay your respects, and swung a Geiger counter around over her coffin? A strange way to pay your respects."

"I can't argue with that, DS Crawley," said Porter. "No harm intended though. Feng said we should use made-up names so as not to embarrass the funeral parlour."

"You touched her and then behaved very oddly," said Crawley pushing on.

Porter was sweating. This was worse than his French oral which, until now, had held the distinction of being Porter's Worst Half Hour Ever.

"I did. Only her hand, and only lightly. The trouble was, I've never seen a dead body before. I was really moved. I touched her hand and was so shocked by the cold I nearly fainted. It brought back bad memories of my mother and father. They died together when I was a kid. Obviously, I wish I hadn't gone."

Feng said, "And that's the truth."

Suspicious silence.

"I'm not sure if any crime has been committed here," said DS Crawley. "Disturbing the peace maybe - but whose peace were you disturbing?"

Porter said, "I'm not sure that would hold even if you charged us…"

"I forgot you were a solicitor. I've seen you here before."

"I've been here a few times, but I don't think we've had the pleasure."

"You're the solicitor they blame for that little girl's death, aren't you?"

"Her name is, was, Janine Crane. Yes, that's me sadly."

"And he wasn't responsible for her death," said Namita. "She died in a fire at a care home."

"Yeah, I read about that," said Crawley. "You have my sympathy. No-one blames the bad parents who put them in care do they?"

"Thank you," said Porter, unused to empathy or sympathy.

"Ok. You're both free to go. I'm thinking of the girl's family here. I don't want them thinking something bad happened to their daughter's body. I'm sure the funeral director won't want any publicity either. Once he's calmed down anyway. But let's be clear - I don't want to hear from either of you two again. And no more touching. Am I understood?"

Feng and Porter nodded assent, looking as guilty as two monks in a confession box.

The group made their way back to reception. As they walked, Crawley chatted to Feng about ghost-hunting, but Namita was silent. Porter knew he was in for an almighty roasting as soon as they got outside.

"What the hell do you think you were playing at?" she shouted on cue as soon as they were clear of the station.

Porter's head was throbbing again, even before Namita began her rant.

"You pulled this stunt before you came to see me this morning? And said nothing?"

"Ms Menon…"

"Be quiet a second and listen to me. You're up to your neck, Porter. You have a good case, but Hitler got better publicity during the Blitz than you're getting right now. What if the Mail gets a sniff and says you've been going around fiddling with corpses?"

"I haven't been -"

"No, and you didn't kill Janine Crane either, but since when did truth sell papers? They hate you."

Feng tried to interrupt. He was silenced by Namita's arm, flung imperiously in his face. The fireball tirade continued.

"Seriously. What were you thinking? Ghost-hunting?"

Porter saw his chance to shut her up. "I *do* believe in ghosts."

"What?"

"I do. Well, I do now, anyway."

"What the hell are you talking about? What's that got to do with anything?"

Feng saw his chance too. "He says he has a ghost-like creature following him around. This morning they were attacked by a poltergeist in your office."

"Feng - don't - please," said Porter, who wanted to shut her up, not drag her in.

"I told you he was a liability," said The Gliss, interested now he'd been brought into the equation.

"Are you two mad?" spluttered Namita. "And you...I thought you said you were a *sceptical ghost-hunter*? I took that to mean you don't believe in the bloody things?"

"I don't," said Feng, "but Porter gave me some interesting readings."

"Porter, I'm worried about your behaviour," said Namita.

"My sister thinks I'm nuts too. But listen! Please! There are too many people talking. Please, all of you, stay quiet for a few sentences - so I can explain!" Eventually, Porter got an indignant silence and tried his best to explain his difficult week. On Stoke Newington High Street, with a crushing headache, he recapped everything.

To her credit, Namita listened carefully. Feng watched her listen. The Gliss hovered over the potholed road, an occasional 243 bus passing through him. Equally to his credit, Porter put in the performance of a lifetime. He explained everything in the right amount of detail, a touch of pathos during the suicide scene, the incredulity of the Quincunx revelation and the shock and pain caused by the sighting of Cartwright. Namita listened carefully and looked up as Porter concluded, "And as mad as that all sounds, I swear I'm telling the truth."

"You, my friend, are a first-class, batshit, crazy loon," said Namita, dropping her professional face. "I've never heard so much twaddle in my entire life."

"He's telling the truth as far as I can tell," said Feng.

"Right, and you are? Oh yeah - another madman - who keeps a Geiger counter in his pocket."

"It's not a Geiger counter, though it does click when it picks up a signal. It's an EMF digifier."

"Of course it is. Porter, look, in all seriousness, I need to speak to Nathan about this. I'm not sure we should be handling your tribunal anymore. To be honest, I don't think we're the type of help you need right now."

Porter took a few seconds and in his calmest voice said, "You're right. I do need help. If The Gliss is right, I have to solve the mystery of Max Cartwright's death. I don't know why or how, but the incident at Quendell's today was connected to all this. Doing this with just Feng on my side is hard. I'd appreciate your continued legal help, Ms Menon, but if you want to duck out on me, I won't blame you."

"I'm sorry, Porter."

There didn't seem anything else to be said. After another second or so of awkward silence, Namita nodded and started to leave.

The Gliss spoke to Porter. "Ask her what's in her locket."

"What?"

"Ask her what's in the locket."

Namita was already five steps away when Porter halted her with her name. She turned.

"Ms Menon, just answer me one question, please. What's in your locket?"

Namita's hand instinctively went to the chain around her neck. "Why do you ask?" Porter looked to The Gliss for guidance.

"Ask her if you can touch it. And then grip it tightly." Porter cottoned on.

"May I touch it please?"

Namita was surprised to hear herself agree. She didn't take it off but gestured him towards it.

Porter's fingers gripped the old gold locket. He had noticed on previous encounters that Namita always wore it. As a man, of course, he had never thought to ask about it. A few years of navigating Tania's magic porridge pot jewellery collection had cured him of trinket curiosity. But as his thumb brushed the locket, he felt an encouraging tingle. The Gliss wouldn't suggest this without reason, surely?

The Gliss said, "This is all about concentration. Don't think about anything else. Ignore me. Ignore the fact you have your hand on a beautiful woman's chest. Let the locket grow bigger in your hand."

Porter obliged and closed his eyes. A tiny black dot formed in his consciousness. It expanded, coming closer to the foreground. But it wasn't yet stable: spinning towards him, spinning away. Eventually, the dot was large enough to come into focus. He could see what it was - a lock of hair - but had no voice to go with it. He didn't wait for a prompt from The Gliss but forced himself to focus, to squash the locket harder.

Faint syllables began to whisper themselves to him. Feng and Namita watched his face. It seemed like he was in pain, grimacing like a child dabbing a graze with lemon juice. Porter was getting something. He tried to pass on what he was hearing.

Nam…after…bits. Nam…look after…bits. His face went up another level of concentration. "Nami look after my rabbits. Is that right? Nami look after my rabbits? What does that mean?" He slowly opened his eyes.

Namita was standing in front of him, open-mouthed.

"Are you ok?" he asked, concerned.

"How did you do that? How could you know?"

"What does it mean?" asked Feng.

"A friend? A cousin? Not your sister?" said Porter, shocked by the inference. "I'm sorry. She passed away when you were young, didn't she? You have a lock of her hair in that?"

Namita looked up. "Sangita. My twin sister. Died of leukaemia when we were six. Those were her dying words to me. No-one else knows them. Not even Mum and Dad."

She wiped her eyes and came to a reluctant decision. "What do you need from me?"

A few hours later, Porter was back at home packing his stuff, listening to the nightly news round-up on BBC Radio 4. The pundits were discussing a bizarre trend among young people to throw themselves into canals, claiming they were pushed. Bizarre. CCTV showed they were alone.

A rent-a-gob MP was blaming social media. "It's one of those crazy Facebook things," she said, with no evidence whatsoever.

"You know something?" Porter said to The Gliss, "this has been a strange day. And this is the strangest way to end it. Running off to Belgium."

"If Crawley hadn't been sympathetic, you could've been on your way to the slammer."

"I'm not though, am I? There's some inevitability about it all. As soon as I read Harry's diary and heard Cartwright, I knew I'd have to go and see Harry's grave in Ypres."

"You still think the cases are connected?"

"They must be. But I want to go see if I can pick-up Harry. He might give me another clue? I want to go for my own sake too. After reading his diary, I feel like I know him a bit." Porter shoved a laptop and charger, a spare jumper and socks into his small Mandarina Duck suitcase.

The Gliss nodded mechanically. "Take a bottle of headache pills. You're going into a cemetery where everyone met an unfortunate end. It'll be loud in there."

The phone rang. It was Feng.

"Are you sure you don't want me to come with you?"

Porter continued packing, wedging the phone between shoulder and ear. "No need, Feng. I've got The Gliss with me. It's a quick journey by Eurotunnel. I'll be back tomorrow night."

"Are you sure? I'm kind of curious…"

"So am I, but this is my family stuff. Let me go alone. I'll see you as planned on Monday morning at the Imperial War Museum with Namita."

"Ok, have a good trip," said Feng, disappointed.

Porter zipped up the last compartment.

"Let's go see if my dead relative is in the mood for talking."

Calais Eurotunnel
Thursday, March 23rd 2017: 11.09pm

The Gliss was back in the front seat on the short drive from the Calais Eurotunnel exit to the smattering of cheap shack 'em ups nearby. Porter had extracted a promise his companion wouldn't attempt to sing.

"What is it with you and musicals?" asked The Gliss. "Is that why you don't have a girlfriend?"

"What? Are you suggesting I'm gay because I like musicals? That's such a stereotype," said Porter. "And you know about Tania. Don't be so provocative."

"Why musical theatre? Why not rock? Or jazz?"

"Who says I don't like those?"

The Gliss raised an eyebrow in such a mechanical way, he looked like a tin Robot toy from the 50s.

"Alright, I don't like rock much. But most of the Great American Songbook is a hybrid of jazz and musical theatre. I quite liked musicals as a kid. Ida took me to see a few. Hated the other boys for being so obvious in their love of sports. Turned the knob up to 11 on the musicals thing. The more they laughed at me, the more I kicked back. Discovered audio restoration work via a friend who repaired 78s for the BBC in the 90s. Got a bit obsessed. That's all."

"So, you're an individualist?" said The Gliss. "They tend to be the most intelligent, but also the most sensitive - a dangerous combination."

"You could be right. I tend to cry at least once in every musical I see."

"What of it? Lots of people do. They're designed to make you cry. I hear 9 out 10 viewers can't hear *Edelweiss* in *The Sound of Music* without blubbing."

"Sure…but *Posh* in *Chitty Chitty Bang Bang*?"

"For why?" said The Gliss.

Porter laughed and then beeped at a badly-driven car, before realising it was he who was in the wrong lane. He cursed *Merde*! and waved an apology. Straightening up, waiting for his heartbeat to return to normal, he realised The Gliss was humming *Posh!*

"How come you know the song *Posh!* - info you presumably got from my head - but you don't know why I like musicals in the first place?"

"Memories and emotions are different beasts," said The Gliss. "Your memories are like keypads on a calculator. Memory is knowledge. It already exists like blocks in your head. I can see those blocks. However, your thoughts and emotions are the sums you do with the keypad, the structures you build with those blocks. Every calculation is unique. I don't get to know your thoughts any quicker than you do."

Porter silenced the sat-nav and reversed into a parking space. "That's a comfort."

As always, he struggled to open the stiff boot of his old racing green Mini Cooper S. He pulled out his case and breathed deeply.

"Ah, La Belle France. I always say that when I get here - a habit I picked up at university. From," he said pointedly, "an old *girl*friend. Still, this isn't exactly the Tarn, is it? I just breathed in a bucket of diesel fumes. Come on, let's go. I'm shattered. I want to set out for Ypres early."

Chapter 19

Ypres, Belgium
Friday, March 24th 2017: 10.45am

Porter strode through the magnificent square at the heart of Ypres town centre, The Gliss hovering by his side. The square is dominated by the colossal Cloth Hall. Cobbles and café society, pastel-painted shop fronts, the clock tower, Belgian chocolate shops. It is a perfect medieval city.

Except it isn't.

Modern-day Ypres is effectively a 1/1 scale model reproduction of the original destroyed during WW1. Ypres was rebuilt in a giant nose-thumbing act of resilience. Unsurprisingly, the city is twinned with Hiroshima. Time had given the re-build a patina that enhanced its perceived authenticity.

After the Great War, many survivors treated Ypres as hallowed ground. Millions of Commonwealth soldiers from across the Empire had passed through it on their way to the frontline. It had been the centre of their trauma and became the centre of their rehabilitation.

Porter was staring up at the Cloth Hall, thinking on this history. He whispered to The Gliss. "Isn't that incredible? This whole building was flattened by shelling. It was remade brick by brick."

"It's ginormous. More like a cathedral than a trading place," said The Gliss.

"We must pop in later. It's home to the In Flanders Fields Museum now."

"What's the plan?"

"I want to go straight to Harry's grave. I can't stay here long. My head is throbbing like a 13-year-old boy at a Little Mix concert."

"We haven't been to the cemetery yet. Painkillers?"

"By the bucket," said Porter, tapping a pocket.

The Gliss had rarely turned to face Porter head-on. But he pivoted on a smooth arc and did so now, causing Porter a jolt of surprise. A woman pulled her child closer in response to Porter's sharp movement.

"Calm down. I think you're right to visit Harry. It's hard to believe the circumstances around Max and Harry's death could be so similar *and* a coincidence. But can I give some advice? Take time to prepare. This is your own family history you're delving into. You may experience this voice differently than a stranger's history."

Porter, shielding his eyes from the sun, nodded. "I know. I've wondered about that: what will these powers allow me to do? The option of checking my family was the first thing I thought of." He put a hand up for silence.

"I get what you're saying. With a history like mine, should I risk standing on my father's grave? I don't remember his voice. And I am more drawn to my father - *there* was the existential pain. He's the one I always wanted an explanation from. Mum can rest in peace."

The Gliss shook his head. "It's the wrong way to think about it. You won't get an explanation. You said it felt like Soraya was trying to talk to you? But that was proximity creating clarity. The people from your past, they will be as faint as Namita's sister or Max."

"If I only get faint echoes, why warn me?"

"Content not volume. Think of his state of mind."

Porter smacked his lips and nodded. "I know. No plans to do it right now, but I am curious."

"Harry is different though," said The Gliss.

"Harry is different," agreed Porter.

After breakfast and a stroll, the pair were heading to Aeroplane Cemetery. It was to the northeast of the town centre, on Zonnebekeseweg, the road connecting Ypres to Zonnebeke.

It was Porter's first trip to Belgium, let alone a war grave. Like most Brits of a certain age, he'd been fed a diet of war films, war poetry, and plenty of war reminiscences from the elderly. Pulling up outside the cemetery, he became conscious of encroaching pain. Not, this time, Quincunx induced. This was the communal, empathetic pain felt by all visitors. Frames from every documentary, the War Poets, Harry's diary, and even *Blackadder*, flickered and pulsed in him. Catching his first glimpse of the hundreds of identical white gravestones, he was choked.

The Gliss diplomatically skipped to the other lurking pain. "The pills working?"

"Not really. They're playing hide and seek in my guts."

"I'll guide you. Aeroplane Cemetery is built on No-Man's Land from the early battles. There must be many body fragments still in the soil. It might sting a bit."

Porter looked out the window and felt something malicious tugging at him. "Oh, it's definitely going to hurt."

"I'll do my best to avoid the hotspots. Ready?"

Porter grabbed a coat from the back of the car, locked up, and squinted through the last of the midday mist clinging to the cemetery gate. He crossed the quiet road. Cars zoomed by infrequently, making each pass an event. His senses were sharpened with feelings of pity and loss. Backlit gravestones heightened his sense of hyper-unreality.

The Gliss stayed quiet. Porter warmed his hands with a rub and entered. You'll probably feel like someone dropped an anvil on you, but at least there are no damn vicars out here if you scream. Come on then, bring it on.

Nothing happened, though the sense of gently malevolent squeeze continued.

"Intense," said Porter, scoping out the rows of stones.

"It's certainly a sight," said The Gliss.

"There are more than 100 of these cemeteries around Ypres alone," said Porter, fresh from skimming through histories of the town in bed last night. "Madness."

"Follow me. I'll pick the cleanest route." The Gliss drifted off, like a Victorian mute at the head of a cortege.

"I've not seen the back of your head before," said Porter. "I was expecting to see *Made in China* or something."

"Is it the white? I've seen millions of images of robots in your head now. When I first manifested, I was aiming for something humanoid, but featureless. I thought this fit the bill rather nicely."

"You look like a cross between a shop mannequin and…"

"… an Imperial Stormtrooper from *Star Wars*? I know."

"Wait - I've never seen *Star Wars*. It's one of those things I've become strangely proud of. How do you know about *Star Wars*?"

"Everyone knows about *Star Wars*," said The Gliss.

Porter laughed. "You could always change your face into something more human. How about Angelina Jolie?"

"I can't. In pottery terms, I've been glazed and fired."

"I expected the supernatural to be a bit more flexible?"

"When you say *supernatural*.... As discussed before, I think you'll find that I'm as much phenomena as you are. One day they'll develop the science to prove it."

"Is that the spingle?"

"Not even close. Two steps to your right, please. There's bad energy from this patch. How you feeling?"

"Getting sore. Let's get this over with. Harry should be around here somewhere. Plot 63."

"I see it...double-back and go around," said The Gliss, pointing out the alternate route. "Don't open yourself up yet. There are many voices in here."

Porter didn't need telling. The cemetery weighed on him – from his mood to his legs. He thought back to the godawful day a PE teacher forced him on a boggy cross-country run, even though he was full of flu.

"Over here," said The Gliss, his hands pointing down an aisle. "There's no way to get to Harry cleanly. Stay closed. Remember what I told you - walk through it. Ready?"

Porter wasn't ready. He was feeling increasingly ill. "Should I run?"

"If you can."

Porter took a deep breath, looked at the 10 graves between him and Harry, and sprinted off.

The long-expected pain came. Unexpectedly, it took myriad forms: sparkly pain, blunt-force pain, stinging pain, burning pain with lights and voices. He was spinning. It felt like his skin was splitting. But the visions were the worst. The damn soldiers.

Porter glimpsed many of their final moments, as limbs separated from bodies and organs exploded. Their hot agonies became his. He could cope with the pictures. It was the voices that got to him. Unimaginable screams, prayers and entreaties. He heard cries of 'mother'. Most disturbing of all, a man whose animal grunts spoke of fearsome pain resisted.

Staggering out of the aisle, Porter fell flat on his face, straight onto Harry's grave. He immediately, blissfully, began sinking into the misty quiet of Harry's dawn execution. Pain continued to churn Porter over, but it slowly morphed away as a new foreground came into focus.

It took longer for Harry to materialise. He looked like a B-Movie monster. Was that a gas mask? On backwards? Was that some kind of sick blindfold?

Paper was pinned on Harry's chest. He appeared oblivious - drunk or drugged. He was gibbering. Blood stained his shirt around his abdomen. Had they fired already? How could they all have missed the target over his heart?

Shockingly, Harry could be heard.

...all that shit.

Porter felt certain the firing squad was about to unleash its deadly volley. They hadn't fired yet. So why the blood? The short sequence began looping.

S'right Harry... did we? ...truth. ...Get.... you...all that shit. Harry was talking to himself.

Nope. Still didn't make any sense. The background pain settled to a mild nag, allowing Porter to focus. He looked at his great-grandfather's uniform. All the insignia had been removed, his disgrace robbing him of military identity. Even the buttons were gone.

S'right Harry...didn't do it, did we? ...the truth. Never forget. It goes with you...all that shit.

Porter wanted to intervene, to comfort. But he wasn't in Harry's world, he was only watching it. The scene looped. Soon, Porter understood all the words.

S'right Harry...didn't do it, did we? You know the truth. Never forget. It goes with you...all that shit.

It didn't mean anything to Porter. The loop ended before any shots. Thank God.

"Porter. Porter. Wake up." It was The Gliss.

With a sigh, Porter forced himself up off the grave. The vision suck-separated itself from him, like pulling a foot from quicksand.

"We have to get out of here," said Porter, now back in the all-too-real pain, of the all-too-real cemetery. "I swear to you, I'm going to die otherwise."

He turned back to Harry's grave. "The truth doesn't go with you, Harry. I heard you. You didn't desert. *Didn't do it,* right? I know you definitely didn't commit suicide now. I'm going to clear you." He was getting ready to go, when he turned back, and said, "I'm going to clear Max Cartwright too."

"Porter, you're getting weaker, let's go."

Porter staggered back to the car, hot knives jabbing him all the way in the form of visions. He saw one soldier crying in the mud, legs missing, arterial blood pumping. A young medic separated into splatter after stepping on a landmine. The horrors came to him in slow-motion. A spray of brain matter from a bullet passing through an African soldier's eye.

He made it back to the Mini, shovelled down some pills and rubbed his head.

"Despite feeling mangled, I should thank you for this gift," said Porter. "It's opened my eyes."

"I keep telling you, I've given you nothing. I'm the messenger."

"It feels like you did. I didn't understand how terrible the trenches were. But now I've seen it, tasted it. No-one can tell me there isn't such a thing as hell on earth."

"There's not much you can do about it bar clear a few names. Ancient history."

"Get out, please. My head is crowded."

"In a sec. Ironically, it's your attempted suicide which means you can now help some people. You might be coming back to life. Porter."

"Maybe. The aspirin bill's going to bankrupt me though."

A few hours later, Porter was admiring the magnificent interior of the Gothic In-Flanders Fields Museum. He had Harry's notebooks with him and was sat scouring. Seated at a small study table with a magnifying glass, he caught the attention of one of the museum's archivists.

"Is that ours?" the man asked with a slight scowl, pointing to the aged document. "I hope not. You should be wearing gloves."

Porter, taken aback by the curt comment, assured the man it belonged to him.

"Ah, you're English?"

"I'm a solicitor from London. Here for family research."

"Do you mind me asking what you're reading?"

Porter told him about Harry and the notebook. He said he wanted to read it in Ypres for resonance. "But I should be wearing gloves?"

"But of course. The oils and sweat on your skin will damage it. Here, borrow mine. May I?"

The man sat down. He was lean, greying and handsome. A few broken veins on his nose suggested he might be fond of a beer or two. He put on some white linen gloves magicked from a pocket somewhere.

"You'll need this. It's virtually illegible," said Porter handing over the magnifying glass. "You work here?"

"I'm so sorry. I get excited when I see historical documents. I'm Cas, Cas Faucheux. Head of the archive department at our beautiful museum."

"Porter Norton. I found the notebooks recently. They've stoked an interest in my great-grandfather's war. I visited his grave at Aeroplane today. Unfortunately, he was shot as a deserter. Personally, I don't think he did desert."

Cas asked why not.

"Oh. It's clear from his diary how committed he was," said Porter, unable to describe the confirmation he got from witnessing Harry's execution and last words. Cas listened. Porter intuited it wasn't the first time Cas had heard this explanation.

"Harry was probably all those things you say - when he wrote it. But so many men succumbed to shell shock. Sometimes they did cut and run."

"I know that. But the diary is lucid and consistent right up until the day of his execution. And if he had deserted earlier than that, it would surely have featured in the diary? We'll never know for sure though, will we?"

Cas studied the notebook, and asked, "So you say, but would you take his case on as a solicitor?"

"Hmmm. Not without a bit more supporting evidence, I admit."

They both laughed. Cas returned to the notebook. He screwed up an eye and wrinkled his nose when the writing proved unusually illegible. Porter smiled. It was like watching David Lynch play Sherlock Holmes.

Cas shut the book and said, "Very interesting. May I photocopy it?"

Porter agreed. He was flattered a tiny bit of his family history was museum-grade.

"I can zoom it up a bit on the copier," said Cas. "I'm hopeless with a magnifying glass. Let's go."

As the photocopier did its noisy work, Cas picked one sheet from the copier and read it. He jabbed at the page and asked, "When do you leave, Mr Norton?"

"Porter, please. First thing tomorrow. Why?"

"This barn your great-grandfather mentions? The one with the Indian soldier?"

"Yes, I know."

"It still exists, can you believe? It's about 4 miles away. I know the owner. I can take you if you like?"

The chance to visit a location Harry had visited was too tempting.

"Are you sure? That's kind of you. I'm supposed to be back in Calais at 8pm tonight. But I guess as long as I'm back in London by Monday morning." Cas nodded.

"I'll call Adalric. He's good with us. The farm's been in his family for several hundred years. The barn was commandeered as a field hospital. You'll find it fascinating."

The Gliss chipped in. "Fascinating and ever so slightly agonising for you? A WW1 field hospital?"

Porter made a dismissive gesture. It was soon settled. Cas and Porter would meet tomorrow at 7.30am to drive out and see the farm. Porter would leave for Calais the following day instead.

Porter said he needed a decent steak, beer and chill-time. Cas left with a handshake.

The Gliss asked, "How are you feeling?"

"I feel a bit battered, to be honest. Nothing a steak and beer won't cure."

"So where are we staying tonight, then? We're supposed to be driving home at the moment."

"Shit."

Porter managed to get a room at a hotel in the square. Top dollar, but convenient. Porter sat in the chilly square under gas lighters, eating his steak, drinking beer. He got chatting at the bar to an American woman wearing a hat, encircled with a silk scarf. She was also researching her family history. They found they had a lot in common. They discussed the Great American Musical too. Porter thought it could be his lucky night. He bought a round. Coming back from the bar, he overheard Sam on the phone. "…yeah, he's cute, but gay, unfortunately."

The Gliss, who had been hanging around all evening like a jealous chaperone, said, "What did I tell you!"

"Bugger off," said Porter, as he came within the woman's hearing range.

"Who? What?" said the American, confused.

"Sorry, I meant my headache." But his heart wasn't in it anymore. He'd blown it. A good excuse to remain faithful to the memory of Tania a little while longer.

Porter fell into bed at midnight, alone, full of beef and beefs. His head was a spinning carousel of falling soldiers, muddy trenches and eviscerating explosions.

"Tomorrow, please be quieter," he said, punching his pillow into shape.

Chapter 20

In-Flanders Fields Museum, Ypres
Saturday, March 25th 2017: 7.40am

Cas gestured for Porter to get into his Land Rover.
"The museum's - useful for field trips."
"Do you have many?"
Cas drove out of the pedestrianised area with an axle-scraping bump. "But of course. There are many thousands of discoveries every year. Most are just war scrap though - bits of old metal - lots of munitions."
"Still? A hundred years later?"
"Of course. Millions of shells came down and sank into the mud. They surface all the time."
"Christ. How well do you know this farmer?"
"Adalric? Very. Neither the farm nor the farmer has changed much in the past 100 years."
"He's 100?"
"No, just a little Belgian joke. He's in his 70s but remembers his grandfather who worked the farm during the war."
They passed under the Menin Gate, the sobering monument containing 55,000 names of the soldiers from the British Empire whose bodies were never found. It turned out to be too small. Another 35,000 UK names were added later to the Tyne Cot Memorial to the Missing.
"They perform the *Last Post* every night at the Menin Gate," said Cas. "You must go before you leave. Very moving."
Porter wondered if Harry or Max had marched along the Menin Road on their own long journeys to the firing squad.
Soon Porter was watching nondescript small villages pass by. They pulled up at the farm. He'd imagined quaintness at the end of a dirt road, hidden from the modern world. This one had a spotless Massey-Ferguson on the drive, parked next to a gleaming steel shed.
Cas picked up on Porter's confusion. "Don't be fooled. The farm's hundreds of years old. It looks different from the other side."

Porter soon saw that the farm buildings formed a U-shape. They had parked on the modern-era curve of the U. Now they walked through a cluster of increasingly dilapidated outbuildings which formed the first of the long sides. They emerged into a rough courtyard. Porter saw the entrance to the farmhouse itself, a few older brick buildings and some tumbledown stables. Opposite these, completing the U-shape, was a magnificent barn. There were splashy patches of mortar repair daubed all over it. The roof appeared newer than the walls.

The Gliss, AWOL since bedtime, popped back into view behind Cas, who had gone to find Adalric.

"How's your head?" asked The Gliss.

"It's growling alright. Bad stuff happened here. I walked past that building and nearly crumpled." Porter gestured at the olde-worlde outbuilding. "Nothing good ever happened there."

The Gliss urged caution. "This was close to the frontline. There would have been mass suffering here. There's a cemetery over the back of that barn."

Cas returned with a short pensioner in white shirt, flat cap and waistcoat. He reminded Porter of the irascible old man in *Asterix*, Geriatrix. His face was the texture and colour of a ginger-nut biscuit. He spoke no English. Cas translated.

"Adalric welcomes you to his farm. He says you are free to go wherever you like."

Porter pointed at the barn.

"Of course," said Cas without checking. "Come."

The three crossed the muddy, pebbled courtyard and stood before the barn. The old man said a few words.

Cas nodded and translated, "He says the barn is exactly as it was 100 years ago except for the roof tiles, which were replaced five years ago. The beams inside are original."

Porter asked Cas to ask if Adalric had grown up knowing the history of the barn.

"But of course, surely," said Cas, translating over the top of Adalric's quiet speech. "Further back than the war even. The barn's 400 years old. The British used it as a field hospital during the war. Tens of thousands of wounded and dying soldiers came here."

Cas paused to catch Adalric's flow. "He's saying many died and were put in the mortuary over there." Cas pointed to the building that made Porter feel sick. "Many were buried a few hundred metres over there," pointing in the direction of the graveyard, which Porter had still not seen.

"That's close to the farm?" said Porter.

"Yes, of course. It makes sense, no?"

"A bit unfortunate for Adalric's family back then. How did they react?"

Adalric, scratching his ears and tilting his cap back and forth, replied while lifting the catch on the barn. The doors swung open. It was pitch inside.

"He says he knew his grandfather well and talked to him a lot as a young man. The barn was filled with medics and the freshly wounded. Adalric's grandmother found the screams upsetting apparently."

There was little to see in the barn: an old rusting tractor; bare bricks; a high ceiling with exposed A-frame beams. But the barn was not empty. Porter sensed a storm of pain, bouncing off the walls like a freshly caged tiger searching for impossible escape. Porter looked at the uneven earth floor of the barn and wondered what horrors lay within and beneath it. You won't be able to stay in here long. It feels like I'm being wrestled.

The pain was getting worse by the second. He tried to find an un-wasted question. "Wasn't it difficult to go back to farming afterwards?" Another exchange between the Belgians.

"No. What other choice was there?"

"I would find it strange - knowing so many died in here. Didn't his family ever feel haunted?" Porter meant haunted *poetic* rather than haunted *ghostly*. When Cas passed on the question, he received a loud tut in reply.

Cas elaborated. "There are no such things as ghosts. What happened, happened."

"Yes, I meant it in a more *casting a shadow* kind of way," said Porter.

"No. Nothing like that."

Porter had failed to get his point across and needed to get out. He tried unsuccessfully to picture Harry on a stretcher somewhere in this barn and the frantic gibbering of the Indian sepoy. His pictures were cheesily Hollywood, a cheap composite of every war film he'd ever seen. The barn was oppressive, even discounting Quincunx pain. Porter took his iPhone out, snapped several shots with the flash, saw that the flash didn't help and bumped the exposure up to try again without. Grainy but better.

He nodded to the others that he was done and took a step towards the barn doors. A grinding noise came from the tractor. Its digger tray, locked in the air to save floor-space, crashed to the floor, narrowly missing Porter's head. The heavy steel teeth brushed his arm as it dropped, ripping his jacket. The force of the tray hitting the floor caused the entire tractor to rock.

"Miljaar! Are you ok?" asked Cas, pulling Porter to safety.

"Fine."

"That could have killed you!"

Adalric, cursing, called for help. Two younger men jogged over. Adalric took no notice of Porter but shouted at his employees. Both shrugged in perplexed and righteous innocence and started arguing loudly with their boss.

The Gliss said, "No coincidence. You know that, right?"

"Definitely, I felt the malevolence," said Porter, forgetting not to speak out loud. Luckily, his speech was lost among the din of the Belgians shouting.

"Let's get out of here and check that arm," said Cas.

Outside the barn, the pair leaned on a gate to a field. Porter saw the cemetery in the middle distance. "The Indian soldier my great-grandfather mentioned could be in there."

"Maybe. There were literally millions of soldiers from the Commonwealth who fought against the Germans. We can wander over if you like?"

Adalric re-joined them. Satisfied Porter wasn't injured, he relaxed and lit up a foul-smelling roll-up. Porter took one too. It tasted no better than it looked.

"Adalric apologises about the tractor," said Cas. "It hasn't been used for eight years. He's been meaning to have it scrapped."

Porter said he was fine. He noticed a pile of rusted metal next to the deserted stables.

"War scrap," said Cas, heading off Porter's question. "It surfaces all the time. This is all from this year. We call it the *Iron Harvest*." They had a quick rifle through it. Bits of cable, barbed wire, tin cans, a bullet casing or two and a larger shell casing. "That looks like a gas canister," said Cas.

Porter examined the shattered metal. Damn thing had probably killed people. Here it was a century later, a mere curio in his hands. Scary. "Don't they have accidents? Diggers hitting shells, that kind of thing?" asked Porter.

"Of course. Three or four hundred people have died in France and Belgium since 1918. There are millions of unexploded bombs still around Ypres alone. It's a real problem and dangerous for the farmers."

"Not to mention dog walkers," quipped Porter.

"Indeed so," said Cas, without smiling.

One of Adalric's workers brought a flask of coffee and a plate of substantial cheese and ham sandwiches. After some thank-yous and a feed, Porter asked Cas if they could walk over to the cemetery. His head felt squashed, his limbs ached, and his chest was bound by iron hoops, but there was no point ducking out now.

"Yes. Let us go please," said Cas, ushering the way.

Adalric decided to keep them company.

They closed the gate behind them and stepped into Adalric's churned up farmland. The farm and the cemetery were connected by a narrow, well-trodden path.

"I presume we're safe here?" said Porter.

"If we stick to the path, sure," said Cas. He double-checked with Adalric. "He says the army cleared this bit 30 years ago. We're ok."

Wind angled noisily across his ears. Porter could make out the sound of his companions breathing as the three of them trudged in single file. The Gliss bobbed along in silence. They reached the cemetery's wrought-iron gate, attached to a post, bound to a large oak tree. Porter looked down. Out of respect, he felt he should clean the clods of mud from his shoes before entering. He leaned forward and put his foot on the gate. Cas and Adalric pulled up behind him and waited. In the shadow of the spreading oak, he managed to knock off some of the mud. The delay saved them.

The explosion was enormous. It came from 20 metres to the right. The bomb blew out a big chunk of the cemetery wall to the east, churning up graves to the west and north. The rest of the blast travelled south along the path of the wall towards the three men, destroying several old monuments in its way. They were sheltered by the tree, its wide girth taking the brunt of the stones, shrapnel and blast waves. Porter guessed it was the only fat tree in Ypres. Few trees here were more than a century old.

All three men stood in shock. Adalric shook his head a few times as if to clear his hearing. Cas gawped at the damage. There was a tinkling sound as tiny slivers of bone and stone tip-tapped their way through the leaves.

Porter checked the tree. It was slashed, torn and denuded. At its base were chunks of skeleton, including two skulls. He knew then he was in trouble. The Quincunx pain had continued to build since leaving the barn. Now it began to burn like fire. A kaleidoscope of new frontline images poured into him. More fragments of tortured voices.

Cas asked Adalric and Porter if they were ok.

"What the hell caused that?" said Porter loudly, trying to talk over the voices only he could hear. Was that one African? That one Indian? It could have been Harry's sepoy. Lots of English and Scottish voices. Shut up. Please shut up. I've got to get out of here before dead soldiers smother me.

"An unexploded shell," intruded Cas.

"Why did it go off now? We're miles away. Can't have been us." Porter was going mad. He needed to get out, right now.

Aging Adalric was still shaking and gestured back to the farm. He said he didn't want his wife worrying. They could see people running from the farm building. All three waved to show the concerned onlookers they were ok.

"Look at them," said Porter, holding out his shaking hands.

"And just the one shell," said Cas.

"I know. I'm not so sure I want to visit the cemetery now."

"Nor I, that's fair to say," said Cas.

They turned to go, to Porter's relief. The Gliss appeared. "Porter, this was an attack. Like the tractor. You've got to get out of here. I don't know what's happening, but I can tell you this - there are hundreds of buried shells between you and the farm. It's time to run."

To the surprise of both Adalric and Cas, Porter took The Gliss at his word and ran. He immediately tripped on an exposed root, falling face first into the mud.

Then the explosions began.

Munitions of all kinds began detonating under the soil. Bullets from pistols and rifles barely registered as they exploded - nothing more than princess burps. Elsewhere, obscene ruptures were corrupting Adalric's field.

Mortar shells, grenades and mines went off one by one. Noise, mud and broken potatoes rained down on Porter as he fled for the safety of the farm. The farm had been used as a hospital because it was near the frontline, not on it. The closer he got to the farm, the safer he was. Thank God for the soldiers who cleared this path. We'd be mincemeat otherwise.

Cas tried to shelter Adalric as the two terrified men began stumbling back to the farm, as fast as the old man could manage. They both saw the explosions were happening in a cluster around Porter, their focus moving as he moved.

Porter's calves were aching and drained. Images of the childhood cross-country run came back to him. The Gliss was shouting, but he couldn't hear. No shrapnel caught him, but a large piece of broken flint skidded across his cheekbone, carving a red worm into it. There was a short lull, though Porter kept running. Now he could hear The Gliss.

"Whatever's doing this can't aim. It can only detonate what's here. Keep straight."

Porter didn't need telling. The explosions began again. Then stopped. Then a few more.

"Whatever's doing this is fading," said The Gliss. "Don't let that stop you running."

A few seconds later, Porter emerged into the farm courtyard, a group of astonished workers and Adalric's wife staring at him. He was sweating, covered in mud, blood pouring from the cheek wound. He also had a tear on his right earlobe, as if someone had torn an earring out. Adrenaline kept the pain away. He heard a woman cry out and turned to see Cas supporting Adalric, arriving through the gate like Derek Redmond and his father. Safe now, the old man was bent, hands on knees coughing up fronds of phlegm. Cas said nothing but looked agitated, sweaty and muddy. It was apparent he too had fallen in the dash for the farm.

"Are you ok?" asked Porter.

"Er, not really. Not fit," said Cas, out of breath. "What was that? It all happened around you."

"Me?"

"The explosions - they followed you. You knew it too. You ran before it even started."

"I wanted to get back."

"Porter, there is…"

Cas' question was neither completed nor answered. A colossal explosion caused everyone to cover their ears and cower. Deep from within the centre of Adalric's field, a small cache of 200lb howitzer shells, abandoned in 1918, detonated. Flame shot from the earth and mud and stone flew in all directions. None of it reached the farm. It didn't have to. All the witnesses were shocked, awed and terrified. All ears were ringing.

"Soddin' Nora," said Porter as the echoes died away. "It's like wartime Ypres has reincarnated itself."

Adalric and his wife looked into their field, dismayed. This year's crop was ruined. Cas shook his head. One of the workers, a young woman in a ragged boiler suit, asked if she should call the army. Adalric nodded.

Cas translated for Porter. "They're calling this in. I think we'd better leave."

No-one blamed Cas and Porter, but no-one was sorry to see them go either. Adalric nodded a silent goodbye. They headed back to the Land Rover.

"You need a stitch. I have a first aid kit. Come."

Porter used the wing mirror to check his injuries, while Cas rummaged in the back. "What was that?" he hissed.

"Someone or something doesn't want you looking into Harry and Max obviously," said The Gliss.

"I could've been killed!"

"Try your best. I never said it was risk-free. Supernatural obviously. Can't be Harry or Max, can it? They're the ones who need your help. It must be someone or something connected to them though."

Porter winced as he touched his ear. "If Cartwright wasn't a spy, someone accused him of it. Or framed him."

"I guess so."

"Its ghost tried to kill me?"

"I don't know. It's a possibility."

Cas came to Porter, waving the green first aid kit.

"Here we are. Let's patch you up. You need a hospital."

"Clean it. I'm going home. I have things to do tomorrow. If I get home early enough tonight, I can pop to my local hospital," said Porter.

"As you wish. Porter, there's something you're not telling me."

Porter winced as the disinfectant bit and said, "Cas, would you believe me if I told you, I have absolutely no idea what happened?"

Cas smiled. "Not really, but I guess I'll have to. For now."

On the short drive back to Ypres, neither man spoke. Porter looked out the window and tried to process what had just happened, his head throbbing. Cas sulked, sure he was being kept out of a loop.

As they were driving under the Menin Gate, Porter had an epiphany of sorts. He'd been under fire, almost died in the barn and heard the final words of a soldier whose words he couldn't understand. For two hours at least, he had experienced what Harry had. He was drawing a strength from the connection.

Cas and Porter said their goodbyes at the museum. Porter promised to stay in touch. Cas reminded him to get the ear seen to.

Showering for the second time that day, Porter didn't mind The Gliss hovering in the bathroom for once. It made him feel safer.

"There's no doubt now, is there?" asked Porter. "After the statue, the tractor and the explosions - something is out to get me."

"I think so. How's your head?"

"Attacked from all sides. Headaches and physical damage too. I look like I've been in a street fight."

"You have been," said The Gliss. "The question is - who with?"

"*What* with. I'm going to avoid cemeteries for the foreseeable future. The pounding in my head...like an elephant had stamped on it. What if I overdose on all these Lemsips and paracetamol?"

With no clean clothes, he rescued his dirty but undamaged clothes from yesterday. He gave them a quick iron and a squirt of aftershave before re-dressing.

Porter looked out the window and asked, "If I solve Max's case, will I be free again? This poltergeist thing - it's very destructive."

The Gliss jiggled his porcelain shoulders, a proto-shrug. "I don't know. I think we carry on until this problem is solved. There may be more though."

Porter's mobile rang. It was Feng.

"Hey, crazy man."

"Look who's talking. How you doing?"

"Have you got a minute? Goff, where do I start?" Feng waffled on about some internal combustion going on within the ranks of the Doves. "What you been doing?"

Porter updated him.

"I can't believe it. Did you get footage? Sounds amazing," said Feng.

"Which part? The bit where I got wounded, or the bit where large chunks of a field blew up, almost killing all three of us?"

"Sorry if I'm insensitive, but either or both obviously."

"There's no footage."

"Oh ok. Just asking."

"You don't believe me, do you?"

"You said that, not me."

"Oh, come on."

"Alright, I'm not sure I believe you. See, I left a little wiggle room. I want to believe you."

Porter wasn't going to judge anyone for raising their eyebrows. "You could speak to Cas if you like? He'll tell you what I told you."

"No need. I'm willing to go along with it. What do you think it means though?"

"Max and Harry both used their last words to say they were innocent. But they got punished anyway. If they were telling the truth, someone was responsible for their frame-ups. I've been appointed to resolve their pain. I have to uncover what happened to them and find out who was responsible."

Feng chipped in. "And you think whoever was responsible for that might now be after you?"

"Sure. Classic mafia tactics. Intimidate or dispose of the cops investigating you."

"How does this person or persons know what you're doing?"

Porter sat on the edge of the bed. "That's the tricky bit. Whatever force brought The Gliss here may have brought this malevolence into being too. Some kind of poltergeist. I don't know. It's had a go at me in three places now. It's not like my idea of a traditional ghost, trapped in a specific place. This one's following me around. My ear's going to need stitches when I get back."

Feng say-whatted. Porter detailed his injuries. "The truth is Feng, I haven't got a clue what's going on. And it's dangerous. And scary."

Porter's phone bleeped. He glanced at the dial.

"It's that journalist at the Mail trying to call me. Again."

"The Daily Mail?"

"Yes. It'll be about my industrial tribunal etc. I'd better take it. See you Monday morning."

By the time Porter had cleared the line and pressed accept, the carbuncle Weekes had hung up. He waited a few minutes to pick up her voicemail. She asked him to call. Nah. He wasn't that keen to speak to the vindictive cow.

Time to go home. He sat on the edge of the bed wondering where the next attack would come from.

Namita Menon's flat, Shoreditch.
Sunday, March 26th 2017: 1.30pm

Namita put the phone down on Barry Hammell and lit up. If anyone could hack into Runyon's system and see if the call between Nick Runyon and Kerry Crane still existed, it was Hammell. Only trouble is, she was breaking the law even commissioning him.

Since the locket incident, Namita was conflicted. She couldn't accept Porter's paranormal gobbledygook, but she couldn't come up with an alternative explanation either. She was still freaked out. How else could he have known all that? No-one knew.

Her sister's death had shaped her life in many ways. She carried her everywhere. She had informed every decision Namita had ever made: dresses to food, holidays to men. She was her sounding board. Recently, she had been pushing Namita to leave Quendell's and set up her own practice. Namita hadn't quite found the time or, if she was honest, the courage to take that step. Sangita was, nonetheless, insistent. *Remember sister, you must live your life for both of us.*

Namita had a tic, nodding in acknowledgement of Sangita's voice. It's stupid if you think about it. Sangita was only six when she died. What did she know of life? You're such a fool Namita.

But it was subtler than that. Sangita had grown up alongside her and become her alter-ego. She occasionally came up with good ideas. It was Sangita who had popped the idea of Hammell into Namita's head.

Hammell was ex-SAS. He was calm and professional on the outside but, Namita suspected, damaged and scary on the inside. He was brilliant at his job, if not expensive.

Part of Namita's worry was how to fund hiring him. It would have to be off-book because it was illegal. Feng had money. He seemed mad enough to cover it. Was she sure she wanted to drag that madman into her conspiracy? It was done now. She'd bring up the subject of money with Porter and Feng when she met them at the Imperial War Museum tomorrow.

Her sister approved. *Backbone. Good for you.*

"Yes Sangita, but what would mother say?"

That stupid cow.

And Namita laughed along and lit another fag.

Chapter 21

Imperial War Museum, London
Monday, March 27th 2017: 10am

Porter wondered if Namita would show. He had imagined her on YouTube, furiously searching for an explanation of Porter's mind-reading trick. It would drive her crazy not knowing how it was done. She's had plenty of time to stew since. Besides, how much of this nonsense do you believe yourself?

But there she was, al fresco, despite the chill, sipping on a coffee and scanning her phone. Red chiffon scarf and sunglasses. Porter had never seen her outside the office and was taken aback by the glam.

He was still gawping when Feng slapped him across the back and said, "Oi Oi."

Porter, coughing from the blow, spluttered, "Flak jacket?"

"Keeping the military theme going. Ah, Ms Menon. She got here first then?"

"That's her job, Feng. She gets everywhere first - to scope out her advantage. Did you see my ear?"

"Your ear?! Look at your cheek!"

Porter had gone straight to Homerton Hospital A&E as soon as he arrived home on Saturday night. Doctors and nurses had tutted, asked questions he couldn't truthfully answer, and then submitted him to a bit of painful repair work. He got home at 2am and spent the rest of Sunday reading books on WW1.

"Please behave yourself today," said Porter.

"What? Is The Gliss here at the moment? I'd love to try and get a reading off him before we go inside."

"I'm talking about you. No, he's not here. And you know he doesn't show up on your gizmo thing. Don't go pulling it out here, please. I don't want to get thrown out."

The pair ambled over to Namita. Her disguise gave her the quality of an Italian film star dodging the Paps. She jumped when Porter called her name.

"Jesus!"

"Ms Menon. We meet again," said Feng.

Namita's sunglasses hid her reaction. Then she spotted Porter's bandages. She whipped off her sunglasses. "What happened to you?"

Within ten minutes, everyone was up to speed on Porter's Ypres adventures. He played down the violence. He needed their help. No point in scaring them off. Porter showed a few iPhone snaps of the barn.

"Creepy," said Namita. "What are we doing today? It'd better be worth it. I told my boss my aunt was dying."

"Is she?"

"I haven't got an aunt. What kind of person would kill off an actual relative for a lame excuse?"

"We need to look up Max and Harry," said Porter interrupting. "The basic stuff: what records exist, how do we get them - that kind of thing." He scribbled down the bare biographical details he had.

"The archivists will know," he concluded. "We'll divide the searches up."

The Gliss appeared. "Focus on Max Cartwright, Porter. Those headaches will kill you otherwise. The only way to stop them is to atone by clearing Max. You can do Harry anytime. My two-penneth worth."

Porter's phone rang. Cherry again and another missed call from the Mail. Cherry could wait. The reporter could sod off.

Namita, a few bristling steps ahead with Feng, shouted, "Porter! Come on."

The Gliss warned, "Remember what I said."

University College Hospital, London
Monday, March 27th 2017: 10.32am

"He's not answering," cursed Cherry. "The little sod's avoiding me."

Orit sighed. Professor Justin Saunders swigged from his plastic coffee cup. "Why do they still make plastic cups?" he said. "Even the cardboard ones burn your fingers. These things…you need oven gloves. Sorry. It's the small things that get you. Seriously, Orit - I do need to speak to this man."

Orit fidgeted. "I know that, Justin. Porter doesn't accept he has a problem yet. He's paranoid and delusional. Intervention *is* required."

"I believe you," said Saunders, "But there are a million hoops to jump through before we can do much. If he's that bad, he may need to be hospitalised. It requires three experts to sign off on a committal. I'm not approaching a judge or clinician until I've assessed him for myself. Sorry, Orit. It's both our reputations at stake."

"I know that Justin," Orit stropped. "I don't want to be standing with Cherry at her brother's funeral in a month because we didn't act today."

"Nor do I," said Cherry.

"Of course not. But we have to do this by the book. Threats of suicide and hallucinations are rarely a good combination - but I need more than your say-so to act. Call him while we finish our tea. If you have no luck, I'll try to persuade him to come in."

Cherry looked at the two psychiatrists. She experienced a momentary twinge of guilt for going behind her brother's back. Then she had a premonition of Porter sprawled dead across his living room floor.

No. This was the right thing to do.

Imperial War Museum, London
Monday, March 27th 2017: 1pm

The three gathered at lunch to share the results of their morning searches.

Feng, messily eating sushi and reading the Evening Standard, sprayed laughter and rice.

"Read your horoscope?" said Porter.

"Silly story. Reminds me of you…some woman has been sectioned after going berserk in Wood Green. She started throwing her arms about, shouting, 'Get off me.' One of the shoppers said she looked like a mad chicken. They had to sedate her.'" Feng looked up. "Funny. Almost sounds like she's possessed."

"Or crazy," said Namita. "If you dare add mind control, possession or Satanism to your list, I'm off."

"I'll get the drinks in," said Porter.

"Americano, milk and one sugar," said Feng.

"Me too," said Namita.

"Me three," said Porter. "All Americanos, with milk and one sugar? That's weird."

"At least you can't screw the order up," said Feng.

"Put a name on each cup anyway. I'm fussy like that," said Namita.

Porter was ready. Feng pulled out a pen and notebook. Namita opened her MacBook Pro. Porter tried to flatten an inadequate, crumpled piece of paper hoicked from his back pocket. He'd left his battered MacBook at home.

Their research covered three areas: documents specifically mentioning Harry or Max, the Worcestershire Regiment, and British executions. There had only been 306 executions, meaning there was a good chance Max or Harry's case had already been written about, especially given the strength and longevity of the Pardon campaign.

They had started the day full of optimism for a quick hit or two. Time to spill. Porter went first. "There's way less archive material than you might imagine. About executions, at least," he teased.

"The British army destroyed all the paperwork in 1924. Wasn't exactly a popular subject with the public." Porter squinted over his notes. "By then, the public had changed its mind about the war. Initially supportive in 1914, four years later, a generation of young men was lost. Soon families were living with the real cost - the dead, obviously, but also those who came home wounded, silent or traumatised."

Porter flipped his sheet of research. "I didn't know this - listen. Although the phrase goes back to Plutarch, it was a book by Capt P.A. Thompson published in 1927 called *Lions Led by Donkeys* that caught the new mood. To this day it's hard to find people who see the Great War as anything other than a senseless and avoidable catastrophe. In the Twenties, no-one seemed to care the army had destroyed all the paperwork." Feng and Namita looked disappointed.

"It does mean the surviving documents are better catalogued and studied." Porter smiled. "For example, a stenographer's record of Max Cartwright's court-martial survived even though the actual records didn't." Namita and Feng did a double-take.

"What's that?" said Feng, spluttering his coffee.

"And the museum has it?" asked Namita.

"The museum has it," confirmed Porter. "And when Labour pardoned all the victims back in 2002, lots of research was done by officials working on the Act of Parliament. The museum still has copies of all of those files."

"Cool," said Feng.

"What's not so cool is I didn't find anything on Harry specifically."

"I've found a few things," said Feng, waving his printout.

"Me too," said Namita. "Though it's all basic stuff."

They headed back into the archive room, still sharing.

A librarian with a fierce stare put fingers to her lips to shush them up.

Feng and Namita's researches had thrown up a haul of references to investigate. They agreed to skip pulling the general war histories because that consisted of hundreds, if not thousands, of books. There were some court records to call up. Potentially more interesting, there were a few digitised letters from other soldiers in the same regiment around the same time as Max and Harry. Good background.

They also had the donated archives of a handful of pardon campaigners, which often included testimony from old soldiers, gathered in the 1970s. Most of this still had to be digitised and needed searching manually. Namita had also printed out a long list of regimental records and sources.

"It's a lot, but I can't wait to see the stenographer's transcription most," said Porter.

Feng and Namita looked at Porter. They looked at the stern librarian.

"Er…your case, your find, you'd better call it up," said Feng.

Porter sighed, got up, and heard the others try not to laugh as he walked across the library towards the scary librarian.

Chapter 22

Imperial War Museum, London
Monday, March 27th 2017: 2.50pm

Later, in a small library, cum-reading room, the three had on white cotton gloves and were eagerly examining a delicate reel of stenotype word clusters - a common shorthand recorded with a special typewriter. None of them understood the markings, which were so faint as to be illegible. Even the typed informal transcription was hard, but not impossible, to read.

"It's a good job this was transcribed," said Feng.

"But so faint," said Namita, squinting.

"It's better than nothing," said Porter protectively, aware he might be hoping for too much from one source.

The documents came from a private collection donated to the museum by Julia Comberville in 1952. The notes that accompanied the material suggested Comberville had been in Ypres during the war on some kind of short-term attachment from the Ministry of Justice. Why she had been covering Max Cartwright's court-martial was unclear. They spent the next half hour going through the transcription, arguing, making notes and discussing their findings. Once they had stopped fighting, Namita typed up a messy summary.

Summary of the Court Martial of Max Cartwright.

The Field General Court Martial (FGCM) was held on March 2nd 1917. Three officers sat in judgement on Cartwright. The president was Major Alfred Guzman. Also sitting were Lieutenant Geoffrey Ayles and Captain Robin Sanderson.

Cartwright was caught coming out of No-Man's Land with highly secretive plans for the battle of Messines, Ypres. He was unwilling or unable to explain himself or say how the docs had ended up in his kit. At least one person suggested Max was hiding something. He appeared cagey and defensive.

Witnesses included three captains, Georges Pelenot, Alexander Wootton and Cecil Braxted and private Alfie Bell. A Reverend Charles Gilpin also gave testimony as well as Corporal Joseph Green and the MP who arrested Cartwright on his return. Star witness was Private Avory, who saw Max in No-Man's Land with a German. Avory shot the German and alerted the authorities.

"Wow," said Porter when he read the witness list. Cecil Braxted. Enfant terrible of Britain's fascist movement in the 30s along with Oswald Mosley and an MP into the 1950s. Right up until his death aged 92, he was a vocal supporter of Enoch Powell. Porter explained Powell to the others.

Feng called up Wikipedia for a quick dip into Braxted's biography. There was a 1969 article from The Times discussing the growing Pardon movement. Braxted reiterated his belief that WW1 sentences should stand. He argued Britain only won the war because of its disciplined army. He had personally met and despised some of the executed. They had put everyone, and the national cause, at risk through their cowardice.

"Nice guy!" said Feng, as they continued putting their summary together.

After a short hearing, Cartwright was found guilty and taken down. Before leaving, Cartwright made some serious unknown accusations about an officer, which the outraged court ordered not be recorded. In Max's absence, he received the death penalty. Confirmation was required from the commander-in-chief, Sir Douglas Haig. Other records confirm that Cartwright was executed at dawn the following day, March 3rd 1917.

"Next day?" said Feng in surprise. "What about the appeals process?"

"There wasn't one," said Porter. "It was purely inquisitorial - did the person do what they were accused of? If they did, then they were guilty. No mitigation."

"The Human Rights Lawyer in me is disgusted by that," said Namita. "But the bombshell is that Cartwright accused an officer of something dodgy. None of his claims get heard, he's attacked by the court for speaking up, and he's killed the next morning. Sounds more like North Korea than Britain."

Porter nodded. "Major Guzman's order that the name of the person Cartwright accused be redacted from the report…I mean, what's that about? We need to go through this and construct a timeline."

Feng and Namita were arguing over whether to use Feng's notepad and pencil or her drawing software. The Gliss faded-in to Porter's view.

"Regular hive of bees. Making progress?"

"I think so," said Porter, causing the other two to stop and stare, before he made a Keep Calm and Carry On gesture at them. "There's certainly something a bit hokey about Cartwright's case. He was tried, found guilty and executed within 24 hours."

"Not that uncommon," said The Gliss.

"True. But the court ordering the records altered, is. The stenographer's transcript looks like a working document used to prepare the actual record. The name has been removed in that. The markings on the Stenotype reel, which presumably did contain the name, have faded, so the only record we have is the redacted trial notes. The official record was destroyed in 1924. There may be a copy in the National Archive but that's unlikely and for now, what we have here is a good account with some of the juicy bits blanked out."

An argumentative hour later and they had their summary.

Field General Court Martial (FGCM) convened.
Capt. Georges Pelenot gives a good character reference.
Capt. Alex Wootton gives a good character reference.
Capt. Cecil Braxted gives an iffy character reference.
Reverend Charles Gilpin gives a so-so reference.
Charges under the Army Act of 1881 read out.
1) Leaving a post without orders (he was missing overnight. Plea: Not Guilty).
2) Treacherously corresponding with the enemy (he was caught in possession of secret documents). Plea: Not Guilty).
3) Knowingly committing an act calculated to imperil the success of His Majesty's Forces. Plea: Not Guilty).

All three charges were capital offences, carrying a death sentence.
* Cartwright caught with the plans for the Messines operation in his kit.

* *Was arrested by Military Police at 0700 on March 2nd returning from No-Man's Land.*

* *Had been reported missing by Private Alfie Bell the night before.*

* *Witness statements from Private Alfie Bell, and two MPs, Corporal James Bracken and Private Cyril Derrell. Another soldier, Private Avory said he heard someone talking in No Man's Land. He fired and saw he had killed a German soldier, but then saw Cartwright leaving the German's body and coming back to the trench.*

* *Cartwright explained he had been on recon in No-Man's Land for Operation Ashbright*

* *Panel asked him what Operation Ashbright was. He said he didn't know but said Capt.____ had ordered him on the mission. (Capt.'s name later deleted on panel's order. See point X below.)*

* *When questioned about this, Cartwright says he was ordered to look for evidence of German offensive preparations, got trapped in No Man's Land, killed a German soldier, and spent the night with the corpse in a crater. He called out to the watch. Private Avory fired at him and the corpse. As soon as he got back in the trench, he was arrested.*

* *Major Guzman: There is no Operation Ashbright. A call is made to HQ to confirm this.*

* *Cartwright - Capt. ____ told him about his mission on the evening of the last day of February. Capt._____ denies this.*

* *How did the plans end up in your kit? Noting he hesitated, Cartwright answered: No idea.*

* *Major Guzman confirms Cartwright must be lying. Guzman was with Capt. ____ that night at a dance at Chateau Ferrie. Lieutenant Ayles was also at the dance for officers and nurses. Ayles confirms Capt. ____ was there all night. The trenches were too far away for the captain to have left and returned in secret.*

* *Cartwright doesn't dispute the papers found on him were Top Secret.*

* *Cartwright appears unable to defend himself, leaving the court no option but to interpret his actions as hostile.*

* *Court is halfway through announcing a guilty verdict when there's unrest, and Cartwright causes a commotion. He is restrained by MPs. Before announcing the verdict, Guzman asks Cartwright to explain himself.*

* Cartwright announces that Capt.____framed him deliberately in an attempt to kill him.
* Outrage in court. Why would Capt. ___ do this? Cartwright: no answer.
* Guzman orders all reference to Capt. ___ to be struck from the testimony. "You are not only a spy and a traitor but a coward and a liar."
* Guilty verdict. Cartwright told he faced death sentence. Removed from court to cells.
* Guzman seeks immediate death next morning.
* Death sentence confirmed by Haig later that day and carried out the next morning.

"You can't say it wasn't fair!" said Feng.

Porter nodded. "The prosecutors only had to prove Cartwright had the documents and wasn't at his post."

"Cartwright was in a bit of a hole," said Namita. "He didn't dispute he had the documents on him."

The Gliss spoke to Porter. "The Quincunx was formed for you to put this right. We know from Max's grave that he was innocent. His claim confirms it. Maybe he was set up?"

"By Capt. Blank presumably. But why? At least we've got new names. We need to look up a few of these characters," said Porter.

"Definitely. I also want to get a bit of background on the Messines Ridge operation," said Feng.

Porter nodded. "I'm guessing the captains who bothered to give character references must have liked Cartwright. I presume, therefore, it's none of them he's talking about?"

Namita shook her head. "It's *more* likely to be one of them, isn't it? How many captains would a private on the frontline have contact with? If they knew him well enough to give him a reference…"

"Yes, but surely if one of them had framed Cartwright they'd want to keep out of the way of the court-martial?" Porter countered.

Feng said, "I'm no lawyer, but I know plenty about backstabbing. If you were covering your tracks, it makes more sense to give a reference than not…"

"Porter, how many times have you seen criminals brazen it out?" asked Namita.

Porter leaned back in his chair. "Maybe. I guess we'll have to look into all of them. Braxted obviously didn't like Cartwright much. What was it he said?"

Namita skimmed back through the transcription and read Braxted's testimony. *Seems decent enough, though I've had to barrack him a few times for sloppy work. Not my first choice for a help, but pretty unlikely to be a spy either.* It's hardly a ringing endorsement, is it?"

"Feng what do you think?" said Porter.

"I'm a sceptic. We need more information."

"He's right. It should be easy enough to find out who Cartwright's captain was from regimental records," said Namita. "I'm also curious about the other captain, Pelenot. Do you think he's one of the famous Pelenots?"

"I was wondering that," said Porter. "Arthur Pelenot, the famous painter?"

"Yes, and Karin Pelenot, the TV historian."

"She's Arthur Pelenot's daughter or granddaughter, I think. I saw them both in The Observer Magazine once," said Porter.

"Excuse me," interrupted a stranger. "I have to apologise, but I've been listening to your conversation…not on purpose, you understand? Sound travels like the Whispering Gallery in here. Darren Griffee. How do you all do?"

He shook hands while they marvelled at his look that mixed bright red shirt, lime green trousers, John Lennon glasses and waxed, Victorian, muscle-man moustache.

"I'm working on a book about deserters," he explained. "So, obviously your conversation was intriguing. I'd have passed you off as civilians doing a family history except…" He gestured at them. Indian. Chinese. English. "Even in our multicultural times, you guys would make one hell of a diverse family. Do you need any help?"

"I like him," said Feng. Porter and Namita sighed.

Griffee twirled his moustache like Dick Dastardly's affable younger brother, while the three of them cobbled together a credible sounding, research story. Porter said the family of one of the executed soldiers had approached them about launching a civil case against the government. Namita said they were starting their research from scratch.

Feng said, "It's a shame he was executed for upsetting an officer, accused of stealing battle plans and spying for the enemy."

Griffee sat up. "What did you say?"

Porter cut in, "Of course, it's all confidential at the moment." But they gave him the bones of the case.

Griffee handed a business card to Feng. "First thing to say is, I'm not surprised your man blurted out an accusation. Purely anecdotal evidence, but this did happen. I guess if you've been sentenced to death, you might as well throw a few punches.

"The second thing is, casualty rates were high amongst all men, including officers. Units were constantly being reinforced. In the heat of battle, separate units might be forced to work together. You may find regimental records that say who your soldier's nominal captain was, but the truth is he may have taken orders from a dozen captains during the whole campaign."

The others let him speak. They were a little bit intimidated by the moustache.

"The third thing that stands out is that your soldier was doomed from the moment the MPs picked him up. Sorties into No Man's Land were a daily occurrence but, of course, had to be authorised. A simple private coming back, *sans* orders, with secret battle plans? The death sentence was a formality. Everyone in court would've known that."

"What if Max Cartwright - sorry, our soldier - had been an officer?" asked Feng.

"Cartwright, eh? I've seen that name. I'm pretty au fait with the list. Don't worry, your secret's safe with me. Only one officer was ever executed. The debate still rages whether WW1 was a *Just War*. However, it's hard to argue it wasn't a *Class War*. That said… battle plans found on him. Definitely not good. I'd love to know more when you feel it's appropriate." He gave more cards to Namita and Porter.

Griffee said his book was about the Class War aspect. "Any new personal family information you've come across…that would be so helpful. Please stay in touch."

As soon as he was gone, with promises and smiles, Namita turned on Feng. "Don't we all sound nuts enough without telling other people what we're doing?"

"He gave us good info," said Feng.

"What am I doing here," Namita plonked herself down in a chair and bashed the table. People looked up.

"Calm down everyone," said Porter. "Let's stick to that story if anyone asks in future. Now we've started the lie, we'd better continue it. Namita, I'm so glad you're here, but if it's really stressing you out, I won't blame you if…"

"No. I'm curious. I'm in. It's just…," she gestured at Feng.

"No offence taken!" said Feng.

"Come on, don't ruin what's been a good day. I'm going to come again tomorrow. I'll widen out the search to include those captains, that stuff about the secret plans etc.," said Porter.

"I'll help with that," said Feng.

"I guess I can take another day off," said Namita. "I suppose I'd better shift my imaginary aunty nearer the precipice."

The Gliss made Porter jump, "The research will take a long time. Everyone had such bad handwriting in those days."

Chapter 23

Mare Street, Hackney
Monday, March 27th 2017: 7.15pm

"The F in TFL must stand for *flipping* - as in *flipping useless*, right?" cursed Porter after a torturous journey back from the museum. One bus, two tubes, one Overground and now, a 10-minute walk from London Fields.

"It's one of those awkward routes," said The Gliss.

"The tube was overcrowded, and the Overground was 10 minutes late."

"Just one of those awkward routes."

Cyclists sped past in the bus lane, rubbing it in. Porter was tempted to pull his phone so he could talk freely to The Gliss but couldn't be bothered. He was excited by the day's researches, but also worn out. He crossed Reading Lane, glancing up at the Empire 50-metres away. Home Sweet Home.

"I can't keep calling you The Gliss - it's uncomfortable. Gliss would be better."

"No. *The*'s part of my name. Don't skip it. It would be like calling you Ter or Por."

"What about TG? It'd make it easier for me."

"Please don't. I'm not a Disney Channel presenter."

"I like it. Hey, TG, let's rescue dead people! Hey, TG, let's buy aspirin! Hey, TG, let's appear completely mental!"

"Who you talking to, Porter?" said Cherry, standing up. Orit and Cherry had been drinking coffee in the Town Hall Square, planning their approach to Porter during this unannounced visit. Porter saw Orit, did the math, and thought quickly.

"I was rehearsing a memory walk. You know - my thing. Trying to remember a list of all the Oscar-winning films since 1929."

"I see," said Cherry. "And in which year did *Completely Mental* win best film?"

"I made a mistake. I got the order of *Bridge on the River Kwai* and *Gigi* mixed up. *Gigi* was 1958 and *Kwai* was 1957. I put Alec Guinness on that bench over there and Leslie Caron on the Town Hall Steps, silly me. It was obviously the other way around. I was just saying to myself, Porter, you are completely mental."

The Gliss coughed. "No-one's doubting that right now. Chill."

Porter clapped his hands. "How you doing, sis?" Then he had a terrible thought. "Ida, she alright?"

"Yes, she's fine. I'm here to see you actually. You remember Orit of course?"

"Of course." Orit waved hello.

"What the hell happened to your face?"

"I got hit by a flying stone."

"Of course you did. And your ear?"

"Another stone."

It was time to change the subject. "Shall we go over to mine? I've no food in, but I can make you fresh coffee?"

They set off, The Gliss continuing to warn Porter, who bit his lip, unable to reply. His sister led the way.

"What's this?" asked Cherry, as Porter prepared tea. She held up Porter's Eurotunnel ticket and his Ypres guidebook, laying skew-whiff across the table.

"I went to Ypres at the weekend. Didn't I mention?"

"No, you didn't. Why were you there?"

"Sightseeing."

Cherry looked at her friend and shrugged. Orit leaned into Cherry and asked if she could smell something? Burning? They sniffed the air. An acrid tang. Like burnt, wet sock. Cherry shrugged and continued her grilling.

"And what did you see?"

"I was digging into our family history if you must know. I was..." He realised his mistake immediately.

Cherry exploded. "What is it with you guys and this family curse bollocks! Scott said he wished he'd never been born this week. How do you think that made me feel? Why can't you be happy with what you've got?"

Porter wanted to ask if Scott was ok, but he was swamped by the rage coming at him across the table.

"I'm sick of this. Stop living in the past. Stop trying to kill yourself before you've even tried living." She stamped her foot. Orit looked uncomfortable. "Nothing's changed since you tried to top yourself after that idiot, Carola. It's always about a woman with you, isn't it? Man-up, brother. Man-up."

"Cherry, shut the flip up," said Porter, audaciously. "Why bring Carola up? I was twenty... girlfriend dumps me...took a minuscule overdose. Hardly uncommon. It's a bit much to have it thrown in my face all the bloody time."

"What were you doing in Ypres then? Don't tell me, that's where you entered a stone-flinging competition?" she said, pointing at his injuries.

"It's the opposite of what you think. I'm not *succumbing* to the stupid curse, I'm trying to put it to bed. I was looking into our great-grandfather, Harry Norton. The one who was executed? I've come across some evidence - he may have been innocent. That's all it was. A bit of research. I can't tell you what for at the moment."

"What did you find out?" asked Orit, looking for an accident-free introduction into the fiery siblings' exchange.

"I found his grave and spoke to some people at the archives there. His case is mentioned in a few documents. It's quite possible he didn't desert after all and was, more or less, murdered by the British Army." Orit nodded politely.

Cherry snorted. "So?" Porter gave up and turned to make the coffee. Still fuming, Cherry looked around. She saw three sealed envelopes propped against an old ceramic teapot. Absentmindedly, she turned them over.

One was addressed to her, one to Tania, another was marked "Porter Norton. Last Will and Testament." Without hesitation or qualm, Cherry dropped them into her bag. She composed herself enough to smile at Orit, who was taking advantage of the lull to pipe up.

"Porter, are you still talking to ghosts?" The room fell silent. "I only ask because the other night you said you were trying to kill yourself. And you were talking to ghosts."

He'd forgotten about the call. In a moment of madness, he said, "The Gliss isn't a ghost, he's a messenger."

"Uh oh, you've done a Gordon Jackson there," said The Gliss.

"What do you mean Porter? Are you seeing a ghost *now*?" said Orit, the inquisitor. Cherry looked up.

"Er no. Nothing now," said Porter.

"You saw something earlier though?"

"Er, No. Not exactly."

"You can tell us," said Orit. The ice in her eyes betrayed the warm listen she was offering.

"You have the right to remain silent," said The Gliss.

Porter looked up and nodded.

Orit's eyes followed Porter's gaze. "You *can* see something, can't you?" she said.

"Of course not. Can you two get off my case?" He rolled up his sleeves, waiting for Orit to tag Cherry back into the ring. But his sister surprised him.

"Come on, Orit. We should leave."

"But, Cherry…"

"Come on."

No sooner were they out the door than The Gliss waded in. "What the hell was that? Stop looking at me! Stop responding to me! Are you stupid or something?"

"She caught me on the hop."

"She's not happy," sighed The Gliss.

Porter plopped down on the sofa. "I know. I wonder why Cherry left rather than screaming abuse at me for another hour? She doesn't normally pass up the chance."

Cherry was with Orit in her parked car on Reading Lane, sniffling despite herself. She handed the letter to Orit.

Dear Cherry,

By the time you read this, you'll know I'm gone. I'm so sorry for the pain this will cause you and the kids. I have tried you know. I've spent the last 10 years trying to ignore how I feel, the feeling of disconnection, of hopelessness and pointlessness.

Janine Crane was the final straw. How am I supposed to live with it on my conscience - everyone staring at me like a murderer? I had a few consolations. You. Scott. Ruby. Tania. But sometimes my sanity felt like a delicately balanced see-saw. Those consolations on one side, Mum, Dad, Janine on the other. Watching Tania finally slide their way... The balance shifted, and I can't think how to shift it back.

Even if I could, it would take more time than I can suffer. What if it took a year? If I woke up every day feeling as physically in pain as I do right now, I would go mad. My fingers sting with electrical shocks, my chest is crushed, my head hurts. I want to vomit all day.

I know this will hit you hard, and you'll be angry with me, but when you're done with that, can you try and remember me as I was as a kid?

Love you, Cherry. Please hug Scott and Ruby for me.
         Your brother, Porter.

Orit was horrified. "That's it. We have to act. He's all over the place. If you support me in speaking to Justin again, we can persuade him to get Porter help. Did you see him? He was hallucinating in front of us."

"I know," said Cherry. "And shouting to himself in public. I need to think. I need to speak to Ida. She's the closest we have to a mum."

The two women sat in silence.

"I've never seen you cry before," said Orit, giving Cherry an awkward shoulder squeeze.

"Maybe this family *is* cursed."

"Not cursed. In need of TLC. We'll sort Porter out. Don't worry."

Chapter 24

Gloucestershire Royal Hospital, Gloucester
Tuesday, March 28th 2017:11am

"Ida, the guilt's killing him," said Cherry, re-arranging various trays and cups on the trolley next to Ida's bed. She plopped a bag of grapes down in a brown paper bag.

"Grapes?"

"It's traditional."

"I don't like grapes."

"They're seedless."

"Seedless or not, I don't like grapes."

"Suit yourself," said Cherry, taking the bag, whipping some out.

"So sad," said Ida, trying to straighten herself a little in the quicksand of soft pillows. "I hope you aren't being too hard on him? You know how you are."

"Me?" Cherry decided to stay quiet about suicide notes, ghosts and committal.

"It's the curse, Ida. He's obsessed with it. Tania; the little girl dying; being struck off. Bad stuff, yes, but we all have slings and arrows to dodge, don't we? The curse allows him to wallow, gives him an excuse. Tania's the worst. He won't accept it's over." Ida tutted as Cherry spoke. "He's been to Ypres to look at our great-grandfather's grave. Harry Norton?"

Ida was shocked. "That's not good. Did he say why?"

"He thinks Harry was wrongly executed or something. I don't know."

"That's bad," said Ida, "very bad. He was here last week and asked about Harry then." Ida rubbed Peter Cushing cheekbones with chicken-foot fingers. She looked at Cherry guiltily. "I might've encouraged him a bit." She recapped the conversation about the box in the attic and Harry's diaries.

"Oh great," said Cherry.

"Have I made things worse?"

Cherry thought about Porter shouting at himself in the street. "Honestly? I don't think things could get much worse."

Ida licked her lips and patted Cherry's hand. "I can't help think of your dad," she said. "When it was obvious your mum wasn't going to get better, he lost his mind. Overnight. He hung his grief on that bloody curse. He said we were all doomed - that the curse was spreading."

"Spreading?"

"Yes. If it only affected men, how come Lis was suffering? I tried to talk to him down, but the inconsolable don't want to hear rough stuff happens. Sorry, love, but it does."

"No need to apologise. I know it does."

"It's not like we pulled punches back then either." Cherry nodded. "Haggerston wasn't like it is now. No trendies. It was violent, poor, scruffy. So was the whole country, really. There wasn't much in the way of cancer treatment. Your mum was born too early. She'd have a chance now. Back then? It's the way it was."

A nurse intruded, updating Ida's charts.

"I did understand your dad though, Cherry. He didn't want to lose the love of his life… It was the earlier signs I should've taken more notice of."

"What earlier signs?"

Ida wrestled with herself for a moment but soon made her mind up. "We lived in a shithole in Dunloe Street, Haggerston. Rough as a badger's tit. Two up, two down. Outside lav. Rough East End birds sitting on their doorsteps, breastfeeding. Poor Geraint couldn't look left or right, or these women would shout to their blokes *Brian! He's looking at me!* Some bruiser would come out and flatten you. Horrible."

"It'd cost you close to a million to buy a house around there now."

"What? They must've spent a bloomin' fortune up B&Q then. The houses were rougher than the women. Mildew, soot up every chimney, woodworm…and that was just the women. The rooms? Shitholes.

"The night after Porter was born, I heard shouting - your mum and dad arguing. I flew up the stairs…what's that Disney film where they hold a lion cub up to the sky? That's it *The Lion King*. It was like a screwed-up version of *The Lion King* - pardon my French - your dad was holding Porter up to the window, shouting and cursing."

"What was he doing?" asked Cherry, appalled.

"Lis was so upset, yelling at him to put the baby down. *'What have I done?'* he said. *'We should only be having girls.'* I stepped in, took Porter away from him and gave him to your mum. 'Downstairs you. *Now*,' I said to Owen. I gave him a good ticking-off in the kitchen."

"I didn't know it was that bad."

"Course you didn't. I didn't want you thinking about all that crap growing up."

"Of course."

"The point is, Cherry, Owen was my son, as well as your father. He was sick, really depressed. We could see it, but who talked about that stuff then? You got on with it. Apart from that bollocking, I never really said anything."

She tapped Cherry's hand, forcing her to look up. "But what if I *had* said something? What if I'd forced him to get help? He might still be here today." Ida stopped as if working out some mental arithmetic. The sum was done. "Do what you think is right. Just don't do nothing, girl."

Sylvester Path, Hackney
Tuesday, March 28th 2017: 6pm

Porter put the phone down from Namita, who was forced to bail from another day at the museum. Couple of crucial cases to work on. Couldn't be helped. Okay to take part another day. Another day with Feng it is. Time for a G'n'T.

"You're really missing out, not being able to have one of these," he said to The Gliss.

"Fizzy water? What's so great about it?"

"It's tonic water. Cool, fizzy, refreshing. Nothing better than a G'n'T that's so ice cold you have to wipe the condensation from the glass. Voila." Porter held up a tall glass filled with ice cubes, gin and tonic. "But the secret ingredient…" he said, turning to the fruit bowl, "…is lemon and lime."

Porter put some onto a chopping board. He selected his favourite knife.

"Two cuts per virgin fruit. One to remove the end, one to create the slice. Give the top a squeeze into the drink. Slide each slice into the drink with a fizzle. Give the drink a stir and, bingo, heaven in a glass."

Which was what usually happened. Not today.

Porter picked up his knife, rolled the citrus around on the chopping board, ready to take the tops off.

The Gliss merely observed, the least interested student in class. He sensed something odd. Suddenly alert, he stared at Porter, who looked odd, hesitant. He had changed from a slicing grip, index finger extended, to a closed grip, like he was holding an axe. Clearly fighting, Porter was bringing his arm up. The serrated blade was edging towards his face. He looked like a man in the middle of an arm-wrestling competition with the Invisible Man. Porter was going to stab himself in the eye.

"Porter! Drop the knife! What are you doing? Drop the knife!"

Silent, Porter continued his battle. The Gliss could see Porter was losing. The knife shook from the struggle.

"You're under attack. Think of Harry and Max. We have to help them."

The knife-cum-dagger inched upwards.

"Soraya Adair. We have to help her too. Porter, this is why you're here: to help people. You can beat this!" Suddenly inspired, "Think of Tania!"

Porter's eyes flickered, no more than could be spared in the heat of battle.

"She will meet someone else, fall in love, get married, have children. With someone else. All because you let yourself die in this kitchen. You don't deserve her."

Porter was sweating and furious. He found a burst of power and with the energy of a steel cable snapping, he flung the knife away. It stuck with a flibber and flap into the wood surround of a bookshelf. The spell was broken.

"What the hell was that?" shouted Porter, before turning on The Gliss. "And screw you too. What a shitty thing to say."

"It worked, didn't it? You'd be one-eyed Jackney of Hackney if I hadn't juiced you up."

"You didn't have to be so…" A lemon thudded into his eyebrow. "What the?"

Then a lime. Then two more lemons. He was being bombarded with fruit.

The Gliss couldn't stop laughing.

"What's so funny?" said Porter, ducking behind the countertop.

"It hasn't got much energy left. Sit it out."

"Ow."

The Gliss was right. The attack was dying down. The last lime in the bowl was gently rocking. It lifted an inch and wobbled to a settle.

"What just happened? Was I nearly assassinated by fruit?"

"No, you were nearly assassinated by yourself. This is a step-change for the worse," said The Gliss.

"Worse? I think nearly being blown up in a field was worse."

"You're not getting it, are you? Once your Quincunx was invoked, who knows what other energies have been introduced in parallel? Bullets and bombs are inanimate. Just now, it controlled your mind."

"Oh great. This force clearly doesn't want justice for Cartwright," said Porter, rubbing a tender spot caused by the hardest lemon.

"Most likely, it's energy formed out of the perpetrator you're trying to find."

"Great. And now it's trying to kill me."

"Look on the bright side. It's only a week since you wanted to kill yourself. Now you're annoyed. That's progress."

"What happens when it gets its energy back?"

"It'll probably take a while to recover. Disturbing though. I would love to physically interact with the world, but I can't. Simply too much energy required from the universe. It must have taken unbelievable amounts of energy to fight you with a knife."

"It wasn't fighting. It had partially taken over my mind. I wasn't fighting *it*, I was fighting *me*."

"You know what this means?"

"No?"

"You're at war, Porter Norton."

Ypres. Officers' Mess
Sunday, 4th March 1917: 2.45am

"Don't mind if I do," said Capt. Alex Wootton holding out a glass as Capt. Georges Pelenot poured from a dusty old bottle. "I don't understand Cartwright," he continued. "I like the fellow. We all do. We gave him opportunities, took him away from frontline duties." He sipped the precious wine and toasted his colleagues. "The fellow must be soft in the head to come up with stuff like that."

"I feel for him," said Pelenot. "He may be suffering from nervous exhaustion."

"Don't talk rubbish, Pelenot," said Braxted. "The bastard barely saw action. He wants to take someone down with him."

"It was a shock hearing that - after turning up to give evidence on his behalf," agreed Wootton.

"You should have seen the snivelling toad when we had a word with him," said Braxted. "Damn fellow refused to apologise. Stood up and said, *I'm telling the truth.*"

"You shouldn't have hit him," said Pelenot.

Wootton swirled the wine in his glass. Pelenot held the stem of his and gazed into it like he was telling a fortune. Braxted downed his with a noisy gargle.

"It's inexplicable," said Wootton. "Mentions in despatches, well-liked, conscientious. Well, he was, until he caught shrapnel in January. Different fellow ever since."

"That's no excuse. He was back quick enough," said Pelenot. "It makes no sense."

"Of course it makes sense," barked Braxted. "The bastard's found with battle plans, caught returning from No-Man's Land? Who would risk that but a spy?"

"We send sorties into No-Man's Land virtually every day," argued Pelenot. "Maybe there was a mix-up?"

"That doesn't make sense either," said Wootton. "No-one goes alone, and why did he have plans on him?"

"There's the key," said Braxted. "I wish you'd stop justifying the blighter. The man was a damn spy for the Bosche, and he's going to get what's coming to him. Good riddance."

"Yet," said Pelenot, "surely he'd have an alibi prepared if he really was spying? Why not dump the papers, if undelivered, in No-Man's Land?"

"I thought that too," said Wootton. "But come on, Georges. You're being very generous." Pelenot shrugged. Braxted was outraged.

"Damn the coward. Those accusations! Against one of us, no less. How dare he spy for the Germans? He could have caused the death of tens of thousands of men if the Germans had got hold of those plans. Good riddance, the miserable little maggot."

"I guess you're right," said Wootton with a sigh.

"I for one, will toast Cartwright a quick and painless end for old times' sake," said Pelenot, lifting his glass, which was ambiguously echoed by a hesitant Wootton.

"Damn the man," said Braxted. "Damn the man to hell and back."

Chapter 25

Imperial War Museum, London
Wednesday, March 29th 2017: 9.00am

Porter stood in front of the giant naval guns that dominated the museum's garden, located Feng, and shook his head. Feng was fiddling with gadgets on a bench, making elaborate attempts to hide them when anyone passed.

"Feng the Inconspicuous," said Porter. "What's with the gizmos?"

"Usual stuff. EMFs. Different gauges."

"Why today? We're researching, not looking for Blackbeard's ghost."

"Be prepared and all that."

"I still can't imagine you as a boy scout."

"I got thrown out."

"Why?"

"Let's put it this way, at 12, I was more interested in the Girl Guides than collecting badges for good behaviour." Off Porter's look, Feng qualified, "That was before I joined the Scouts, nudge nudge."

"Yes, I got that one. I shudder to think what you did with your woggle."

They sat together like Cold War spies on a bench rendezvous. "I nearly got killed again last night," said Porter.

"Killed?"

"By a ghost…or something."

Porter showed Feng small bruises on his face caused by the fruits.

"Not as impressive as the cuts from the explosions."

"No, but I've been attacked three times since Thursday, each a few days apart: the bouncing bronze, the exploding farm, and the mind control last night."

"Mind control?"

"I took a kitchen knife and tried to gouge my own eyes out. If The Gliss hadn't given me a bit of strength by winding me up about my ex, I'd be dead."

"And the bruises?"

"Once it realised it had lost, it started chucking fruit at me."

"Was that likely to kill you?"

"An expression of rage probably. Nice bruises though. But it's no laughing matter, is it? At this rate, in a day or two, I'll probably get killed. Whatever is behind this, it's getting stronger."

"Let's hope I'm around for the next attack. I'd love to see it, to measure it."

"Oh ta. Thanks for the concern."

Porter halted on the museum steps. "I'm going to have a quick look into Harry today. The Gliss is all "only-look-at-Max" – but Harry's case is really bugging me."

"Because they're so similar?" Feng queried.

The Gliss appeared and answered for Porter. "No. Because you still don't believe Harry committed suicide, do you?"

"Nope. I saw him get shot."

Feng instantly fumbled to turn on one of his devices.

"Porter," said The Gliss, "the Quincunx couldn't have been activated without Harry's suicide."

"It is The Gliss, right? What's he up to?" asked Feng, swinging his box about.

"He doesn't like me asking questions."

"That you're not listening to reason," corrected The Gliss. "By all means look at Harry one day but, for now, concentrate on Max, or you'll suffer."

"Funny thing is," said Porter, "I don't actually have much of a headache today. Maybe I'm getting used to it? Look, he's family. I need to check Harry out for myself, ok? I'll be fine." Porter patted his pockets. "I have enough pills to fill a mattress."

Sandra Belloc, the archivist, shushed an excited Japanese researcher who had dared to whisper. He looked up, astonished and mouthed "Me?" She nodded, lips scalloped like amateur pastry, which was enough to quell any disturbance. He shook his head disbelievingly, looked at his co-researcher and laughed – but just to be on the safe side, silently.

She ignored him. As long as he was *virtually* silent. Silence was her mantra and companion. There was a small semi-circle around her desk in which she tolerated whispered enquiries, but that was it. As far as Belloc was concerned, and she had no science to back her up, noise was as significant a threat to the museum's collections as bookworms and daylight.

She heard something wicked this way coming from the corridor and hurried over, ready to cut whoever it was off. With a podgy no-no finger ready, she arrived at the swing doors as the transgressors did. But Porter had spotted her early. With a tug of Feng's sleeve, he guillotined their conversation just in time for them to arrive in silence, looking angelic.

The librarian was left redundantly waggling a finger, mouth open, ready to chastise. Feng and Porter nodded politely and smirked at her squinted hate.

The pair went straight to her desk where she was forced to hand over their requested documents, and pairs of white gloves, which she slapped down as if challenging them to a duel.

Feng and Porter rummaged. There was a bundle of letters and other documents donated by the family of Second Lieutenant Stephen Hellwether. He had been in the same battalion as Harry Norton, around the same time. Porter wasn't hopeful they would be of much direct use. He pointed out a battalion had up to 1,000 men, and Harry and Hellwether were also separated by rank and class. But they might give a flavour of Harry's life in the trenches.

They also had a few items from Thomas Mitchell's collection. A famous Pardon campaigner, he had donated his diaries and working notes to the museum in 1967. As well as dry legal material, his notes also contained verbatim veteran interviews. There was also a pile of Xeroxes of several official documents. The originals had been destroyed by a fire in the Public Records Office in Chancery Lane in 1958.

There were also some records from the Worcesters which should rightfully have been with the regimental museum. Luckily and usefully, they had found their way to the Imperial War Museum instead.

"That's probably not a bad thing, would probably all be gone otherwise. I found out lots of interesting stuff researching Harry last week," said Porter.

"Such as?"

"The Worcestershire Regiment doesn't exist anymore. Lots of regiments were folded in the 90s. The Worcesters were folded into the new Mercian Regiment."

"Does that make a difference?" said Feng.

"Sure. In World War One, the Worcesters sent 20+ battalions to The Front – that's 20,000 men. Bearing in mind the Worcesters were set up in the 1600s, that would be a lot of paperwork to store. Probably better if it ends up here and the National Archive."

"Let's hope this lot's worth ploughing through."

"I'm hoping the regimental diaries will also help. They have an incomplete run here, but there are some from 1917 which cover our period."

It took a while to tune into the handwritten documents. It reminded Porter of reading Chaucer for the first time. It was an hour before Porter and Feng felt like they were making any progress.

It was Feng who got excited first. "Oh, my Goff. Look at this!" It was a page from the regimental diary covering August 1917.

"Christ alive!" said Porter.

The document was yellow, stained and faded. It detailed the movements of the Worcesters on August 15th 1917. There were references to orders and manoeuvres being carried out by various battalions. A few sorties to report. It seemed to be a typical day.

At Zero Hour, smoke bombs were thrown by those in our left front sub-section. Mixed with the fog, it provided some cover. Enemy sent machine gun fire back. 8 wounded, 2 fatalities. A mine was exploded under the forward lip of the "Edward Somers" crater. Mop up successful.

There was no hint as to the author of the document. It was detached, even when describing the battle. It came as a shock to read the following paragraph.

Military Police arrested Private Harry Norton of 3rd Bn who was found in a comms trench 2 miles from the front. He was discovered near a Fullerton telegraph machine without authorisation or justification.

When it could not be proven that he had used the device, an initial charge of Aiding the Enemy was changed to Desertion. However, both are Capital Offences. A court-martial was convened. Private Norton protested innocence of spying but then changed his plea to guilty when the charge was altered to desertion. There was no evidence required, therefore. The private was sentenced to death by firing squad, to be carried out the following morning.

In a sure sign of his guilt, the Private tried to stab himself in the stomach before the execution was carried out, shortly after receiving a visit from Gilpin, our chaplain. Men from 3rd Bn were ordered to form a firing squad of 12.

The next day's entry carried another succinct line about Harry.

The death sentence on Private Harry Norton was carried out at dawn on Aug 16th.

"There you go," said Feng. "It's right there in black and white. The Gliss has his wires crossed. He was *killed* by firing squad after *trying* to stab himself. Attempted suicide at best."

Porter shook his head, the truth dawning.

"No. Harry changed his plea to guilty. That guaranteed he would die. The Gliss was right. He did commit suicide. By firing squad. He was a coward after all."

"Didn't you say you tried to commit suicide recently? Is that what it was? Cowardice?"

"I didn't mean to say that. I'm disappointed."

"There's no shame here," said Feng. "If that's what happened, he obviously couldn't cope. Maybe he even deserted hoping he would get caught and killed?"

"There's one thing," said Porter.

"Yes?"

"It still doesn't square up with the person I've come to know through his notebooks."

"Ok, but why would someone kill themselves if not because of depression, illness or exhaustion?"

"I don't know. But I heard him at the grave. His soul is still troubled a century later. Something's not right. His spirit is reaching out the same way that Max and Soraya did." Feng gave him a look.

"I know what you're thinking," said Porter. "That I'm obsessed by Harry. I guess I am. I feel a connection. If we keep going, I'm sure we'll find something to prove me right."

"Or wrong," said Feng. "To be honest, seeing this, I think we *have* found something. You just don't like what that something is."

"Maybe he was framed like Cartwright?"

"There's no mention or suggestion of that anywhere – in his notebooks, in Beale's letter, or this. Maybe he was abducted by aliens?"

"I wish we had his court-martial records. But even those are no use if he pleaded guilty."

"In spite of my misgivings, I'll go with your gut on this," said Feng equitably. "Let's agree to keep an open mind. For now."

Porter clapped him on the arm, a polite gesture of thanks.

"I trust you've spotted our other lead, Feng?" Porter pulled Harry's diary from his rucksack. He ran his finger down the list of names in Harry's diary. "Yes, look. Charles Gilpin."

"Cecil Braxted comes up in both cases too. He gave the ambivalent evidence at Max's court-martial, but Harry speaks well of him in his diary," said Feng. "Here he is. Braxted. July 14th 1917. Let's double-check something." Feng pulled out the copy they'd made of Cartwright's trial notes. "Yes, here they both are in Cartwright's trial. Braxted and Gilpin. That's a connection, a proper, demonstrable connection between Max and Harry."

"Yes, but not a particularly strong one," countered Porter. "All this says is 'some officers who knew Max also knew Harry.' But Harry and Max didn't know each other. Max was executed before Harry turned up in the same trench. There's no automatic tie-up between the two cases. But it's a lead."

The pair agreed to hasten their previously discussed searches on Gilpin, Braxted, Wootton and Pelenot. Maybe they had firmer connections to Harry? Feng, re-reading Namita's court-martial summary, said he also wanted to research the plans Max was supposed to have stolen.

"The stenography transcript mentioned the Messines offensive," said Feng. "I wonder if they went ahead with whatever that was, knowing their plans had been compromised?"

"Who knows. It's not a priority though. Let's start with the personal stuff," said Porter.

Fired up, they both sat at terminals and began browsing the museum's extensive database. Within an hour or so, both had leads to follow. The infamous Braxted generated a good few newspaper references. Gilpin generated just one lead, but it was potential dynamite. He had privately published a book of war memoirs in the Thirties. The museum had a copy.

"Exciting. Hard to imagine he won't mention Harry's execution. It must have been fairly traumatic watching your own men die," said Porter.

"Worth a diary entry at least," said Feng. "Your turn or mine?"

They both looked up at the librarian, who was glaring, daring them to make another order.

Ypres. Holding cell
Thursday, 16th August 1917: 4.30am

"You know Reverend, I grew up with my mother saying we were a cursed family," said Harry. "My father was crushed under a horse and cart delivering beer barrels. Ironic seeing as how he liked the drink. Caused no end of problems for us. Made mother take a dim view of all men. She wouldn't be so surprised to see me here."

Charles Gilpin had come to like, even admire, Harry over the last hour or so. He was 90 minutes away from the firing squad but was steady and reflective. His hand shook occasionally but otherwise was as calm as Gilpin, who had little to worry about in the middle of the night.

"Do you have family of your own?" Gilpin asked.

"A wife and four children," said Harry.

"How sad for them."

"I was only ever trying to do the right thing. Seems a bit harsh. I didn't do what I'm accused of, but I can see why the system needs me to die."

"I don't. If you weren't spying, why were you adjudged guilty?"

"And you a man of the cloth? What did Jesus do wrong exactly?"

"Don't blaspheme," said Gilpin, shocked.

"Hasn't this war touched your faith at all, Reverend? I'm not a believer, but I always allowed there *might* be a God. Till I got here anyway. Now I know there's no such thing. Or if there is, it's cruel and pointless."

"For heaven's sake man. Remember who you're speaking to."

"You can take it. If you're right, I'll be getting my eternal punishment in just over an hour, won't I? You didn't answer my question."

Gilpin was in no mood to. Secretly, he 100 per cent agreed with Harry. He now only prayed in the hope he would survive this Hell. His only wish was to get back to the old comfy job. He would never confess otherwise, to anyone.

"This war is a great challenge to any man of faith," he said carefully. "I still see small mercies everywhere. That's in spite of this horror, which was created and perpetrated by Man alone."

"What does *challenge* mean in this context? Have the words *Does God really exist?* popped into your head or is it a feeling of spiritual discomfort that you can't pin down? Explain it to me please."

"I think we should be using this short time to discuss your situation, not mine." Gilpin took out his penknife and an apple. "Do you mind if I...? You say you're not guilty. Another man said that to me recently. I was almost swayed. When I looked into it, his guilt was plain enough. Why should I believe you? I'm curious. Sadly, I can't do anything but prepare you to meet your maker."

Harry eyed the chaplain, chipping away at a delicious red apple with his penknife. For once, he wasn't envious. He was about to relieve Gilpin of it.

"It's all done. I don't want to go into it. Can I ask you for a favour please, Reverend? I've written a note to my wife. I have a few belongings. Could you please make sure they all get home?" Harry gestured to a small pile of tat - a couple of notebooks, a hip flask, a cigar tube and an envelope. "The note, especially."

"I'll come back for it all, er, later."

"Thank you." Harry picked the envelope off the table and headed towards Gilpin. With a cry, he tripped and crashed into the chaplain. Both fell to the duckboards with a crump and an oomph. The half-peeled apple rolled across the floor. Harry immediately got up and apologised, helping Gilpin to his feet.

"I'm so sorry, Reverend, I must be more nervous than I thought."

Winded, Gilpin waved him away. The apple, covered in dust, was wasted.

"I understand. I have something for you." He handed Harry a piece of cloth. Wrapped up inside were four white pills. He opened a leather satchel and brought out a bottle of whisky.

"If you take the pills and have a swig or two of whisky, you'll be pretty dopey and won't feel much. I can't leave you the glass bottle. Do you have a beaker?"

"I have the hip flask, Reverend. It would be nice to fill it one last time."

"Give it to me." Gilpin filled it to the brim. "Do you need anything else?"

Harry took the first of his swigs and swallowed one pill. "You've given me all I need, Reverend. Thank you."

"I'll be back with the others to collect you in an hour or so." He wondered whether he should say something about prayer? Looking at Harry's I-dare-you face, he settled for an inappropriate, "Good luck, Harry Norton."

Harry waited until the chaplain had closed the door. "And good luck to you too, Reverend. Hope you make it home."

Left alone, Harry worked his way through the pills, tossing each down with a glug of whisky. He examined Gilpin's penknife. The blade still smelled of apple. Harry licked the juice, nicking his tongue. The rusty blood ruined the tiny flash of apple he had been savouring. He washed his mouth with another swig of stinging whisky. The apple on the floor was dusty but edible.

So, it had come to this? Dusty apples and death by firing squad. So much for trying to do the right thing. Time for one last cigar Harry, you old sinner.

He took the tube that had been his constant companion since leaving England, unscrewed the top and inhaled. He slipped out an imaginary cigar and pictured himself back home, enjoying a smoke and a drink with the lads in The Martyred Bishop.

A clang from outside brought him back to reality. He put the tube on the table alongside the flask.

It was time. Soon he would be too incapacitated. He would have the final, albeit pyrrhic, victory. Alice, I'm so sorry it's ended like this, but I won't go to their damn firing squad that easy. I don't like the thought of what I'm about to do, but it's the only way I can think of. Kiss the children for me.

He picked up the penknife again. It wasn't especially large, but it was sharp. Where to plunge it for best and quickest effect? He checked for arteries but had only learned their positions from witnessing battlefield wounds. He hoped he got this right, he didn't want to suffer too much or too long.

Lifting his shirt, he took the blade, winced and plunged the knife into his gut as deep as it would go, slicing and cutting to make sure the job was done. It took longer, was messier and more painful than he could ever have imagined. Despite the morphine and whisky, he gave way to the agony.

Before the job was thoroughly done, Harry could hold back no more. He began screaming. Guards came running.

"He's trying to kill himself!"

"Get the medic."

"He's not here yet. Get me a suture kit and a dressing."

And there on the floor of the condemned man's cell, two prison guards saved Harry's life. With no sense of irony, they patched up the man they were escorting to his death in 20 minutes.

Chapter 26

Imperial War Museum, London
Wednesday, March 29th 2017: 3pm

"Here she comes," said Feng.

The librarian pushed through the double-doors with what looked like a hostess trolley, tottering with books, folders and boxes. She unloaded all the items onto her desk and began scanning them.

The librarian screamed. Everyone in the library looked up.

She had been holding a tan quarto volume and forced to drop it. Smoke was pouring from the book.

Feng and Porter were slow to react, but others ran to help, snatching fire blankets and extinguishers from the wall. A David Attenborough doppelganger threw a blanket over the book. The lady, a Laura Ashley curtain catalogue made flesh, fiddled with the extinguisher.

"No foam!" said the librarian, making practical her philosophy that books are more important than burnt fingers.

"What happened?" said Porter.

"One of your books caught fire," said Belloc, the librarian. "The scanner must be broken or something. Damp it down quick before the sprinklers go off. They'll ruin everything."

Feng, guessing another attack might be on its way, shouted, "Duck!"

On edge, everyone did. Nothing happened.

"Why on earth did you say that?" complained Belloc. "I banged my head."

Porter looked to Feng for an explanation. "I don't know," said Feng, chastened.

"Heavens above! Look at this!" said Attenborough. He flicked through the smouldering memoirs of the Rev. Charles Gilpin. The leather and paper frame of the book was intact. The ink had not fared so well. All the print had been neatly burned away.

"What the hell…" said Belloc. Every single word was gone. The pages looked like mouldy lace. Feng and Porter exchanged meaningful glances.

"This is a rare volume…privately printed," gasped Belloc. "Virtually irreplaceable." She held it like a child embracing a wounded puppy.

"Crap," said Porter. "Has it been digitised?"

"No."

"Double crap," said Feng.

The Gliss appeared. "It would take a ton of energy to do something that focused and energy-sapping. By obliterating the text, your pursuer makes clear he/she values anonymity then. It appears to be getting stronger."

Porter nodded. "Between us, we'll have to find another copy." He asked for their other documents. Belloc, a woman who would have been happy to never open the library to the public again, realised there was nothing she could do.

"I will bring the rest of your order over," she said, with a look that could have qualified as harassment.

Everyone watched with degrees of interest and nervousness as, after a few tests, she scanned the remaining documents on the trolley without incident. Ten minutes later Porter and Feng had their docs. The librarian turned the burnt book over, puzzling it out.

The pair sifted the ragbag of new material: stuff about the three captains and the battle plans.

"How come there are lots of letters from the soldiers but no letters from sweethearts and parents?" said Feng. "The traffic's all one-way."

"Those that weren't blown to bits with their owners helped solve the toilet paper shortage," said Porter. "Letters soothed hearts, then arses. Sometimes it was a month or two without paper."

The loss of Gilpin's book was keenly felt. There wasn't much else. There were a few newspaper articles on Braxted, documenting his rise in public life. One Daily Telegraph clipping reported that Alex Wootton was named in despatches. They also found his death notice in The Times. He died on the Menin Road, two weeks after Cartwright's trial and long before Harry arrived in Ypres. There was nothing at all about Georges Pelenot in his own right. However, the librarian had pulled a few interview pieces with the famous artist Arthur Pelenot, who had talked about his father Georges in a couple of interviews.

They began with Braxted because neither Feng nor Porter liked the sound of him. They discovered they were the latest in a long line of people to research him. A small card attached to the folder showed that the papers were last called up ten months ago by Darren Griffee, Old Scary-Moustache they had met on Monday.

They were struck by how Braxted's World War 1 experiences had coloured his life. He'd become a vocal supporter of Oswald Mosley, particularly about immigration and the *problem of Zion*. He had vociferously opposed the proposed abolition of capital punishment. He'd advocated internment and armed response as the only solution to the Irish insurgency. Porter and Feng came across many quotes linking any issue you could think of back to his Great War.

From The Times. February 1937.

What the Irish have to understand is that Northern Ireland belongs to Great Britain. Its people want to be with us. The fact that Eire and the Province share the same piece of land is inconsequential. Do not France and Germany share the same piece of land if looked at in the broadest sense? If you think that's too wide a definition, then take a look at how the Bosche and Herr Hitler have continued to complain about losing Alsace-Lorraine to France after Versailles. Culturally that region has always been French, though there are many German-speaking people there.

It is entirely possible for the Germans to articulate an internally coherent sentence such as 'Alsace-Lorraine is German', but that doesn't make it a fact, no more than if I said 'Alsace-Lorraine is British.'

It makes sense only as an idea in fiction or deluded reality. We did not fight in the trenches of Verdun, The Somme and Passchendaele only to have the Nazis try to undo the consequences of their country's just punishment in 1918.

"He's scarred and angry. He was supposed to be talking about Ireland, but most of the interview is about the Germans," said Porter.

"Wodehouse wrote about a tin-pot dictator with the sort of eye that could open an oyster at 60 paces," said Feng. "This is him, isn't it?"

"Does sound like it." Porter jabbed at another piece of evidence. A 1945 Daily Telegraph article, when Braxted was in the House of Lords. It was similarly no-nonsense about the then-nascent pardon campaign.

It's an outrage. Those of us who stood firm in the trenches, under horrendous conditions, cannot understand why people are so keen to make heroes of cowards who refused to stand-by their colleagues or their country. It's easy for armchair libertarians to play the whiny-outrage card, but the reality is: we won that war. And we won it because our men were as hard as nails and brilliantly disciplined by their senior officers. If we had dished out cupcakes and cuddles, we'd have lost. It was a war, not a kindergarten day-out.

"Lovely fellow," said Feng. "All that discipline. He'd have been popular on Tinder or Grindr if he was around."

"Do those sites work?"

"Yeah. But not if you're Cary Grant hoping to sail off into the sunset with Audrey Hepburn."

"You've used those sites, then?"

"They should rename them *Kneetremble*," said Feng.

"And how often do you use it?"

"No more than 10 times a month."

"Good grief. Successfully?"

"Mostly."

"Meaning?"

"Eight out of 10."

"Eight? That's *all* the notches on *my* bedpost. And for you, it's a month's takings?"

They read the interviews with Pelenot's famous son, Arthur. One of these was in *Candles*, a short-lived arts magazine that ran for a few editions in 1964.

The *Candles* profile celebrated Arthur Pelenot as a major player in the new wave of British Art. The scene, like him, was young, vibrant and adventurous. His fluorescent swirls and ripples hurt the eyes, but they became ubiquitous - the symbol of black and white's demise as the de facto colour of life. When The Beatles' second film *Help!* came out in 1965, the film and London were finally in colour.

Arthur Pelenot - or The Pel as he was known - had been one of its most famous children, up there with David Bailey, Twiggy, Peter Cook and Terence Stamp. The only *Candles* reference to Georges was Arthur acknowledging his father served in The Great War.

The second article was from a magazine called *The Rave*. Porter loved the fisheye photo of The Pel on a beanbag, in a swinging pad, overlooking Battersea Power Station. The headline was *Hyperion's Revenge - The Pel on Light* – a pretentious 60s feature on function and form in art.

"In many ways, to create art, a vision through art, is to mandate oneself as God," said The Pel. "I re-create the world in my image, my omniscient vision. As the fly sees the world differently through eight eyes, the Artist filters the world through his lens. Once seen, his vision cannot be unseen."

"Pretentious burk," said Feng. Porter agreed. They skimmed, looking for the reference to Georges. They scanned the article twice before finding it.

"The Americans and the Russians seem determined we should all die in a nuclear holocaust," said The Pel, toking on his Egyptian cigarette.

"Egyptian cigarette. Whatever," said Feng, miming a stoned hippy.

"Yet, for all the hysterical fears, it's self-evidently true that, so far, neither has inflicted Armageddon upon us. My father Georges fought in the trenches during World War I. He and his friends were the ones who faced real Armageddon. The young like to make out that we have it bad - but we don't. We have it good compared to them. My art is just one of a thousand heralds, each screaming prophecies of a new future for the young. My art is merely the precursor. It is not the future itself. In any case, I'd hate to be trapped on a museum wall 100 years from now - pinned and analysed to death. My work is in bloom now. It will not suit being pressed."

The final article, from 2007, when Pelenot was 68, was an in-depth feature for The Sunday Times Magazine. The photos were shot in his country house in Surrey. Pelenot was pictured in the study, kitchen and garden. In some, he was accompanied by his granddaughter Karin Pelenot. She was well-known across the UK as the no-nonsense, sleeves-up, metal-cahoned presenter of Channel 4's *History ThisStory* programme. Arthur was now in a wheelchair. He had long ago abandoned day-glo for more traditional oils and acrylics. If he wasn't exactly *chocolate box*, his final works were at least *biscuit tin*.

"I don't regret my early work, of course not," he snapped. "It was appropriate to the culture of the time and also to my own mind and state of being. Things change, however."

You could almost sense the impatience of the journalist waiting to get another question in.

I wondered how Pelenot felt about being constantly asked about his early work.
"Where did you go on your summer break when you were 16?" was his strange reply.
Puzzled, I took a few seconds. "My mum and dad took me to Boscastle in Cornwall. It was very beautiful," I volunteered.
"What was the weather like the first Tuesday you got there? How did your mother dress? What did your father say that upset you? How did you resolve it? What colour was your toothbrush? What did you think of the Cornish coastline? How did the Cornish pasty you had on the first Monday affect your thoughts on pastry over the next 50 years?"
He carried on angrily for a few more minutes.
"That's how I feel," he said, crossing his arms as if to say, "subject closed."

The journalist moved to safer ground.

I asked if he was pleased that, in spite of his contempt for traditional concepts of prestige and public approval, he had been given a retrospective at the National Gallery.

"It's nice to get some official recognition. But it's odd seeing my work on the wall. It was only ever supposed to be ephemeral."

Pelenot went on to explain how disability had left him dependent on his granddaughter and an army of carers.

"I'm so grateful to Karin. She knows it's my dearest wish to die at home, surrounded by my books and paintings. She has pulled out so many stops to keep me here, despite the pressures of her own amazing career."

There was also a quote from the famous Karin.

"I hardly knew my own father, David. He died from cancer in 1971. In his absence, Arthur's been a great father to me. And the ideals of the Sixties do live on in me: it's all been about love, never duty."

There was a quote from Arthur which brought the two strands together and mentioned Georges Pelenot finally.

"It's been such a pleasure sharing my life with my granddaughter. My own father, Georges Pelenot, was a captain in Belgium during the Great War and was an unhappy and damaged man. I was scared of him, to be honest. Exactly the opposite of my relationship with Karin."

Almost closing time. They hadn't even started on the essential histories of Messines' battles yet.

"Didn't learn much today, did we?" worried Feng.

Porter shook his head. "Not true. Braxted was a bastard. Pelenot sounds like he was damaged too. Wootton died before Harry even got to Ypres. And we know that whatever's attacking me definitely doesn't want us to read Gilpin's book."

"I've been on abebooks.co.uk," said Feng. "Great site. It's like being connected to half the booksellers in the world. Two copies came up. £176 and £224. I've ordered both."

"Surely one will do? At that cost anyway."

"What? And have it burnt again? The Gliss said it takes a lot of power for the poltergeist to do that, right? Having two copies might give me time to read and photograph them in case I get a visit from your pyromaniac friend."

"Thanks for doing that, Feng. I'm broke. I've also had an idea. I'm going to write to Karin Pelenot."

"Why?"

"She's a historian and author. If anyone knows anything about Georges, it'll be her. For all we know, she's sitting on all his personal papers. They're a posh bunch by the looks of the house - prone to self-importance. I think The Pel himself is dead, unfortunately."

"No, but he hasn't spoken for five years. I looked him up on Wikipedia."

"I'll get in touch with Karin through social media." Feng nodded. "She's on Twitter and has a contact button on her website."

Feng and Porter took a collective deep breath and approached the librarian.

"We're back tomorrow," said Feng. "Could we get these please?" He showed her the rest of the Braxted list.

The Gliss saw her look of suspicion. "You have another enemy here. The librarian hates you both."

Porter shrugged. "Supposing we do find something connecting one of the captains with Max? What next? How will that free up Cartwright?"

"We go where we go, and we see what we see."

Canterbury, Kent
Wednesday, March 29th 2017: 7.30pm

Cherry put the phone down after authorising Saunders and Neave to find another doctor to start the process of getting her brother sectioned. "You should have returned the doctor's calls brother," she said out loud, sneaking a cigarette from the cupboard where she kept her secret stash.

She had re-iterated to Saunders that Porter was ignoring every call, had left a suicide note, was talking to *ghosts*, and had picked up cuts and bruises that made him look like a tramp on a bender. She wanted it to stop. She had the blessing of their adoptive mother.

Orit and Ida had convinced her it was better to piss Porter off now than be reading his eulogy. Cherry agreed he was in physical and mental danger. *Just don't do nothing.*

Cherry picked up the photo of her and Porter again. This time one eye moistened, but all fledgling tears were quickly blinked away.

Bloody cigarette smoke. Always getting in your eyes.

Chapter 27

Chartwell House, Surrey
Wednesday, March 29th 2017: 7.30pm

Karin Pelenot wheeled her grandfather into the lounge of their ancestral home. The house was too big for just the two of them, but the Pelenots had been here since before the Regency. It had more staff than residents. A trap of a kind. On the plus side, it was American-tourist-wet-dream beautiful. She tucked Arthur in, turned on the TV, and organised tea. He squeezed her hand as she left, his once great mind silenced by a mix of early Alzheimer's and undiagnosed ennui.

Karin was once a prominent left-wing activist. She still felt pangs of embarrassment at the accident of birth that put her in such stately surroundings. But if not her, who? Chartwell wasn't historically significant. It would become a hotel or conference centre if she sold it. She shuddered. It would kill Arthur to leave. For better or worse it was home. For now.

He may have needed Chartwell, but it was hard on Arthur, day-to-day. The Stanna chairlift only partially helped. The first-floor landing had several single-step drops and rises. Karin placed planks over the spans so she could wheel Arthur about.

She refused to tamper with the structure. She was thinking ahead to when Arthur was gone, and buyers would cough-up more for authenticity.

Misgivings over privilege aside, she adored the house. Her study overlooked immaculate gardens. And that room was the most special place in the world. Jane Austen, her first true heroine, had once slept in it. Austen stayed at Chartwell for one night during a trip with her sister. Karin had staked her claim on the room aged 12. Now it was the most active space in the house. She was usually either working on a paper, a book or a script for *History ThisStory*.

Recently, she had begun researching her family history for a Durham University project coinciding with the Great War centennial commemorations.

So it was a strange coincidence to sit at her desk and find an email from some random man asking about her family during WWI.

Dear Professor Pelenot,

You don't know me, but my name is Porter Norton. I'm a solicitor based in London. I've watched History ThisStory a few times - my favourite episode was the one where you argued that Anne Boleyn may have had female lovers. But this isn't a fan letter, though I am one.

Myself and a friend, Feng Tiān, are currently looking into a little bit of my family history regarding World War 1. My great-grandfather, Harry Norton, was executed for desertion in Ypres. During our researches, the name of your great-grandfather, Georges Pelenot, came up. According to Harry's trench notebooks, Georges was a captain and Harry served under him. In fact, your relative may even have been present at Harry's execution.

We have tried to research Georges at the Imperial War Museum but drew a blank. We were wondering if your family archive contained any personal papers relating to him - even a photograph would be a help - which might help us build up a picture of what happened to Harry.

If you are in London anytime, I would love to buy you a coffee to discuss. You can reach me on…

Karin's eyebrows raised. He had struck a nerve. Her family archive was extensive and complete. Except for the papers of this one man. There were a few artefacts of Georges stored upstairs, but zero paperwork. Arthur's archive, recently donated to the Bodleian, filled several tea chests. So would hers - if anyone should ever want it. Even her parents had left a cupboard's worth. Paperwork by the ton had been the family form for several hundred years. But Georges Pelenot…nada.

She concluded his archive was destroyed. It was the only way to explain the loss of everything. And this man Norton had notebooks from someone who served under him. Long shot but…

She opened an A4 Moleskine notebook, full of immaculate notes, handwritten during research for the Durham University project.

Georges Pelenot. Survived four years at the front, in theatres ranging from Greece to Ypres.

According to family legend, he was almost unique in WW1 in attending three executions of his own men. Worse, all three had been botched. Poor Georges had been forced to deliver the *coup de graces*. This could explain the lack of material. Most men who returned from the Trenches never spoke of the horror. Georges had seen the same horrors but also killed three of his own command. If that didn't cause PTSD, what did?

And she had no sources. Arthur, even in the years before his illness, had never spoken of his father. In truth, she had little to show or tell Porter. A quick email would cover it. However, she was curious to know what sources had put Georges on this man's radar. And then there was this man Harry's notebooks. Her nose for a story got the better of her.

Dear Porter, thanks so much for your email and your kind words about my programme. I'm afraid I'm going to be a disappointment and say I have little to add to what you already know. I can supply a photograph of Georges Pelenot (attached). However, I would still like to talk to you as I'm currently researching my own family history - Busman's Holiday and all that! - and maybe talking to you will also help me?

Would you, by any luck, be around tomorrow morning for coffee? I have a meeting at the Wellcome Institute in Euston at 10.30am and could meet you for a quick chat about 9am in Euston.

All the best,
Karin Pelenot

She pressed send. Two minutes later, Porter agreed to meet. Starbucks. Opposite Warren Street station.

Sylvester Path, Hackney
Wednesday, March 29th 2017: 8pm

Porter dropped Feng a text to say he'd be late tomorrow morning as he was meeting Karin Pelenot. The TV presenter! A little star-struck, he returned to his computer to chill. A rare night off.

Cleaning up old 78s was one of the most relaxing things in the world, at least the equal of a good game of five-a-side. Porter had no-one to kick a ball around with, so tonight it was all about the music. Mission: to create a stereo mix of Sonny Bryars' Delta Blues classic, *Ain't Got No Nuthin'*.

Collectors all over the world recognised Porter for his faux stereo mixes. Hobbyists sought his approval on their handiwork. Others sent him raw audio files, curious to see if he could do anything with them.

He arrived home today to find that Oriel J. Larkwilliam in Detroit had done both. He had sent two versions of Sonny Bryar's track and his own attempt at creating a stereo file. It was amateurish to say the least, so Porter decided to create his own from the same sources.

Larkwilliam had done him a favour. After this week's madness, he was desperate for music. He loaded in the files, launched Izotope's RX audio restoration software and stuck on a very expensive pair of monitoring headphones. Ready.

There was a heavy pummelling on his front door. What now? Opening the door in annoyance, he was astonished to see Robbie Crane. Janine Crane's dad.

"Norton."

"Mr Crane. What are you doing here? Can I help?" Porter's mind was racing. How the hell did Crane find out where he lived? He was ex-directory as a precaution against over-zealous clients and mortal enemies alike.

"I want a word with you."

"Robbie - I can't. You shouldn't come here like this. We're still in the middle of the case. You know that."

"Don't give me that shit," said Robbie, pawing the ground.

I hope he's not on speed, thought Porter, the reluctant matador.

"You don't call back. You're a rude sod, aren't you?"

"Oh, for flip's sake. Come in, get it off your chest." Porter waved him in with a sigh, but knew it wouldn't go well. On the bright side, Porter had caught Crane off-guard - he no longer needed to kick his way in. Maybe he could sort things out amicably.

"Weekes told me you're getting struck off," said Crane, waving an official letter around.

So that's how he found his address. The bitch. "The case is ongoing. I should report you for this, but I won't. Come in, sit down. Let's talk about it. Tea?"

"I don't want your tea."

"I didn't kill Janine. I made a small mistake. The fire killed her. I've barely slept since, wondering what we could've done differently."

"Bullshit."

"It's not. I can't talk freely because of the case. But even if I could, what would I say? It's the worst thing that ever happened to me. I'm thinking of quitting as a solicitor whether they strike me off or not."

"You're full of it, Norton."

Porter paused. He fought the urge to say something about Crane's culpability. "Let me show you something," he said. Porter gestured for Crane to follow him. They walked past Porter's audio set-up.

"What's all this crap?"

"I restore old records. Look." Porter pointed out the photo of Janine. "I keep this here to remind me of the debt I owe your daughter. I won't rest till I've done something to make it up to her."

Robbie was stunned. "Are you kidding me? Take that down! How fucking dare you!"

"I'm not doing that. This picture reminds me that I still have to get justice for her."

Robbie was angry and vile. But not stupid. The tumblers clicked. "Are you saying it's *my* fault now?"

Porter retreated from his misstep. "I'm thinking about the landlords - their legal obligations re fire protection. There was a fire, Robbie, and neither you nor I caused that."

Crane was livid. "You're trying to get out of it!" He reached for the photo.

Porter stopped him. "No, Robbie. The picture stays. I'm a black belt in karate. I will put you down."

"Yeah? You can try," said Robbie, unfazed. "I'll flatten you, so help me. Record restoring? You'll need someone to restore you when I've finished."

Porter assumed a defensive karate stance, picked up from many teenage nights watching Bruce Lee movies. He had no karate skills past that but had used the trick once to deter a mugger. It didn't work this time.

Robbie reached out, grabbed the nearest thing to hand - a 78 of *Autumn Leaves* by the Melachrino Strings, and swung it hard. It shattered over Porter's head.

"That hurt," yelped Porter, revealing he wasn't going to put up much of a fight after all.

Robbie attacked. His lumpen fist bust open the cheek gash. Crane picked up a stack of 78s and dropped them on Porter's head. Those that didn't break on him, broke on the floor. Porter barely registered the damage. He was too busy bleeding and trying to breathe.

Robbie eventually stopped and sat down. Quiet as a post-coital lion, he murmured, "Sorry, Norton. Had to be done." He seemed to have enjoyed the violence more than the vengeance.

Porter managed a half-hearted, "I understand." Then passed out.

He came to. Through the blur, he saw a smashed chair and broken 78s, strewn about like roof tiles after a tornado. Most upsetting of all, a space where the framed cutting of Janine had rested.

He rinsed his mouth and spat pink liquid into the sink. His face was sorer and lumpier than usual. He staggered to the mirror. One eye was bleeding, his lip was cut. There was snot, blood and spittle, but otherwise, his head was ok. It hurt, but he was getting used to that. His mobile rang.

"Mr Norton? Tawney Weekes, Daily Mail."

"You've got a nerve." His voice sounded strange - like his tongue had been accidentally injected with novocaine. "Gave him my address, didn't you?"

"He just called. Said he'd been over and had a word with you. Are you ok?"

"You don't deny it then. I'm ok. No thanks to you."

"What happened?"

"Had a chat."

"That's all?"

"That's all. Did he imply something else?"

"He says he beat you up and feels bad about it."

"No, we had a nice little chat."

"You categorically deny any fighting took place?"

"I do."

"Why are you protecting him?"

"Publish and be damned," said Porter.

Chapter 28

Imperial War Museum, London
Wednesday, March 29th 2017: 8.30pm

Sandra Belloc double-checked her trolley. There were a lot of papers relating to Cecil Braxted. Some had been consulted by someone called Griffee recently. They were still pulled together as a collection, housed in one of the *Return to* drawers, ready for processing. Each giant metal drawer was the size of a small bath. She looked down at the Braxted pile and sighed. It would all need pulling, re-scanning and sticking onto her trolley. So much for her date with Arnie Helfson tonight. He could wait.

As she bent to pick up the first of the folders, her cheekbone cracked against the cabinet's metal frame. Someone had pushed her with such violence that her feet left the ground.

"What the hell? That hurt!" she shouted, swivelling herself back to her feet. There was no-one there. She reached deep within herself and cursed. But she never got to finish the surprisingly robust obscenity she had planned.

Her guts were booted hard by an unseen foot. Not just any foot. A giant's foot. In steel-capped DMs. An elephant. Unable to breath, she also heaved. Acid flooded her mouth. Belloc sank to her knees. Elephant kick after elephant kick landed on her arms, her thighs, her stomach, her breasts, her face. She felt muscles tearing. But there was no-one there. Why wouldn't she pass out? Please, can I pass out?

Then, she was upside down, then falling. Box files edges cut into her lips and nose. Belloc could smell the must of old papers. The Braxted files.

The cabinet door began slamming violently. It was the third slam that snapped her spine. Sandra Belloc, the matriarch of her department, saw and felt no more. By the time the assault stopped, her torso had been all but chopped into two. Matter leaked from an aperture in her right temple.

There was a small whoofing sound. Ignition. The last crash of the drawer had crushed the lighter in her pocket, the grinding metal causing a spark.

If she could have survived 10 minutes more, she might have been surprised to find that the museum's sprinkler system was, contrary to her opinion, pretty good at putting out fires after all.

Chapter 29

Starbucks, Warren Street, London
Thursday, March 30th 2017: 8.55am

A patched-up Porter arrived early at Starbucks. He found Karin seated, reading the Daily Mail. Disappointing. He'd never met anyone who'd admitted to reading the damn thing. That his nemesis, the dread Ms Weekes, also wrote for it, didn't help.

He had recognised Karin immediately. Her perfect-for-quirky-TV face, framed by a mousey bob, had been a staple of British TV for more than a decade. Others in the shop clearly recognised her too, nudging each other. She seemed oblivious.

"Professor Pelenot?"

"Karin, please. Hi, Mr Norton."

"Porter please."

They shook. She folded the paper up.

"Thanks for meeting with me," said Porter. "Hope it's not a waste of your time."

She took a sip, looked Porter directly in his swollen eye and said, "I've been reading about your *accident*." She gestured at the newspaper.

"Don't tell me she wrote something then? Bloody hacks."

"I'm a journalist too. Occasionally." laughed Karin. "What happened?"

Porter outlined his history with Weekes and last night's encounter with Robbie.

"You should've called the police," said Karin.

"What would that achieve? It would damage any case to come. I've also got a tribunal coming up - gross misconduct. It's not looking good for me professionally, but being accused of fighting with Crane... I thought I'd let him get it out of his system. He's suffered as well as caused suffering."

"Very humane of you."

"He also broke a pile of my 78s. Most of them on me."

"I won't ask. What's all this about my great-grandfather being at your relative's execution?"

"His name popped up when I looked into two executions in the same area, around the same time. I've been trying to piece it together, but the official record is scanty."

"Scanty! Great word. A man after my own heart," said Karin. "Let's start a campaign to use more words like scanty."

"I need words alright," said Porter, smiling. "If only correspondence would fall from the sky to help me research this case… Considering how few soldiers were executed, you'd think there would be written testimony about all of them, somewhere. But no. You say you have nothing from Georges Pelenot?"

Karin hesitated. "Porter, this might come as a shock, but there's every chance Georges Pelenot performed the *coup de grace* on your relative - Harry was it?"

"Yes. Good grief."

"No hard evidence, I'm afraid, but family legend has it he performed three, poor devil. It goes against all logic to assume, with 300 or so executions during the whole war, that Georges could have been in the vicinity of four."

"No hard evidence? No diaries? No papers?"

"No, and that is strange in itself. Georges' archive is, well, scanty. One can only assume he was so traumatised, he destroyed everything."

"Damn."

"Indeed. It's frustrating for me too because my project was inspired by the BBC's *Who Do You Think You Are?* Not dissimilar in tone to my Channel 4 stuff."

"I really do enjoy that."

"Thanks. It's hard work but fun."

Porter popped a couple of paracetamol with his latte.

"Tell me about your project," said Karin. "How else can I help?"

Porter spent 15 minutes detailing what he had so far. He showed her a couple of scans surreptitiously taken at the museum on his iPhone. He told her about the family curse. He told her about Harry's diaries.

"I'd love to see them," said Karin.

"Of course. Harry's diaries leave me sure he didn't desert as we'd normally understand it. He may have committed suicide by firing squad for a reason. I think he got caught up in something."

Karin raised a tell-me-more eyebrow.

Porter, encouraged, said, "It's all obtuse but Harry was definitely documenting something in his diary. Unfortunately, trying to solve it now is like trying to solve the Jack the Ripper murders: It's too late. There just aren't enough sources."

Karin was beginning a reply when The Gliss appeared. "Porter, don't look up, don't say anything. I'm getting seriously bad vibes."

Porter assumed he meant from Karin, but, no, she was just talking. He almost missed that she was offering help.

"…and it suits me to dig a little on this for you. After all, if our relatives er…interacted in Flanders, then their stories are connected."

"Sure, sure," said Porter, looking around nervously, not sure what he was agreeing with.

"I do have a few of Georges' belongings - his pistol for a start. They're still in the attic. It might be sad for you to have a picture of the pistol used to put poor Harry out of his misery, but that's history for you. Objects tell stories, even if the stories turn out to be tragic. Poor Georges. It was his job and in no way makes him culpable for anything that happened to Harry or this other soldier - er Max, correct?

"Max Cartwright. Definitely not. There's no question that –"

It was as far as Porter got.

A table overturned with an ear-shredding clatter. Muffins, toasties and mugs crashed to the floor.

The Gliss shouted for Porter to warn everyone.

Porter jumped to his feet. "Everyone! Get down! Get out! Quick!"

"What?" Karin barely had time to get the exclamation out, before table after table began tipping over violently. Amid the screams and hubbub, the entire mass of topsy-turvy furniture began to move in a broad circle. People scrambled to get out of the way. Legs and knees received hefty whacks from metal chair and table legs as they picked up speed.

The Gliss shouted, "Get out now!"

But it was too late. The tables and chairs were now moving as one giant mace, before lifting off the floor and spinning like a carousel at full pelt. Everyone quickly saw they had to either pin against the wall or lay flat on the floor to avoid being clipped.

A lone Japanese student walked into the shop, headphones on, head down, checking his phone. He wasn't so lucky, walking straight into the maelstrom. He was thrown against the wall like mud pie in a playground.

Bits of countertop and glass joined the swirling mass, as chairs and tables bit into everything they smashed past. Unsure of the trajectory of the storm, people began screaming and crying, the wails of those about to die.

Porter's phone had fallen when their table overturned. He shouted to a teenager lying on the floor with an iPhone in his hand. "Film this! Do you hear me? Film this!"

The whirling furniture was making a peculiar wind-howling-in-the-bushes noise. A woman, several feet clear of the perverse cyclone, stood and held her phone up. She pressed Facebook Live. As soon as she did, everything in the air fell back to the floor with a smash.

People got back to their feet, stunned. There were a few groans and some crying. One woman stared accusingly at Porter.

"What did you do that for? Shouting and stuff."

"Me? It wasn't me! You all saw that, right?" said Porter.

"I'm calling the police," said the manager.

A bruiser in an Arsenal top charged and threw himself at Porter.

"I said it wasn't me!" said Porter, as the rugby tackle landed.

"Stay down geezer," said his attacker. All Porter could see was the word Giroud written across the back of the man's shirt. The shouting began as people checked for injuries, called the police and, in a couple of cases, directed blame at the man who had warned them to duck.

The Gliss watched on, powerless, shaking his head.

Karin dusted herself off. She appeared unruffled and made no effort to exonerate Porter in the eyes of the mob. She picked up her bag. "You do seem to attract trouble, don't you Mr Norton?" she said, with the tone of an aunt on holiday from Blandings.

Imperial War Museum, London
Thursday, March 30th 2017: 9.20am

Simultaneously, Feng was standing outside the Imperial War Museum unable to get in.

The entire entrance had been marked off with police tape. Damn. He was peachy keen to make a start on the Braxted papers before Porter arrived.

"You won't get in today," said Darren Griffee, appearing at his elbow. "Someone was murdered in there last night. One of the librarians."

Feng prickled all over but said nothing. Shoot.

"More research on the execution?" said Griffee, carrying on as if murders in museums were an everyday occurrence.

"Yes. We're looking into Cecil Braxted," said Feng, desperate to know more about the dead librarian.

"That bastard! Why him?"

"One of the deaths we're researching is a soldier called Max Cartwright. Braxted was probably his captain. There's a small possibility that Braxted may have framed him."

"Braxted was a Class A bastard. That wouldn't surprise me at all," said Griffee.

Feng said he was shocked about the murder, and disappointed not to be able to continue his researches. Griffee slapped him on the arm.

"I've got some good news for you. I've got copies of some of the Braxted archive - and my notes, of course. You're welcome to have a look if that helps."

"You have them on you?"

"No, I finished months ago. But my flat's not too far away, if you're free?"

"How kind of you," said Feng, walking off with Griffee, texting Porter an update.

"Don't expect to find anything as dramatic as a confession. I've been through it all, and there's nothing like that."

"Even so."

"Onward Christian Soldiers then!" said Griffee, proving that a voice can be fully as ostentatious as its owner's sartorial choices.

"What a nutter," thought Feng, patting his rucksack full of ghost-hunting tools.

Chapter 30

Stoke Newington Police Station
Thursday, March 30th 2017: 11am

Porter gratefully watched DCI Bob Crawley remove the handcuffs. He wanted his hands back. His wrists were on fire from chafing. But that was nothing, compared to his fragmenting headache. There was something evil about this bloody station. He was sure of it.

"Thought I said I didn't want to see you again," said Crawley.

"I haven't done anything. Again." Porter rubbed his temples.

Crawley looked down at the charge sheet. "Modest, aren't we? Criminal damage, grievous bodily harm, and causing an affray."

Porter looked up to the ceiling and sighed. "I really need an aspirin or something."

"You look like you've gone ten rounds with Wladimir Klitschko. What happened?"

"Off the record? I don't want to press charges. Ok with you?"

"No promises."

"The little girl they say I killed?" Crawley nodded. "Her dad decided to have a word with me last night. Gave me a kick or two. It feels like karma, I can deal with it," said Porter. "It's all in today's Mail if you're curious. All my quotes are made up of course."

Crawley sized Porter up.

"You shouldn't be here by rights - Westminster is supposed to have you. But the G7 protests in Marble Arch have used up all the cell spaces in Camden and Westminster. They put out a message - *anyone with a spare cell?* I saw your name and couldn't resist."

"Thanks for the interest."

"All part of the service." He gestured for Porter to sit. "You know, I've been a cop for 30 years. I know trouble when I see it. I don't see it here. What's going on? Coffee?"

"Please. The last one was rudely interrupted. Can I get an aspirin or something? I'm not joking about the headache."

"Will do. Starbucks. Odd place to stage a terrorist incident."

"Terrorist incident? You can't be serious?"

"I'm not. Just joshing. Right, let's have it. Beginning to end, no mucking about."

Porter did his best to explain. He decided his best bet was to describe precisely what happened, painting himself as the person who tried to get everyone out of the way. Which was the truth.

Crawley took notes in silence and listened attentively. "What do you think caused it then?"

"It looked like a cyclone or tornado."

Crawley raised an eyebrow.

"Are you suggesting there was a cyclone in Starbucks? *Wizard of Oz*-style?"

"No idea. Check the CCTV. Read the witness statements."

"CCTV was out. Various witnesses described something like a cyclone too. However, they suggest you caused it."

"How?"

"You tell me."

"I couldn't, could I? I'd need a wind machine or something. Was one found?"

"No reports of one, true."

"So how would I do it then? Where's the proof?"

Porter decided to break the uncomfortable silence. "I saw a bloke get hit by the chairs. Is he ok?"

"He's at UCH. He'll be alright. Concussion and a broken nose. A few others got hit by flying glass. Miracle no-one had their block knocked off, by the sounds of it."

"It was pretty scary," agreed Porter.

Crawley nodded. "None of it makes sense. I'll have to hold you while we work out what happened."

Porter groaned. "Let me make my phone call."

"I'll write you up. Let's go to reception, make your call, and then it's holding cell number three for you, I'm afraid." Crawley looked at Porter. "Do you smoke? Most of the solicitors who come in here do."

"Sometimes," Porter admitted.

"Let's nip out the back and have one. I'll treat you."

"Not afraid I'll run off?"

"Not really, no."

Ten minutes later, Porter was holed up again. He liked Crawley, pretty decent for an older cop. Solicitor Porter understood police officers had to decide early on whether to work in cynicism or in empathy. Encountering the worst of people pushed most towards the former. Solicitors weren't much different. Crawley was an old-school cop who could judge guilt or stupidity with a fair degree of accuracy. They had that in common.

Cherry, however, did not. She was upset to get Porter's call from prison. After exhausting herself shouting labels of stupid, dumbass, irresponsible down the phone at him, she promised to visit later.

"Porter you should get a nameplate made for that door," said The Gliss.

"You. Made me jump."

"Apologies. Time to discuss what happened this morning. We're agreed now that something is trying to kill you - presumably, the ghost of whoever framed Cartwright."

Porter shrugged. So far, so insane.

"But, the intensity…burning Gilpin's book, spinning that furniture around… I'd love to have corporeal form, but I think it would take beyond-nuclear levels of power to give me the power to do something as simple as touch you. Whatever did this can explode bombs, spin furniture, control minds. Luckily, it seems to need time to recuperate or recharge. But it tightens our deadline. If it continues to gain power…"

"Agreed," said Porter. "What can we do about it?"

"Get out quickly and carry on with the mission."

"Crawley seems decent enough. I told them to speak to Karin Pelenot. She must think I'm odd, but she knows I didn't start anything."

"Call her. Speed things up."

"I only have her email."

"Ask Feng to track her down?"

"You think that's a good idea?"

"Mmmm. Ok, Namita Menon."

"I'll have a word with Crawley. Jeez, I feel dreadful. There's something wrong with this building."

Bliston Avenue, Kennington
Thursday, March 30th 2017: 11.35am

While Griffee poured coffee, Feng glanced around the room, a treasure trove of World War 1 memorabilia. Dominating the living room was a mannequin. It was dressed as a British Tommy.

"All real," said Griffee. "Took me years to piece together."

"Cartwright would have looked like this?"

"Within a 10% margin of error, sure."

Griffee showed Feng his notes on Braxted's archive.

"I'm writing a book," said Griffee. "Braxted was a bog-standard captain during the war. He became famous - should I say infamous? - much later. Then he was interviewed a lot. I think he treated the war like others did university."

"Yes, we noticed that."

"It defined a lot of soldiers' later lives. From both sides. Hard for us to imagine what they went through."

Feng sat up waving a piece of paper from Griffee's files. For the first time in 10 years, he used the G word. "Good God. Griffee! Look!"

Feng waved a Xeroxed letter. Griffee squinted through his Lennon specs. "Ah yes, interesting that. It's a copy of a letter Braxted sent to one of his constituents. It details Braxted's thinking on pardons. He was dead against them. He's explaining to his constituent why he wouldn't support moves in parliament to issue pardons."

"Yes," said Feng, "but reread it. Look who he's talking about."

Stannington Villas, W9

Dear Mr Grimes,
Thank you for your letter dated Oct 12.
I read it with interest but am afraid I cannot agree with you. I fully intend to vote against any motion in the House of Commons regarding the campaign to "exonerate" the men executed by the British Army during the Great War.
I understand this will cause you some vexation, so I wanted to lay out my reasons.

As you may know, I served myself as a captain with the Worcesters during the war. I fought in the Somme, at Ypres, and saw action in Turkey.

I saw acts of bravery which, even now, shock and fill me with pride. I saw men stagger to certain death in a bid to rescue injured comrades from No-Man's Land. I saw men lead a battalion into slaughter - every soldier knowing that their only function was to decoy while larger movements of men attacked further down the line.

I only met two men who were executed. In each case, their crimes were so heinous that they would have served long sentences if tried back in England. One would have gone to the gallows.

It is not the case that they were punished solely because they were soldiers in an overly-strict regime. They deserved to be punished.

All soldiers operating in the Great War were aware of the rules - they were all read the Riot Act on conscription.

There were the rules, and there was the practical application of them. A death sentence was never applied without awareness. In the vast majority of cases, compassion was shown. Some 30,000 men were sentenced to death. As you may know, only 300 or so were executed. They were the worst of the worst.

Let me give you the examples I saw.

Private Joe Brown served well until mid-1915 when he attempted a mutiny. He stood in the centre of his trench, like some Southern Baptist preacher, gathered soldiers around, and urged them to throw down their arms and march with him back to England. His own disgusted comrades reported him. What if he had been successful? What if tens of thousands had joined him? It was an open and shut case. Mutiny imperils everyone. Widespread insurrection could ultimately have prevented the British from defeating the wicked Germans.

We had another case which affected me deeply. A young private called Maximilian Cartwright alleged that one of my colleagues, a thoroughly upright man, had perversely assaulted him in the most vile and indecent way. He only made the terrible accusation after being caught spying for the Germans. It was well understood that the captain – a man of honour and unquestionable standing - had been elsewhere at the time of the alleged assault.

The cowardly Cartwright attempted to pass on Top Secret information to the Germans. Once the court martial's guilty verdict was delivered, he picked the first authority figure he saw and made his outrageous allegation.

And here's the shame of it: the man he accused was only in court to give the accused a good character reference. Cartwright had no concern for his comrades. He could have caused my fellow officer to have been court-martialled himself had it not been clear by experience and evidence that he was innocent. Fortunately, no-one believed a word of it. The accused captain went on to have an honourable and brave war.

You ask me, Mr Grimes, if I would support the vote to pardon these men? I would never do so. It would be a betrayal of all the real heroes I fought alongside.

With my best regards,
Cecil Braxted MP.

"He's talking about Pelenot or Wootton," muttered Feng to himself.

Griffee asked, "Important?"

"You bet!"

Feng fumbled for his phone, in a rush to share his information. But Porter's phone, shoved in a police locker, rang out, unanswered. He tried Namita. She picked up.

 "I've got news," said Feng.

"Old news. I already know Porter's back behind bars."

"Say, what?"

"He didn't call you? Called me 10-minutes ago. Looks like our poltergeist has been at it again. Caused some sort of mayhem in Starbucks this morning. Guess who got the blame?"

"Was he hurt?"

"*He* wasn't. Some Japanese guy was badly injured, and half the café ended up with lacerations and spilt lattes. GBH charges could follow. He asked me to get in touch with Karin Pelenot of all people. Says she'll be able to clear him."

"Goff. It's getting violent. There was a murder last night at the Imperial War Museum."

"What's that got to do with Porter?" asked Namita, warily.

"Nothing. Happened hours after we left yesterday. But it's a coincidence, right? There are no details on the news yet."

"You think it was connected to us? To, er, you guys?"

"I don't believe in coincidence. And, yes, I did pick up on that subtle distancing - thanks for the moral support."

"I'll look into it. Karin is the great-granddaughter of one of our three suspects."

"Two suspects." Feng filled Karin in on Braxted's letter.

"Braxted says Cartwright accused Pelenot or Wootton of sexual assault?"

"It's hard to tell from what we have here. But, unless Braxted was really sneaky, he didn't frame Cartwright. His comments suggest it was someone else."

The cynical solicitor snorted. "The guilty always blame others."

"But this letter should have been seen by only one person: the recipient. It's not a public declaration of innocence. Why bring it up at all if he wanted to disassociate himself from it?"

"Possibly. I'm going to try and get in touch with Karin. If Porter's right, she'll get him out. Hopefully, by teatime."

"In the meantime, myself and Mr Griffee, will continue to research. I'm popping out to buy some books later. I'll send you what I've found via email. It might help if you talk to this Karin woman."

"I have a million TV presenters' numbers just laying around my office. I'll see. Don't do anything that will make things worse," said Namita.

"Like what?" said Feng, more amused than offended.

"I don't know. Whatever it is, don't do it."

Stoke Newington Police Station
Thursday, March 30th 2017: 3pm

Porter looked around his cell. Nothing to do. Nothing to see. It wasn't Alcatraz. Inmates, in for the night mostly, hadn't scratched days served into the wall. No-one had ever considered tunnelling out. It was what it was supposed to be: A Dull Trap.

A door clanged. Good. Someone to talk to. Maybe Karin had done her bit, and he was about to be released. He stood up and grabbed the bars the way prisoners were supposed to and stared at a small convoy making its way towards him. There was DCI Crawley, Cherry, her friend Orit, and a man and a woman he didn't recognise.

"Oh, Porter," said Cherry in a surprisingly tender voice.

"Hi yourself. Hi, Orit. To what do I owe the pleasure?"

Orit flicked her hair and sought permission to speak. The group nodded.

"Porter Norton - myself, Dr Saunders and Dr Gershon are here to section you under the Mental Health Act..." She got no further. Porter himself stared, but DCI Crawley interrupted. "Hey, no-one said anything about this. What kind of stunt are you pulling? There's nothing wrong with this guy. I should know. I've seen him a lot lately."

Orit rounded on the DCI. "It's none of your business. It's all in order. Three doctors have said it would be in the patient's best interests to be sectioned and placed under medical care. He's been suicidal and acting irrationally - seeing ghosts, causing trouble."

"Cherry! Why are you doing this? I'm perfectly sane, and you know it."

"I spoke to Ida. Even she told me I should do this."

"Rubbish."

"She did, I'm afraid. I told her what you'd been up to. She told me to do what I had to do. This is what I have to do."

Orit turned to DCI Crawley. "Can you release him into our custody, please."

"No."

"We have all the paperwork."

"He's safe here. I've seen no evidence that this man is a danger to himself."

"You're not privy to everything - being just a cop an' all."

"Is that so?" said Crawley, bridling. "If the patient objects to your diagnosis, then you will have to hold a Mental Health Tribunal before you can take him away. Mr Norton, I presume you object to their diagnosis?"

"Er yes, I object," said Porter, catching on.

"There it is. If you want him, you'll have to convene a tribunal. With a judge, a psychiatrist, and someone with a social care background before you can take him away. Sorry, I'm only an ignorant cop, but that's the way it is."

Porter smiled at him. Cherry, Orit and the two doctors, conferred and exchanged angry whispers. Porter saw the man Saunders shrug. He apparently wasn't that bothered.

Orit, however, was apoplectic. She stepped back into the ring. "All of us mental health professionals and his own family think it's in his best interests to be sectioned. What right do you have to intervene?"

Crawley rubbed his face, serene and untroubled. "If you're serious, you'd better get on with finding your panel."

"Let's go upstairs and sort this out then," said Saunders, the calmest of the visitors. "DCI Crawley perhaps you could give us a bit of space to consult in? Would coffee be a stretch?"

"Sure. The coffee's rough though."

They left. Cherry, head down, looking at the floor, refused to turn and talk with her brother. As soon as they were gone, The Gliss appeared. "You need to fight, Porter. Good job you have Crawley looking out for you."

"It's a disaster. He'll hold them up a day at most. I've been through similar situations with clients before."

"Don't be defeatist. You still don't want the mission. You'll lose like this."

"S.O.D.O.F.F. will you," said Porter, sticking his hands in his pocket, hunching his shoulder and kicking the wall.

"Ok. Buck up." And he was gone.

"Hey. Wait. Come back! I haven't finished. What do I do now?" The cell was silent.

Chapter 31

Cafe Del Pietro, Russell Square, London
Thursday, March 30th 2017: 3.30pm

Namita had no problem tracking down Karin. She called the Wellcome Institute and was put through to Karin's host. He gave out Karin's mobile number after Namita used her patented *bluff 'n' muff* technique on him. (Recipe: Take one simple-minded man, add one hot-sounding woman, stir in a legal job title, add white lies to taste. Pull result out of the oven).

Karin was fiddling with her keys at the NCP when she took the call and agreed to meet Namita near the British Museum.

"How is Mr Norton?" asked Karin.

"He's in Stoke Newington nick," said Namita. "I'm trying to get him out."

"What on earth are they holding him on?" Namita detailed the pending charges.

"That's nonsense. Norton might be a bit odd, but he definitely wasn't responsible for that mess in Starbucks."

"Great. Can I put you on the phone to Stokey nick?"

"If it'll help. I gave a statement this morning, but I didn't hang around. I had a meeting to go to, and there were plenty of other witnesses. He was cuffed and out of there in under five minutes, but I presumed that was routine."

"Actually, no other witness gave him the all-clear."

"Really? I shouldn't be surprised. It was so odd, so freaky, I guess people saw what they wanted to see. He was the only one shouting and making a fuss, so he did stand out."

Namita was having a crisis of rationality. She had been genuinely shocked by Norton's trick with the locket a few days' earlier. But her natural scepticism had soon returned. She had no idea how Porter had done it. She was still describing it to herself as *a trick* - a clever one, but definitely *a trick*.

However, she also knew Porter wasn't responsible for either the mess in her office or the Starbucks incident. Something was, but she was not keen to admit a supernatural cause. But she was tenacious: for her clients, as well as herself. Porter was innocent, so she had a professional duty to represent him. Being a bit mad wasn't a good enough reason to desert him.

Her problem now was how to tell Pelenot what had been going on without sounding a bit mad herself. On the way over, she had argued it out with Sangita. Tell Karin. Tell her about the ghosts. Don't be stupid. She'll laugh at you. But it doesn't make sense *unless* you do. It doesn't make sense *if* I do.

As she wondered what she would say, the other half of her brain listened politely. To Namita's surprise, Karin solved the problem for her. Karin piped up, "If I didn't know better, I'd say I'd seen a poltergeist at work. Obviously not, of course. I can't think of a rational explanation for it."

Namita took her chance. "What *if* - and I mean *if*, you were right - what if what you saw *was* a poltergeist at work?"

"Why? Do you think it was?" said Karin, widening her eyes.

"Er. It might be."

"I see. What makes you say that?"

"You're going to leave in a second. This is so stupid. Well, it might be the ghost of your great-grandfather, Capt. Pelenot. If not him, someone close to him. There was a Capt. Alex Wootton it could be too."

"Go on." Karin's tone was neutral.

"It sounds ridiculous. I can barely believe I'm saying it."

"I'll try not to judge. You might as well tell me now you've started."

Namita did her best. Her digest included Porter's mission, his family curse, the suggestion of links between Max Cartwright and Harry Norton, Harry's diary, the exploding munitions in Ypres, the research on Braxted, The Gliss... everything she could remember.

Karin didn't react as dismissively as Namita had expected. "I can take or leave that ghost stuff," said Karin. "But I don't have a major problem believing Georges Pelenot was up to no good in the Great War."

Startled, Namita asked why.

"Because everything about him is hidden. He's the only Pelenot in 200 years not to have kept an archive. There were dark rumours about him when I was a child. No-one said it out loud, but I assumed he beat his wife."

"You're talking about The Pel's mother?" There was no need to explain how she knew who Arthur was. Everyone over 30 did.

"Yes. I'm not sure Arthur had any contact with Georges once the divorce came through. Arthur never spoke about his father. And family never featured in his work."

"No," said Namita, unthinkingly. "His sixties work was impersonal in the extreme, wasn't it? Fluorescent swirls, that's about all it was."

"I love his sixties work." Before Namita could cover herself, Karin added, "But art is in the eye of the beholder. I love it. You don't have to. Relax."

Namita apologised anyway. Karin trundled on. "Of course, it's a long way from saying Georges committed some heinous crime during the war. He probably did. But to say his ghost is trying to kill people *now*…"

"I know, I know."

"It's an interesting narrative though. I'll take the ghost stuff on advisement at the moment, but I'll keep my promise to Porter. We have no papers at all from Georges, just a few objects in the attic. I said I'd dig them out. I'll call Stoke Newington police too. See if I can amend my statement or something."

Namita thanked her on Porter's behalf.

"Will you call me if you find anything?"

"Oh, I'll definitely call," said Karin. "Just don't expect too much."

Stoke Newington Police Station, London
Thursday, March 30th 2017: 4.00pm

An elephant, the size of a zeppelin, was sitting on Porter's head. Some headache. Dead soldiers, Tania and imprisonment, had ganged up to do a number on him.

"She isn't coming back," said The Gliss.

"My sister?"

"Oh, she'll be back, mob-handed and spitting. I meant Tania."

"You're back - reincarnated as a relationship counsellor. Great," said Porter, rolling his eyes.

Au fait with Woody Allen from Porter's head, The Gliss did his best nebbish shrug. "When you're busy, she barely crosses your frontal lobe. As soon as you're alone, in she comes. She's the darkness of your past, not the light of your future."

Porter nodded. "Do you have to poke around my head like that? Haven't you heard of Data Protection? True, she doesn't share my feelings at the moment. But I can't just give her up. I love her, I really do. Isn't this where you usually burst into song?"

"It's too sad to sing about. Move on. You have people to save."

"I've been thinking about that. Am I one of them?"

"I think you are. The Quincunx is your second chance. Namita seems nice. Can't you show an interest in her?"

"Namita's not my type. Imagine what she'd say if she saw my flat? She'd either bring in a Romanian cleaner or walk out in disgust citing hygiene violations."

Bob Crawley sidled up to the bars, chewing gum. "What's with your sister? You must have really pissed her off."

Porter sighed. "Nothing sinister. She's always been over-protective. Drives me mad. But we do love each other. My recent behaviour has tapped into her biggest fear."

"Which is?"

Porter decided to tell Bob all about the Norton family curse and how his recent experiences fed her paranoia.

"It's all about Scott, her son. In a strange way, she believes in the curse more than I do. It's why she's so gung-ho about getting me sectioned. In her heart, she knows I'm as sane as she is. But Scott said stuff recently which freaked her out. She can't control that, so she's trying to control this."

Crawley pulled up a chair. "I don't have any of that crap going on in my family. We get together for barbecues and send each other birthday cards."

"Sounds good."

"You know what? It is."

Porter asked if Cherry and her cronies were still in the building.

"I'm afraid so. I can hold them up, but I don't want to obstruct them either. The posse is up there now, drinking our bad coffee, frantically ringing around trying to set up your tribunal."

Porter felt another ribbon of pain unfurling through his head. He winced.

"You ok?" asked Crawley.

"It's this station," said Porter. "It's so oppressive. Can't you feel it? Like something really heavy happened here."

Crawley laughed. "Don't tell me you're a psychic now? Apart from a few deaths in reception at the old Stoke Newington Police Station, this building has a fairly quiet history. Next door? That's a different matter."

"What happened next door?"

"Victorian Road. One of the worst disasters of the Blitz. People were taking shelter in the basement of the parade of shops. Direct hit. 170 dead. There's a memorial to them in Abney Park Cemetery up the road."

Porter groaned inwardly. No wonder he was picking up bad vibes.

"Of course," continued Crawley, "there's almost a quarter of a million people buried there too."

"Is that right?" said Porter. "That's great. I've got to get out of here you know."

"I'm holding you for your own protection now. Once you're out, they can section you with what they have. I'm only delaying the inevitable. Dr Neave is hell-bent on locking you up." Porter nodded. "Want some good news? I've spoken to Karin Pelenot. She said you had nothing to do with Starbucks. Your best bet is that the Mental Health Tribunal comes down on your side."

"Thanks, DCI Crawley."

"I've got to go. There's a special task force been set up to deal with that murder at the Imperial War Museum, and I've been asked to donate DS Breeze. The whole Met is so squeezed this week because of the G7 protest. Breeze will love it. She's a bit of a specialist on the grizzly stuff."

"What murder would that be?" said Porter, his pulse racing.

"Some librarian got smashed to a pulp in her own filing cabinet by an intruder after-hours yesterday. Quite gruesome really."

Porter slumped down on his bench. "That's horrible," was all he could say.

"Here, you can read about it if you want." Crawley passed him a copy of the Evening Standard.

Porter thanked him. The newspaper burned hot in his hand. As soon as Crawley was gone, Porter tore into it, to see if his worst suspicions were confirmed. They were.

Librarian murdered at Imperial War Museum
By Edwin Harris

A senior librarian was found murdered and her remains partially burned in a filing cabinet at the Imperial War Museum last night.

Sandra Belloc, 52, was found with multiple injuries and post mortem burns. Several documents were damaged, but the museum's sprinkler system stopped the fire from spreading.

DCI Alan Braithwaite said an examination of the museum's CCTV had revealed nothing. The cameras appeared to be faulty for the duration of the attack.

"It looks like a deliberate act by someone familiar with the security system. Our investigation is looking in that direction. There were no signs of a break-in."

Elspeth Parrish, the Imperial War Museum's Director, said the building would remain closed for the rest of the week while police carried out forensic searches.

"We are all in shock," said Ms Parrish. "Sandra had been at the museum for 23 years and was a highly regarded member of the team."

A friend of Belloc said the librarian was a decent woman but had been on a worrying number of dating sites recently. The friend feared she may have met her killer online.

"This was a cowardly attack by a very dangerous person," said DCI Braithwaite. "We have put together a special murder inquiry team using some of the best detectives in London to get to the bottom of this as quickly as possible."

Porter guessed what had happened. "Where are you? TG come here at once. Eric?"

"You called, oh master," said The Gliss, his white hands in mock salutation like a plastic Genie of the Lamp.

"Have you seen this?"

"I don't need to. It's in your head now. It's exactly what I warned about earlier. This force is getting stronger and deadlier by the day."

"What happens now? I can't do anything from here."

"There's not much we can do," said The Gliss.

"I hope the others have seen this and know to be on their guard."

"Let's hope so indeed."

Chapter 32

Denizens occult bookshop, Clerkenwell
Thursday, March 30th 2017: 4.20pm

Feng tutted, crossing the threshold of London's infamous Denizens - the last of the great musty and dusty occult bookshops.

A place for idiots and the gullible: The Supernatural, the Occult, Religion - three great imposters stopping humans from fulfilling their potential. Like a lot of atheists, Feng was intrigued anyway.

He had zero belief himself, but the imposters still informed the so-called thinking of most of the world's citizens. Know thine enemy. He knew that Religion and the Occult (why differentiate? - they were the same bloody thing) would never be eradicated. The Supernatural though… He dreamt of one day writing the tract that would debunk the whole thing. Going along with Porter's insanity was a blip.

Today, he hoped to find illumination. His own collection of books wasn't up to much, so Denizens it was.

The bookshop had been there since 1879. So had most of its stock. And, on first glance, its owner too. Polly Greengross was Miss Haversham in tweed. Evidently, she was the only person left in the world still using a lorgnette? She looked through it now and studied the man who had appeared with a tinkle of the shop bell.

"Hello there," said Feng. His voice sounded muffled in the anechoic chamber created by so many fat leather-bound books.

"I've told you before," said the shop owner, "I'm keeping the A-board outside no matter how many times you fine me."

"Good for you," said Feng. "I'm sorry, but I have no idea what you're talking about."

"Aren't you from the council?"

Images of a line of black-hooded wizards sitting at a table draped in scarlet crossed his mind. "No. I'm a customer. Potentially."

"We get more health and safety officers than customers. They say my A-board's a danger to the public. A blind person could walk into it, you see. They don't mind putting up parking meters though, do they? I presume the blind are expected to just drift through those? Blood-suckers."

"I see."

"Well?"

Feng was confused. She addressed him with the *get-thee-hence* disdain of a headteacher at home-time confronted by a crying child. She had spent at least 50 years laughing at the concept of *the customer is always right*.

"Just browsing."

"I thought you said you were a customer?"

"After I've browsed…maybe."

"Don't waste your time browsing. It's bloody chaos in here. There are skeletons out the back of people who never found their way out. Tell me what you want. I can soon tell you if we've got anything germane."

Feng hesitated, wondering how to define his search. Greengross tutted with impatience. "Out with it. Are you looking for spells and potions? A love potion perhaps? No need to be coy. We get all kinds of weirdos in here. Perhaps you're looking for woodcuts of naked devil-worshippers prancing about with goats? Most people of the really weird ones are."

"No, no," said Feng, getting more irritated by the second. "I'm researching poltergeists. Or things like them."

Greengross seemed disappointed. "Oh that. There's a section over there. How's your Latin? No? There's a smaller section over there then. Don't touch the Pan paperbacks. You won't learn anything from them. I do have some good woodcuts of nude satanic ladies if you're interested? No? Then those two shelves it is."

Feng sauntered over and was confronted by a beautiful mountain range of old spines, intriguing title after title. *Mysterious, Murderous and Malign* by Edward Akerson. *Hell on Earth: Those Who Come Back* by Prof A. J. Karzakian. *Evil Spirits: A Compendium* by Hilversum Press.

He pulled the latter volume, its binding a dark-unto-black leather, scraped and scratched to a Jackson Pollock texture in the 180 years since it was published. Its pages were thick and smelled of wet cat. Polly Greengross farted loudly.

"Apologies. I'm of advanced years, and the clench is not what it was," she pre-empted.

"No problem." He moved the book a little closer to his face, wet cat the lesser of two evils. He read. The text was flowery and vague. Disappointed, he put the book back. Greengross was humming *The Rose of Picardy*. She was so old-fashioned her teeth were probably made from Bakelite.

The next five books were no better. His phone rang. Namita. The I-dare-you face of the shop owner made him instantly hit the decline button. His eye caught a more recent cover - something from the sixties or seventies, in hardback, called *Poltergeists: A History* by Peregrine Zouche.

"At least it'll be in readable English," Feng muttered, more in hope than expectation.

It was. There was plenty of good background material, some illustrations and a glossary. Feng flipped straight to the back to check the author profile on the flyleaf. Judging by the grainy photo, Zouche had gone out of his way to impersonate a frog, and the blurb made ludicrous claims about his occult credibility. However, a quick skim-read showed Zouche not only knew his onions but also his sprites, elves and all manner of other ghoogly-whooglies. Feng decided to buy the book.

"How much?" he shouted.

"£5"

"Bargain. Thanks. I'll take it."

"I meant £6 - £10 if you take some woodcuts."

In a nearby coffee shop, Feng began to read. It was a pretentious, but useful, mix of personal anecdote, seventies-style new-age ramblings and some hard info. He soon found an intriguing passage, entitled: *Profugus - King of the Poltergeists*.

We have discussed the common or garden poltergeists that most people have heard of. Many experts associate violent apparitions with the emotional stirrings of an adolescent living in a house said to be malignly haunted. These are distinct from "ghosts" - commonly considered to be troubled historical figures leaving relatively benign echoes or footprints. There is, however, a far rarer form of poltergeist, The Profugus (Latin: the outsider) which has made occasional appearances throughout history and is capable of astonishing damage, able to kill and create pandemonium unless quickly dealt with.

There have only been a handful of recorded instances in history where a Profugus was considered to be at work. They differ from the general poltergeist in being seen to show sentience. They pick targets. There are reports that some can even communicate. They are manipulative and malign. The handful identified have all shown traits carried over from their pre-formation when they were human. They are perverse, murderous and capricious in the extreme. They come into being through a traumatic event and grow in power until a way is found to stop them. In short, they are a threat to any and everyone but luckily seem to be a once a century event. Due to the difficulties of diagnosis, they may have appeared more frequently with their effects and works concluded to be more natural phenomena.

Feng smiled. This was more like it. He ordered another cappuccino and moved the bag of revolting woodcut prints to one side. His sister's birthday present sorted. Feng hated his sister.

Quendell's & Co, Dalston Junction, Hackney
Thursday, March 30th 2017: 5.15pm

Namita demanded to be put through to DCI Bob Crawley.
"Ms Menon. How can I help?"
"You've spoken with Karin Pelenot, I hope?"
"I have. I'm as sure as can be that Porter Norton is innocent of the Starbucks incident."
"Great. I presume he's been released?"
"No. I'm holding him for his own protection at the moment."
Namita gasped. "As his solicitor I demand you release him right now. This is –"
"Ms Menon, I'm holding him with his full permission." And he explained.
Why me? You going to have another ciggie then? Yes, Sangita, I bloody well am.

Chartwell House, Surrey
Thursday, March 30th 2017: 6.32pm

Karin watched her grandfather sitting in the lounge, engrossed in re-runs of *The Antiques Roadshow*. This foreshadowing of her own dotage prematurely terrified her.

Arthur's had been a great mind, though Karin still believed he'd underused it. His status as a celebrity artist had allowed him to float without exploring the deepest waters. But now? He was physically shrunken too. He could hear, understand and gesture. He could not - or, she suspected - would not, speak.

This was always annoying, but doubly so right now. The day's conversations had unsettled her. She needed to talk to Arthur.

She thought back to the start of her Durham University project, and the day she announced it to Arthur. She assumed he would be pleased. Instead, a flicker of something like pain had warped his face. He said nothing, of course. She remembered the reaction again now.

He heard her, smiled, raised one hand, and then let it fall back on the wheelchair's armrest.

"Arthur, darling. I have to ask you a question."

He reached for the remote control and muted the sound.

"I told you I've been looking into our family history? I'm having problems. There's nothing on your father. Literally nothing. Why is that?"

To her astonishment, Arthur shook his head, his eyes watering.

Karin rushed over. "Arthur. I'm sorry. What's the matter?"

He shook his head and his lips parted. He was trying to speak. It wasn't easy. His impotent throat struggled to emit more than a rasping hiss.

"Easy, Arthur."

"Karin." And there it was - his first word in more than five years.

"Arthur, you don't know what it means to hear you!"

He squeezed her hand. "Karin," he said again, a tad more definition to the word. "No. Please."

"What, Arthur? Don't look into the history? What is it?"

"Father. No. Bad. Bad. Bad." His face had changed. There was resolve in it, a fight to overcome his withered muscle. He shook his head to reinforce the fragile "don't" of his words. "Please."

Karin took a chance. "Let me tell you why I'm doing it. Is that ok?" He closed his eyes but signalled no objection.

"A man came to me saying Georges may have performed a *coup de grace* on his own great-grandfather during the war. Prepare yourself - there's also the possibility he sexually abused at least one soldier. There were no charges at the time but…"

Arthur looked into her eyes, nodding slowly.

In icy dread, Karin asked, "And how do you know?"

Arthur held her gaze. He tapped his own chest.

"Me. Me," was all he could manage, his voice fizzling back to nothing.

Chapter 33

Quendell's & Co, Dalston Junction, Hackney
Thursday, March 30th 2017: 6.46pm

Namita tried Feng again. Come on idiot. Pick up.

"Namita. I'm so sorry I couldn't get back to you. I've been researching. I found out a few things today. Top stuff."

Namita cut him off.

"Porter's sister is trying to get him sectioned. The only reason he's not in a straitjacket right now is that the police are blocking him from leaving. They're keeping him in overnight while his sister and a bunch of doctors arrange a Mental Health Tribunal for him."

"Goff!"

"What?"

"Goff. I refuse to say God."

"You just did."

"Leave it to me," said Feng.

"You? What can you do?"

"The nose knows," said Feng, tapping his. Realising Namita couldn't see him, he converted the tap into a scratch to save face with himself.

"Stop being an idiot. He's in trouble."

"As I say, leave it to me."

"What did you find out?" asked Namita.

Feng told her about the Profugus. "Not much detail in the book, unfortunately. I looked up the author, Peregrine Zouche. He's rotting in a retirement home in Oxford. I'm going to see him tomorrow."

"More supernatural guff."

"Maybe. Zouche says a Profugus can be killed or neutralised though. Some kind of exorcism ritual. Guff, agreed. But I'd better check."

Namita said she hoped to hear from Karin Pelenot later.

"Good luck," said Feng. "I've had an email from DPD saying they've left packages with my neighbour. That'll be Gilpin's books. I'm on my way now." He took her email address so he could share his research through Dropbox.

Namita hung up, reclined with a sigh, and shook her head. What on earth have you got into? Sangita laughed at her.

"You don't need to say a damn thing Sang. I'm right there with you."

"Talking to yourself again?" asked Nathan Caiger, poking his head in, straightening his tie. "Fancy a glass of vino at Despicables?"

"Not tonight, Nathan."

"Suit yourself," said Caiger, marching off to try and pull a secretary instead.

Chartwell House, Surrey
Thursday, March 30th 2017: 7.44pm

With the help of Arthur's carer, Karin managed to soothe Arthur to sleep. Lucky him. She was far from soothed.

Abused by his own father. No wonder Georges had been wiped from the family record. She pictured her beloved Arthur's suffering as a child. It hurt to do so. It provoked a flash of insight. That's where the self-destructive streak came from. Mary Whitehouse had once famously demanded The Pel be banned from British TV. She didn't approve of him ingesting a Peruvian tribal hallucinogenic, live on ITV.

She smiled for a second before reverting to angry historian. She was determined to correct the record. Damn the family name. In this mission, she was in sympathy with Porter – irrespective of whether Georges had anything to do with his case. She'd definitely help him. Starting now.

It was time to go back to the House of Horrors that was Chartwell's attic.

She changed into decorating clothes, essential for anyone brave enough to enter. A Maglite in her pocket, she pulled down the ladder and climbed. She used an ancient key to unlock the heavy oak door in the ceiling. Grunting, she pushed up and over, catching her pinky in a hinge. She sucked her finger, lit the torch and clambered in.

Stacks of boxes and tea chests were veiled in Grade I-listed cobwebs, fronds of dust flapping gently in the draught from the door. She heard mice scuttle away. She was no baby but shuddered anyway.

The Georges Pelenot box was easy to find. She'd had it out just three months ago. It rattled as she pulled it towards her, brightly lit by the Maglite's narrow beam.

She undid the worn gilt catch and opened the box. The Webley service revolver lay in crushed red velvet. She thought of the family legend of Pelenot's three executions. Three British men, three *coup de grace*, snuffed out by their comrade - her relative. It was a tough thought.

Karin weighed the gun in her hand. It was surprisingly heavy. She checked the chambers. Empty, of course. She did what everyone does with a pistol in their hand: lifted it, sighted it and squeezed the trigger. It clicked. The chamber advanced by one. Her arm shook. The gun was heavy.

The first box hit her in the back. The second, a tea chest edged with metal strips, scraped across her calf. Winded and hurt, Karin dropped to the attic floor. She caught her breath. What the hell just happened? She checked nothing was broken and picked herself up, brushing off the mice droppings embedded in her palm. Three crates had been stacked, and the top box had fallen. Full-to-the-brim, it had dragged the second crate down with it. The *what* she was clear on. The *how* was a mystery. She'd been a metre away at least. You'd need a hurricane to move a box that obese, but how? A mouse-fart would have been considered a dramatic wind event up here. The attic was as hot and still as a greenhouse.

Karin winced, rolling the dungarees up to check her leg. She'd have a bruise the size of Lake Windermere. She cursed. The broken skin was bunched into a line of tags, leaving only dots of blood. Nothing she couldn't handle.

The revolver had fallen into a cobwebbed hole in the floor. Thick webs stuck to her fingers as she pulled it out.

Odd. The pistol looked different - cleaner, newer. She stared for a few seconds and then to her horror, found herself turning it around. The barrel was pointing at her head.

Come on, this is stupid. Point it away.

But she couldn't. Now, the barrel was resting on her temple. Her lust for life was intense. It wasn't her doing this. Heaven knows what was, but it felt like she was fighting something. At least the gun was empty. She struggled to move the barrel away from her temple. Instead, her finger tightened on the trigger. What was that smell? Gunpowder? The gun, her instinct told her, was now loaded.

Karin fought to break the alien will inside her. She was flushed and pricking with sweat. "Come on Karin, Arthur needs you. You need you." With the thought of Arthur, her will re-exerted itself. The barrel swung away to the right. She pulled the trigger. A deafening blast, a searing light and a hole appeared in the roof.

Her ears rang like a pinball machine thrown down a mineshaft. Dazed but aware, she opened the pistol. The chamber was empty. No spent round, and now she looked again, no hole in the roof. She smelled the barrel. Nothing. She had imagined it all then? The effect of fear on her body was real enough. Her legs were shaking.

She put the gun back in its box and slammed the lid tight. She shovelled all of Georges' belongings into a Waitrose bag and climbed down the ladder. "I'm going to find out who you were Georges Parry Pelenot. You try and stop me."

She lowered her head, tying the bag to the ladder. The second she did so, the heavy door to the attic slammed violently shut. The force of the downdraft ruffled the bag and her hair, but not her new resolve.

"Missed again," said Karin, her sleeves well and truly rolled up.

Church Lane, Walthamstow
Thursday, March 30th 2017: 7.57pm

Feng picked up his packages and rushed home to read Gilpin's book. Like the ex-Boy Scout he was, he had prepared. An IKEA fire extinguisher stood next to a bowl of water, dampened tea-towels and a camera. If the poltergeist was in the mood for a book-burning, Feng was ready for his Nazi ass.

It started well. He tore open both packages, laid the books out and immediately began photographing the pages. He didn't stop to read. He got to page 36-37 before tiny smoke tendrils drifted from the first book.

"I'm ready for you, sunshine," shouted Feng. Snap! Another shot. Some of the writing was singed but legible. Snap! Page 38-39. More smoke. More damp cloth. 40-41. Snap!

The other book showed signs of heating up. Throwing another wet tea towel over book one, he switched his attention to book two. Going for broke, he plunged the whole book into the bowl of water. Book one was now smoking again.

"Screw you!" said Feng.

With a whirr of air-buzz, the fire extinguisher flew at him. Feng ducked, the red torpedo smashing past him into a cabinet full of his mother's old ornaments.

The extinguisher had buried itself deep into the wall, and Feng watched warily as the canister violently tried to wiggle loose. It was stuck. He yanked the tea towel off book one. Smoke, but enough time to get 42-43. Snap!

"Bring it on!" 44-45. Snap! Oh shit. Book one burst into flames. Fury overtook Feng. He threw it out of the window. No point trying to save it.

There was a loud "Oi!" from outside. Sounded like Bartek from next door. Feng wasted seconds rushing over to peer out the window. The flaming book lay next to Bartek, his poodle and a small puddle of dog wee.

"Sorry, Bartek. Flat's on fire." He ducked back inside and resumed.

Turning to book two, Feng found there was just enough room to open it and photograph its distorted pages through the water. The poltergeist wasn't ready to give up. Cups, books and chairs flew at Feng in a random and dangerous barrage. This was hopeless.

Grabbing the bowl and camera, he fled to his sparse bathroom. Something thudded against the door. Feng grabbed every loose item in the room and shoved the lot down his toilet bowl, slammed the lid shut and sat on it. He continued to photograph. 46-47, 48-49, 50-51. Snap! Snap! Snap! The toilet seat bobbed angrily beneath him.

Snap! Snap! Snap!

With a fizzing whoosh, the shower attachment in his bath leapt up like a snake and careened off his head with a donk. But it could only sting, not kill. Feng sprang at it like Tarzan, yanking the snaking hose free from its mooring, throwing it out of the bathroom window. Left loose, it would have made a good garrotte.

The poltergeist ran out of energy or gave up, Feng couldn't tell. He photographed the remaining 50 pages with no problem. The physical book was ruined but its contents preserved. His camera was equipped with wi-fi backup.

He stayed on the toilet seat for another 30 minutes until he was sure every picture had gone to his iCloud storage. "I'll swallow the damn SD card if I have to! I'm reading this book!" Only his echo came back.

Feng poked his head around the bathroom door. The flat smelt of smoke. His living room looked like a saloon after a mass brawl. Feeling safer, he sat at his computer and put copies of the photos in Dropbox. The images were mirrored to several iCloud and Dropbox servers around the world by now. "You lose," he felt brave enough to taunt.

Opening file roll 202_001.jpg, he was faced for the first time with the Reverend Charles Gilpin's privately printed memories of his time at the front 1914-1918. Feng skim read for about an hour before he hit the jackpot.

The thorny issue of home executions has vexed many commentators and civilians in the dozen years since the Armistice was signed. I have pondered long and hard on the subject. I still feel the same as I did during the fighting: it was a necessary, and always to be deplored, evil that helped the British Army triumph over the evil Germans.

As a chaplain, it was my privileged, though unfortunate duty, to offer solace and comfort to condemned men in the hours before they met their grim fate. I had to administer to three such men altogether. All are seared into my memory. I will spare their families further pain by changing their names. Otherwise, the following accounts are based on the details in my notebooks from the time.

Feng wondered whether the notebooks had survived. Unlikely, but worth a dig around.

Private Penhaligon was a clear-cut case. As a civilian, he would also have died for his crimes. I belong to that school of church which believes in an "eye for an eye, a tooth for a tooth." Penhaligon's decision to shoot a fellow private in an argument over smokes meant there could only ever be one outcome. And who could argue otherwise?

I met the fellow in his cell the night before. He was violent and abusive. I was pushed up against the wall. The scoundrel threatened devilish punishments on my kith and kin if I did not leave him be. He objected that "religion is a waste of brain." Perhaps unwisely, I reminded him that without God there was no Devil. Threatening to retaliate from an afterlife he did not believe in was illogical. He punched me in the gut, which left me winded.

A guard arrived and restrained the brute. I left shortly afterwards and, in an admittedly un-Christian act, "forgot" to leave him the "presents" I had brought. It has troubled me ever since, but one cannot undo the past.

The "presents" were a bottle of whisky and a handful of morphine tablets to help ease a condemned man's pain at the end.

These gifts weren't welcome at my second vigil either. A young private from the Worcesters, by the name of Goodchild, had been accused of spying for the Germans. It was most against character, and I felt sorry for the lad's predicament, misguided as he was. When I brought out my presents, he told me he didn't drink. I advised him that tonight would be a good time to start.

He drank to ill effect and told me an extraordinary story - all lies of course - about a Capt. George who had forced him into unnatural intercourse. He claimed to have resisted, but in doing so had become a threat to the captain. This explained, he said, why the captain framed him for the spying charge by sending him on a non-existent mission into No-Man's Land. I asked him why he had not said anything until the end of his court-martial yesterday when he had begun blurting out accusations in a wild and emotional state. He said, "And who would have believed me, Reverend?" As it turned out, because of who he accused in his outrageous outburst in court, no-one did believe him. Goodchild was clear on the time and date the alleged perversion had occurred. But it could be comprehensively proven that this Capt. George fellow had been miles away from Goodchild that night. There were many witnesses to that.

He went to meet his Maker as he deserved and only one thing about the case troubles me still. When I turned up at the cell to comfort Goodchild, Capt. George and another captain were having, at the least, 'strong words' with the condemned. I a-hemmed my way into the cell, and they departed, but the scene left me feeling uneasy. I have never believed in vigilante justice.

It changed nothing of Goodchild's obvious guilt, of course. The court-martial had seen all the evidence. I dismissed the allegations as they had. I knew the captain in question and had never seen anything in his behaviour to suggest he was capable of such a crime against Man and Heaven.

I think the young private was probably lashing out at his last possible moment when he realised his despicable actions in aiding the enemy were to forfeit his life. A strange accusation to make and I can only guess the boy was a latent sodomite, the lie an expression of some dark fantasy. This account may be distasteful to the gentle reader but is an accurate account of my life in the trenches.

I attended Goodchild's execution the next day, and the boy suffered a little because only two of the 12 rifles hit their targets. This was often the case. The firing squad comprised members of the condemned man's own unit, a practice which may seem callous viewed from the comforts of peacetime. However, it ensured the demands of honour and discipline spread to the broader audience of our Tommies. Yet, it has to be admitted that it was flawed too: many of the men in those squads had no stomach to fire on their own. So they deliberately missed.

In an ironic coincidence not lost on me, the captain who stepped forward to deliver the coup de grace was the same man Goodchild had accused: Capt. George himself. However, far from relishing the job - as might be expected were Goodchild's accusations founded in truth - the charitable and decent captain seemed distraught at his role in this unpleasant end to the affair. It confirmed to me, at least, that he was the humane and considerate officer I had hitherto seen enacting his duties. I had only ever heard solicitous praise from his own men.

Tragically, the same Capt. George had to perform the exact same function a few months later on August 16th 1917, when the third of the unfortunates I attended met his untimely end.

Private Horton had also been caught spying. This, he too denied. After some investigation, the charges were downgraded to desertion. This had no impact on the soldier's ultimate punishment. Then, as now, desertion was a Capital offence, punishable by death by firing squad. Apparently, no reprieve or pardon was sought or asked for by the prisoner.

I attended this man too. I was put at ease by his charm and intelligence, though, I realised later, he was playing me for a fool. Horton engineered a situation in which he was able to steal a penknife from me.

Come the execution, it was clear he had used my presents to maximum effect. He arrived dopey and bleeding with injuries I had not seen just two hours before. The foolish man, his senses overcome with drink and morphine, had used my penknife to try and end his own life, in an insane attempt to commit what the Japanese Samurai call, Hari Kiri. They, however, use long lethal blades. Horton achieved nothing but a painful gash to his stomach which, when discovered, was quickly bandaged. It did not delay the execution.

He too fell victim to a less than enthusiastic firing squad. As mentioned, Capt. George once again stepped in to perform the coup de grace. This may have hit George worse than Goodchild's coup de grace: Horton had been George's batman for the past few months. I saw in Capt. George's face a pitiful look that said, "I could have prevented this."

So it was, that thrice I saw this sad duty performed, thrice it troubled my conscience. Many nights since I have seen these terrible acts of mercy re-enacted in my dreams. More than once I have said a prayer on behalf of the gallant Capt. George for the trauma he must have gone through.

Feng pushed his mouse to one side.

"You bastard Pelenot," said Feng, all clear to him at last. "I shall bring you down somehow." He waited for a blow from the poltergeist. None came.

Feng typed up his notes and sent an email to Porter and Namita.

Pelenot was involved in both cases and executed both men's coup de grace. We now have a motive for the framing of Cartwright. Harry was Pelenot's batman. He may have become aware of what happened to Cartwright and tried to do something about it. Pelenot's motives for framing both men are clear: either man could have exposed him as a predatory sexual pervert, so he set them up to ensure they faced the firing squad.

Feng summarised his learning about the Profugus and detailed the attack in his flat.

In my opinion, the poltergeist we have been dealing with is known as a Profugus. I will find out more about this tomorrow when I visit the occult author Peregrine Zouche in Oxford. It's clear the Profugus doesn't want us to uncover the details of his wartime crimes.

Pelenot was a sexual sadist - I should know, I've met a few - and therefore based on all our experiences so far, we should assume that he is still evil, still dangerous and, most importantly, still here.

I have spent the day uploading all our documents to Dropbox. Link attached. You can read everything in there and upload anything you have found yourselves.

Feng surveyed his broken flat. I'll do it in the morning. I'm knackered.

It was only when he went for a pee and lifted the toilet lid, he realised he was going to have to replace every unction, tube and lotion he owned.

Chapter 34

Quendell's & Co, Dalston Junction, Hackney
Friday, March 31st 2017: 9.20am

Where the hell did that woman from the Daily Mail keep getting
her information from?
Janine Death Solicitor to be sent to Mental Hospital
Namita hoped Porter hadn't seen it. Mind you, that was only
delaying the inevitable, wasn't it? Other papers would follow-up.
With Porter otherwise detained, she would get the calls. You need to
be ready.
The thorough solicitor skimmed Porter's file. How on earth did
he get himself into such a preventable mess? Was it any wonder his
sister thought he was nuts? Anyone could crack in this situation. He
seems pretty healthy to me. Under the cosh, alright. His confusion
was understandable, even if talk of World War 1 ghosts wasn't.
No, if she doubted anyone's sanity right now, it was her own.
Supporting Porter and Feng's quest was entirely out of character.
She was quite enjoying it. She had been dying slowly at Quendell's
for years. Same office and caseload, week after week, year after
year.
"You're onboard because you're bored," said Sangita.
"I guess so. Actually, I spoke to Shahnaz Uddin last week.
We're still thinking of going it alone."
"Stop thinking, start doing."
Lighting a cigarette, she sifted through some more papers, quickly
got bored, and stared out of the window.
Namita ruminated on Cherry's attempt to get Porter sectioned.
Not many options there. She would have to let the process happen
and get him out on appeal. Two of the doctors hadn't formally
assessed Porter at all, and the third had only had informal
conversations with him. It would be overturned pretty fast. But it
couldn't be done before the sectioning. DCI Crawley was right:
Porter was safer in a cell right now.
Cherry told Namita her brother would probably be transferred on
Sunday morning to Horseferry Road magistrates. An emergency
Mental Health Tribunal would take place.

Her phone pinged: Feng asking if she'd read his email from last night yet? She hadn't, so she did now. She had no idea what to make of Feng's supernatural theories. She forwarded it on to Karin with the message, "See what I'm dealing with? Find anything last night?" She leaned back in her chair.

"Sod it," said Namita. "I'm getting coffee."

Chartwell House, Surrey
Friday, March 31st 2017: 9.32am

Karin was taking a late breakfast in Chartwell's sunny dining room. The windows were three metres high and ran in a large semi-circle, giving beautiful views of the gardens. She had a corking bruise on her leg from last night. She was massaging it and reading The Times when her phone pinged. It was an email from Namita Menon.

She read it with interest and opened Feng's forwarded Dropbox link. They think Georges framed Cartwright? She read the first document: Namita's summary of the Cartwright court-martial. There was a scan of the actual document too. She read the opening description of attendees with interest. It was one of the first official documents she'd seen that mentioned her paper-shy great-grandfather. She found Namita's summary easier to read on her phone's small screen.

> *Field General Court Martial (FGCM) convened.*
> *Capt. Georges Pelenot gives a good character reference.*
> *Capt. Alex Wootton gives a good character reference.*
> *Capt. Cecil Braxted gives an iffy character reference.*
> *Reverend Charles Gilpin gives a so-so reference.*
> *Charges under the Army Act of 1881 read out…*

Karin nearly choked on her toast when she got to Namita's summary of Cartwright's defence statement.

> ** Cartwright explained he had been on recon in No-Man's Land for Operation Ashbright*
> ** Panel asked him what Operation Ashbright was. He said he didn't know all the details but said Capt. ____ had ordered him on the mission.*

** When questioned about this, Cartwright says he was ordered to look for evidence of German offensive preparations, got trapped in No Man's Land, killed a German soldier and spent the night with the corpse against a crater.*

** Major Guzman: There is no Operation Ashbright. HQ confirmed this.*

Over the coming hours, she would eagerly read everything in Feng's Dropbox. But for now, she just got up and walked to the window and gazed out onto the garden.

In the centre of the lawn was an ancient oak. It was already hundreds of years old in 1720 when it was struck by lightning. Tended by generations of gardeners since, it was still named after the groundsman who had saved it after the lightning strike. It had been known ever since as The Ashbright, in honour of Thomas Ashbright.

Still staring at the majestic tree, she shook her head. "Georges Pelenot. You were a very bad man. A very bad man indeed. But what the hell are you now?"

Stoke Newington Police Station
Friday, March 31st 2017: 9.48am

The Gliss had abandoned him. No amount of name-calling could fetch him forth.

Porter was thoroughly cheesed off. He understood why but was frustrated and bored to be behind bars. Crawley had given him a couple of painkillers, refusing to provide him with a whole bottle. Porter realised, with irony, he was on suicide watch. Because of the unusual circumstances, he had been given the contents of his rucksack, bar his phone. He had Harry Norton's diary. Bored, Porter decided to re-read it.

The entry for July 4th 1917. What? No. Surely not?

He angled the paper a few different ways and examined it with a squint. The mysterious list of crossed/uncrossed people. And there it was. The entry for George Blenof in Harry's minuscule scribble. It dawned on Porter The Gliss may have been right from the start. What had he said? *They had terrible handwriting in those days.*

The *B* of Blenof was really a crushed *Pe*. The *f* was a distorted *t*. George Pelenot.

Harry probably never even realised there was an *s* on the end of the *George*.

Porter grew restless with excitement. It was obvious now: Harry knew of Pelenot - maybe even knew him. Blenof/Pelenot hadn't been crossed out.

Porter had always assumed this was Harry's list of suspects. The crossings-out were in different inks, made as and when he eliminated people. At the time of his death, Harry still suspected Pelenot. What had The Pel said of his father? He was, "*...a very unhappy and damaged man. I was scared of him, to be honest.*"

Damn, Porter needed to speak to Feng right now.

Riverview Nursing Home, Oxford
Friday, March 31st 2017: 11.40am

Feng expected to find a doddery old man, wrapped in blankets, dribbling. He was met, instead, by a chipper bald-headed man, with monstrous tentacles of nasal hair. He was smoking a cigar on the porch and wore a large-lapelled purple shirt, topped by a light blue-and-white check dressing gown. His white eyebrows were the size of slippers. More hair than Barry Gibb in his prime – none of it on top.

"Are you the ghost-hunter?" he asked, as Feng strode up the path.

"Mr Zouche? Yes, I am. Is it that obvious?"

"It's a Jewish residential home, and you're not. A Jew that is. And you're too old to be a new orderly. Ergo…"

"Just so," said Feng, holding out a hand.

"Besides, we don't get many Chinkies in here."

Feng decided punching the old bastard might make getting information harder.

"Shall we go in?" said Feng.

"Hold your horses, sunshine. You ain't going nowhere. From what you've told me you're messing with a Profugus. Even talking to you puts me at risk too. They're pretty damn evil. You're not coming in here and dragging one across my threshold, thanks. I like to sleep at night. And in the afternoons. And sometimes the mornings."

"We meet out here?"

"I haven't got long. Lunch soon. It's worse than National Service here. Breakfast, lunch and dinner, same time every day. Chop, chop. What do you want to know?"

Feng pulled out Peregrine's old book on poltergeists.

Zouche laughed. "That old piece of shit. Where did you find that?"

"Denizens."

"Is that place still going? Is Greengross still running it? She should be in one of these by now," said Zouche, thumbing over his shoulder.

"She's still there."

"I'm all ears. Fire away, Fu Manchu."

Feng made a wish for Zouche's next bed bath to be made with iced water.

"You write about the Profugus," said Feng. "I've done a bit of research. You're the only one I can find who's ever mentioned it in a book. Is it real? Or did you make the whole thing up?"

"Cheeky sod. Of course I didn't make it up. How's your Latin?"

"I wish people wouldn't keep asking me that."

"You can't delve into this shit without Latin. The medieval monks were the first to record this stuff in an age where people both expected and dreaded to see the supernatural manifest. Their eyes were open. Not like today with their google glass and AR. There are many old references to them. I could give you a few tomes to research, but you don't have Latin - what's the point? Let me give you a digest. Then you can see what you're dealing with."

In fact, began Zouche, he didn't think Feng and co were dealing with the classic Profugus at all, but something much worse: A Profugus with The Saevita - literal meaning, the outsider with the rage. A super rare animal. Only two examples generally credited during the past 3,000 years - all of recorded history, basically. A few early historians suggested Noah's 40 days and 40 nights storm, was a Profugus with The Saevita mucking about with the weather.

"But most scholars later accepted they can't influence meteorological or geological events. So that's probably bollocks. The first generally accepted example was the one that lit the Great Fire of London."

Feng was disappointed. "Even I know that was started by a baker's fire in Pudding Lane."

"Not that one, you dolt," said Zouche. "The one in 1212 which killed thousands of people."

"Oh. I didn't know there was a Great Fire in 1212," said Feng.

"So what? Now you do."

"What was the other example?" said Feng, finding the conversation more annoying by the second.

"The aftermath of the Great Kanto earthquake in Tokyo in 1923," said Zouche.

"I thought they can't affect geological events?" said Feng, exasperated.

"Are you listening? Not the earthquake - what happened *after*. The Dragon Twist."

"Dragons?" said Feng.

"Not Dragons. *Dragon Twist*. A freak pillar of fire. When the earthquake came, everyone in Tokyo was having lunch, food cooked over portable fires on wheels. The PWTS capitalised on the quake by upsetting braziers all over the city. The wooden houses lit up in a flash. More than 140,000 people burned to death, including 44,000 people who took shelter by the Sumida River, only to be burned alive in the Dragon Twist."

"140,000?" said Feng, astonished.

"At least." Feng's internal projector recreated the scene.

"What's interesting is that historians generally acknowledge the fire had terrible side effects – something even the PWTS couldn't have planned. In the aftermath, the political and religious Right in Japan were emboldened to reject Western-style democracy. It was the philosophy that eventually took the Japanese into World War II."

"No way! What happened to the Profugus in these cases?"

"Profugus with The Saevita," Zouche corrected. "They were annihilated. They must have been, in both cases, because otherwise civilisation would have been destroyed in time as their powers increased."

"How were they destroyed?"

"I'm going to look into that for you. I'll have to try and remember my Latin and call some books up. This place has a computer. I can also get stuff from the British Library. As to details, I can't remember exactly. I saw an account of Tokyo, but the old bonce isn't as reliable as it was. Let me show you something."

Feng looked at a couple of brown notebooks that Zouche magicked from his robe.

"I still keep a scrapbook. It's hard to give up completely."

Feng looked through them eagerly. He was expecting to see copies of old Latin text but was surprised to find they were full of newspaper clippings, the latest, all-too-familiar cutting, from a few days ago.

He recognised several stories from recent times - children throwing themselves into canals, a woman going berserk in a shopping centre and, most recently, an account of the table whirlwind in Starbucks in London.

"This is amazing. You know, we are involved in this one," said Feng pointing to the Starbucks story. And he related the full story, updated to include Porter's incarceration.

"This is not good news, though it makes me feel smug," said Zouche. "I had a feeling these might all be connected. You see, the Profugus, in all forms, can interact with both the living and the dead. Your average ghosty-whosty would give its non-corporeal right arm to actually touch things or talk. These had to be a Profugus. Way too dramatic for a stroppy Poltergeist. Only the Profugus can pull off shit like this."

Feng told him about the burnt books, the murder of Sandra Belloc and the exploding munitions in Ypres. Zouche looked concerned. Something of the serious scholar appeared in his face for the first time.

"They're not Bond villains with a masterplan. They're the spiritual equivalent of a plague. They wreak massive harm. They're not out to conquer the world. They are pure malevolence and thrive on chaos. It's their undeniable nature. There's no reasoning or talking with them. Do you understand? Basic protocol when dealing with a Profugus is to run like the wind and hide your sorry arse in the deepest cave you can find."

Zouche took his notebook back and flipped through it. "All these years, I've tracked weird phenomena in case a PWTS should appear in my time. What you're telling me suggests one might have."

Feng nodded. "I'm a sceptic myself."

"What are you talking about, you blithering idiot? These things exist. You've described seeing stuff with your own eyes. Why are you still describing yourself as a sceptic? You're lucky. This one is just getting started. It's not talking to anyone yet. It isn't close to full power. If you start to hear words from it, you're in trouble. Glad you haven't. You - *we,* if I can help - haven't got long to stop it."

"How exactly? In your book, you said it could be destroyed by a kind of exorcism? Using the same method of killing it used in life?"

"Yes, but I've forgotten the precise details. Sod this fog." Zouche slapped a hand against his temple in frustration. "It won't take me long to catch up. I don't want to advise you wrongly now. If I remember rightly, there's an account of an exorcism carried out by a Samurai in Tokyo which ended that one's reign of terror."

As much as he disliked Zouche, Feng pitied the look on his face. It was the face of a man who had once known everything but was now struggling to accept the blurring and bleeding of his condition.

"The thing that's crucial to remember - the PWTS was once human. It had a human life. It would have been a truly evil one. The man would have murdered at the very least. As the PWTS it will have the memories of its embryonic human form and the ability to talk and reason like a human, but this is a trap for its hunter. Under no circumstances should you treat it as if it's still human, the person it was born out of."

"Apart from the method of killing it?"

"Yes, apart from that."

A matronly woman arrived and told Zouche it was time for lunch. Zouche looked torn but then got up to make his way to the dining hall.

"Look, I'm only human. They give KZ rations here. I can't miss my nosh, or I'll waste away by teatime. Can you toddle off and come back in a bit?"

Feng agreed and spent a worried hour pottering the streets and colleges of Oxford. The gargoyles and statues seemed to leer down at him.

When he arrived back at Riverview, Zouche was waiting for him. This time he had on half-moon spectacles and was reading in a deckchair.

"There's something else," he said as if they had not broken their conversation. "I mentioned the Profugus with the Saevita can communicate with the dead and the living? This is important because it's one of their greatest weapons.

"First-hand accounts from the Great Kanto incident suggest that when the PWTS communicate with the dead, they can raise them and bend them to their will." Feng nodded, deciding it was safer to let Zouche continue than interrupt the racist old fool.

"Some early medieval theologians thought the Four Horsemen of the Apocalypse would be four of these bastards. They can manipulate humans too – just look at these cuttings? Luckily many humans - God bless our truculent little souls – can't be hypnotised. The dead aren't so independent. I hesitate to use the word *army* because these massed spirits would more resemble a swarm of locusts…but you get the idea."

Feng whistled. "Porter - the man I'm working with - has been given powers through something called the Quincunx. It means he can hear the dead. I was sceptical but have seen evidence he's telling the truth. Maybe that'll help?"

"All sounds interesting. I've not heard of that phenomenon before. Do you think I could meet him at some point? If true, it'll certainly put this Porter bloke - and you as his sidekick - on the PWTS' radar."

Feng assured him that he would bring Porter to see him soon. "It all sounds a tad scary."

"A tad scary? Are you studying for a Phd in Understatement, majoring in Ignorance? If one of these bloody things got to full power now…just think how different the world is from 1923, the last time one appeared. There are nuclear and chemical weapons now. If yours gets to its full power… It would take seconds for it to realise it should go after the man with the nuclear football. Look who's holding that. He's barely got a mind to control, but I'm guessing, what there is of it, would be easy prey." Zouche let that sink in.

"Right, I've done enough talking until I've done more research. Tell me everything. Take my lack of prejudice for granted. From the beginning. Chop-chop, Hong Kong Phooey."

Through gritted teeth, Feng began with Porter's attempted suicide, The Gliss and the Quincunx, before summarising their adventures.

Zouche nodded. "I think the Profugus and the Quincunx are connected; they are opposite but parallel magicks. The one has come into being because of the other."

Feng thought about this for a second. "Sounds like we must act quickly?"

"Quicker than a stir-fry," said Zouche, giving the last words enough shade to offend as intended.

Chapter 35

Paddington Station, London
Friday, March 31st 2017: 3.10pm

On the train back to London, Feng called Namita. Namita called Karin. Karin called Feng. A quick exchange of updates and all three agreed to meet at 4pm at Stoke Newington police station. It was time to update Porter.

Feng's stomach bubbled and churned all the way home. At first, he put it down to the lukewarm Cornish pasty he had bought in Oxford. Then he realised it was fear.

He had always been a sceptic, but Zouche had a point: Was that the right position to hold in light of recent events? It's hard to be logical in an illogical situation, Feng, you old fruit. He decided he would like to remain a staunch rationalist for a few days more and take things as they come, without prejudice. The Doves would have a field day mocking him when they found out he was going along with this. It couldn't be helped.

He picked up a free copy of Metro on the way out and saw another of those strange stories Zouche thought was evidence of the Profugus with Saevita.

Police reported that three men had been sexually assaulted in London parks in as many days. None of the men had seen their attacker. All claimed to have been pinned down and penetrated, despite wearing trousers throughout their ordeal. In all three cases, when the men felt free to look up, the perpetrator had vanished. One of the attacks was in the middle of Hyde Park, in broad daylight, and not a tree within 200m of the attack. Yet the victim saw no-one escaping. All of the men were respectable, unremarkable in every other way, neither drunk nor on drugs. All had injuries consistent with their accounts. Police were investigating.

"I hope we're not too late to stop this," Feng muttered. "These weren't sexual assaults. They were power trips. Pelenot's memories are fuelling the Profugus, building its power up based on his perverse life."

Watching Newington Green pass by from the top deck of a 73 bus, Feng called Riverview.

"I had to leave in a hurry but just wanted to say thanks for your time." He told Zouche about the attacks in the park.

"Sounds like the Profugus," confirmed Zouche. "Watch your Chinky arse."

Feng jumped off on Stoke Newington Church Street. It seemed like an age since he and Porter had visited Mustham & Sons.

Walking towards the station, he saw Namita.

"Ms Menon."

"Ah, it's you."

"Nice to see you too."

"I enjoyed your research. Sort of," she said, in her version of a conciliatory voice.

"Thanks. I've got a lot more to tell you now."

"Let's wait till we get there."

"Any news on Porter?"

"He'll be transferred to Horseferry Road magistrates Sunday morning at nine for the hearing. It gives us a day or so to decide what to do next."

"I have a plan."

"There's really nothing we can do," said Namita, annoyed at anyone who dared meddle in her sphere.

"There's nothing *you* can do. Best not to discuss. As I keep saying, leave it to me."

"Don't make things worse."

"Extreme situations call for extreme solutions."

"Don't say another word."

"Client confidentiality."

"You're not my client."

They arrived in Stoke Newington Police Station reception and found Karin Pelenot reading a book. They introduced themselves. Namita asked for DCI Crawley.

"Look who it is," said Crawley on seeing Feng. "Who are you impersonating today?"

"Just myself. Look I'm sorry about that silliness the other day. All innocent, even if a bit insensitive of us. We're all here to see Porter."

"I gathered that. Hello again, Ms Menon." And then in shock, "Karin Pelenot? The missus and I love your show. You with these two?"

"Thanks. Yes. I'm a friend of Mr Norton too."

"Are you indeed? He's fine. As you know, I'm only holding him for his own safety. Would you like me to organise a meeting room? Coffee anyone? I seem to have become his doctor and confidante. I might as well become his waiter too."

He asked for them all to hand over their mobiles and gave them a tag, apologising for playing it by the book. They handed over their phones without complaint and placed coffee orders. Crawley showed them to a dingy meeting room, eerily lit by dying fluorescent tubes. A screen saver on a desktop threw a pale blue cast over one corner of the room.

"Give me a minute, I'll get him," said Crawley. "Make yourselves comfortable. If you can. Comfort's not exactly our forte."

The three stared at the walls, awaiting Porter. He arrived unkempt and unslept.

"Hi. All together for the first time. It must have been like this the day Ringo joined the Beatles."

"I'm Paul then," said Namita. "You know, the cute, talented one."

"Then I'm John," said Karin. "The loud, arrogant one."

"I'm definitely George," said Porter. "Quiet but sophisticated."

"Come on. Don't make me Ringo. Who wants to be Ringo?" said Feng.

"He was the backbeat, and you're the researcher providing the pulse of this case," said Karin. "No Ringo, no Beatles."

"Then I must be Brian Epstein, the manager," said The Gliss.

"Oh you. Welcome back. Where have you been?" asked Porter.

"You know when you pause a computer game, turn the electricity off at the mains, but when you come back to it, you pick up where you left off?"

"Yes?"

"Wondering about me is like wondering what the game characters are doing while you're asleep."

"That's not very satisfying."

Porter felt obliged to translate, to arched eyebrows from Karin. Namita asked her to go along with this. If she still wanted to be involved at the end of this meeting, great. If not, she was free to quit the band citing musical differences.

"I think we've exhausted the Beatles metaphor," said Ringo, sulking.

Crawley came back, dumped the coffees, and made his excuses. Actual police business to attend to.

"So," said Porter, excitedly. "I think I know who Cartwright accused at his court-martial. And, I think Harry knew him too."

"Georges Pelenot," said Feng and Karin at precisely the same time.

"What?" said Porter. "You knew?"

"You go first, Feng. I saw your brief email. I'm curious to know what you found," said Karin.

Feng spent ten minutes outlining his findings from Gilpin's book, his surmises and a precis of Zouche's thoughts. All eyes turned immediately to Karin. What could she say to top that?

Two days ago, Karin would have walked out if confronted by this supernatural gobbledygook. But two days ago, she hadn't been assaulted by unseen hands and pushed into mock suicide. She told her story. Showed them the injuries to her calf and a photo of the gun, how she had imagined it going off, the non-existent hole in the roof.

"It was as real as a hallucination could be. You'll be glad to hear I left the gun locked up in my safe," said Karin.

Porter finally got his moment. "I feel a bit deflated now. You've all found out more than me. But I did find this. I misread Harry's diary. Look." He showed them the Blenof/Pelenot error. "You see - it all fits. Pelenot assaulted Cartwright. Max fought back in some way. Pelenot forced a fake mission on him hoping he would die in No-Man's Land. But he made it back and was accused of spying. Poor Max. No-one believed he had been framed by Pelenot."

"Ok," said Namita, "But where does your Harry come in?"

"He and Cartwright served together?" said Karin.

"Not at all," said Namita. "Harry arrived in Ypres months after Cartwright was killed."

"Gilpin's book says Harry was Pelenot's batman," said Feng.

"It's not that hard to explain then," said Porter. "Think about Harry's list and his comments about it *not being right* and *he must be stopped*."

"Harry, working for Georges, became aware of what happened to Cartwright and maybe some others," said Karin.

"Yes," said Feng. "Harry had a list of presumed suspects in his diary. He was eliminating people from his inquiries. A risky game."

"Fatal," said Namita.

"So, let me get this right," said Karin. "Harry had my great-grandfather in his sights. Somehow ended up working for him. Later your great-grandfather is accused of spying…"

"…desertion eventually," said Porter.

"…spying then desertion," continued Karin. "He ends up in a botched execution and my great-grandfather performs the *coup de grace*. Is that right?"

"Pelenot found out that Harry knew. Harry was framed at the very least. Maybe he was assaulted too?" said Porter.

"In either case, why didn't Harry just spill the beans and shop Pelenot?" asked Namita.

"That's not clear," admitted Porter.

"Pretty clear, if you ask me," said Feng. "What proof did he have? He'd have been in no better than position than Max if he went to the top brass and accused Pelenot."

"Some narrative," said Karin. "Even if we skip the ghost bits, there's a definite story in there for me. I'll help expose this. I'm on the side of justice, not blind family honour."

Feng recapped on Zouche's theory about the Profugus with Saevita and how it had been birthed by the Quincunx, activated by Porter's attempted suicide. Porter tried to wave away the idea, embarrassed.

"Zouche says if this Profugus is allowed to carry on, it could cause problems on a global scale."

"That's just what I want to hear, with North Korea tooling up," said Namita.

"How do we kill this Profugus thing?" asked Karin.

A tiny bit of family loyalty must still linger, thought Porter. She never says Pelenot. Always Georges or The Profugus.

"Zouche's looking into it," replied Feng. "He's a bit old and decrepit - and an old-school racist. He's forgotten a lot of the detail - of the exorcism, not how to be racist. But, yes, there is a ritual in which the Profugus is killed in the same way it killed in life."

Karin looked up, instantly alert. "Don't you see? The *coup de grace*. Carried out with his pistol. No wonder he didn't want me to take his gun from the attic. It could destroy him." They all whistled.

"The problem is," said Namita. "If there's any truth to any of this, Pelenot must be aware of what we're doing. And no-one's actually seen him yet?"

"We're all in danger," said Feng, with a little too much delight. "Real, proper, poo-your-pants danger."

"You're ok for now," said The Gliss. "I've been able to sense his presence every time so far, and...DUCK! Everyone DUCK!"

Porter, the only one who could hear the warning, threw himself violently to the floor. Feng, who saw the panic in Porter's face, fell almost simultaneously. Mid-dive, Porter screamed a warning to Namita and Karin, who obediently dropped like stones.

As they hit the concrete, every lightbulb and window pane in the room shattered. The desktop computer exploded. Shards of debris hovered mid-air, defying gravity and logic.

"What the hell?" said Namita, finally seeing an example of the weirdness for herself.

The glass didn't hang about. A cloud of vicious splinters moved in a murmuration, before rocketing towards the four of them huddled on the floor.

"Under the table, now!" warned The Gliss.

Porter leading, the group moved as one, cracking heads, as hundreds of dings and tings signalled the table top was under attack. Porter had a leg protruding, Karin an arm. Both received hits from the glass and plastic shrapnel. Debris smashed into the wall at the far end of the room.

Elsewhere in the building every light, computer and phone had blown. Crawley, who was in the men's room peeing, jumped back in horror as a full-length mirror turned into a solar system of hovering, shiny fragments that swirled before spraying against the far wall with the ferocious patter of a Sten gun.

A short stunned silence in the meeting room, was broken by Karin."What the hell was that!"

"That," said Feng, "was probably, your extremely pissed off relative."

"Not *probably*," said Namita, pointing to the wall.

Gouged out of the paint and plaster were the initials G.P.P.

"Georges Parry Pelenot," said Karin. "Bloody hell."

"He knows we know. Why hide any longer?" said Namita.

A loud buzzing and clicking hurt their ears.

"Look at the reading on this," said Feng. One of his meters was spitting like pig fat on a bonfire.

"Turn it off, you're deafening us," said Porter, who was getting used to the sight of blood dripping off his extremities.

"I wonder what the hell Crawley's going to say when he sees this mess?" said Namita.

On cue, Crawley burst into the room, saw them under the shredded table, the initials on the wall, and said, "You too?"

Chapter 36

Ypres, Western Front
March 1st 1917: 10.31pm

Capt. Georges Parry Pelenot leaned back into a folding trench chair in his office and wished things had turned out differently.

He was waiting for Private Max Cartwright to arrive. It would be a difficult but necessary conversation. By the end of the night, the problem would be solved. It was a pity because he liked Cartwright. He'd genuinely enjoyed dallying him two weeks ago. Such a shame the bastard had resisted. Cartwright had been on the verge of either shooting or reporting him ever since. There's always one. Other privates had taken it like men and avoided him forever after. Forever could be measured in weeks in Ypres.

Few of Pelenot's victims were left to complain. Cartwright was the one who looked like he could cause problems. Nothing for it but to act in pre-emptive self-defence.

It didn't have to be like this. From the first, the pair had got on because Pelenot was, outwardly, caring and a good commander. Cartwright was flattered to be taken under Pelenot's wing. Both had been involved in a messy recon op that went wrong on February 1st. Both had been brave beyond the comprehension of non-soldiers. Both had made it back to the trenches in one piece. Cartwright was flattered when Pelenot bought him a drink and toasted him in front of the other soldiers a few days later.

He offered Cartwright a position as his batman, the previous one having had his brains shot out. Never a good idea to put your head above the parapet for a drunken piss.

A few weeks later on Valentine's Day, the pair had been drinking together. Pelenot had leaned over and kissed Cartwright on the lips. Cartwright was outraged, lashed out and landed a corker of a right hook on Pelenot's jaw. It escalated quickly.

From the floor, dazed and furious, Pelenot pulled his pistol, cocked it and ordered Cartwright to drop his trousers. He smiled now, remembering the private bent over the table, gun to head. Compliant but livid, Cartwright gripped the wooden sides, while Pelenot had his way.

"Get dressed," said Pelenot, as if nothing had happened. "You can go now."

From that day, Cartwright was visibly a constant threat. The private knew assaulting an officer could land him the death penalty. He gave the impression of biding his time.

Until the situation resolved, Pelenot knew it was in his interests to try and smooth the waters. He apologised, said it would never happen again. He asked for forgiveness and lied that he would make it up to Cartwright. He shamelessly used his own wife to form an excuse narrative. "I love my wife. It's this war. It brings out the brute. Forgive me." But Cartwright, no coward, was cold and bitter. He spoke to Pelenot in self-protective duty only when there was an audience.

Cartwright must die. And here he was now, about to execute the plan that would see the private dead by morning.

Last night's officers' dance had left a bit of a hangover. He smiled at the thought of the nurse he had pinned to the wall. She had begged and cried, "No Sir, no sir." Bitch had loved every second his hand was down her pants, though she had screamed when he pulled on her pubes. What was she going to say? Nothing.

His head hurt like the devil. Postponing wasn't an option. You want to survive this war? Cartwright has to go. Better over and done with.

Cartwright arrived. He kept as far away from Pelenot as possible.

"I know there's bad blood between us, but you have to put it to one side," said Pelenot. "Take a seat, man. You're perfectly safe. There are people outside."

Cartwright stayed where he was.

Pelenot smiled but scowled inwardly. You'll pay for this insolence. He took his revolver out. Cartwright's icy brood cracked. Pelenot gestured calm, emptied the chambers and threw the bullets to one side. He laid the Webley top-break service revolver down on the table.

"Pax, man, pax," said Pelenot. "Put your bag down. Nothing's going to happen. This is work."

Cartwright remained wary and listened.

"You've been selected for a mission by HQ," said Pelenot. He tapped a communiqué lying open next to him. He hoped Cartwright would show enough deference not to demand to see the orders. That would be bad. They didn't exist. "Top brass. Nothing to do with me."

"Screw you," said Cartwright.

"Enough. Plumer wants some intel. We intercepted a German message suggesting the Bosche are planning a big offensive tomorrow. We urgently need to find out if there's any truth to this."

Cartwright ground his jaws together.

"Operation Ashbright - top secret, need to know etc.," said Pelenot, tapping the paper again for emphasis. "All along the line tonight we are sending a dozen recon men into No-Man's Land. Nosey up to Jerry and listen-in on their trench talk." Pelenot tapped at the HQ paper on the desk again. "Ashbright intel will ensure we have artillery in the right place, ready to pre-empt their attack."

Cartwright nodded. He understood, but he didn't like it one bit.

"Plumer asked me to choose a man and, despite the coolness between us, you're the best and most experienced man for the job," said Pelenot.

"What do you want me to do?" The lack of a *Sir* irritated Pelenot.

"If they're preparing a major attack, the trenches will be busy. If they're not, they'll be quiet at this time of night. Plumer has agreed to send a barrage at 10.54pm to distract them while you chaps sneak out. They won't be expecting that. We've deliberately chosen a time that has no significance. They're always more alert on the hour. It's a 200-yard crawl. Go slow, wear a cape, you'll be fine."

Cartwright glanced at Pelenot's wind-up clock. "That's in 20-minutes."

"You'd better get your cape then."

Cartwright knew better than to refuse. He bent to grab his bag.

"Leave it," said Pelenot. "You'll go faster without."

At 10.49pm, Cartwright stood at a trench ladder position often used to launch recon ops. It led to No-Man's land. This was different from all the others. This one led to mats that cut through the barbed wire defences, allowing belly crawls. Most importantly, there was a raised mound of mud about 10 yards out. It formed a protective lip dubbed Connaught's Hollow in memory of a soldier who fell there in 1915. So many men had died along this stretch since, there was not one person left who had known Connaught, but the name had stuck.

Cartwright grabbed some mud from the wall of the trench and camouflaged his face and hands. He pulled his rubber cape about himself and stared with hatred at Pelenot.

"How many times do I have to apologise?" said Pelenot, holding out his hand.

Cartwright ignored it. He took his bag back from Pelenot's outstretched arm. Pelenot glanced at his watch. 10.50pm.

"Go now before the barrage," said Pelenot. "Less light. Good luck, man. Get to Connaught's before the barrage, and you'll be fine."

Cartwright climbed the ladder and, in slow-motion, slid over the top as noiselessly as a snake.

Cartwright smelled the mud in his nostrils. It was rank. The weather had been cold and wet for weeks. No Man's Land had been churned like buttermilk by the ruptures of artillery. Worse, every inch contained the mincemeat of man and horse, giving off a gangrenous odour. It was worse than usual, nose to the ground.

He inched forward, his uniform soaked in seconds. His exposed wrist was scratched by a snapped human jawbone that had been picked clean by rats.

Even if you get back, you'll still die of tetanus. The sanctuary of Connaught's was about three yards away. For five minutes or more he slithered, inch by terrifying inch. Where the hell was the barrage? Typical. His best hope was to be firmly lodged by Connaught's when the shells crashed into the German trenches.

Cartwright moved forward. The best eyes in the German army could not have seen him. All was quiet, though he could still hear the faint chatter of some of his colleagues getting ready to take cover for sleep.

Two yards to go. No barrage. If this was a genuine attempt to send 12 men out, he would have heard shells. He realised what he had already suspected: he was on his own. Pelenot did not expect him to come back.

You wait till I get back.

He wedged against the sanctuary of the mound. He moved some earth to one side and created a little more space for himself. The lip resembled the slope of a mini-volcano. It wouldn't survive a hit from anything bigger than a rifle bullet, but it gave visual cover. He covered himself with earth and waited. Just in case that barrage came. Some chance. What now? Death still lay in wait in his own trenches for a coward's return. He decided to move forward anyway. Experience had taught him to obey even the most suicidal of orders.

He began to edge sideways, half-inch by half-inch, when he heard a pfffft sound.

A flare exploded into the air, directly above where he lay. It had to be Pelenot. Confirmation. Not only was no covering fire coming, but he was being made visible for the Germans to spot and take out. Cartwright watched the flare reach its zenith. It fell back to earth, spreading its light, wider and brighter. It was going to drop close by. Pelenot had known precisely where to launch it. Connaught's Hollow.

Max was protected by the lip of mud from most eyes, but it would only take one flash of light to zip across his boots, cape or helmet to give him away to the extreme left or right of his position. *If I ever get back, you're a dead man, Pelenot.*

A curious German machine gunner, watching the flare fall, sprayed the other side of the Connaught. The German hadn't seen anything specific. Better safe than sorry. Cartwright felt the pressure of rounds slamming into the mound protecting him. None made it through the dense, wet mud but Max felt each bullet like a punch to the ribs. The gunner got bored and halted.

Moving further forward was now off the agenda. Scarcely daring to breathe, Max used his hands to scoop and drag small amounts of earth to cover himself.

Twenty scoops in, he almost gave himself away with a cry, when a partially denuded arm flopped in front of him. The arm - most of the flesh gone - dangled in front of his face like a pendulum. He held his breath. Lookouts took pot-shots at any movement. Many a rat had paid the ultimate price for squeaking in No Man's Land.

His best bet was to stay still for a few hours. By 1am, all but the Watch would be getting what sleep they could.

There was a noise. He recognised it instantly. It was the whisper-quiet rustle of a man crawling on his belly. Cartwright was confused. Pelenot said other men would be sent out along the line. If there *were* any others on this mission, it made no sense. No point getting intelligence from two sources too close to each other. It was with a creeping horror he realised it was no Tommy, but a German conducting a mirror-image of the same suicide mission he was on. He thanked the heavens he was covered and invisible. He wasn't scared of hand-to-hand fighting, but noise would bring artillery down from both sides.

He made tiny head movements in the direction of the rustle. His enemy was creating one hell of a din for No Man's Land. The damn fool could kill them both.

The German's trajectory curved towards his hiding place. What was the idiot doing? Cartwright realised he was looking for a safe place too. The German was no more than 4ft away, oblivious to the danger he was in.

What do I do now? If I shoot him, we're both dead within seconds. If I bayonet him, his cries will give us away.

A sudden realisation. *No-one else on my side knows I'm here. Who was on watch tonight? Avory? Trigger happy.* One sound from here, the area would light up with machine gun fire. *Shit.* Connaught's was only cover if your side knew you were there.

One hope. Survive the night and be visible to the Watch at first light. True, once he left Connaught's he would be visible to the Germans too, but Connaught's height would shield him from direct-gaze. His chances were at least 50-50.

What to do about this soldier? If he continued on this path, they would be toe-to-toe, spooning within minutes. He had to kill him. Silently. He gently flexed his outstretched hand and felt around. Nothing. In mud studded to capacity with battle debris, he couldn't find so much as a nail. His own weapons were encased in mud too far down his body for him to reach without alerting the other soldier. The German continued to move. His head, turned away from Cartwright, was moving closer to his own. Finally, he lay with his back to Cartwright staring at the British front line, working out his own next move.

Cartwright hadn't breathed for 30 secs. The three inches of mud that separated him from the German would shift violently when he eventually gave up and was forced to gasp for air. *Now or never.*

With a sudden pull of arm that surprised the German, Cartwright clapped a handful of foul mud over the German's nose and mouth. With his other hand, he felt for the German's weapons. *A bayonet. Thank you Lord.* In two seconds, the serrated blade was whipped out and plunged into the German's guts. Cartwright pulled upwards, rotating the enemy's bayonet around his chest cavity. Arteries were severed, vitals sliced. Welcome warmth flooded over both Cartwright's hands as the German's blood flowed. He could afford to let go of the bayonet, leaving it protruding. The mouth of mud had dulled his enemy's screams but, in fear for his own life, Cartwright used both hands to smother any noise. Suffocation and exsanguination it was.

And there, five and a half hours later, they both still lay at the first light of day.

Max realised the most dangerous moment had come. Moving the cold corpse to one side could attract attention from either trench, but it had to be done. The first thing his side would see was the German uniform. He had to be quick. He flexed his aching and frozen muscles and moved the German slowly. Rifle fire broke the dawn silence as several rounds were fired from the British side. The German's body shook with their impact. Cartwright prayed for luck not to desert him.

"Who goes there?" shouted Avory. Cartwright knew better than to answer immediately. The Germans would hear the conversation and blast the area. Absolute stillness. Ten minutes later, Cartwright attempted an impression of a casual trench voice. The Germans heard those all the time. No-one would be mad enough to talk in No Man's Land after all.

"Avory, good morning. It's Max Cartwright. Act normally, please. Trapped by Connaught's. Stop firing for a second, would you?"

"Cartwright? What ya doing out there?"

"Recon gone wrong. I'm coming in. Got to move the Bosche you shot first. I was in the middle of bayonetting him when you started shooting."

"I'll get help."

"Good man."

Ten agonising minutes later, Cartwright, once again protected by Connaught's, belly-flopped across the matting and into the trenches. He had made it! Alive!

He was pulled roughly to his feet by two MPs. One held a pistol on him.

"Don't move. You'll only make it worse for yourself."

"Officer, I…"

"Not a word, you louse. Here it is, Jim. Like Pelenot said it would be."

The second MP was rummaging in Cartwright's bag. The one Pelenot had handed back to him before he left. From it, the MP pulled a manila envelope. They glanced inside and shook their head in disgust.

"What's that?" said Cartwright, the truth slowly dawning.

For answer, Jim kneed Cartwright in the balls, kicking him in the gut as he lay retching on the floor.

"You lousy traitor," said the one who wasn't Jim.

"He was out there with a German I pegged," said Avory. "I saw them together, the bastard trying to hand over papers."

Cartwright heard Avory's comment and realised, despite his work overnight, he was going to die anyway.

Chapter 37

Chartwell House, Surrey
Friday, March 31st 2017: 8.10pm

What on earth had she seen today? It couldn't be real? Surely*?*

Karin's profession enabled her to move forward without full understanding. Sometimes it took a year of research on a paper before a conclusion manifested itself. She was not frightened of the intellectual dark. But...even so.

There was one source on Georges she hadn't re-visited: Pelenot's mother, Rose. They had some of her papers, including diaries. Karin had made some notes a few months back for the Durham University project. She was disappointed only to find trivial domesticity documented. Karin was keen to re-read the papers and see if she had missed anything.

She picked up her large Moleskine. It listed the documents and their location. It also served as a diary of the project. She opened it to record today's events.

What the...?

Smoke poured from its pages. Karin dropped it and stamped on it, infuriated. All of her research was being destroyed. The pages were spontaneously combusting. *Wait. No.* Letters were appearing on the first blank page, cauterised into the paper. Is that you, Georges? She watched in fascination as words formed in smoky brown cursive.

Harry's pages. Le Petite Chat farm. Black brick well. Walk 9ft, dig 3ft. You are my apostle, relative. G.P.P.

She reached for her iPhone to take pictures, but the notebook and research flared into flames and crumbled into ashes.

She shouted in fury. "Apostle? You really *are* a Pelenot, aren't you? You arrogant bastard."

However, the historian's motor was now up-and-running. A treasure hunt. No need to think: she was going after those papers. She googled Le Petite Chat's location in Flanders.

She quickly came across an article mentioning a farm of that name. If it was the same one, it had long since been renamed La Cheval Noir. *If* it was the same one. I can always look around once I get there.

Within 20 minutes, the co-ordinates were in a map and Eurotunnel booked.

Karin called Namita. She could pass the news on to the others.

"I'd like to come with you," said Namita, surprising herself.

"I don't think that's a good idea," said Karin, a solo operator by nature.

"Why not?"

"Don't you need to be here? For Porter?"

"I can't do anything tomorrow. As long as I'm back for the special hearing on Sunday morning."

Karin mulled the prospect. Ok. Some company might be nice. So might legal representation if forced to explain to a Belgian farmer why she was digging up his garden. "You need your passport. Get to me for 5.30am." She gave Namita Chartwell's address.

Exhausted, Karin sat down. The cuts on her elbow and calf were all too painful a reminder of the danger she was in. Was this really happening? Maybe the menopause was starting early? Maybe she'd eaten some dodgy seafood? Something weird was happening, that's for sure.

"Karin, darling, this is a once in a lifetime opportunity to go mad. Enjoy it. Jane Austen would have written a good book about it."

She pulled her skirt over her knees and stared out into the garden at the tree that had spelt doom for a young private in 1917. Damn, I'll never enjoy this view again.

Chapter 38

Chartwell House, Surrey
Saturday, April 1st 2017: 5.40am

Karin stood impatiently by her car, waiting for Namita's cab to arrive.

She checked the boot. Wellies, waterproofs, a shovel, a spade. In the spare tyre compartment, a wooden box with a worn gilt catch, marked G.P.P.

She wasn't sure why she was taking the pistol. If there was a ritual to get rid of the Profugus, they didn't have it yet. But better safe than sorry. Customs checks were minimal on Eurotunnel. Besides, her celebrity usually got her a free pass for most things in return for a selfie or autograph.

A car pulled onto the gravel drive, depositing Namita, who emerged in a stylish red plastic mac.

"So much for incognito," sighed Karin, waving hello.

They chucked her bag in the boot and were off.

"After yesterday, it seems like a stupid question," said Namita. "But how much danger do you think we're in?"

"We're probably safer than the others. It's clear Georges wants Harry's notes to be found and sees me as his emissary. Probably sees them as a religious artefact. I think he believes the notes will give his story some oomph when he goes public. That being so, there's no point killing us if we find them. Or at least, until we find them."

"He tried to destroy all the other evidence. Why do you think he changed his mind this time?"

"Because we found out. He's swapped from hiding to using us. You don't have to come if you're frightened."

Namita snorted. "Did you tell Feng we were going?"

"No, sorry. I thought you would?"

"Bit early to call now. When's our train?"

"8am."

Feng didn't answer. He was in the shower singing *I Am What I Am* when Namita called. She left a message.

Karin and Namita, sitting in the passenger section of the car ferry train, went into the tunnel and lost their signal as expected. If they could have drilled down into the microprocessors of their smartphones, they would have seen surges of electrical energy burning their way through the components. They didn't know it yet, but they were cut off.

Church Lane, Walthamstow
Saturday, April 1st 2017: 8.10am

Feng returned Namita's call. It went straight to voicemail. He listened to her message. She explained where they were going and why. They would be back this evening. She would check in on Porter later today.

Feng looked up their destination. Something bugged him about it. But he couldn't pin it down. It would come. He printed off a copy of the map.

For now, he had other things to worry about. Like getting Porter out of jail.

He had arranged a meeting of the Doves that morning in Hackney Central, at a little Turkish café just off the Narrow Way. He had a cunning plan. Not a fool-proof one, but if he threw enough bodies at it, it might just work.

He had till 9am tomorrow to make sure it did.

Efe's, Amhurst Road, Hackney
Saturday, April 1st 2017: 9.10am

The Doves arrived in quick succession. Feng had commandeered the most discreet table. Susie, Dolan and Carson sat like the three unwise monkeys, each of them with the word Misfit tattooed on the back of their neck.

"What's this all about, Feng?" said Carson. "I'm supposed to be at work."

"I thought you'd been fired?" said Susie.

"I'm supposed to be *looking* for work," said Carson, unabashed.

"No magnifying glass big enough," said Dolan.

"Leave it out," said Feng. "This is *big*. Change-the-world *big*."

Something in his tone stalled the bickering. The misfits listened.

"I've seen a ghost."

Susie laughed. "What you? Don't be silly."

"I've seen it, and I've been attacked by it." There was no smirk, no shade, no sarcasm. For the first time, Feng sounded like he was on their side, not just sniping from the margins.

"Go on," said Carson.

"Yeah, spit it out," said Dolan.

And Feng did. His initial disbelief, his own experiences, and what had happened to Porter - the instigator and medium.

"And now, we have to break Porter out of jail," said Feng.

Calais Eurotunnel terminal
Saturday, April 1st 2017: 8.50am

"My phone's not working," said Namita, bashing it on the dashboard.

"Check mine," said Karin. It wouldn't turn on either.

"Is this where we say *crap* a lot?" said Namita.

"Let's plough on."

"Thelma and Louise it is."

They set off towards Ypres via Dunkirk on the French A16. Six miles later the car ground to a halt, the engine making farting noises.

"Crap again," said Namita, punching her knee for emphasis.

They shivered. There was no doubt about it now: they were phoneless, car-less, cold and alone.

Efe's, Amhurst Road, Hackney
Saturday, April 1st 2017: 9.46am

"Let me get this straight," said Carson. "You want us to hijack an ambulance?"

"That's right," said Feng. "Not for long obviously. We don't want a car chase."

"I don't like this," said Susie.

"Don't worry. You're the getaway driver. You don't have to touch the ambulance."

"You must be mad," said Dolan. "We'll get banged up like this Porter bloke."

"No. He's only being transferred. The second the driver puts him in the back, jump in and skedaddle. You drive two streets. We chuck him in Susie's car and quietly drive away. We do a second handover, under the arches. Carson drives Porter and I off into the sunset, we're out and scot-free. It barely counts as a borrow, let alone a hijack."

Such was Feng's plan. It didn't go down well. There was so much shouting and arguing that Efe came over and asked them to leave. They had spent a lot on muffins, true, but he had to consider the other customers.

The Doves walked around the corner, still arguing loudly. They sat in St John-at-Hackney's churchyard. People with prams crossed to the other side of the park, preferring to walk past East European homeless men with cans of lager than grown-ups shouting.

"Why should we do something this stupid just because you think you've seen a ghost?" said Dolan, his mouth full of croissant, ignoring his mother's childhood advice never to speak with your mouth full. He looked like a cement mixer processing porridge.

"Not a ghost. A Profugus with the Saevita," said Feng. He concluded his *case-for* by showing off the graze from the station attack yesterday. It impressed no-one.

"It's a graze, Feng. Not an amputation," said Susie.

"It could work," said Dolan. "Risky, but doable. I can hear the Laurel and Hardy theme sound-tracking the whole thing though."

Feng shook his head. "By the time they've radioed for help, we'll have dropped the ambulance and be on our way. I've found the perfect spot for the handover. A small cul-de-sac near Princess May school. Completely CCTV free. Two turnings from the nick. Susie will drop Porter off at the second location, next to Hackney Downs. We'll put him in Carson's car and be off. Seriously, we'll be out of Hackney before they've finished calling for help."

"They'll put out an APB on him," said Carson. "They'll be searching for us the length and breadth of the country."

"This isn't *Kojak*," said Feng. "The cop at Stokey knows Porter isn't mad. He'll probably tell the doctors they should've taken more care of him."

"What about the stolen ambulance?"

"They'll have it back 5 minutes later. They have tracking devices. It'll be undamaged and safe. Really, it's child's play."

Dolan was the first to come on board. "I want to drive the ambulance."

"Of course," said Feng, brushing crumbs from Dolan's lapel. "I wouldn't consider anyone else."

The A16, near Merck
Saturday, April 1st 2017: 1.09pm

Namita and Karin watched the unappetizing bum-crack of a middle-aged French arse as its owner tinkered under their bonnet. It had taken an hour to find a garage; two more waiting for the mechanic to get to them. He'd wasted another half an hour chatting them both up in broken English.

He emerged, shaking his head. He said two words and both women groaned. "Le garage."

"So much for a quick in-and-out," said Karin.

"What shall we do?"

"Let's get the car fixed. If not, let's hire a car. We have to do this."

"As long as I'm back by tonight."

The mechanic finished clamping the car to the back of his truck. With a grin, he gestured for them to climb up in the cab.

"Bagsy you go in the middle," said Karin.

Church Lane, Walthamstow
Saturday, April 1st 2017: 4pm

Feng arrived home with a sigh. He had the Doves onside but, my Goff, what a pestilential bunch of buffoons they were. He made himself at home and called his cousin William in Broadstairs. "William, it's Feng."

"Feng, you old goat. How are you?"

"Good, good. Mrs Hoang still in fine fettle I hope?"

"She's in Beijing for a wedding. Cat's away and all that."

"Why, what are you up to?"

"Nothing obviously," said William with a sigh. "She took my claws out years ago."

"I need a favour."

"Guns? Money? Drugs? Dancing girls?"

"Keys."

"Keys?"

"To your cottage. And your old camper van."

"And then the dancing girls? Am I right?"

"I'm more dancing boys, remember?"

"Whatever lights your candle."

"Nothing like that William. I'm hosting a couple of friends, and we need a place to stay for a few nights."

"The door keys are under the mat, camper van keys on a hook by the door. You know the drill."

Feng thanked him.

"And Feng?"

"Yes?"

"You're not going to make me regret this are you?"

"Me?"

"It's just that my delightful wife still has *her* claws. You know what I mean?"

"Check that. All innocent," he lied.

"Enjoy then. I'm off - promised to have the decking creosoted by the time she gets back."

Feng hung up on his hen-pecked cousin and considered how best to fill his evening. He had re-tried both Namita and Karin's mobiles. Still dead. It reminded him of the niggle he had about their destination. *Le Petite Chat.*

As he was preparing green tea, he remembered where he'd seen the name before. It was in one of the books about the fighting in Ypres. Which one? He picked up a few volumes, sat back in his armchair, took a sip of tea and opened the first.

He was asleep 15 minutes later.

He woke up at 11pm with a cricked neck to find he'd dropped the book on the floor. It had landed on top of another book, *Ypres: The Battle of Messines.* Cartwright had been accused of trying to give plans for that battle to the Germans. He had meant to read about it for background. Boring, no doubt.

He looked up Le Petite Chat.

It was 3am when he put the book down, its contents excitedly devoured, his imagination working overtime.

"Damn," he said, giving the book its shortest review ever.

Hotel Du Lac, Merck, France
Saturday, April 1st 2017: midnight

"What a disaster," said Namita. "I'm supposed to be back preparing, ready to represent Porter tomorrow morning. We're going to end up in prison ourselves at this rate."

"I know what you mean," said Karin. "Who'd have thought we'd cause so much destruction? Thanks Georges."

Every phone they had tried today had combusted, melted or exploded. The public payphones emitted booms and sparks. The mechanic's mobile had gone up in smoke. Half a dozen hotel phones had fried. It was a minor miracle they weren't being charged with criminal damage.

"Clearly Georges doesn't want us in contact with the others. Yet he hasn't attacked us directly," said Karin. "I wonder what he's playing at?"

"Why interfere with our journey at all? If he'd left the car alone, he could've had the papers and finished us off by now."

"I don't know," said Karin. "I guess we just have to stay on guard and see."

Chapter 39

Stoke Newington Police Station
Sunday, April 2nd 2017: 8.20am

"You're free to go," said Crawley, handing a coffee to Porter.
"Really? What happened?"
"April Fool."
"That was yesterday. Very funny."
"Sorry about that. Your sister and friends are on their way. They said to have you ready at 9am sharp." He took a sip from his own cup of liquid tar and winced. "I'm really sorry about this Porter. I was hoping your solicitor would come up with something."
"Have you even heard from her? She said she'd be here."
"No, I haven't. Sorry."
"A good day to disappear."
Crawley shrugged. "I've held up your sister's crew as long as I can."
"I know." There was a slight pause. "Feng?"
"Sorry."
"Don't worry about it. I'm only being sent to the loony bin by my sister. It's not like I need the support."
Crawley shrugged, unable to help.
"Even The Gliss has gone," muttered Porter, distracted.
"The *what* has *what*?"
"Nothing. Just one more sign the universe has it in for me today."

Opposite Stoke Newington Police Station
Sunday, April 2nd 2017: 8.27am

Feng sat with Dolan in another Turkish café.
"Nervous?" Feng asked.
"Only of getting caught, going to prison and becoming someone's bitch."
"Not of stealing the ambulance itself?"
"How hard can that be?"
"Remind me," said Feng. "What's your favourite film again?"

"*The Italian Job*. Why?"

"Nothing." Incipient regret is a real stomach churner.

Dolan bit his nails. He spat one out, looked sheepishly about and scrabbled to pick it up.

"I should think so," said Feng. "That was disgusting."

"Oh, it's not that. I don't want to leave DNA."

"Oh, come on… Quit with the *CSI* fetish. They're not going to run DNA searches over a joyride."

"It's kidnap, Feng."

"We're springing him, that's all. He can call in later and let Crawley know he's ok. We're not sending bits of him back in a box."

"It wouldn't surprise me if that was your real plan."

The two lapsed into quiet. Dolan nibbled his third doughnut of the session, Feng sipped his fourth coffee.

"How did Porter react to your plan," said Dolan, wiping sugar from his mouth.

"Ah, about that."

"You did tell him, right?"

"Not in so many words."

"Which means?"

"No. I didn't tell him."

"Why not? He might jump me while I'm driving. He doesn't know me. He might think I'm Mossad or something."

"Unlikely. Just tell him Feng sent you."

"I don't like this."

"It'll be fine."

"Where will you be?"

"Here, then with Susie. I'll jump out when she drops us to Carson."

"How you doing that? I intend to floor it, and I bet Susie does too. You don't look like a sprinter."

"I've got a cab waiting. As soon as –"

Feng saw a private ambulance 100 metres down the road.

"That could be them. Ready? Let's go."

By the time Feng had paid up, a large Volvo was parked outside the station with its flashers on.

"That's probably the doctors. They're all here then. Hope they get a ticket for parking on the red route," said Feng. He handed a plastic bag to Dolan. "Don't forget to tip this shit in the back when you dump the ambulance."

"What is it?"

"Old needles and some used heroin wraps. Decoy. Not difficult to find where I live."

Feng started off towards Princess May Road and the waiting Susie. He looked back and had a widescreen overview. Porter's sister, her female doctor friend and another official, stood arguing with DCI Crawley on the steps of the station. The other side of the road, Dolan was walking in circles and biting his nails. He looked about as innocent as Trump at a pool party.

"Damn fool," said Feng. "Look at him. I've seen hungry zoo lions pacing less than that."

Something was happening on the station steps. A woman in a suit was signalling to the ambulance driver. A woman with a blonde ponytail, wearing a green boiler suit, got out of the ambulance and slammed the door behind her. Good. She hadn't locked it. He watched Porter emerge blinking into his first daylight for three days. Crawley patted him on the back.

Damn. Feng's waiting cab had gone. The driver decided he was better off taking two jobs than waiting around for Feng's potential one.

Shitty, shitty, shitty-poos. A quick calculation. It would take 10 mins brisk walking to get to Susie. He didn't have his bus pass. No choice. Run. He started off, instantly huffy-puffy. He heard a commotion and glanced back.

Porter, still shouting at his sister, was being shoved into the back of the ambulance. The woman in the suit was climbing into the rear of the Volvo. With a loud flooring of the accelerator, the £150,000 ambulance shot off.

"Oi," shouted the driver, running uselessly to the spot where her vehicle had stood.

"Hey," shouted DCI Crawley reaching for his radio.

"Ow!" shouted Porter who was thrown forward and almost onto the street but was batted back by the heavy, flapping door.

Dolan burned rubber. The ambulance caught up with jogging Feng, its back-doors still banging and flapping. The rear right door was swinging dangerously into oncoming traffic. The vehicle screeched to another rubber-burning halt. The door swung inwards, knocking Porter flat again.

"Get in the back!" Dolan screamed to Feng from the cab. Feng didn't need telling twice and hopped in the back of the ambulance, which once again set about breaking the land speed record.

One minute and two turns later, the ambulance braked violently. Porter and Feng - rowing loudly - jumped out and got into Susie's car. Susie threw Dolan a cap and jacket. Dolan wiped the steering wheel down with wet wipes. He chucked his flimsy disguise on and strolled nervously back onto the High Street in the direction of Stokey nick.

"That's the one place they won't be looking for you," Feng had explained. "Dump the keys and go home."

Two minutes after the kidnap, all were on their respective ways. Susie drove sensibly and quietly. She said they would be with Carson in five.

"Will you tell me what the hell is going on?" shouted Porter. "What do you think you're doing?"

"There's plenty of time for you to go to the loony bin," said Feng, "but not so much time to solve this case. Had to get you out."

"You know, until 5 minutes ago I hadn't done anything wrong. Now I'm a fugitive!"

"The ambulance is more important than you. Believe me, they'll be looking for that first, giving it the once over to see what drugs have gone missing. They'll only start looking for you once they've realised everything is fine. By then, we'll be on our way to Broadstairs."

"Broadstairs? What are you talking about? Are you mad?"

"We've got to go and rescue Karin Pelenot and Namita. They went looking for Harry's missing diary pages and have gone missing."

"What missing diary pages?"

Feng tutted. "Because you've been putting your feet up, doesn't mean the rest of us have."

"Now, now people. No violence in this car," said Susie. "Here he is."

Carson was pacing up and down in the little cul-de-sac at the back of Sandford Terrace. They weren't far from the police station at all.

"We're only a minute from the station and it's my third vehicle in 10 minutes," said Porter, climbing into Carson's jalopy. "Oh, it's you," he said spotting Carson, remembering their first meeting at St Briavels. Carson nodded.

"That's the beauty," said Feng. "No-one's looking for this car, especially not here. Keep your head down and we'll be fine." And he was right. They drove sensibly as if nothing had happened and were passed by several blue flashing lights. The cops had already found the ambulance. The relieved driver was on her way to collect it. It had been off-grid for less than 10 minutes.

Feng tried to re-assure Porter he had a holdall full of clothes for him. Porter seemed less bothered about a change of clothes than the how's and why's of the rescue operation.

"If this will shut you up, take this," said Feng, handing over an old phone. "Call DCI Crawley and let him know you're safe. I picked this up just for you." Porter barely remembered how to work the cheap, old-fashioned mobile phone. "He can't trace you on this," Feng reassured. But if he hoped the phone would end Porter's griping, he was wrong.

"This is madness. Namita could've gotten me out in a few days. This will cause all kinds of problems," said Porter.

"She might have. If she hadn't gone missing," said Feng. "This is best. Come on. Call Crawley."

"What do you mean, *gone missing*?"

It was a difficult phone-call. Crawley was part-amused, part-angry about the ambulance.

"Somebody might have died because of that," he said. "I don't suppose you're going to tell me where you are?"

"I had nothing to do with it, Bob. You know that. I've been with you for days. Couple of junkies trying to find some drugs. But now I'm out, I'm not coming back while my sister is after me."

"And it was nothing to do with Mr Tiān?"

"No!" shouted Feng, unable to resist chipping in.

"Tiān? Is that you? I'm expected to believe that your presence AND the first ambulance heist in Stoke Newington's history, is a complete coincidence?"

"I bumped into him in the street right after the junkies chucked him out the back. *Call Bob Crawley,* I said, or he'll think you've done a jailbreak."

"You've created a hell of a mess for us," complained Crawley. "I'll leave you to it, but, Porter - come back in as soon as you can. It'll help with my paperwork."

"Will do, Bob. I owe you. There's something we have to do first."

"Good luck then. Don't leave the country."

"I won't." Porter hung up. "So, what do we do now, Feng?"

"Leave the country," said Feng.

Porter handled the drive to Broadstairs. Feng explained what had happened and why he thought Namita and Karin were in danger.

"They told me where they were going. I looked it up."

"Messines? The battle plans Cartwright was accused of slipping to the Germans?"

"Right. We should have looked it up before. Do you know how the Battle of Messines started?"

Porter shrugged.

Feng pulled out his notebook. "In 1915, the British Army had the crazy idea of tunnelling under the German frontline and filling the tunnels with high explosives," he summarised from his book without looking up. "Over the next 2 years, the British, with help from Australian tunnelling troops, dug 26 huge caverns under the German frontline."

He stopped to face Porter. "The idea was to detonate them all in one go, decimate the defences and pour in for the mop up."

"Sounds like a big plan," said Porter. "No wonder Cartwright was executed if they thought he was trying to expose that."

"Exactly."

"Did it ever happen?'

"Sure did. On June 7th 1917, at 3.10am, the British set off the mines. Nineteen of them."

"How much high explosive are we talking?"

"About 55,000lbs per mine. More than a 1,000,000lbs overall."

"Must have been noisy," said Porter.

"Immense. They heard it in Downing Street. In Switzerland, seismologists registered a small quake in Belgium. It was the biggest explosion of all time before the American A-bomb tests of 1945," said Feng.

"More than 10,000 Germans died. Those that survived were so shocked, they were easily killed by the advancing British. I read a story about some British soldiers who stumbled into a room full of dead German officers playing cards around a table. The shockwaves had killed them where they sat. There wasn't a mark on their bodies."

Porter mulled it for a few seconds. His face screamed I'm-not-getting-this. "Help me here. What's the connection with Karin and Namita, again?"

"I said 19 mines were detonated. But 26 were dug. All but two were filled with explosives before being discovered, marked as not required or damaged. Three of the mines were cleared after the war. Two fell into disrepair while the war was going on. They were abandoned without being primed. The final two were completed, ready to blow, but never detonated. I think the Germans found them and filled them in."

"But they were cleared years ago?" said Porter.

"That's it though. They never were. One of them, near a place called Le Pelegrin, was hit by lightning in 1955 and blew up. No-one was killed, fortunately."

"Which, if my maths is correct, leaves one," said Porter.

"Discovered by the Germans and filled in, but the explosives were too unstable to move."

"And it's still there? Really?"

"Really. Under a farm on the Messines Ridge called La Cheval Noir. And guess where Karin and Namita are heading?"

"To the farm? How did he send them there? What was that you said about Harry's missing diary? Sod it, Feng, I wish you'd kept me more up to date."

Feng shushed him. "It's easier if you listen to Namita's message, then you'll know what I know."

Feng, it's Namita. I'm with Karin. We're heading off for the day to Ypres to go and get the missing pages from Harry's diary. Yep, we didn't know there were any either, but Karin got a message from the ghost thing last night. It claims to be Pelenot. He's given her instructions to go to a place called La Cheval Noir, used to be a farm in Flanders called Le Petite Chat.

We've got to find a well in the garden and dig a hole nearby where he buried the papers after Harry's death. I know this all sounds mad, but Karin really wants those papers so Pelenot can't make a religious artefact out of them after he destroys the world or something. I'm along for the ride. I'll be back this evening. Call me if you or Porter need anything.

"And you haven't heard from them?" said Porter.

"Their phones are dead, and they didn't come back last night."

"Shit."

"Something like that. On the plus side, there's been nothing on the news about a big explosion in Belgium."

"What are we talking about here? You think Pelenot is trying to lure them to the farm to blow them up? Seems a bit elaborate."

"I thought that. One thing's for sure, if what I read in that book is anything to go by, they're in real danger and so is everything within a few miles."

"How bad?"

Feng opened his rucksack and pulled out the book about the Messines Ridge operation. "I found this. It's a quote from General Sir Charles Harrington talking to various journalists the night before the explosion. He said, 'Gentleman, we may not make history tomorrow, but we shall certainly change the geography.' And take a look at this."

Feng held out the book to show Porter a large pool. "This crater is 250 yards wide and is now filled with water and known as a peace memorial. One of the ones that blew in 1917."

"Shit."

"I presume you agree we need to head the women off at the pass?"

"Definitely."

"As you are the one who brought him into being and, hopefully, will be the one to send him back one day, I'm guessing you are probably his main target. Let's hope we all make it back in one piece."

"Why are we going to Broadstairs?"

"To pick up our escape pod."

St Christopher's Place, London
Sunday, April 2nd 2017: 1.30pm

"And then, one of his friends hijacked the ambulance, and now he's on the run," said Cherry, finishing her account with a sip of Montrachet.

"You're kidding?" said Tania. "Are the police looking for him?"

"Of course not. If anything, I thought the copper in charge was on Porter's bloody side. Trouble is, he hasn't actually done anything illegal. He was kidnapped. He's on the run from us. The people trying to make him better."

"Is he that bad?"

"He started investigating the family curse. He tried to commit suicide. Porter wrote us both suicide notes. He's talking to himself. He says he sees ghosts."

"I hope this is nothing to do with me?" said Tania, artfully making the situation about herself.

"To be honest," said Cherry, choosing her words carefully, "it's hard to divorce all this from, well, your *divorce*. He's obsessed with getting back with you."

"Not gonna happen. I told you that," said Tania, poking an olive with a toothpick. "I love the guy, you know that, but we're completely incompatible. If I have to hear him talk about Jerome bloody Kern one more time or how the playback timbre of 78s is part of the aesthetic architecture of how we imagine the past, I'll kill him." She flicked her immaculate hair and smiled at the handsome young waiter who was too busy to notice the middle-aged lady on table seven.

"We went to *Lovebox* last year. Porter was like - *how can you listen to that Boom Boom! Boom! Boom! music?* He's stuck in the thirties," said Tania.

Cherry surprised herself. "He's not clueless. He's very contemporary actually. No-one knows more about computers than him. He just happens to like old music too."

"Sure," said Tania, "but it was awful. I sit down for a bit of *EastEnders* and on comes Bing Crosby at full blast singing *Leilani*. I mean, come on!?" After calming a little: "Where do you think he is?"

Cherry shifted uncomfortably. "No idea. He knows we're trying to have him sectioned. He's not going to rush to come forward. You know Orit, don't you? She's furious. She went out on a limb to help him. She's keeping an eye on his flat as we speak, but I don't think he'll go there in a hurry."

"You make it sound like a spy film."

"*Keystone Cops* more like. You should have seen that ambulance - doors swinging, careening about like an outtake from *The Fast and Furious*. My stupid brother was bouncing about in the back like a wallaby on speed. If nothing else, I bet his arse is the colour of a plum."

"Greengage?"

"Damson. From the bruising."

"I hope he's ok, wherever he is. You don't think he'll be home tomorrow then? I've got to pick some stuff up from the flat. He said he'd stay away, but I don't believe him. I guess he won't show his face now."

"Can't show it. If he does, Orit will bust his plummy arse. What are you picking up?"

"My vinyl. He'll be glad when it's gone. David Guetta remixes are not exactly his thing. Don't repeat any of this if he gets in touch. I really don't want him to know we're still talking."

Cherry bridled. "Yes, I can keep a secret, Tania."

"Make sure you do. Dessert?"

Chapter 40

Eurotunnel exit Calais, France
Sunday, April 2nd 2017: 2.48pm

Clear of customs and police, Feng pulled over in William's red VW camper and yanked out the boxes he had stacked on top of Porter.

"Comfy? Time to get you out," said Feng, with a smile.

Porter was unsmiling. He had been wedged in for over an hour. Houdini would have thought it a tough ask. "I think I'm getting gangrene." With a few grunts and ows, he emerged in roughly the same shape he went in. "That was agony," he said. "My kneecaps have a migraine."

"It got you here without a passport."

"Are you even insured?"

"I put myself on William's yesterday. I don't drive regularly, so my no claims bonus is sensational. It was a bit scary getting this thing on and off the train though. I scraped a few walls. I'm glad you're taking over again."

"What now?" said Porter, grabbing the flask of tea Feng pushed over to him.

"We've got to find Namita and Karin. We'll deal with Pelenot when he comes. What does The Gliss say?"

"Nothing. He's disappeared. For good this time. I did some thinking in my cell. It was quite therapeutic, if uncomfortable."

"Any therapy that's any good is uncomfortable."

"I meant the bed, Feng. But you're right. I admitted to myself that I've been depressed. Maybe Cherry was right? I should be locked up while they sort me out? It's really bugging me: have I been hallucinating The Gliss?"

Porter turned the cup around in his hands as a distraction. "He doesn't show up on your machines, no-one else can hear him. I can't be sure I'm not imagining him. He certainly looks like a composite of every damn robot I ever saw. If he's supposed to be some kind of guide, where is he? Where did he come from? Figment or not, I need him now."

Feng shook his head. "I thought you were disturbed when we first met. But now…I've seen strange things that are nothing to do with you. You didn't burn those books or suspend all that glass mid-air. *Something's* happening. I even told The Doves I'd seen a ghost. The loss of face was excruciating."

Feng took a swig of tea. "And yes, I admit, none of this makes much sense, but think how much we've uncovered because The Gliss told you about Cartwright. That's all real. Where did that all come from if The Gliss is only your delusion?"

Porter nodded, shaking out an arm, to fill the last bloodless inch. Feng slapped it in a sympathetic gesture, aimed at restoring circulation. It stung instead.

"Sorry about that," said Feng, as Porter wiped tea from his lap. "The Gliss must exist, Porter. You're just disappointed the rest of us can't see him/it. That's fair enough."

Porter sipped the last of his tea. "Let's get going. It's going to take a few hours before I stop feeling like a spatchcock chicken, however long you pummel me."

"It's not the most scenic of journeys, but Ypres - here we come."

"I'm not as enthusiastic as you. I just hope Karin and Namita are ok," said Porter.

Messines, Ypres
Sunday, April 2nd 2017: 2.48pm

Karin and Namita were ok, but fed up, annoyed with each other and considerably poorer than when they left England.

The engine problem turned out to be entirely un-supernatural in origin, but entirely to be expected if you don't have your car serviced regularly. Karin, who was paid £40,000 per episode of *History ThisStory,* was not poor. However, she had picked up the wrong bag and left her credit cards at home. She was forced to ask Namita to stump up the extortionate car and hotel bills.

Namita agreed. She would have declined anyone else. She wasn't exactly in awe of her famous new acquaintance, but something about Karin made her feel inadequate. Fame has that effect.

Namita was also painfully aware of their respective salaries. She expected to run her own legal practice one day but had seen the tabloid stories: Karin pulled in more per episode of *History ThisStory* than Namita earned in a year.

There was also the mundane question of whether she had funds available. Her parents had enticed her to New Delhi for a family wedding in January. She wasn't sure how much financial wiggle room she had left. She heard her card scream with every new swipe.

The car engine now worked again. The sat-nav, however, was kaput. After wasting an aimless hour, they found a map in a service station.

"Analogue it is," said Karin.

"I'm a terrible map reader," said Namita.

"Remember that the blue lines are rivers and we'll be fine," said Karin.

They had entirely given up on electronics and phones. Earlier, Karin had bought a TomTom with Namita's card. It fizzled out the second they turned it on. The petrol station manager had refused to give them a refund. More than a dozen pay-phones had shorted along their route.

"Karin, why are we trying so hard to contact Porter? He'll have been transferred by now, and I can't help anyway. Feng knows where we're heading. If he doesn't hear from us soon, he's the kind of person who'll send out a search party."

"He's a bit…er eccentric, don't you think?"

"Not eccentric, no. He's barking mad. A sceptical ghost-hunter. What's that all about?"

"Namita?"

"Yes?"

"What are we doing here then?"

Silence.

"I don't know about you," said Karin, "but I still want to phone home to check how my grandfather is. You got anyone special?"

"Not really."

"Meaning?"

"No."

"Me neither, if you don't count Arthur."

Namita, itching to bring up Karin's career and fame, seized her chance.

"Doesn't being on TV mean you get hit on more often?"

"No, funnily enough, I think it scares people off. I get lots of attention, but no-one hits on me."

Perhaps, if she sorted her hair out, toned down the smell of tweed and dropped the strict schoolteacher act, they would? Namita wasn't having a good trip. Looking out the window, she caught her reflection in the wing mirror and sighed. Not even a grandfather to go home to. Karin put a CD on. Brahms. "How come the CD player works but nothing else?" said Namita, who preferred hard EDM to Western Classical.

"Georges seems to only mess with comms equipment," said Karin, turning up the volume. "He doesn't appear to mind us enjoying ourselves."

Not that Brahms had anything to do with "enjoyment" as far as Namita was concerned. She watched the Belgian countryside whizz past and asked herself the question that had troubled her for years: Why were the English so bloody obsessed with the two World Wars? She could understand it if you'd lived through one of them. But those people were nearly all dead.

Her Hindu family had suffered during Partition and had fled Pakistan for India. Several members of her extended family had died, generations had lost access to their ancestral homeland, and a natural enmity of Muslims was born which Namita secretly carried to this day. Yet, she had no compulsion to watch endless programmes about Partition, read books or see movies glorifying the violence of the time.

The British though… whole TV channels and walls of bookshops devoted to the two conflicts. So many movies! Harry Patch, the last WW1 soldier, was long dead. The Queen, who was in her 90s, was a teenager during World War II. That's how long ago it was. Get over it! And yet, here she was, despite her cynicism, caught up in a madman's nonsensical wartime obsession. Ridiculous.

Karin was also stewing. She had regretted bringing Namita from the first. She was everything she disliked; angry, bitter and her ambition reeked like a teenager's aftershave. She expected Namita to give her a card any minute and say, "If you ever need a solicitor…"

Karin glanced at her passenger who was letting the wind blow through her hair. Ok, maybe she wasn't that bad. She caught a reflection of her own make-up-free face. *You're just jealous, aren't you? Doing that imperious snob thing, again. Stop it.*

Namita opened the map. Winds, swirling around the car, caught it with a punch. "The map's tricky," she said, narrowly stopping it from flying out the window. "My research on Wikipedia and Google threw up answers with French names. Out here, the signs are in Flemish. It's taken me over an hour to realise Ieper is Ypres. Sorry. Messines, I think is, Mesen. If that's the case, the farm will be about three miles ahead. Are we on Ploegsteert?"

"I saw something like that. What will we do when we find it? It won't be dark for another couple of hours," said Karin. "We can't go up to the farmer and tell him we're digging up his field."

"We'll sneak it in the dark," said Namita. "If we get caught, we'll say we're history buffs."

"I guess that wouldn't make me a liar anyway. Bet they have a bloody dog."

There was neither dog nor farmer. The family were away for a wedding in Bruges. However, as the farmer hadn't put up a sign advertising this, Karin and Namita were doomed to spend a couple of hours needlessly scoping the area out.

"They're out," Namita concluded eventually.

"Any CCTV?"

"Too old-fashioned."

"Yeah, they could've filmed *The Hobbit* here. Ready?"

"Not really, no," said Namita, eyeing the farm with great suspicion.

"Me neither. Come on."

Namita lifted a pitted iron hoop holding a rotten wooden gate in place, and swung it open with an alarming creak. In they went.

They had passed similar unremarkable farms earlier. But they weren't trespassing on those. This empty building felt dark and dangerous - nothing like the modern farms both had sometimes seen on TV. Those were full of shiny Massey-Fergusons, spotless milking facilities, and farmers in white aprons and hairnets. This farm, in contrast, was evidently run by Ma and Pa Larkin.

"It's got a touch of The Wurzels," said Karin, showing her age.

"Does it? What's that then?"

"Nothing."

Karin flicked a switch. Her torch worked fine. Georges' largesse extended to their torch batteries. Maybe he really did want them to find the papers?

"Are you getting bad vibes? Or is it just me?" asked Namita.

"We've been sent here by a malevolent ghost. A touch of bad vibe is probably *de rigeur*."

A large barn loomed to their left.

"Let's check that out," said Karin.

They squelched and skidded on the messy combo of mud and grit, before rounding the top of the barn to face an open field.

"Look!" said Namita. "Is that it? Put your light over there."

"Well I never," said Karin. The small brick well was three metres from the end of the barn. It was circular and dilapidated.

"If that has a black brick, I'm going to have to re-think my entire life," said Namita.

"You and me both."

Knee-high weeds and grass obscured the base. They pulled out as much as they could and examined the well. It was Namita who saw it first. "I can't believe it. Look." There was one black brick.

Karin whistled. "We're not in Kansas anymore, are we, Dorothy? I guess we can assume the diary pages really do exist then?"

"I hope he wrapped them up good. They've had a century to rot."

"Yes, I did wonder. Everything checks out so far," said Karin. "But stay on guard. Georges may try and kill us immediately we get the pages. Look what happened to Porter last time. Georges wants them, but maybe he wants to find them just to destroy them."

"What direction do we have to pace?"

"He didn't say. Let's go perpendicular from the brick."

Namita looked at the sky, imagining lightning striking them in the open, and shuddered. "You're the historian. Do you want to dig, or do you need a hand? I can stand back a bit and keep watch?"

"I've got trowels with me. It'd be quicker if you dug too."

They followed Georges' instructions precisely. Karin did the pacing. With her back to the well, she walked a 9ft straight line. The pair got to their knees and checked for any obvious booby trap.

"Looks like grass to me," said Namita.

"Me too. Let's dig."

They had no way of knowing if they were in the exact area Georges intended, so they marked out a 2m^2 target. For the next hour, they excavated the square, kneeling and digging from outside the deepening pit. Sterile. Nothing but worms and pebbles.

When the stretching got uncomfortable, first Karin, then Namita, jumped in.

"My hands are sore," said Namita. "Do you develop archaeologist digging chops doing this all the time?"

"Definitely. But I ache too: I'm the face of popular archaeology, not its hands." She sighed nostalgically. "I do miss slopping around in the mud. In the absence of chops, I'll have to grit my teeth."

About half a metre down, Karin hit something. It made an ominous *ching* sound. "Oh great."

"What is it?"

"A shell."

"Unexploded?"

"Will check the cap. Yep." Karin sat back on her haunches and sighed.

"Damn," said Namita.

"We have to move it."

"Isn't that dangerous? Do you think Pelenot knew it was there? I'm frightened."

"Probably but he could have detonated it any time in the last 10 minutes. We'd be steaming mincemeat. I've read a bit about this; there's only a tiny chance it'll go off. The army moves hundreds every week. Don't stress. C'mon - jump out. I'll do it. I'm used to getting delicate stuff out of the ground."

"Are you sure about that? It'll slow us down a bit if it's just you, but, ok, if you insist," said Namita, only too happy to take a few steps back.

"Better slow than dead."

Namita, stood a good 12 paces back from the hole, waiting impatiently, checking her watch and wishing she had a warmer coat.

"Give me your scarf please," Karin barked.

"My scarf?"

"Come on. I've got to move this thing. I need a sling."

"It was expensive."

"Ok, I'll throw this shell to you…"

"Ok, ok," Namita chuntered, unwrapping as she went.

Karin lifted the 12-inch shell delicately onto the scarf, keeping it as close to its original orientation as possible. "I've no idea whether the fuse is intact, missing or damaged," she said. "Let's try not to disturb it."

She made a fragile Christmas cracker out of the scarf, and the pair took an end each. "The scarf should absorb some of the shock of moving it," said Karin, deftly using one hand to stop the shell from rolling in the sling.

Gingerly, they took the casing to the other side of the barn. Lowering it gently, Karin shaped some mud to create a cradle. With fingers of ice dragging down their backs, the two of them sprinted back to the other side of the large barn.

"If it does go off, the barn will shield us," said Karin. Silence. The pair resumed digging.

"Can you hear something?" said Karin, halting the excavation.

"It's the ground," said Namita. "I can hear some kind of rumbling."

Karin knelt down further and put her ear to the ground. "Yes, you're right. There's something below us, it sounds like sucking? I think we –" She got no further.

The mud gave way. Both women found themselves tumbling into air, bashing their heads against each other, rocks and roots. The fall seemed to last forever before they hit the ground.

Karin hit the wet floor first, Namita a second later, already unconscious from head-butting a rock. Karin spat out some dirt and groped around until she found her companion. "Namita, are you ok?" She checked the limp body for a pulse. Relieved to find one, she immediately abandoned Namita to grope around for the torch. They were in trouble if she didn't find it. She grunted with relief when her fingertips brushed the barrel of the torch.

Flicking it on, she looked straight up. She could see the sky through a ragged hole. It was, what? 6m, 7m, 8m above? Difficult to tell. The subtle echoes she'd heard from her voice suggested it was a big man-made space. She turned to see if she could work out where she was.

The scanning torch revealed a massive cavern, its roof supported by rotting wooden beams. Great. Going further afield, Karin saw what looked like the world's biggest collection of Toblerone bars. What the...? She moved some of the cobwebs and dust aside and shone the torch at the chocolate boxes. *Amatol* was printed on the side. High explosive blocks. There appeared to be about a million of them.

"Oh shit. Oh shit. Oh shit. Now you're in trouble, Karin Pelenot." Her voice echoed around the abandoned mine. Namita's ghostly moans as she regained consciousness did nothing to calm Karin's unease.

Messines, Ypres
Sunday, April 2nd 2017: 3.40pm

"These Belgian motorways aren't as good as their chocolates," said Feng, stuffing his face from a tin picked up from services.

"That should be Godiva's new slogan," said Porter, whose arms were tired. The old VW had been restored but still handled like a pig with a saddle.

"I bought the Godivas as a thank-you for Griffee, but to be honest, I'm starving," admitted Feng.

"We're only an hour from Ypres. If we're lucky, we'll find the girls quickly."

"I wouldn't call them *girls* to their face."

"Nor would I. I wonder why I said that?"

Feng was about to explain his theories about casual sexism when a Fiat Uno in the lane opposite, lost control and veered across the road into their path. Porter managed to dodge it, swerving into the hard shoulder. The Fiat skidded to a halt in the road, the driver throwing his hands in the air in shock.

"What the hell was he playing at!" blasted Feng. "We could've been killed."

"Porter," said The Gliss, appearing on cue for the next disaster. "Err... how good were you on the dodgems?"

"I tried to hit everything, why?" said Porter.

Feng's antenna was straight up. "Shit. The Gliss. That was no accident, was it?"

"Nor is this," said Porter wide-eyed, springing to attention.

The north and southbound lanes were separated by a small concrete curb, and 1m of grass, as close as this road got to a central reservation. 100 metres ahead, a red Volvo estate accelerated and swerved into the curb. The angle was too shallow and the car, driven by a surprised-looking brunette, bounced into the air and corkscrewed back onto the motorway, landing on its roof and sliding into a mini.

"Get away! Drive faster!" screamed Feng.

"Are you serious? I've been in faster shopping trolleys. Crap. Look."

Further down the road, a white van, driven by two fierce-looking young men had reversed and parked. It was now sitting on the hard shoulder, at right angles to the road, facing the central reservation head on.

"They're waiting for us," said Porter. "Feng, can you be rear gunner and make sure nothing comes at us from behind."

"It's all about the timing," said Feng, eyeing the white van. "Vary your speed, or they'll have you."

Porter slammed the brakes on as the white van began revving up its engine.

"If we were on the M1, we'd be donating organs by now," said Feng. "Thank God it's quiet. Nothing behind."

The Gliss moved to the dashboard area. Porter wasn't sure whether this was a comfort or not.

"Mind control," said The Gliss. "This is how powerful this thing has become. It was struggling to get you to poke your eye out a week ago. Now it's turning drivers kamikaze."

"Maybe it'll run out of power in a second?" said Porter.

"Maybe. Probably. But you've got to outrun it first."

Porter revved up, gunning the accelerator like he was stamping out fire. The VW picked up what speed it could. On cue, the white van's wheels started spinning, brakes still on, rubber smoke drifting onto the motorway. It was 100 metres, 90 metres, 80 metres, away.

"Either speed the flip up or slow the flip down," shouted Feng.

At 50 metres away, the driver of the van took his brakes off. It left stasis like a greyhound springing from the traps.

"It's gonna hit us!" screamed Feng.

Porter maintained a straight line. The van would hit them square on at about 70mph. When the trailer was five metres away, Porter swung the steering wheel violently to the left. The VW virtually left the road but cut inside the van's trajectory. The driver saw Porter's move at the last moment and corrected to the right. He was too late. The van clipped the back of the VW, causing a window frame to pop, and Feng to shout, "Watch it!" as he was thrown from side to side, taking hits to face, guts, bollocks. The enemy's impetus carried their van into the central reservation, the front axle breaking with a loud snap.

Porter, to his amazement, found he was still alive, still driving. The reduction in speed after the swerve allowed him to straighten up on the hard shoulder. "Where's power steering when you need it," he said, sweating. "You ok, Feng?"

"I feel like a kitten in a blender," Feng managed, his hands massaging his bruised groin.

"Nothing's coming right now. Are we safe?" Porter asked The Gliss.

"You're nearly there," The Gliss replied. "I'd get off this road if I were you."

"I hope Namita and Karin are having an easier time of it," said Porter.

They weren't.

Chapter 41

Messines, Ypres
Sunday, April 2nd 2017: 5.22pm

The attack came as a shock. Georges Pelenot's invisible hands were suddenly everywhere. Jabbing and penetrating, he pinched and probed Karin and Namita's skins and spaces as effortlessly as if they were tied down and naked. How could they fight what they could not see? Windmilling arms, kicking and screaming: none of it made any difference. Pelenot wasn't just winning - there were no other competitors in the room.

Namita, still hurting from the fall, carried another disadvantage, bordering on a disability: she was weak from a lifetime of familial love. Her life just hadn't been tough enough to breed a warrior. In contrast, Karin had survived boarding school, absent parents - and years of dealing with TV commissioners. Her skin was already inches thick and freed her to fight a battle of wills with anyone or anything.

Her mental resistance infuriated her sadistic ancestor. Pelenot stole mean pinches for punishment. Unseen lobster-claw fingers grabbed at Karin's breasts. One twist of skin on her arm made her yelp and lose concentration. *Hold that picture, Karin. Don't let him in. Remember the gun in the attic – it's not real.* But the searing pain made it hard to maintain her defences in an unbroken line.

At least you're not Namita, poor bitch. The solicitor was partially lit whenever she jig-jagged through the torch beam. Karin heard her screaming obscenities, crying out for help from…*Sangita? Who the hell is Sangita? Did I miss something?*

Namita was pushing hands away from her groin but the yelps and screams suggested jab after jab, pinch after pinch, were hitting home. Karin had no time to empathise. Georges grabbed her bob, yanking her to the floor. A strand of hair fluttered away like a sycamore seed, eerily backlit by her Maglite. Through her own pain, she saw Namita again, scarcely human now, whirling and screaming.

Karin hurt like she'd been whipped with barbed wire, but regained her focus. *Pain? Yes. Fear? God, yes.* She understood this was a battle of wills. In a flash of inspiration, she pictured Georges' gun. She aimed it at him but didn't get to fire. The image broke as another jolt of pain wilted her concentration. She fell backwards, sharp rocks slicing into her knee and leg as she tumbled. But pain could not hide what she had just sensed: George's panic when the revolver was levelled at him. And a sensation of something changing within him: *Gears slipping on a bike. Was that all it took to weaken him? Was Georges really scared of his own gun? Maybe Feng had been right about something, at least?*

Close to vomiting, she re-imagined the pistol. *No time to waste.* She imagined Georges in his photo, took aim and fired six shots into his gut.

The physical assault on her stopped immediately, giving Karin the opportunity to shout, "It's all in your head, Namita. Just picture him. Kill him in your mind. He's weak. Push back, Namita!"

It went unheard and unacknowledged. The solicitor screamed again, brushing at her stomach and groin as though she was being tattooed with acid.

Karin watched in frustration. She'd seen a video of a boy after a Box Jellyfish attack. Writhing and screaming, his heart stopped twice as bystanders tried to save him. He looked like he was getting a pleasing massage compared to Namita's suffering now. Karin shouted further instructions and encouragements, but Namita didn't or couldn't hear. *C'mon Georges – what's your game here? Sate yourself and go away.*

The attack finished abruptly when Namita was thrown with force against the wall of the chamber. Mud and dirt dislodged. Karin eyed the explosives with fear. Clumps fell from the roof to the ancient duckboards. Namita's head came to rest on her chest. She was unconscious. *God, she's out again.*

Karin caught her breath and wondered if anything could be more terrifying than the last ten minutes. *Oh, great. Yes, it could.*

Georges Pelenot appeared in person. He shimmered, a barely-flickering, transparent figure, floating over Namita's body. It was undoubtedly him, dressed in full uniform.

Karin shuddered and looked for somewhere to hide, though she knew there was nowhere to go. George's appearance made her crave somewhere safe - like her mother's childhood embrace. Or next best thing: a cave in Tora Bora with bomb-proof doors.

To her horror, the apparition spoke. "Nice try with my pistol. It will not work. I grow stronger by the hour. Next time you see me, you both die - you and your idiot friends, galloping for you like white knights of old."

Were Porter and Feng on their way then? Karin's heart beat a little faster.

"Why?" managed Karin. "If you just want to kill us, what was all that crap about Harry Norton's diary?"

Georges smiled. "You're the only ones who know. Why not in a reprise of our greatest pre-Versailles moment?"

"Only ones who know what? What pre-Versailles moment? Stop talking in riddles."

"As for the pages story... what better way to attract a busy-body librarian like you?"

"Why would you do this? What's wrong with you?" Karin spat the words out, as much condemnation as enquiry.

"Because I was maltreated at Eton as a boy," said Georges.

"Really?"

"Of course not. Humans. Always looking for a pat answer."

"You are human. Well, were. What was it then? The trenches? They caused this derangement?"

"That word implies a progression from normality to insanity. But I never knew different, dear relative. I killed animals for fun as a child. I pushed a friend to his death out of a tree when I was 11. I took one of our maids when I was 16 - holding a kitchen knife to her Mound of Venus. She never dared protest, never said a word, just took another berth. The war was made for people like me."

"Mad then, mad now - is that it?" said Karin.

There was a flicker. His anger brought a surge of power to the apparition which quickly faded again. *His strength is ebbing. Keep him angry.*

"A mad, deluded, small-dicked incompetent whom no-one loved. Not your children, your wife. Or parents."

Another flicker. Another weakening.

"What do you know, harlot?"

"I've seen your mother's papers. You barely get a mention. You were an inconvenience, the biological mistake that ruined her life."

"Whore," said Pelenot. "You're so linear, so stupid. I wasn't demonised or traumatised by the war. I was happy. With each trigger pull, I felt ecstasy. I never cared whether the brains belonged to our side or theirs."

Karin curled a lip and shook her head. "A soulless, murdering misanthrope. Nothing else."

Fading fast, he managed one last threat.

"You die shortly - but not before I rip you…" And was gone.

When you say rip?… Actually, I'd rather not think about it.

"Hurry up, Porter, before this maniac gets his strength back," said Karin out loud, rushing to tend to Namita.

Services near Messines, Ypres
Sunday, April 2nd 2017: 6.07pm

Feng and Porter parked up the battered VW and checked it for damage. The *dangerous* mission had just been upgraded to *potentially lethal*.

"What mission?" said Porter. "This isn't the *A Team*."

"Come now," said Feng. "I don't want to die, true, but did you see that? Zouche said a Profugus could exercise mind control, but you've got to admit, that was awesome. Vans and cars coming at us like pickpockets in Rome."

"It scared me shitless."

"Me too. How exciting."

"You make me feel boring."

"You're depressed. Life's lost its taste. It'll come back. For me, it's one big buzz."

The pair picked at coffees and croissants on a chilly table outside the service station. Porter frowned.

"What's up?" said Feng.

"If the Profugus could do that to us, what's he done to Karin and Namita?"

"We'll be at La Cheval Noir in 20 minutes. We'll find out soon enough."

"That's what worries me."

The pair enjoyed their break. A butterfly landed on Porter's head.

"You've got a butterfly on your head." Porter swatted it away as if it were a hornet. Feng admired it as it flew around. "That's a Holly Blue. How lovely."

"You an expert or something? I can just about identify a Cabbage White."

"No, I just like them." Brushing crumbs from his hands, Feng stood. "Time to go. I'll drive."

"We'll be lucky if the van still works. That last swerve had the cabin going one way and the wheels another. There can't be a stable rivet left."

"If that van survived hippies dragging it to Afghanistan in the 60s, it'll cope with a measly Profugus with the Saevita. The farm's literally down the road. If we drive quick, Pelenot won't be able to pull the same prank."

The Gliss, motionless and hovering, said Pelenot would be weak after the exertion. "But he's getting stronger. He's recovering quicker each time. You need to move."

Porter, with a touch of whiplash, rubbed his neck, grimaced and got to his feet. "I think I preferred writing solicitor's letters reminding companies of consumer rights, if I'm honest," he said.

"Nonsense. I'm in Indiana Jones. Totally exhilarating," said Feng.

"You're a strange man."

"It's on my business card."

"Yes. It might yet end up on your tombstone."

N365, near Messines, Ypres
Sunday, April 2nd 2017: 6.18pm

Back on the road, Porter scowled. "Listen, if they do need rescuing, let me do it," he said. "It's my damn fault they're in this mess. Keep your distance from me. Stay on the road while I'm off it. If he starts exploding shells again, he could take both of us out in an instant. Remember where we are."

"Talking of which," said Feng, "how's your head?"

"Low-level headache only at the mo. The real pain will come when I get near the cemeteries and battlefields." He checked his directions. "One mile on this road, to the left."

"I really think I should come with you."

"Not a good idea. All eggs, one basket etc."

"I can film and record the whole thing."

Porter shook his head. "Waste of time. This damn thing screws up recording equipment. Think about the CCTV at Namita's office, the Starbucks store etc. Everything goes on the blink when he pulls his stunts."

"What you're saying is that I've been wasting my time as a ghost-hunter if I'm seeking a proof?"

"No, I'm saying you'll never get any proof on video. But at least you know the truth now. Now help me bring the damn thing down without both of us getting killed."

"So, I stand at the back and you do the heroics, is that it?" said Feng, disappointed.

"Pull over."

"What?" said Feng, gearing up for a row.

"We need real distance between us, Feng," explained Porter. "Let me go explore the farm. If I'm not back in two hours, come and get me."

Feng argued, but Porter won.

"I'm not happy about it," said Feng, kicking one of the VW's tyres.

"Don't think of it that way. More like a second line of attack. It'll only take me 15 minutes to walk. God knows how long it will take me to find them – if they're here."

"Good luck, Porter. Come and get me as soon as you can."

The pair faced the dark, hedge-lined road that lay in front. Like a lame soldier trailing his battalion, Porter set off. He didn't know it yet, but he was involved in more than one campaign.

Messines, Ypres
Sunday, April 2nd 2017: 6.57pm

Namita stared at the mountain of high explosive in terror. Karin wasn't happy either but did her best to shut the vision out. "Look on the bright side," she said, attempting to complete Namita's thought: "If it does go off, we won't feel anything. It's been here since the First World War. I doubt it's about to go off accidentally now."

"What the hell is it? How come it's still here?" said Namita, massaging her groin.

"Who knows? Clearly, Pelenot knew all about it. Why he's lured us here just to blow us up, when he could have killed us anywhere, I don't know."

Namita considered this. "It doesn't make much sense though. Porter said Pelenot blew up a whole field on his first trip to Ypres. He'd only have to detonate one of these for them all to go, surely? Domino effect."

"I'm sure he could do that. Probably intends to. One can only assume his conditions for setting it off haven't been met yet."

"What do you mean?"

"Pelenot said something earlier which implied Feng and Porter were on our trail."

"Really?" The relief was palpable.

"Maybe he's waiting for them to get here," said Karin. "Remember the White Witch in Narnia wanting all four of the Sons of Adam, Daughters of Eve? Who knows how the supernatural scales work? Maybe Georges needs to get us all in one spot first? Kaboom."

"Shit. Do you think? What else did he say? God, I hurt."

Karin, still bruised and sore herself, wondered how much she should tell Namita. In the earlier battle, Namita had proved to be weak-willed. Would it make things worse to update her that Georges was indeed a mass-murdering sexual sadist?

"Well," said Karin hesitantly, "he said…"

She was cut off by a rushing noise, a massive crash and then groaning. Karin swung the beam of the torch to the centre of the cavern in panic. There, flat on his face, winded and struggling to breathe, lay Porter.

He looked up into the dazzle, saw Karin dimly, and just about managed to raise a hand in greeting.

"Ow," he said.

Chapter 42

Messines, Ypres
Sunday, April 2nd 2017: 6.48pm

Feng sat in the back of the VW camper swigging green tea. He wasn't happy. The girls were dead for all he knew. And yet here he was, side-lined, while Porter walked straight into the same trap. It was obviously a trap, wasn't it?

He stood too quickly and banged his head on the ceiling. He put the pop-top up. Once he had some headroom, Feng pulled out the table, opened his laptop and connected a wi-fi dongle. To his delight, he got a signal. He checked his email.

*From: **pzouche@hotmail.com***
*To: Tiān, Feng <**TF@chizzwhit.com**>*
Attachment: 1

Feng. Hope I'm not interrupting your sweet and sour pork balls or whatever.

You're in trouble, sunshine.

The longer I thought about it, the more I remembered. I got hold of an old amigo, Skelton Ridgeway, who specialised in exorcism back in the day when we were both working at Charing Cross Library. I always tried to keep religion out of my stuff. However, Ridgeway was convinced ghosts and the occult were an essential part of understanding God.

*I was amazed to find the old bugger still alive and peddling his tosh via a website called **OpenThePortal.com**. Anyway, we had an interesting chat.*

He confirmed what I suspected. Profugus with the Saevita. But he knew much more and was able to point me towards the only detailed report of the historic Tokyo case we discussed.

There's an archive in Kyoto which has an account by a famous Japanese occultist, Yori Nakamoto, about the Tokyo fire. He sent me a link. I downloaded a transcription of that, see attached. It's important to read because it contains the incantation - Skelton would call it an exorcism - that can get rid of this thing. And you must get rid of it. That asteroid that killed the dinosaurs? Yeah. That bad. Old Nakamoto was beheaded for his beliefs in the 30s - you're Chinky so you know how handy the Nips can be with their swords - remember Manchuria! - but luckily his records survived.

That particular PWTS was destroyed by a suicidal Samurai, who performed the ritual and just about slew it. How? This is the scary thing, my old chum. The ritual made the PWTS manifest in physical form. And then the Samurai had to kill its physical body using the same method the PWTS had killed as a human before it turned. The pair duelled, the Samurai was mortally wounded but managed to douse the PWTS with oil from a lamp and set fire to it. The Samurai burned alive along with the Profugus. Basically, it's a dangerous business.

If you read the attachment, you will find the incantation you need. Ridgeway said it's like the antibiotic of exorcism. Few have it. He said to use it wisely.

If you want to talk through any of this give me a call.
Zouche

Feng read the attachment. At least the incantation was in English. It was a pile of doggerel. Buffy's scriptwriters could have improved it no end. It didn't scan and was far from poetic.

He pressed the Facetime button. Zouche appeared, picking his nose, with the gusto of the Seven Dwarves digging for diamonds. "I got your email," said Feng. "Thanks."

"Isn't this amazing," said Zouche, shaking his head. "Straight out of *Star Trek*. I can see you!"

"Don't you have young relatives? Video calls have been around a while now."

"No. I was a whole flock of black sheep in my family. Totally on my own for the end of days. Suits me. At least I put myself in here. Wasn't packed off by someone out for an early inheritance."

He wiped his fingers on his blanket, as he realised - if he could see Feng, Feng could see him. "No need to say thanks. I should thank you. The days do get fuzzy here. Doing a bit of research has blown away a little fog. I think I might have given up on all that a bit too soon."

"I've got a few questions."

"Thought you might."

Feng pulled up the incantation. "The way I read it, this verse could give any ghost some sort of physical form?"

"Agreed," said Zouche. "Exactly how I read it."

"Bringing people back from the dead? Wouldn't that change the world?"

Zouche shook his head. "No, Feng, it's only a temporary fix. Maybe the spirit turns physical for a minute or two? It fits my own wider theory that every person has two possible forms - physical and paranormal. They are mutually exclusive. You can only be in one state or the other at any specific point in time. What this incantation does, I think, is act as a revolving door, pushing the paranormal version back to the physical version and vice versa - but only for minutes."

"Long enough to pour oil over it and destroy it with fire for example?" said Feng.

"Just so," said Zouche.

"What about the non-evil ghosts?"

"No idea."

"If this Profugus with the Saevita *is* Pelenot, he killed people by sticking his revolver to their heads. Karin, his granddaughter, still has his pistol from World War 1."

"That's good," said Zouche. "That's a big headstart. And lucky. You'll damn well need it."

"Yeah, he's a master at mind control though," said Feng, recalling the battering-ram cars. He could make us turn the gun on ourselves."

"One of the risks."

Feng updated him on recent events: how he was now the only one of the four investigators he could account for. Zouche frowned when he heard about the unused explosives under La Cheval Noir.

"He'll blow that for sure. Why wouldn't he?" said Zouche. "Probably wants to kill you all, together. Ultimately that's just an explosion - a farm-destroying explosion for sure - but small fry. My big fear has always been a Profugus with the Saevita in a world with nuclear and chemical weapons. Remember, they are sentient."

"I know. I had nightmares about those research facilities where they store all the killer viruses. Bend one nutty professor into opening all the hatches... but what can I do?" said Feng. "Porter's gone off, I'm stuck on my own, and I've no idea where the girls are."

"Read, read, read, while you wait," said Zouche, annoyed. "You're not dealing with a common or garden thug; you're dealing with one of the most powerful forces the planet has ever seen. You can't be over-prepared. Weren't you ever a boy scout?"

"I was actually." And Feng recounted a story about a tent, a flashlight and a scoutmaster that turned Zouche's stomach.

Feng tried Porter's phone. Dead. Of course. Another hour and a half before he was allowed to search for Porter. Reluctantly, he decided to stick to their bargain.

To fill time, he flicked through his research folder, re-reading some of their notes plus a few chunks of Harry Norton's diary. No matter how exciting the past fortnight's adventures had been, he could not believe there really were extant unseen pages from Harry's diary. Where would they have been kept all these years? Ypres had been flattened and rebuilt brick by brick. The ground had been mercilessly churned up by a billion shells. Even Harry's final words, as Porter heard them - "the truth goes with me" - were a sad admission of failure: the truth would never be known. No, whatever had happened to those torn-out pages, they were almost certainly lost to history now.

Feng looked at the photo Porter had taken of his great-grandfather's grave. He envied him this connection to his ancestor. Porter was right. It's important to know where people are buried. He had no idea where he could find the grave of his own father - a Beijing university lecturer who fell foul of Mao Tse Tung during the Cultural Revolution.

Hang on. Wasn't Harry Norton buried in Aeroplane Cemetery? Feng checked and found it was only a few miles away. Rather than sit here like a ninny, he could drive 10 minutes down the road and see for himself? He might as well pay his respects while Porter was playing Indiana Jones. Paying your respects is good. Wait…Jesus H Christ.

An idea spurred him. He dove for his laptop, cursing the snail-slow dongle. He looked up a list of all the cemeteries around Ypres. And who was buried there.

La Cheval Noir Farm, Messines, Ypres
Sunday, April 2nd 2017: 7.08pm

"Not much of a rescue, is it?" said Namita, bashing her head against the wall.

"Easy!" said Karin, as a little more dirt dislodged. "Are you on your own?" she asked Porter. "Is Feng up there?"

"With a rope?" added Namita. "Please tell me he has a rope?"

As soon as Porter put his head in his hands, both women groaned.

"Where is he?" said Karin.

"A mile or so up the road," said Porter, massaging his ankle. "I didn't want to make us an obvious target by coming together. Your great-grandfather tried to kill us on the way here. We're a bit shaken up, to be honest."

Both women looked down at the ground. Porter had an inkling what that might mean. "How bad? I'm sorry. We did try and get here to help."

Namita gestured to Porter to look behind him at the endless mound of high explosives. He did.

"Ah."

"Is that all you've got to say?" said Namita. The air chilled around her.

"Feng said you were heading to the explosives."

"Did he? And he was going to tell us when?" Icicles were forming like a picket fence.

"Namita, our phones weren't working, remember?" chided Karin. "I'm sure they tried."

"Dozens of times," said Porter. "Feng got your message, Namita, realised what it meant and set off to find you. I guess it's no coincidence your phones are out?"

"Not *our* phones, *every* phone we tried," said Namita. "We're here now, with no way out, and a huge pile of explosives sitting opposite us. What was this? An army store?"

Porter told them about the Messines campaign. Karin, sparing the worst for Namita's sake, summarised what had happened to them. "How did you find us?" said Karin.

"I knew you were here somewhere because I saw a car outside with your Wellcome Institute visitor pass on the dashboard. I wandered around the back, didn't see the hole. And here I am." Porter alternated between massaging his head and his ankle.

"You ok?" asked Karin.

"If you believe me now about The Gliss and being able to hear the dead speak…"

"We believe you."

"…well, we're in the middle of a battlefield. There are fragments of dead soldiers all around us, recycled into the earth. That's giving me a blinding headache. No voices, just a giant background hum. It's worse than a migraine."

"And where's The Gliss?" asked Namita. "Maybe he can help us out?"

"He's not a pet dog, unfortunately. I tried calling for him for some advice - but nothing."

Karen tutted. "It would have been good to have something supernatural batting for us right now."

Namita, unconscious throughout Karin's confrontation with Pelenot, looked up. "Now Pelenot can make himself visible and talk," she said, "does that mean I can punch the bastard?"

"I don't think so," said Karin. "But we know he can exercise mind-control, can move physical things, and we know he's gaining strength. I think we'd probably better get out of here as fast as we can."

"You're not going to like this," said Porter. "I think our best way out of here is to move some of the explosives, build a platform, and climb out."

"Are you nuts, Porter?" said Namita. "That stuff's 100 years old. It's unstable."

"You're right. But when the two hours run out and Feng gets here as planned to check I'm ok… well, then all four of us are here. Based on the field he exploded around me, Pelenot can easily detonate one of these blocks."

"How long have we got before he gets here?" said Karin.

"Ninety minutes at most. Then…boom."

The three scrambled to their aching feet, the clock ticking.

A lay-by, Ypres
Sunday, April 2nd 2017: 7.09pm

Feng re-read the incantation ritual. Utter gobbledygook. Carson might have written it. As if reading this bollocks out loud would bring anything back from the dead.

He'd always said The Doves were nutcases. Yet here he was. "Goff. Porter, Zouche - they've really suckered you in," he whispered to the night.

His initial plan had been to head to Harry's grave at Aeroplane Cemetery. But as soon as he passed another deserted cemetery, he realised he could test out the incantation anywhere. He didn't expect it to work and didn't want to feel foolish giving the gobbledygook text its big debut untested in front of the others. If they weren't dead already, that is.

The road around the small cemetery was deserted. Feng jumped the low brick wall. Following the well-maintained path, he soon found himself among tombstones. He picked one at random.

429-675 Rifleman Graham Smith. City of London Rifles 16th September 1917.
Aged 24.

At the bottom of the stone, a further inscription.

Faithful unto death. May he rest in peace.

This one was as good as any. He pulled up Zouche's email and read the verse out loud, shaking his head as he went. Scepticism was his marrow, his DNA, his psyche. It physically hurt him to take this seriously.

Graham Smith, City of London Rifles, wake, wake, wake.
Three times I call you in the name of Hisporatus.
Graham Smith, City of London Rifles, wake, wake, wake.
I give you this short time cycle to return one last time.

"This is stupid. It doesn't scan. There's no poetry. Hisporatus, my arse. They made this stuff up." Aside from his angry whispers, all around was silence. He continued.

Graham Smith, City of London Rifles, wake, wake, wake.
You are welcome to return, I call you now.

"Do you know the password?" said a voice from behind.

Feng, turned, staring in shock at a short, handsome young man dressed as a British Tommy, who was offering him a cigarette. As soon as he smiled, Feng knew he was for real. His teeth looked like someone had put his face-on-fire out with a shovel.

"Where are you from, friend? China? I always wanted to go to China." He held out his hand. "Graham."

"I'm Feng Tiān. Are you really *the* Graham Smith?" Feng gestured at the grave.

"I don't know. I'm *a* Graham Smith. City of London Rifles. But I can't be here *and* in that grave, right? What time is it?"

"2017," said Feng.

"My shift starts at 2030, so I'd better be off."

"Private Smith," said Feng, softly. "I meant, it's 2017, 100 years after you died during the fighting in Ypres. I'm sorry."

The soldier studied Feng. Instead of blowing up in rage or crumpling in despair, a look of acceptance and wisdom blossomed in his face. "I can believe that. I feel as if I've been somewhere else. I can't describe where or how. Where am I now?"

"Ypres. I'm afraid you never left."

"No. That makes sense too." The soldier knelt down on his own grave and traced the lettering on his tombstone. "Do you think my mother ever got to see this?"

"We're standing in the battlefields," said Feng. "They managed to put the landscape back together - eventually. The graves were dug after the war ended. I *hope* your mother saw it."

"I hope so too, Mr Tiān. Is it really 100 years later? What happened? Did we win?"

"Yes, you won. The war ended a year after you died."

"I don't think I could have taken another year," said Private Smith. "You don't seem frightened to see me? I'm not a ghost then?" Feng stepped forward and held out his hand. Private Smith took it and shook it. "Well met," he said with a smile. "Why am I back? Wait... we're about to say goodbye already? I feel it."

"I think that's the way it works. I just wanted to ask if there's anything I can do for you?"

"I'm ok. Nice to have some quiet. Still stings a bit." He gestured down. His intestines were hanging over his belt.

"Was it not quiet, where you were?" stammered Feng.

"Here is all I remember. Last time I was here, it wasn't quiet."

"No."

"Please, take this." Smith pulled a brass button from his coat and a hair from his head. He inserted the hair inside the ball-like button. "You can do me this favour. I grew up near Canizaro Park, Wimbledon. My mother was Prudence Smith, of 254 Worple Road. Please, find her grave and bury this near her headstone? It would be wonderful to know a bit of me made it home."

Surname Smith? Sure. Piece of research cake. "I promise. Thank you, Private Smith."

"Please...Graham, I think. Yes, I want to say my last goodbye as Graham. The military life wasn't for me."

"Thank you, Graham. I promise to do this for you." Feng held up the button with one hand. With his other, he went to shake hands again. There was no-one there.

Feng tucked the button into his shirt breast pocket. "Well, well, well," was all he could say. So he said it again. "Well, well, well."

Chapter 43

La Cheval Noir Farm, Messines, Ypres
Sunday, April 2nd 2017: 8.22pm

The hole was smack-bang in the middle of the roof. This was a problem. There was no wall to prop their lethal bricks against. They would have to build high and wide to have any chance. The platform would be unstable, desperately dangerous, and time-consuming.

Some of the Amatol containers had rotted away. Every block represented a potentially messy end for all three. However, driven by panic and cushioned by luck, within half an hour they had made good progress.

"This is like the Romans trying to get into Masada," said Karin.

"Sure is," said Porter. "Like them, we'll need to build a ramp to one side. Without one, past about two metres, we won't be able to build any higher."

The plan was simple. Build a wide platform about 4 metres high. Ramp structure on one side. Porter was already on top, taking new bricks from Karin and Namita. Within reach of the roof, Porter would be able to stick Karin or Namita on his shoulders.

"How unstable is this stuff?" asked Namita, halfway up the narrow ramp. She held out the next block like a child forced to hold a spider.

"No idea. What choice do we have?" said Porter, taking the block in a swift but gentle motion. His back hurt already.

"Look on the bright side," said Karin. "Someone carried this in here. It didn't go off then?"

"I doubt it's become more stable over the years," cautioned Porter. "If I lift one of you out, we should be ok. I saw plenty of hose, rope, chains lying around up there."

They carried on in silence. The Maglite gave just enough light for them to sense each other's positions. Cartons fell apart in their hands. A small clump of unusable explosive began to amass alongside their structure.

And then the air chilled. They all felt it. Namita's skin crawled. Karin double-checked she could still picture a gun. Porter felt nothing but dread.

"What is that?" he whispered.

"I think you can guess," said Karin, speaking with firm clarity. "Ready everyone, ready." It wasn't a warning; it was an instruction.

"Oh no, not again," said Namita.

No less dramatic for a silent entrance, the apparition of Pelenot stepped forward. Still transparent, he had enough of a glow to flicker and shimmer in the blackest recesses of the mine. Karin had her mental cocoon ready, but no attack came.

Pelenot stood erect, his hands behind his back as if inspecting the troops. Nobody dared move. Georges broke the silence, his Victorian inflexion almost as great a shock as his appearance.

"It has much in common with developing a muscle," said Pelenot. "Kindergarten steps for now. Thought I should say hello."

"You mean, you're not powerful enough to get it up yet?" sneered Porter.

"Don't concern yourselves. It's coming. As is your end."

"Naturally. I presume you mean to blow us up?"

"Yes indeed. Though it will look in appearance, and will be in substance, suicide."

"Porter, he'll try to control your mind," warned Karin. "Build a wall against him."

"Yes, I know all about that. Tried to make me take my eye out with a fruit knife. I'm ready."

Pelenot, unconcerned, shifted a fraction and turned his gaze upon Karin. "Not everyone is as strong as you."

Porter and Karin both instinctively turned to the pale shape of Namita, 1.5 metres up the ramp. She coolly picked up one of the blocks and threw it to the floor. Karin and Porter both cried out and ducked, but the block landed harmlessly on the boards below.

"A dud. They won't all be. Carry on building by all means," said Pelenot.

"Namita!" shouted Karin. "Get down now."

Whatever spell Pelenot had cast, had already worn off and Namita, crying, jumped from the ramp. "I'm sorry, I'm so sorry."

"Stop it. No time for this. Can you carry on? Or should I tie you up?" said Karin matter-of-factly.

"I can carry on, I think."

"Good. Come on. This is going to be a long hour."

Pelenot watched as the three continued to build, the cavern silent bar the rustle of their clothes. All understood that overheard communication might become a weapon against them.

"Ah, your friend is here," said Pelenot. The three looked to the hole, hoping to see Feng. All they could see were the stars.

"He means me," said The Gliss. "You must move as fast as you can. He's gaining strength all the time."

"Yes, thanks for that," said Porter. "It hadn't occurred to me."

"The Gliss is here?" said Namita, looking up hopefully. "What's he saying we should do?"

"Move quicker," groaned Porter. "Useful tip."

Brick after brick passed along the line. The platform inched higher, painful-layer after painful-layer. Pelenot stood and watched impassively. "You remind me of Harry Norton quite a lot," he said finally. "Decent man, out of his depth."

"You're a murdering bastard," said Porter.

"I don't deny it. Thank you."

"There never were any missing pages from his diary, were there? It's all been a wild goose chase."

"Ah, you're wrong about that. Damned if I could find them, but they existed, alright. They were torn out of Norton's notebook before I could get to them."

"What was in them?"

"I never did find out. The meddler had been investigating me. The fool even tried to frame me. He was far too naive to best me."

Porter was breathless as he quickly, but carefully, added to the pile. "How did he try to frame you?"

"You want answers? Tempting though it is to boast, I think I'll deny you the relief."

"If you're not going to cough up, why waste your time here?"

"It's always pleasant to watch suffering before death."

Namita retreated into her own head, only to encounter Sangita dishing out a bollocking. "What is it with you? Stand up to him. You're better than this."

Karin and Porter both noticed that Namita had stopped moving. What they could not see, was Pelenot at work in her head.

Namita was choking her sister with both hands. *Nami, you're killing me. Sorry, Sangita - I'm trying.* She managed to pull one hand away from her dead sister's windpipe but, almost immediately, it sprung back to squeeze again.

Karin shouted, "Namita, snap out of it."

Porter put down the block he was holding and started down the ramp towards Namita. If nothing else, he could sit on her. Without warning, Namita broke from her hypnotic state, ran at the mound of Amatol and threw herself against it.

"I think you should hurry up," said The Gliss. "The explosive isn't the only unstable thing in here."

"Will you kindly stop stating the bleeding obvious?" shouted Porter. "With Namita swapping sides every second, we'd worked that out for ourselves, thanks."

"That's it. I'm tying her up," said Karin.

"With what?" said Porter. "You might have noticed we're a bit short on rope?"

"I'll tear my blouse into strips if I have to. Namita?"

"I'm ok again," said Namita. "He was in my head. He tried to get me to kill my sister. If I could get my hands on him…"

Karin and Porter exchanged puzzled shrugs. Pelenot calmly put up one hand and commanded, "Silence, whore."

Namita brought up both her hands to once again fight off invisible hands twisting and pinching her skin. Though no-one was near her, Namita was lifted off her feet, flew backwards and shuddered into the pile of explosives again.

"You're going to get us all killed! You've got to fight him off," said Karin, hands on hips, as defiant as the Colossus.

Pelenot turned calmly to her. "You're a Pelenot. You're bloody-minded like so many of our line. But you can't fight me forever. I shall enjoy dispatching you when the time comes."

Karin stopped for a second. She closed her eyes. With all the calm imagination she could rustle up, she walked over to Georges and blasted his head with his own pistol.

He turned to her, all suave and coolness gone. His head seemed to swell and distort with anger. If hatred had a sound, it was Pelenot's hiss. He emitted a loud and piercing one, then disappeared.

"Well done Ms Pelenot!" cheered The Gliss.

"Good work, Karin," said Porter, patting her on the back.

"What did you do?" asked Namita.

"I shot his brains out," said Karin. She tapped her head. "We can only fight him up here."

"Tell me how," said Namita.

La Cheval Noir Farm, Messines, Ypres
Sunday, April 2nd 2017: 8.59pm

Feng pulled up outside the farm. All was quiet. "On the Western Front," he said, completing the phrase, unduly pleased with himself. "By Goff it's chilly." Voluminous evergreens funnelled the wind. "Now, where is the silly bugger?"

Feng moved cautiously towards the farm. All the lights were off. A good thing? A truck trundled towards him. He turned to face it. Like a nude seeking the cover of a fig leaf, he whipped his phone out and put it to his ear to look less suspicious. The lorry passed by without using him for target practice.

Counting to three for courage, he clambered over the gate and assessed the yard. The house stared him down. Folding his arms, he spoke to the building. "You know what...offence is the best form of defence." He strode up to the house and rapped the lion-head knocker. I'll just say I'm lost if there's anyone in, he reassured himself.

His first rap was pathetic enough, but soon he was giving it as much welly as he could, in a Bonham-esque barrage, triple-checking the farmhouse was empty before going further.

"Stare all you want, Bubba," he shouted at the frowning farmhouse. "I'm off for a ramble in your grounds, and there ain't nothing you can do about it."

It didn't take him long to find the well. He also found the hole, luckily by sight, rather than by falling through it. He put his ear to the ragged entrance and heard shuffling.

"Porter?" he bellowed. The shuffling stopped. "Porter, is that you?"

"Feng?"

"What on earth are you doing down there?"

"Get us out. Now! This place is full of dynamite."

"Oh, you've found the mine. How interesting."

"Get us out! Now!"

"Us?"

"Yes, we're all down here - including, on and off, Georges Yes-He-Does-Exist Pelenot. He's going to blow us up any frigging minute."

Feng was delighted. "Pelenot! Time is of the essence - got it. There's rope in the van. Give me a sec."

Feng sprinted off to the VW and had a good rummage for a blue nylon rope he'd spotted earlier. It was a bit frayed and wispy at the edges, but long, strong and make-do suitable.

He kicked open the farm gate, ran back to the VW and reversed it into the yard, taking out a post and a bucket in the process. He backed across the uneven weeds until he was a metre from the hole.

Tying one end of the rope around the van's towing bar, he dangled the other end into the hole.

"Not before soddin' time. Karin's coming up first," said Porter.

The Gliss a-hemmed. "I think you should go first. It's you he seems to want the most."

"Ladies first."

"Chivalrous. But stupid and possibly sexist."

"I'm front of the queue because I'm strong enough to pull you two out, not because it's Ladies First," said Karin, reacting as though she had heard The Gliss.

"Two against one it is," said Porter. "Feng. Karin coming first."

Feng didn't fancy creating inescapable furrows in the mud driving backwards and forwards. He'd haul by hand. It proved harder than it looked. Five long, painful minutes dragged by before Karin's bob appeared at the hole.

"Hello again," she said.

"Nice to see you too. I won't shake," he said, blowing onto his hands.

"My palms look like crinkle-cut beetroot too," she replied, holding them up.

Feng was helping untie Karin when they heard a scream from below. They bent down and peered into the hole.

"What the hell happened?" shouted Feng.

"Is Georges back?" said Karin, alarmed as the screaming continued.

"It's Namita," replied Porter. "She fell off the platform. Crap. I think she's broken her arm."

"Get her tied up anyway," said Karin. "No time to lose." Porter followed orders, while Karin and Feng stood impatiently watching the kettle boil from up top. There were sounds of a struggle going on, punctuated by Namita's screams. They reminded Karin of an ear-splitting experience she once had on a bus: a woman with a burst appendix, howling at the medics not to move her.

"Sounds bad," said Feng.

"There's a mountain of explosive down there. If Georges comes back and triggers it as promised, it'll hurt her a whole lot more before we're finished."

Porter obviously won the battle. "Pull!"

This time the process was both easier and harder. Two people pulling, despite their burnt hands, made it easier, but Namita was a dead weight, unable to help.

Porter watched as Namita spun helplessly above him. She looked like a drunken aerialist, spinning slowly towards the hole. She screamed, but attempted to follow Porter's command to stay vertical.

It took a good 10 minutes to get her out.

Karin stamped the ground and cursed at the delay. Feng told her to go to the hole. He adopted his best tug-of-war brace. With good arm outstretched, Namita reached through the hole. Karin grabbed her hand with a wince. Feng nodded. *Ready.* Karin let go of the rope and freed up her other hand. Namita fell back a few inches thanks to the reduced anchor. Feng grunted at the strain it put on his shoulder. Karin skidded in the dirt, shushing Namita, whose agonising could surely be heard for miles. But after a long, wet slog of tugs and tears, Namita popped out of the earth, as awkwardly as a baby born sideways. Karin let go of her as soon as she was through.

"How bad's her arm?" said Feng, struggling to see in the gloom.

"Sticking out the skin," said Karin. She knelt down and examined Namita. An impromptu sling held Namita's damaged limb in place. "Is that your shirt, Porter?" shouted Karin.

"Does that mean you're coming up naked?" Feng shouted down the hole as he threw the rope back down.

"Topless, yes, but if you could keep your perverted fantasies to yourself at this particular point in time, I'd be most grateful," said Porter.

Porter was a metre short of the hole, six or seven metres in the air, when a chilling voice cooed impossibly in his ear.

"Hello, Porter."

It was Pelenot. "Oh hi," said Porter, a sinking feeling in his chest. He looked up to the moonlight. "Pull! As hard as you can! He's back!"

"I wanted a moment alone," said Pelenot. "Before you die."

"The Gliss is here. I'm not alone."

"The Gliss is you. Or some part of you. Who cares?"

"I wouldn't take his word on that if I were you," said The Gliss. "Pelenot's present in voice only. The Amatol hasn't exploded. He's still not strong enough." Porter nodded. There was still a chance.

"I know what you're thinking," said Pelenot. "You're half right. To tell the truth, I wasn't expecting your friend to be so efficient. A shame. I like to put on a show. I apologise for my déshabillé, though of course, you are more literally in that state."

The rope, hard as a poker, chafed painfully against Porter's out-of-shape midriff. Pelenot watched it and said, "I trust this rope is hurting you? It looks painful."

Porter was tantalisingly close to the exit now. "The rope's hurting," admitted Porter, "but if you're going to kill us, how about you get on with it. You're quite a boring fellow, old chap," said Porter, doing a bad impersonation of a posh Victorian.

"Yes, blow us all up. Unless you would like to tell us what your plan is first?" tried The Gliss.

"Fool," said Pelenot, dismissively. "However, in a manner of speaking, you are my father, Porter Norton."

"What the hell are you talking about?" said Porter.

"Come now. Not literally. But I did want to thank you before I kill you."

"Oedipal, sexual sadist, psychopath. Are you collecting the certificates? You mean, I presume, that the Quincunx is your father?"

"Exactly. Your selfish little attempt to end your own pointless life brought me back in my purest form. Newton's Third Law."

"Equal and opposite reaction. We figured that out already."

"Like you, I can see the magic but not the magician. I don't know how the trick was performed, but here I am, complete with my companion, The Gliss."

"Mine's called The Gliss!"

"So is mine."

Porter was furious at the revelation. "You dirty double-crosser! Is that where you've been going? You been playing away with the guy trying to kill me? Thanks a bunch, The Gliss."

Pelenot laughed. "I don't think they're the same being. Mine is such a fit with my thinking, I don't see how it could also be linked to anyone else. Dogs assume the characters of their owners, correct?"

"What are you saying? I'm in some way like The Gliss? Kill me now." Porter reached up and clasped Karin's hand. On contact, Porter expected Pelenot to either launch a tirade or attempt to detonate a block or two. He felt sick. But Porter didn't vomit. Nor did any bombs go off. And when he spoke again, Pelenot was just as quiet and calm.

"You're getting out of the hole. Well done. But, of course, you are literally in a minefield. I'm not short of ammunition."

"Er, Porter," said The Gliss. "He's gone quiet to conserve energy. I can feel it. He's about to unleash something. Run for it the second you land."

Porter felt the air on his cheeks. His hands found purchase on a root. Feng let go of the rope. Porter was pulled through.

"Pelenot's here," gasped Porter. "Leg it. Leg it now."

"Porter, I haven't finished yet," said Pelenot.

The others, shovelling Namita into the VW in the blurred background, stopped to listen to Pelenot.

"Before you die, I wanted you to know something. You're responsible. Whole countries will burn because of your pathetic self-pity. Too wrapped up in your own petty problems to think of the world. I've been in many minds since you brought me back. I lived long enough to see the Atomic Bomb. I lived the start of the nuclear arms race. I know how many missiles there are now. I know where they are. I even know who has the keys."

Damn. Feng was right about that too, thought Porter.

"And it's all your doing," said Pelenot. "I've been in your head. What a mish-mash of childish delusion is contained therein. There is no curse on your family bar the one you brought into it by birthing me. Harry Norton was a brave man. You let a fiction guide your hand towards self-destruction. What happened? *I* happened. The symmetry is beautiful."

Feng was gunning the engine. Porter stumbled towards the van's open door.

"Your whole life, Norton: it was all nonsense." Pelenot's form began to materialise again. It looked bolder and more lifelike than ever before. "And now, you can all die. Goodbye."

Chapter 44

La Cheval Noir Farm, Messines, Ypres
Sunday, April 2nd, 2017: 9.49pm

The cliché is that your life flashes before your eyes before you die. The cliché turned out to be true.

Porter saw himself as a child, building sandcastles at Weston-Super-Mare. He saw Frobisher, his fourth-year teacher, reciting a poem at the front of class. He saw Cherry holding up a squirrel with a homemade arrow jutting out of its still-heaving belly. He saw Martin Harris, his first boss, bollocking him for stealing a bag of sweets from the Post Office storeroom. He saw Lily Moss, his first girlfriend, breathing hard as she put her hand down his pants on Christchurch Road. He saw Lionel Bart giving him an autograph backstage in 1975 at the Theatre Royal, Stratford. He saw himself sweating in Old Street Magistrates as he presented evidence in court for the first time. He saw Tania's face, covered in tears, as they made love for the first time. He saw Feng laughing like a lunatic. He saw Feng and the others as the van picked up speed.

Wait a minute, that wasn't a flashback, that was the future, about to happen. He could see Feng gunning the engine and trying to remember which pedal did what. His heart skipped a beat in hope.

Porter discovered another truth about the cliché. It's possible to experience the cliché without death actually following - if miracles intervene. So, it was this night.

In the cavern, half a dozen blocks fizzed sequentially, but none exploded. Two popped with a phutt! - like the dud fireworks they were. Pelenot tried others. All dead - inert after a century of rotting damp.

"C'mon Feng, do your best F1 impression. Floor it," said Porter.

"He's ready! Full strength!" said The Gliss. "Fly you fools!"

"Schumacher meets Gandalf, here I come," said Feng, finally remembering to take off the handbrake.

The van crossed the threshold of the farm with a crash onto a cattle grid. Namita screamed as the break in her arm shook. They had the wrong driver. Feng ground his way through the gears. They also had the wrong vehicle, but they were making progress. 100 yards. 200 yards. 300 yards. 400 yards. The combo of a terrible driver and a clapped-out vehicle was tense for everyone. There was shouting, tumbling, guts churning in fear. 500 yards.

"Porter, can't you go a tad faster?" said The Gliss.

"He's driving!" shouted Porter, cussing at Feng, who was busily whipping the steering wheel backwards and forwards.

600 yards.

"Can you stop bouncing us around? Her bloody arm's coming off," said Karin, sick of being thrown side to side.

700 yards.

They never made 800 yards.

The blinding light came first. A few seconds later came the head-squeezing, belly-crushing, ear-popping, sub-sonic whoompf! Ears were shredded by a treble-heavy grinding, that sounded like *shattle and spettang*. The VW's windows shattered like fine crystal thrown into a jet engine. The van lifted off the ground. It was gliding out of control. Feng and the camper were mutually ill-equipped to deal with roundabouts, let alone catastrophic explosions. The whole escape pod veered towards a centuries-old, stone wall.

Rubble began to fall. Earth, brick, timber, iron. It cascaded in a crushing waterfall from the sky. The blast, slowest of the explosion's three terrors, overtook them tsunami-style, bringing the vehicle to a flattening halt. The few van windows left intact, shattered. Karin was knocked senseless into the Formica cupboard over the sink. Namita, already on the floor, was covered, rather than hit, by the mud and debris that flowed through the window. The force shifted her fracture excruciatingly. She too passed out. Feng slumped over the large uncovered steering wheel. He was unconscious after hitting the farm wall at 45mph. The steering wheel broke his lower ribs.

Porter was the only conscious person in the van. And he was cut and shaking. Sensing the first blast had been coming, he'd put his hands up to ward off the rubble. Glass and a tear of aluminium wall lining shredded his palms. He yelped like a dog snagged by the belly on barbed wire.

The surreal ringing blotted out all sound but his own amped-up breathing. Flailing, Porter failed to help Namita up. His lacerated hands had to settle for making her a rest from the mud. He laid her fractured arm gently on it. He brushed the hair from her eyes, mingling his blood with hers.

Karin was face down in a pile of earth, suffocating. He pulled her torn bare shoulders up from the dirt and placed her in the recovery position, leaving bloody handprints on her bleeding shoulder. He called to Feng. No reply. Was he dead? The debris rain settled to the pitter-patter of mud and small stones, thrown highest by the blast, the final detritus to gently bounce off the roof.

With the last of his energy, Porter made it to Feng, grabbed his hand and pulled him upright. More blood. Feng's hand was gashed open too. A tea towel on the dashboard used to clear condensation from the ancient VW, made-do as a temporary bandage. Between his and Feng's blood, it looked like the finale of *Saw*.

There was nothing more he could do. He flopped backwards, exhausted. The Gliss appeared. "You need to get up, Porter. Your night's work isn't finished."

"Go away. You didn't tell me Pelenot had one of you too."

"It was news to me."

"It's not you?"

"It's not me. Get up, will you. That blast was seen for miles. Emergency services will be here soon."

"Good. We're all screwed. Look at us."

"Leave Namita. She needs the hospital. The rest of you are concussed. I mean it. Get up. Karin's car is still here. Go get it."

Porter stirred a little and looked at Namita. She was regaining consciousness and crying.

"Namita. Can you hear me?" said Porter. "The Gliss wants me to find Karin's car. An ambulance will be here soon. Is it ok to leave you so you can get treatment?"

Dazed, she nodded.

"You need to wake Karin up," said The Gliss. "She has the keys."

With a groan, Porter started up again. All he wanted to do was lay down and sleep.

Five minutes later, Porter had roused Karin and Feng. Both were as foggy as he was, and Feng was spitting blood through muddy gums. "I think I've broken my ribs," he said. "Nothing fatal but I won't be doing tantric yoga anytime soon."

"Blood's not a good sign," said Karin.

"I haven't punctured a lung. I think I've lost a tooth."

"The Gliss says I have to find your car," said Porter. "If it survived that."

"I doubt it," said Karin. "And that's not good. I've got Georges' pistol in my boot."

"And I've got the incantation that can bring him to life so you can shoot the sod for real," said Feng. "We've got to get that pistol."

"How are your hands?" said Karin, taking Porter's and turning them over. She winced, avoiding looking at the vicious tiger-claw scrapes across his chest.

"Not good," admitted Porter, "but I don't have time to worry about them now."

They agreed Feng should stay and comfort Namita while Karin and Porter set off to find the car. Porter found a zip-up hoodie of William's in the mud. It was a bit tight but better than nothing.

Out of the van, a terrible sight lay before them. Where the farm, the barn and the well had stood for centuries, a giant crater now dominated the landscape. They could feel its malign presence, though its furthest edge was out of sight in the dark. It was the kind of hole that, if you fell in, you woke up in Sydney. The moonlight backlit intense smoke spewing from the burning caldera. What was left of the road was covered in mud, rocks and unidentifiable debris.

"There is zero chance of finding my car," stated Karin.

"Yet the VW survived," said Porter. "The Gliss is usually right about this type of thing. Over there wasn't it?" They moved closer to where the farm had stood.

"What did Georges say to you?" asked Karin.

"Nothing much. Blamed me for all this."

"You? How so?" Porter told her about the suicide attempt and the family curse. "My family sounds more cursed than yours," said Karin. She patted him on the arm. It was difficult to navigate, but both agreed they'd found the spot where the car had been. It wasn't there. "I've only just repaired it," said Karin ruefully.

"What's that? Is that it?" said Porter, pointing into a field opposite where the farm had stood.

"What's left of it anyway."

They ran. As they arrived at the field, Porter pulled up. "If I go out there, he'll have me where he wants me."

"Say no more," said Karin. She set off for the wrecked car.

Alone, Porter looked around. The damage was incredible. He had seen a million war films, half-a-million war documentaries, yet nothing had prepared him for that detonation. He was surprised to find himself thinking about Syria, not Flanders.

"Got it!" Karin was waving at him in the distance. He signalled back.

Karin emerged from the verge holding a wooden box. "Car's a write-off obviously, but I got it: Georges' pistol. Let's go kill the bastard."

Without a blink, Porter said, "Let's go."

Karin took the pistol out as she walked and handed the box to Porter. She spun the chamber like a pro, cocked and fired.

Porter flinched. "No bullets?"

"No, but even in my head, he was scared of the damn thing."

They arrived at the van, amazed no help had yet come. Odd. Mesen wasn't that far away. In the quiet of the country night, the explosion must have been heard 50 miles away. Maybe it was difficult to pinpoint the sound in the empty landscape?

"We have to go to Harry Norton's grave," said Feng, on seeing them.

"This is no time for sightseeing, Feng," said Porter. "Namita has to go to hospital. Now."

"I think Porter should get his hands seen to," said Karin.

"We need to end this. We have the gun and the incantation. We can do this at Harry's grave," Feng ploughed on.

"Hospital. I insist," said Porter.

Karin coughed. "Err, we don't have transport for either option."

"What about that?" Feng pointed to an old Land Rover a few hundred yards down the road. It had been dented in the explosion, the windows were out, but it looked driveable.

"You're not suggesting we steal a jeep now?" sighed Karin.

"In the circumstances," said Feng, pointing in a circular motion that encompassed the ex-farm and the wounded solicitor, "I think we'd be able to justify hotwiring it if we got pulled over. If Ms Pelenot was to put away that pistol, what are we? Just four tourists caught up in a freak WW1 explosion, needing to get to a hospital?"

"Why do we have to go to Harry's grave?" said Porter.

"It's simple," said Feng, picking up a large chunk of timber. Without warning, he hit Porter on the side of his head. Porter slumped to the floor. "Because I said so."

Two seconds later Feng joined Porter on the floor, KO'd, as Karin swung an equally large slab of wood at Feng's head. Surveying her three travelling companions, Karin, swore. "Thanks, Georges. Now I've got to do this all by myself. Am I the only one with any kind of willpower around here?"

She found some cable ties in the back of the VW and lashed up Feng and Porter's hands. She hot-wired the jeep, backed it up and after much huffing and puffing, got the boys inside. She sure was getting a workout. Namita was more of a problem. She was delirious, and the ugly splintered bone poked nauseatingly through her skin.

A faint flashing blue light began pulsing in the distance. Thank God. "Don't worry, Namita," said Karin, stroking her head. "You'll be fine in a minute."

Fifteen minutes to be exact. In that time, she had explained herself to the police (who reacted as Feng said they would), helped put Namita in the ambulance, and assured everyone she was fine, albeit muddy. She would drive her jeep to the hospital. The police, who were keen to seal the area off until the military arrived, merely took her name and sent her on her way.

The initial trickle of emergency vehicles turned into a full-scale flash-flood. She watched in amazement as she passed them, eventually pulling up at a closed service station.

"Are you two dopes awake yet?" she called to the back of the jeep.

"What happened?" said Porter. "Did Feng hit me?!"

"Georges did," said Karin. "Looks like Feng is as susceptible as Namita."

"Why am I tied up then?"

"I'm not taking any more chances with either of you. Not until I've worked out what we're supposed to do. What does The Gliss say?"

"He's gone again."

"Why does Feng want to go to Harry's grave? Where is it?"

"I don't have a clue why he wants to perform the exorcism there. But it's a place called Aeroplane Cemetery. If you can get to Ypres, I think I can get us there. I drove there with the guy from the museum. It's on Zonnesbeekseweg."

"How's your head?" said Karin.

"Between the explosions, the dead bodies and the iron-bar-posing-as-wood-whack-around-my-head, it feels like it's wedged under a slow-moving, caterpillar-tracked tank. Thanks for asking."

"Here take these," Karin threw a packet of paracetamol out of the glove compartment.

"My hands are tied," reminded Porter.

Karin sighed, stopped, fed Porter his tablets and drove on. Porter tried to muscle up some spit for lubrication, but his mouth was drier than a Saharan beach towel.

Feng gradually came to. "What happened?" he groaned.

"You got taken over by Pelenot and hit me around my sodding head is what happened," said Porter, miffed.

"Sorry, chum. Why am I tied up?"

"Have a guess," said Karin. "I'm not taking any chances."

"Where's Namita then?" asked Feng, looking around the jeep.

"In hospital, where she needs to be."

"The Beatles have become Peter, Paul and Mary."

"You're the only Mary in here," said Porter, making both men laugh painfully.

"We need to crack on," said Karin, who was not fluent in Banter.

"We need to pinch some shovels," said Feng. "Drive to Aeroplane Cemetery. We've got to dig up Harry Norton's body."

Chapter 45

Aeroplane Cemetery, Ypres
Sunday, April 2nd 2017: 10.55pm

One stolen jeep, two shovels taken from front gardens, three-quarters of an hour later, the trio stood over the grave of Private Harry Norton. Each was bruised, battered and bloody. Each was struggling with their conscience.

Porter's head was on fire. He had run to Harry's grave taking the same Gliss Approved Route as before and for the second time in an hour been bombarded painfully, this time by agonised voices from the past. He preferred, when it came down to it, being caught in the mine blast. Feng's theory was all well and good but if they got caught desecrating a war grave…prison-bound, no doubt about it. His few days in a cell had taught Porter he was allergic to them.

Karin considered her professional standing. At St Maude's School for Girls, she had gained a reputation as the sensible, strong, reliable one. Everyone had left her alone. These days, in *academe,* she was the same: robust, intelligent, aloof. She took no part in the personal politics and rivalries that took up 50% of the other professors' time. She was an obelisk in a turbulent river: always there, always reliable, immovable and inscrutable. Her production teams cherished her TV professionalism. Rigour, no compromise for infotainment's sake, integrity and respect for the subject.

She knew all this, so had to ask herself why the hell was she standing here with a stolen shovel about to dig up a dead soldier? She had experienced the inexplicable today and couldn't dismiss the supernatural as she would have done in the past. But this imminent desecration struck somewhere deep: her own self-respect as a custodian of history was at stake.

Feng's conscience ached too. He shouldn't have brought these two with him. He could see their hesitations, their struggles. Screw that! After everything he had seen, digging up Norton was necessary. It's not as if they wouldn't re-bury him. Historians dig up bodies all the time. Why so fastidious now?

Feng put his spade into the earth. The starting gun had been fired and the other two, making whatever quick accommodation they could with conscience, began to dig too. The going was quick in the sodden ground, but still far from easy. Porter kept quiet as he dug, hearing Harry's final disturbing words again. The loop was getting louder all the time. Feng's broken ribs made him exhale painful *oohs* and *ahs*. Karin was thinking of Arthur and imagining how he had suffered at the hands of Georges. Maybe she was hurting the worst of the three.

"I don't believe it." It was Porter who found the first bone. It looked like a femur.

Karin immediately ordered the other two to stop digging. "This is my field, leave it to me." She worked methodically, scraping away mud, exposing the skull. There were holes in the temple and diagonally opposite in the back.

"Georges' handiwork," said Karin. "I'm sorry, this must be upsetting for you."

"I'm ok," said Porter. "I can hear his last words going around in my head. I've got to get out of here soon, or I'll go mad."

"No coffin then? That's a surprise," said Feng.

"Sacking probably. I doubt there were enough trees for building coffins mid-war," said Porter.

"No," said Karin. "Most of the soldiers here will be in coffins. This cemetery was put together after the war, and bodies re-interred. Maybe Harry didn't deserve one as a deserter."

Karin, using the femur and skull to triangulate a rough position, moved to what she calculated was the middle of the corpse. With bare hands, she moved dirt and rotten fibres. She resembled a vet pulling a calf from a cow, hands buried deep, feeling rather than looking.

"Wait a minute… What's this? My God. Feng, I think you're right." She wrestled something from the ground, scraped away the cloying mud and held the object up.

"Wow," said Porter.

"Say hello," said Feng, "to your relative's long-lost cigar tube. The one he carried with him throughout the war. The one in which he stuffed his final confession."

"And cut himself open with Gilpin's penknife to shove into his own body," said Karin. "I thought it was a bit of a stretch when you proposed it, but…"

"It was the butterfly," said Feng.

"What butterfly?"

"The Holly Blue. The Butterfly. Papillon, in French. See?"

"I've no idea what you're talking about."

"My goodness," twigged Karin. "Did you never see the film, Porter? Steve McQueen and Dustin Hoffman? Storing cigar tubes in their rectum?"

"What happened to humidors," grimaced Porter.

"They were prisoners – using the tubes to hide their valuables."

"I never saw it. Sounds grim. *The truth goes with me*. So that's what you meant, Harry? Jesus."

"I got the feeling from Gilpin's diary that Harry was hiding something," said Feng, "but it wasn't till the Holly Blue…hiding, the tube, butterflies. It just all clicked."

"Blimey. I struggle to do the Concise Crosswords," said Porter. "You're the King of Cryptic."

The three of them looked at the tube. Porter tried to open it. It was stuck. "Look on the bright side," said Feng. "This was stored in his abdomen, not in his rectum."

"I'd say that was only marginally better. We need to get out of here," Porter reminded. "If we get caught, we're all going down."

"Do you want to say a prayer or something before we fill the grave back in?" said Karin.

"God no. What makes you ask that?" exclaimed Porter.

"You said you were an atheist a few days ago, but you're *Jesus* this, *Jesus* that, *God almighty*, etc.…"

"Let's fill this in and get out of here."

Driving towards Ypres, they spotted the B'n'B De Potzye. The reluctant landlord, sizing up their blood and mud-covered clothes, eyed them warily. They told him about the explosion. It calmed him. He'd heard the boom, but of course. He gave them a nip of whisky, less from largesse than an excuse to quiz them. He offered to lend them dressing gowns while he put their clothes in the washing machine.

Half an hour of showering later, saw them sitting like three Hugh Hefners in Porter's room. "I still can't get the lid off this cigar tube," said Feng. "It's completely rusted shut."

"Let me try," said Porter. It wouldn't budge. The lid of the tube still contained traces of grave – including the decomposed body of Harry Norton. Faint images and sounds flickered in Porter's head: a ragged and thin version of Harry's last moments.

"What now?" said Karin.

"We're in Ypres," said Porter. "I met the chief archivist at the In Flanders Fields Museum last week. He'll be interested in the cigar tube. They'll have facilities there. They can get it open for us and sort things out if the paper's degraded. We'll go first thing."

Feng said he would dump the jeep a mile up the road before they set off by cab.

"We'd better stop in and see how Namita's getting on first," said Porter.

"I suppose we'd better," said Karin.

"Where the hell do you find grapes around here?" said Feng.

Ward 4, Jan Yperman Hospital, Ypres
Monday, April 3rd 2017: 8am

Namita looked pale but restful, asleep, dosed up with morphine. The room smelled of antiseptic. The three of them shuffled and stared, not knowing what to do. "We could leave a note?" Feng suggested.

Porter went to reception and rustled up pen and paper. The Gliss appeared. "Oh, so the Mighty One blesses us with his presence now that he's no flipping use to anyone," whispered Porter. "Where were you last night?"

"I'm a guide, not a guide dog. I'm not supposed to be here all the time. I'm more alarm clock than wristwatch."

Porter opened the door back into Ward 3, still whispering. "We could do with a bit more guidance than…" Feng and Karin sprang up so fast they almost lost their shadows.

"What the hell is that?" said Feng, pointing up at The Gliss.

"Is it Georges?" gasped Karin.

Porter did a double take. "The Gliss? You can see The Gliss?"

"Ah this is embarrassing," said the apparition. "I feel a trifle naked now."

"Goff in hell. What's going on?"

"Mingling. Oh dear. This wasn't supposed to happen," said The Gliss, to blank looks. "Porter's hands. Helping you all. There was a bit of mingling of blood."

"I hope none of you has anything contagious," said Karin, her pulse beating in the early 200s.

"I must be hallucinating," said Feng. "Karin, are you really seeing this too."

"I am."

"Goff."

Porter turned to look at Namita. "She's going to get a shock when she wakes up. I left blood all over her forehead too."

"Scribble that note quick," said Karin. "Let's get out of here before she wakes up. She's had enough shocks for one day."

"Yes, the woman most likely to scream her head off at the sight of a ghost: contender number one," said Feng, gesturing at the bed.

"You're right," said Porter. "Let's go to the museum."

In Flanders Fields Museum, Ypres
Monday, April 3rd 2017: 10am

En route, Karin and Feng quizzed The Gliss about who, why and what he was. They got the usual litany of non-information and snarkiness. Porter watched the grilling with surprising envy. This was his thing surely? Now he had to share?

Disappointingly, Cas Faucheux wasn't in the building. The three of them milled about uselessly in the reception, wondering what to do next. Porter recognised a woman he'd seen on his last visit. He explained he was a friend of Cas and would she mind texting him? She asked them to wait in the café. Twenty minutes later, she found them and said Cas would be driving in.

Karin broke off a piece of crumbling fruit cake. "I think this was made the year Harry died."

"This croissant deserves listed status too," said Feng, whose tooth injury had left his mouth throbbing angrily since last night. He jammed in a piece of chewing gum to protect the nerve from the air.

"Let's hope Cas has a store of the hard stuff - fluffy pastries and all," said Porter, surprising himself with the sarcasm. "We're lucky to be alive, people. A good breakfast would only be a bonus."

Cas greeted Porter and friends warmly.

"So, what's this all about? I've been up the road helping the military. We had a huge explosion in Mesen yesterday. Were you still here? Did you hear it?" He registered their cuts. "Wait? You weren't caught up in it?"

"I should think everyone in Europe heard it. Yes - our car got hit. Luckily, we were far enough away." said Porter. "Are you involved in the clean-up?"

"But of course. Can you imagine how much has been revealed by the explosion? It will take some time, so I can't spend too long here. You should stay out of Belgium, Porter - explosions seem to like you."

"I need to show you something," said Porter. "I told you about my great-grandparent, Harry Norton? Executed for desertion? Do you remember how he carried an empty hip-flask and cigar tube with him to remind him of home while he was in the trenches? This is it."

"We have hundreds of such artefacts in this museum. It has no monetary value if that's what you want to know." Cas looked slightly annoyed to have been called in for something so trivial.

"We can't get it open."

"It is empty, no?"

"We don't think so, no."

"A cigar would not have survived all this time, Porter."

Porter shook his head, willing explanation and understanding to come faster. "We think it contains some missing pages from Harry's diary - pages in which he accuses a British officer of terrible crimes in the trenches."

"Where did you find it? Why bring it here? Wouldn't your own Imperial War Museum be interested?"

Porter tapped a spoon against his cup. "We traced it to a hidden spot through the letters of another soldier," said Porter, improvising a lie. "We think the crimes committed were so outrageous that, even now, we could run into problems with the British military establishment."

"And you're impatient, of course."

"A bit of that, yes, but here does seem the safest place to investigate the contents. Besides, you did seem interested when we last spoke."

"I am, I am. But tracing and finding it. The odds against it are incredible. There's something you're not telling me. This mud, it is fresh, no? I hope you haven't been digging over here?"

"No, no. Nothing like that I assure you. We brought it from England. We wanted to read it for the first time at Harry's grave but couldn't get it open."

Cas moved the tube around in his fingers. He tried a quick twist but had no more luck than they had. "It will need cutting open. It's been in the ground for almost a century. Let's head to our archival rooms."

After tap-tap-tapping their way through various echo-ing corridors, they emerged into a room that was half lab, half workshop. A low hum made it sound like the command deck of a movie spaceship.

Cas introduced everyone to Jean, a thirty-something nerd with glasses. "Jean is, as they say in France, *Le Homme.*"

Jean dipped his head in the least energetic show of "nice to meet you" Porter had ever seen.

All five gathered around a lightbox. Attached to it was a magnifying glass, held in place by a gooseneck clamp. Cas placed the cigar tube on the lightbox and examined the rusted cap. Jean looked too. He tutted.

"I think there has been some kind of reaction in the metal. This isn't just jammed shut, it's like it's welded shut. Still, first things first." Jean wandered off and came back with a pair of pliers. He gently placed the tube in a small wooden vice attached to one of the tables and tried to use the pliers to worry the cap loose. No luck.

"I'm sorry, we'll have to cut it open," said Cas, nodding in agreement with Jean. "It's a shame because we'll lose the tube. It's rare to get an artefact like this that we can back up with written testimony like Harry's diary."

Feng, Porter and Karin stood around like gooseberries while Jean and Cas did their thing. The cigar tube was re-clamped. A hacksaw was used to cut open a section of the cannister. Jean used a pair of needle-nosed pliers to peel back the lid. Cas dropped to his haunches and using a small LED light, examined inside.

"Ah yes," he said. "The tube is filled with notepaper."

Feng whooped, Karin goody-clapped and Porter leaned back on a work surface and blew air from his cheeks.

The Gliss said, "It looks like you're one step nearer to solving one of your atonements at least."

"It's gonna take time to get used to *that, him, it,*" Feng said to Karin.

"Not so much of the *That,* if you don't mind," said The Gliss. "I'm not supposed to be talking to you."

"Hold your horses, no?" said Cas, so focused on the tube he didn't notice the strange conversation going on. Jean was the one who looked around the room, puzzled. "We have to get it out first. After a century in the ground, it may not be so clear as a kindle."

Chapter 46

The torn-out pages. Written in Harry Norton's holding cell, Ypres
Thursday, 16th August 1917: 1am

Dear Alice,
You'll never get to see this, but who else should I write to?
You and the children are on my mind all the time. I feel terrible my actions and decisions will leave you without a husband and the children without a father. I have only tried to do the right thing, and yet it has been my undoing.

You will hear bad things about me. They will say I spied for the Germans or that I deserted. Neither is true, of course not. But this is my sad fate. After dodging so many German bullets over three long years, in as many hours I shall die at the hands of my unfortunate friends. Don't blame them. I don't.

I have to put down in writing how it was I came to be in this predicament and the deeds of the vile man who put me here.

Not long after I was transferred to the frontline in Ypres, I had a terrible experience. I met a young private by the name of Al Hobbs. He was wandering around the yard, muttering and wiping his forehead. I watched as he sat down on a verge and saw him put the barrel of his rifle in his mouth, start crying, remove the barrel and weep some more.

I sat with him and asked what the trouble was. Over a cigarette or two, he told me some of his story. I brought out my hipflask and offered him a swig. He laughed when he realised it was empty. I think it broke the ice.

He told me something I found hard to believe. He said that one of our captains had forced himself upon him at gunpoint. I wasn't clear what he meant at first, but eventually, he spelt it out in all its horror: sodomy.

I asked him which captain, but he was too scared to tell me.

I tried not to judge without evidence and offered him words of consolation. A few hours later he was dead. The poor blighter took a hand grenade and detonated it in his mouth, dying instantly.

I could hardly forget the story but, of course, there was no way to find out who the captain was.

A month later, I was helping Capt. Braxted, one of our best captains, into bed after he arrived back at the trench worse for drink. Braxted complimented me on my work in the trenches. Then he began ranting about a soldier who did not fit his ideal.

"You're good. Not like that weasel…Cartwright was it? Max Cartwright, that's it. A bastard through and through."

"I don't know him."

"Firing squad was too good for him."

"Why, Sir? What did he do?"

"Caught spying for the Germans and then had the cheek to try and get out of it by claiming Capt. Pelenot had buggered him. Buggered him, mind. Said it out loud at his court-martial to his face. Pelenot was only there to give the damn man a good reference."

Why would two unconnected soldiers make up the same, unlikely story? I concluded they must have spoken the truth and that Capt. Pelenot had abused his position and preyed on them. I was filled with rage.

Pelenot is all charm and, I have to admit, a great captain. I started watching him. It wasn't easy to believe. I saw Pelenot display great leadership. How could such a perversion even be possible in a man so otherwise virtuous? When poor Jimmy Shand developed the shakes and was in danger of being accused of malingering, Pelenot took off his own cape in the pouring rain and draped it around Shand so that a passing group of officers could not see his condition. He not only saved his life but took Shand in and gave him brandy.

When Weston lost a leg in No-Man's Land, Pelenot took it on himself to go through the fusillade to retrieve him. Alas, Weston died from gangrene a few days later, but none forgot Pelenot's bravery.

I might have stayed in this state of confused indignation forever but for two more incidents.

A month ago, Private Paul Rubinstein, appeared to lose his mind. Shouting out the name of Capt. Pelenot and crying, Rubinstein climbed one of the ladders and ran into No Man's Land. We all wondered what the cry of "Pelenot" meant, but only I thought I had the answer. I could not share it of course.

Rubinstein's death affected my spirits. How many more young men might this evil man destroy if no-one did anything to stop him? After a lifetime of living with the consequences of a weak father, a man who tolerated the bullying that caused nothing but misery, I couldn't let it go. I quietly began to bring up Pelenot in conversation with others. "Such a great officer," I would say. "A soldier can always rely on Capt. Pelenot." I shook nothing loose.

One day my friend Bill said, "You always talk up Pelenot, but I know someone who's not so fond of him." And he told me about Johnnie Eaves from 1st Btn. He disliked Pelenot so much that he stuttered in his presence. Eaves was now known as "Stutty" by his mates.

It wasn't much, but I contrived to meet Eaves and tried the old "isn't Pelenot great?" spiel. He stuttered, "I...I...i...if you s...s...s...say so."

I didn't know how to proceed, so I chose to lie. I pulled the saddest face I could and said, "Damn. Not you too. The bastard." And I made to look down in grief. Eaves shot me a look of panic and almost jumped 5ft backwards. He knew exactly what I was talking about. A day later, I saw Eaves again, and he came over to me and said, "Don't let it get you down." We shook hands. You can imagine how terrible I felt pretending to have suffered the same ordeal. I had to get justice for Cartwright, Hobbs, Rubinstein and Eaves. But how?

In the meantime, the most curious thing happened. I was surprised one evening, to be visited by Capt. Pelenot himself.

For a second, I worried he had me in his perverted sight, but soon realised he had come on a very different mission.

"I'm flattered to hear that you have been singing my praises in the trenches, Norton. Thank you. It means a lot. It's not an easy job. I hear good things about you too. Capt. Braxted says you're a good man."

I was still nervous as you might imagine. None of the men I knew about would have submitted to Pelenot's vile attacks without some violence on his part. Here we were alone.

"Well Sir, good leadership means a lot to us." In this at least, I was not lying. He was a good captain.

"We lost Jackson yesterday. He was my batman. Would you take his place? It's slightly safer than being a general infantryman, and there are benefits. Not least an extra drink or two."

Providence had given me the chance to get close to this vile man. My route to justice had been obscure, but this represented a clearer path. I said yes.

I won't bore you with the details of the first month of my new duties. I occasionally got out of the trenches to accompany him. I had light tasks such as cleaning his boots before important gatherings at HQ. I got extra food and a swig or two of real whisky. Pelenot himself was excellent, considerate and well-liked by the majority of men. I even came to question whether I had made a mistake.

One day I found myself at HQ with him. He wanted to loan me for the day to the General who needed help with an unexpected admin task requested by London.

The task, which concerned the court-martial records of everyone who had been executed along our stretch, was to make copies of all the documents held there and send them back to London. Privy to inside information, I was pleased to see there were only half a dozen cases on record. Six too many but not as bad as the rumours.

I worked alone with the files, including all the paperwork relating to the unfortunate Max Cartwright. There it was in black and white. The accusation made at the end of the trial. Cartwright claimed Pelenot had forced himself upon him. The court-martial ordered the accusation struck from the account. The General himself reminded me to make sure Pelenot's name was kept out of the copy for London.

Cartwright said the attempted murder, the night Pelenot sent him into No Man's Land on a pretend mission, took place on the last day of February. The court pointed out that on the last day of February, Pelenot had been at a dance, miles away with virtually everyone currently in the court. It had sealed his fate. I looked it up. It was a leap year. Cartwright no doubt got his dates mixed up but it made him sound less credible.

I cannot begin to tell you how this fired me. I was determined to bring Pelenot to justice. You will have to forgive me for what happened next.

There was no point in hoping that Pelenot would be accused again publically. As far as I knew, only Eaves could make the accusation. He had no spine. In any case, it is doubtful any man would give such evidence unless, like Cartwright, a sentence of death had already been passed. Shame is a powerful force.

So, I decided Pelenot had to die like his unfortunate victim, Private Max Cartwright. By firing squad. Executed for spying. The army had no problem dealing with men on that score. It was up to me to frame the bastard.

My secondment went well, and the General borrowed me on a couple of other occasions. This was to prove my inspiration as well as my undoing. I now had occasional access to HQ where there were plenty of documents that could be taken, planted on Pelenot and reported missing. All I had to do was find a way to tip-off Command that Pelenot had them and was aiming to use them.

Over the next month, I grew closer to Pelenot and then came the fateful night, when I caught him full roule-par-terre, blind drunk, rolling on the floor. I found him in the act of masturbation. It was a disgusting sight but not uncommon. I have lost all desire since arriving in the trenches. But this man was writhing like a beast, tugging and pulling.

He saw me, grinned and continued as if I wasn't there. Inspiration struck. "Sir, let me." May the Lord forgive me, Alice, but I bent down and finished him off with my shaking hand.

In Flanders Fields Museum, Ypres
Monday, April 3rd 2017: 1pm

"Flip," said Porter. "That's grim."

"This is an extraordinary document," said Cas.

The Gliss looked at Porter and did his *I-told-you-so* face. It looked like the apparition had indigestion.

Cas said his eyes were straining to read the higgledy-piggledy writing and begged for a coffee break. "The document is in remarkable condition all things considered. It will need preserving. I can send it to our team tomorrow, though they will be busy after the explosion."

"We'll need a copy today," said Porter.

"You'll have to take pictures on your phones."

Feng still had his. They agreed.

"As long as it's emailed to all of us, that will be fine," said Karin.

Feng snapped a few pictures and uploaded them, insurance against the book-burning Pelenot. Cas watched and said, "It's not difficult to see how Harry Norton ended up in front of a firing squad, no? His plan went sideways, as they say."

"Harry was executed for desertion," said Feng.

"But only after trying to bring Georges to justice," said Karin.

"Pelenot claimed another victim. Poor Harry," said Porter.

Holding cell, Ypres
Thursday 16th August 1917: 2.30am

I don't have long left to get my story down, Alice. Our chaplain is coming to visit me at 4am. I shall be escorted to my doom at dawn.

I know you will never see this and that is good, for what husband wants to reveal the depths he sank to, to bring about the downfall of the vilest man on the planet? It has been a comfort to picture you listening to me as I write though, and that justifies putting your name on the header of these sad notes.

The next evening, we were alone again.

"Norton. What happened last night…"

"Say no more, Sir," said I. Perhaps something in my voice emboldened the monster, for his demeanour immediately changed, and I saw the red mists of lust had descended upon him.

"I would like more actually." He backed against the door and unbuttoned his flies.

"Just the hand, Norton, just the hand." And I stood there again, watching his face up-close as I did my odious job.

"Thank you, Norton. Don't you ever need relieving yourself?"

"I couldn't ask that of you, Sir."

"That's not what I meant. A man's balls could turn blue in a place like this."

"They could, Sir. Yes, sir. I have my moments."

"Let me see."

The fiend had only just spent but now was expecting me to do the same, in his full view. I decided to play along, anything to keep the disgusting man in my long-term sights. He sat in his chair, watching, while I failed to stiffen. Nothing could have been less arousing to me.

"You prefer to get your jollies watching others rather than being watched? Put it away." And with that gesture, I never had to perform in front of him again. It was as if I had been excused, as well as made accomplice.

I was definitely not free. Almost every night after, I was required to milk the bastard. He never touched me. He would mutter in his ecstasies, disgusting stories of horror and rape; men, women, boys, girls and even animals. It was sickening. Beyond sickening. I prayed they were fantasies and not memories re-enacted, but I suspected the worst.

One night, sure of the bond between us, he said he needed a good jump. "If there aren't any lassies, a laddie will always do," he voiced his vile motto. As ever, I was ready to fight than submit to him. But, as it turned out, I was destined to be his partner in crime, not his victim.

"There's a young private - you know Eaves? I have taken him before, not by his choice, but he has remained quiet. I have a yen to take him again. This time you can join in. It's about time you got a portion." How sickened I was that Pelenot considered me as crazed as he, but at last, I saw my chance.

"Really, sir? That sounds good." Five words and yet I sealed my fate with their utterance.

"I'll leave it to you to arrange. He won't come to see me, but he'll come to see you."

"Yes, sir. Leave it to me."

Time was running out, so I immediately went to see Eaves. I had no choice but to take him into my confidence and told him of Pelenot's vile plan.

"What to do, sir?" said Eaves, horrified, but deferring to me as Pelenot's batman. "If he does this again, I shall wander into No Man's Land and let the Bosche finish the job he started. I cannot bear it again."

"You'll do no such thing. I will have him brought to justice. You will not be mentioned. I have a plan."

Dear Alice, as history now shows, it was not a good plan.

Close to our trenches, was the Chateau Ferrie. A beautiful building with bare damage. The officers used it to socialise on occasion. Its primary function was as an adjunct to HQ. Nearby was a disused communications trench not currently in use due to the success of recent advances.

I was in the perfect position to take papers from HQ, put them in Pelenot's gear, entice him out to the chateau on the pretence of attacking Eaves in seclusion, while actually using the Fullerton to telegraph HQ that Pelenot was a spy - on a rendezvous with a German agent.

Eaves was rightfully terrified, lest his part was discovered.

"You don't have to do anything but stay here," I said. "I'm only telling you in case Pelenot checks with you. Tomorrow night I will tell him that you and I are to go to the chateau. I will find a reason for delay. He will be expecting you so he can conduct his dirty business and I am to join in."

Eaves gave me a look of horror.

"Calm yourself," I said. "You will be here, and I would never do such a thing. I'd kill him first. I will radio the coordinates, head back to the trenches and the MPs will catch him, in the shadows, holding the papers."

It took some convincing to get Eaves to acquiesce. But agree he did. And my heart beat louder for it. I knew I had the one chance to get it right. Get it wrong, and I was a dead man.

The times were arranged carefully. I would tell Pelenot to meet me at the servants' entrance to the chateau at 7.45pm, with Pelenot expecting Eaves to join us at 8pm. But Eaves would still be in the trenches, and I would be in the comms trench, radioing HQ to let them know of Pelenot's treachery. Once caught alone and with the papers, he would be quickly court-martialled.

Eaves was scared but thanked me for my plan and for warning him. I promised to take some papers the next morning and ensure they were on Pelenot's person.

Fear is a peculiar thing, dear Alice. It can inspire a man to greater heights of courage than you could believe. I have seen it here often. Men quaking against a wall, terrified of going over the top. Some crying, kissing crosses. But I had rarely seen men refuse to actually go when the whistle came. Up ladders they go, and through barbed wire, they crawl. Any second could mean instant death or the beginning of a drawn-out agony.

But sometimes, fear can dull people to the point where they don't know what they are doing: where the shortest route becomes the only choice.

So, it turned out with Eaves. It became clear to me later, as I waited to face my court martial, that in the cold light of day, fear had taken the boy for his own. And who could blame him? I fancy he ran straight to Pelenot and told him all. I do not know whether he was rewarded or punished for his candour. Pelenot, who saw a way of getting rid of someone who knew too much, allowed my planned day to fall out as arranged. I retrieved the papers. I put them in Pelenot's case. I warned Eaves to go into hiding. I set off for the communications trench unaware Pelenot was at HQ putting the papers back, not en route to the chateau after all.

Yes, Alice, I was the only one who was now exposed. I had left my trench without orders, and Pelenot knew the exact time I would be in the communications trench, unauthorised, making a call.

The MPs came for me. Luckily, I was nowhere near the actual machine when they arrived, and I had no incriminating papers on me. They could only suspect, not prove, I was spying.

What was I to do? I could not blame Eaves. I was dead three ways, whatever my choice. Desertion was enough to see me dead. If I then attempted to accuse an officer without proof? Mutiny. If not that, then a trumped-up charge of using the Fullerton would be enough to see me dead.

There was nothing else to be done. If Eaves was to survive, and it was my fault he was in this new predicament, then I should have to perish. Ironically, I took the opposite path to my father but arrived at the same destination.

I will leave this note here, for I now have to write you the official note that I know you will see. No-one will ever see this letter, but I felt it had to be written down.

Fear is, as I say, a peculiar thing. I never once stopped to think that I shouldn't bring Pelenot down, whatever the cost to me. I have won in a way. Not to fight is to condone. At least, I have chosen my own death. I trust my pals to aim true and end it fast for me.

I hope someone, somewhere, sometime, has the power to do what I failed to do and bring this vile man to justice.

Harry Norton.

Chapter 47

In Flanders Fields Museum, Ypres
Monday, April 3rd 2017: 3.53pm

There was silence.

"Extraordinary," said Cas.

"This changes everything," said Porter. The legend of the Five Suicide Curse had become two suicides, an accident, an execution and his own pathetic *attempt* at suicide. It's gone, you silly bugger. There is no, was no, curse. You're free.

Feng cleared his throat. "Porter, Karin? We have to go…*remember?*"

Cas folded his arms. "What is it that you're not telling me?"

Karin stepped forward. "Cas, I need your help. May we speak in private?" The pair went off to a side room.

"What's that all about?" said Feng, archly.

"I don't know, but if she needs Cas, I'm sure it's for a good reason."

Feng took a couple more backup photos, emailing them to the Doves and Dropbox for safekeeping.

Karin and Cas returned.

"There's a great deal of trust involved here," said Cas, "but of course, even here in Belgium your reputation is well-known."

"Thank you, Cas. I won't let you down," said Karin.

Everyone shook hands. Porter and Cas promised to keep each other updated. The trio and The Gliss halted in reception, to assess each other. Feng straightened his clothes. "Are you ready for a showdown?"

Ward 4, Jan Yperman Hospital, Ypres
Monday, April 3rd 2017: 4.20pm

Namita was woken by a nurse putting a call through to her bedside phone. It was Hammell.

"I hear you've done your arm in?" he said, skipping the formalities.

"Yes. Bone was poking out the skin. You'd have loved it. What do you want?"

"I found the message. Nick Runyon's initial call to Kerry Crane. Like you said. Doddle really."

Namita shifted uncomfortably. She'd have preferred to have this chat about illegal investigations in person.

"Keep it brief."

"Entre nous and all that. Gotcha. The system had a backup of the backup. Easy to get into. Sorry about the broken window."

"I won't ask. Text me the computer's location. I can order a detailed witness summons under section 34(b). Runyon will have to disclose it. If he doesn't, we can produce our copy and show he is perverting the course of justice. This is good news for Porter either way. Thank you, Hammell."

"The bill's in the post. No tennis for you for a while then?"

"I said *thank you,* Hammell."

"Charming."

He was about to hang-up when Namita had a thought.

"Wait. Hammell, don't you have contacts in the MOD?"

"That's right. Why do you ask?"

"I want you to look at something for me. Back in World War 1, there was a captain in the Worcesters who fought at Ypres. His name was Georges Parry Pelenot. That's George with an s on the end. See what you can find on him," said Namita.

"What? There'll be loads of stuff."

"I'm looking for scandal, Hammell. I don't need his shoe size."

"Your wish is my command. Oh, and it won't be cheap."

Aeroplane Cemetery, Ypres
Monday, April 3rd 2017: 5.47pm

Porter stood over Harry Norton's grave for the third time in as many weeks. "Harry, I promised you I'd sort this out for you, and today I hope we will." Porter was doing his best to block out the storm of cemetery voices, topped by Harry's last words, which still tracked his every visit.

"Your mission's only just beginning," said The Gliss. "You must be able to sense that?"

"Maybe."

"Is this a private conversation, or can I chip in?" said Feng.

"Private," said Porter and The Gliss, simultaneously.

Feng and Karin took the hint and moved a few yards back. Porter and The Gliss needed a few minutes.

"Do you think this really will work?" Karin asked. She was moved, watching Porter talk over his great-grandfather's grave.

"I don't know. I spent a few minutes with a young soldier called Graham Smith after reciting the incantation Zouche gave me. It was the most goose-pimply thing I've ever experienced."

He reached into his pocket and removed the button. "He gave me this. It's got one of his hairs in it. I'm going to bury it in his mother's grave when I get back to England. Isn't that something?"

"We've seen how dangerous Georges is," said Karin. "Making him physical, even for a short time..."

"He won't be the Profugus with the Saevita for those few minutes," said Feng. "He'll be human again. He can't be both at the same time. It gives us a few minutes to kill him with that pistol of yours. Hopefully, saying *bang!* and pointing will do the trick."

"I think I can do better than that." She pulled the pistol from her bag and opened the chamber. There, sitting in one of the holes, was a single bullet.

"Where the hell did you get that?" said Feng, clapping a hand to his head.

"Cas."

"You sneaky devil." He pushed her, playfully.

"I agreed to come back and base a *History ThisStory* around the museum," she said, ruefully. "A small price to pay for going up against Georges armed. He's a real sadist, Feng. Namita nearly lost her mind when he tortured her in the mine. He tore her hair out."

"I didn't see any missing patches on her head...Oh, you mean?"

"What about you, Karin?" said Porter, re-joining them.

"Maybe I don't have a mind to lose. It hurt, but I fought him off, so I wasn't assaulted as badly as Namita. But, let's put it this way. I'm still sore." She folded her arms across her chest.

"I'm really sorry to hear that. I didn't know how much you and Namita had suffered," said Porter.

"I'm sure she doesn't want you to," said Karin. "Anyway, we have our plan now."

"Let's hope it does the trick. The Kyoto script is clear: a Profugus can only be killed in the way it killed in life."

Karin weighed the pistol in her hand. "It's why he was so afraid of this when I used it in my mind. He shot Max and Harry through the head. He knows if I get his head, it's the end."

"Can you shoot?"

"Definitely."

Feng decided not to probe.

"You need to get on with it," said The Gliss. "Pelenot's batteries are recharging. He'll be back as soon as he can."

"The absences are worse than when he's here. I'm on tenterhooks all the time," said Karin.

"We can call Pelenot up here, even though his grave is in England," said Feng, "Harry's grave is symbolically the right place to do it."

"And quiet," said Karin. "I suppose I'd better get psyched up to shoot."

"Are you both ready?" said Feng, proudly taking out his incantation.

> *Georges Parry Pelenot of the Worcesters, wake, wake, wake.*
> *Three times I call you in the name of Hisporatus.*

Karin and Porter sniggered.

"Look no-one said it was poetry," said Feng, annoyed.

> *Georges Parry Pelenot of the Worcesters, wake, wake, wake.*
> *I give you this short time cycle to return one last time*
> *Georges Parry Pelenot of the Worcesters, wake, wake, wake.*
> *You are welcome to return, I call you now.*

"And you think you can beat me with this?" said Pelenot, who appeared immediately.

The script was wrong. The assumptions they had made were false. Pelenot was human no longer. He was outlined in green fire, the size of a lion standing on its hind legs, leaking rage and fury like spittle flung from a rabid dog's jaws. On the whole, they would have preferred the dog to the psychedelic monstrosity in front of them.

"Ah," said Feng. "What have we done?"

"What you have done," said Pelenot, "is complete me. No more fading in and out like a badly tuned radio. I have ascended! When you are dead, I shall raise all these soldiers. We will move at will. We will pillage and destroy."

"What's the point?" asked Karin, bitterly. "What will you achieve?"

"Achieve? Pain for pain's sake, death for death's sake, lust for lust's sake. Don't tell me you've never longed to indulge these most basic of human desires? Humans are so small. They harbour bad thoughts about their neighbour's wife. They wish a bad end on a business rival. But they *do* nothing. The neighbour's wife goes unmolested, the business rival unchecked. You *dream*. I *do*."

Karin fingered the pistol behind her back. She removed the safety catch.

"What happened to you?" said Feng." Did they drop you on your head as a baby or something?"

"I learnt how to draw out suffering in others to extend my own pleasure. That is true living," said Pelenot.

In a flash, in full Emma Peel mode, Karin swung the pistol and fired. They all watched as the bullet penetrated the fire, straight through Pelenot's forehead.

Feng hoped the bullet would create the mystical equivalent of a fireworks display. Karin wished for a Wicked Witch of the West style dissipation. Porter was more of a *punctured tyre* kind of guy. So long as Pelenot went down and stayed down, he didn't care about the theatre of the execution.

They were all disappointed. Pelenot stood defiant, laughing. "Really, relative, is that the best you can do?" He flung an arm out. Karin lifted from the floor, flew backwards five metres, and crashed against a gravestone. They all heard the sickening snap.

The Gliss warned, "Porter, he's coming for you next."

"Porter Norton. Another sad little person trying to right the wrongs of his ancestors." Pelenot plunged his hand into Harry's grave.

"Leave him alone!" shouted Porter. But the ground churned as Pelenot's arm extended deep into the soil. He excavated deep and messily, emerging with a good chunk of Harry's bones and skull in his palm.

"He was nothing then, and nothing now," said the fully-formed Profugus with the Saevita. Pelenot crushed the bones effortlessly and threw the resulting powder and shrapnel at Porter with huge force. "Take Harry. He's all yours now."

Porter stung, blinded and revolted in equal measure, spat dust and bone from his mouth, trying to rub his eyes clean.

"And now for your friend," said Pelenot.

Feng almost peed himself in terror and closed his eyes, awaiting the blow. Nothing happened. The next thing he registered was Porter shouting.

"Not The Gliss! Leave him alone!" Feng spun, opening his eyes wide in shock.

The Gliss' plastic visage was no longer white. It was turning black. Thin red lava-like lines appeared and expanded everywhere across his surface. The Gliss' face stretched grotesquely. His features disappeared, breaking up like the print on a squeezed balloon. The Gliss shattered into a billion pieces, without a word. Feng and Porter watched a cloud of fine dust falling from the air to the ground.

"Look what you've done," shouted Porter.

"He's killed The Gliss," said Feng, gawping. He realised he was probably next, turned and ran.

"Feng, you bastard, come back!" shouted Porter. But the ghost-hunter was already vaulting the wall.

"Ignore him," said Pelenot, coolly. "He's going nowhere. No-one can hide from me now."

"You miserable, pathetic bastard –"

Another outstretched hand. This time, it was Porter who was thrown against a gravestone. He was winded so severely he couldn't breathe. If he could just catch some air –

He felt the first stone smash into his hand. Before he could scream, before he could raise his hand to soothe it, another small stone hit him like a bullet in the arm. He heard Karin's muffled scream as stones and pebbles hit her too.

There was a sickening pop. Porter glanced over. Blood and eyeball fluid trickled down her cheek. The rocks kept coming. Porter saw the scarlet on Karin's face. He instinctively brought his arms up to avoid the same fate. A stone crashed with nerve-destroying force into his exposed elbow. He heard a banshee wail and realised it was coming from him.

Porter had a flash of a YouTube video. A young African girl accused of witchcraft, stoned to death by angry villagers. He'd stumbled on it and watched the whole damn thing in sick fascination, desperate to look away. It had damaged him. He remembered her agonies often, awake and in his nightmares. And now this was to be his end too?

A stone caught him on the hip. He vomited. The junctions of bone and flesh were the worst hits. He knew bones had snapped but had lost count of how many. Karin's wails were almost inhuman beside him. "Please," stammered Porter. "Pl...pl...please don't kill me."

Pelenot laughed. The fusillade stopped. "I thought you wanted to die?"

"No. Please. Not now."

"And now you know how Harry felt when the firing squad fired," said Pelenot. "She's wounded. Go to your friend's aid. Help her, if you can." The voice was almost tender, but beneath it, Porter detected a taunt. With what little energy he had left, he crawled to Karin. She was descending into delirium. Porter put her in the recovery position, on her side. To his horror he found himself undoing her belt. *Wait! What? No!*

"You're so weak. So easy. Go on, do it. Can't you feel her desire for you? Are you so blind? Take it. It's yours." Pelenot continued his sick ranting while Porter, disgusted fought to gain control of his own actions.

"Look at you," sneered Pelenot. "And you think you're better than me."

"Lies! Karin, I'm so sorry," said Porter, caressing her head with one hand.

Karin turned and said, "Porter, *I'm* sorry." With her last ounce of energy, she clattered him in the temple with an orange-sized rock. He fell, poleaxed, the skin splitting across his temple. Karin passed out.

"That was disappointing," said Pelenot. "I shall take you both, in time."

Chapter 48

Aeroplane Cemetery, Ypres
Monday, April 3rd 2017: 8.55pm

"Did you get bullied at school, Pelenot? Or were you always a sad little sadist? Probably started with a pigeon and worked your way up to people. Am I right?"

Pelenot's blazing form turned to face Feng in a fury. "You dare to come back?"

"I don't get it," said Feng. "I never understand it when people want to take over the world. ISIS, the Russians, McDonald's."

"You dare to compare me with humans?"

"Look at you. Sure, you're all green fire and teeth, but you've still got trousers on and a moustache." Feng whipped out his EMF meter.

"You can't kill me with a machine," hissed Pelenot.

"You're a bit behind the times, *old chum*. This only gives me a reading, it measures your energy."

"I am unmeasurable. I am all."

"No, you're actually giving off about the same amount of energy as an electric scooter."

"And now you insult me? Insect." Pelenot went to fling an arm out, but it locked mid-fling. There was a flicker on the EMF.

"Oh, look, you can measure confusion," taunted Feng. "And, what do you know, fear too." His machine tocked a little faster.

Either side of him stood two men in Military Police uniform. One of the tunics was burnt and shredded and its owner, James Wells MP, was burnt and shredded too. The other MP, Thomas Griffiths, was in as pristine condition as the day he died of a heart attack in 1915. They stepped forward, guns outstretched.

"You see, Mr Pelenot, I did a lot of thinking about you before we met. A lot. How many people did you kill? Why did you kill them? How did you kill them?" The Military Police continued to stride towards Pelenot. "When I found out about the Profugus with the Saevita I was told it could only be destroyed the way it killed in life. With a murdering bastard like you, that gave me several options."

Pelenot was fixed to the spot. His eyes were brighter than the sun, powered by hate and fury.

"It's true that you performed the *coup de grace* on both Harry Norton and Max Cartwright with your pistol, but that was incidental to their deaths, wasn't it? They were already dying at your hand when you finished them off. They were dead the second you engineered their court martials."

The MPs stepped forward. The hatred pouring from the eyes of the paralysed Profugus with Saevita was palpable. "And now, *old boy*," Feng spat the last two words out, "it's your turn. Gentlemen, do your duty."

"Capt. Georges Parry Pelenot, by the powers invested in me," said James Wells, "I arrest you for the murder of Privates Maximilian Cartwright and Harold Norton."

The flames of green turned orange and a final look of hatred, fear and disappointment, spread across Pelenot's face. Pinned between the two MPs, Pelenot was unable to move, held in check by the power of the incantation. Even the flames appeared to be slowing to a freeze.

Thomas Griffiths turned back towards Feng. "Thank you, Sir. The buttons, don't forget the buttons, Sir." And they were gone, all three of them, back to wherever justice would be carried out. Feng put the two new buttons in his pocket.

Feng ran over to Karin first. She was in a mess but breathing. For the second time in two days, she was in the recovery position. Porter was bleeding profusely from his temple and not breathing.

Feng tried to remember CPR but found he was wasting time on trying to remember the details rather than doing anything. He put his mouth over Porter's, pinched his nose, and began pumping his chest. A man walking his dog shouted something at him in Flemish."He must think we're cottaging or something in this light," said Feng, before shouting and waving him over. He continued pumping Porter's chest as the man ran over, assessed the situation and called for a blessed ambulance.

Chapter 49

ICU, Jan Yperman Hospital, Ypres
Tuesday, April 4th 2017: 2.36pm

The doctors brought Karin back to consciousness early afternoon the next day. The surgery and antibiotics had saved her from sepsis, but her eye was lost. A bandage covered it for now. The patch, that was to increase her celebrity to international heights, yet to be made.

Namita, Feng and Porter stood at her bedside, a mixture of pity and awkwardness draping them like widow's weeds.

"I've lost it, haven't I?" were Karin's first words. She was too weak to move her arm and check for herself. Porter put his hand over hers and nodded.

"I'm afraid so Karin. I'm so sorry for getting you mixed up in this."

"God, Porter. No need to patronise me. He's my relative."

"*Was* your relative," said Namita, "thanks to Mr Tiān here."

"Yes, he's gone for good it seems," said Porter.

"How? Why? What did you do? He seemed invincible."

"I brought a couple of MPs back to life and had him arrested and sent for court-martial," said Feng. "Simple really."

Karin thought about laughing but wasn't sure all her ribs were back in the right place yet, so stifled the urge. "That's good. I always hated guns. I was wondering how it would affect me, shooting him in the head."

"Your collar bone is broken too," said Porter. "Sorry."

"What about you, Porter?"

"Feng gave me CPR. He probably counts that as a snog. I've got a couple of broken ribs and enough cuts and bruises to start a shop, but I'm ok."

A nurse came into the ward. "Is there a Mr Norton here? You have a phone call on reception?"

"Porter. Hi, it's Tawney Weekes."

"You've got to be kidding. You know what you can do, right?" Porter picked up a biro and stabbed a pad of Post-It notes.

"I was wondering if you'd like to give me a quote about Karin Pelenot and the explosion."

On the other side of the reception desk lay a party hat, some streamers and an air-horn - the remnants of a rowdy birthday party last night. He shouldn't. He mustn't. Of course not. Sod it. Porter gave the journalist a blast of air-horn and then apologised to all the nurses, especially the one who dropped her coffee mug.

Back in the ward, the trio looked up expectantly.

"Did you hear that?" asked Porter. "I gave that bastard from *The Daily Mail* an earful. Literally."

Karin told Porter she had a proposition for him. Would he like to collaborate with her on a book about Harry and the WW1 scandal of Georges Pelenot?

"Change the subject, why don't you. What would *I* do?"

"Co-research and write it of course. It's both our story. It must be told. It'll give you something to do once you get struck off." She smiled.

"Ah, about that," said Namita, revealing that Barry Hammell had tracked down the missing recording of Runyon and Kerry Crane.

"But that's amazing," said Porter. "How did he do that?"

"Trade secret," said Namita.

Karin laughed this time in spite of the pain. "Don't mess with the Tiger. Look at the state of us. Everyone else ok?"

"My arm's going to take a while, Feng's got broken ribs, and Porter is a giant bruise with a thousand cuts and fractures aplenty, but yes, we'll all live."

"It looks like only The Gliss actually died," said Porter. "I'll miss him."

"I thought he got on your nerves?" said Namita, "And he wasn't exactly on hand when you most needed him."

"Shame you were unconscious when he died," said Feng to Namita. "Karin and I got to see and hear him. You got some of Porter's blood too. You'd have been able to see him too apparently."

"I'm rather glad I didn't," she said. "I've had my fill of ghosts and ghouls."

"I'm still not 100% sure he even existed," said Porter. "He was somehow a part of my depression. When I say he died, I think I mean his death symbolises something died within me. The Norton curse is over. In fact, I now know it never even existed, though I guess The Gliss was right that Harry's father Mortimer must have killed himself. He was the first of the four suicides."

"Maybe Mortimer did commit suicide, but the rest of your theory is rubbish, Porter. I definitely saw The Gliss," said Karin. "White and ceramic as a toilet bowl." Her eye was closing, the morphine sending her back to sleep. Before she passed out, they heard her mutter, "The last casualty of the battlefields of World War 1. Typical."

The other three returned to Namita's room and discussed their plans. Porter said, "I need to go to Harry's grave one last time. I want to hear his voice again, but I've got to go back to England. My gran is dying."

Feng said he had to sort out the insurance on his cousin's camper van but would head to Paris with Porter to get the Eurostar home. "Next week, I'm supposed to be going to Scotland to join the Doves looking for one of the UK's many White Lady ghosts. It'll be a bit of a disappointment after all this."

"Don't you have a real job, Feng?" asked Namita.

"I'll let you in on a little secret. I'm quite rich," he replied.

"Good for you. Quendell's are a bit pissed off with me. I had to pretend my sick aunt lives in Belgium. Nathan called me a bull-shitter but couldn't exactly sack me with everyone writing about the explosion, my arm in a sling, and a doctor's note. I've got to go back sooner than later though."

Earlier, Karin had given them all leave to go home. She would be in the hospital for a few weeks at least. Her recuperation would give her some protection from the unwanted publicity her injuries had attracted. There was plenty of it, all unwanted, since Channel 4 had put out a press release confirming their presenter had lost an eye in Belgium. She was front-page news at home and abroad. Porter and Feng agreed to visit Arthur Pelenot and check with his carer that he was ok.

Porter called Cherry and told her he had been injured in the explosion and that he was coming home. "I want to see you, Cherry, but, so help me, none of this sectioning crap. I'm fine. It was a secret, but I've been working with Karin Pelenot on an episode of *History ThisStory* - and a book, can you believe? Hence the secrecy and the acting weird."

"I saw the news. So, you've been mixing with the stars then? I'm sort of impressed."

"She's become a friend actually," said Porter.

"Porter," she said, gently, "you need to go and see Ida. She's near the end. Can you meet me in Gloucester?"

"I'll be back in the UK too late tonight…I could be there by 11am tomorrow?"

"Ok, do that. I'm there already. I'll tell her you're coming."

Gloucestershire Royal Hospital, Gloucester
Wednesday, April 5th 2017: 11.40am

No hugs. No handshakes. No kisses. A nod and hi. And there they sat; brother leaning back, sister slumping forward, both waiting for the other to break the silence.

Cherry caved. "So, you made it. Eventually. You look a right state."

"It's been a long couple of days, Cherry, don't start. How is she?"

"Yes, don't worry yourself, you're in time. They're giving her a bath at the moment."

Awkwardness patrolled their corridor like a Pac-Man. "It's probably best if I go first," said Porter. "I've been working on a book with Karin. I uncovered revelations about our great-grandfathers. Hers murdered ours. Conspiracy stuff. She got involved, so we've been researching it for a while - me mostly here, Karin mostly in Belgium. Luckily, those junkies nicked the ambulance…"

Cherry gave him a look, which was registered and ignored.
"…so, once I was free, I thought, *as I can't trust my sister anymore*, might as well go join Karin in Belgium. Then, by bad luck, we got caught up in the explosion. Karin, the poor devil, lost her eye. Me? You can see for yourself. Cuts and bruises mostly. I came home."

"Are you going to make me say sorry?"

"Yes, I am."

"Sorry."

"That's ok."

"How bad is it?" he said, gesturing to the room.

"She's 99, Porter."

Porter saw Cherry was holding herself back. Change subject. "I've got my hearing next Monday. Namita has found some new evidence, but I could still get struck off. Funnily enough, now that I'm working with Karin on the book, I don't really care."

"Maybe you'll make a better author than solicitor?"

"Thanks for the support."

A nurse emerged from the room. "You can see her now."

They went in together, Porter put his hand on Cherry's shoulder as if to say, *no hard feelings*. Ida was awake but weak. She smiled when she saw them. "God, am I that ill? Both of you?"

"Hi, Mum," said Porter, attracting another look from Cherry.

"Hi, love. Lord - what happened to you?"

Porter ignored the question and sat down, pulling out Harry's diary.

"I've got a story to tell you both. I want you both to know there's no curse on our family. Never was." He put his hand up to silence them.

"No, this is really important. I've been looking into Harry Norton. It was all bollocks. The whole Norton Curse. Utter bollocks. In fact, it's literally the opposite of the truth." Porter's assurance and defiance ensured a quiet audience. "In Belgium, we found some missing pages from Harry's diary. You need to listen to this."

Porter ran through the less traumatic bits of Harry's account. Both women set personal bests for staying silent. "Yes, he did commit a suicide of sorts by sacrificing himself for Private Eaves, but there was no-one braver or more principled in the First World War.

"Sadly, I also discovered that his father, Mortimer, didn't die from an accident. He did kill himself. Couldn't take the bullying." Porter had no direct evidence for this but had to accept it was four suicides if The Gliss was correct about the Quincunx. "Cherry, you must go home and tell Scott about his great, great-grandfather. It's time to turn these lifetimes of negative into at least the one really positive role model."

Cherry nodded. She had nothing to add to Porter's narrative. Tears welled in Ida's eyes. "So, my poor Geraint, my poor Owen. All their actions based on a lie then? How sad."

"Yes, about Geraint," said Porter, stroking her brittle hand. "But I think my Dad just wanted to be with my Mum. I don't think anyone could have helped him."

Ida was emboldened. "It's not much, and my mind isn't what it was, but I remembered something the other day. Maybe it's the kind of story I should've told you two earlier. I'm sorry for my mistakes."

"You were great Ida. Don't fret," said Cherry, glancing at the heart monitor.

"I turned up at your house once. The door was open, so I came straight in. No-one was around. I went upstairs. There you all were - Owen and Lis curled up on the bed asleep - you two wrapped around them, sleeping too. Yes, Owen went mad with grief when Lis died, but half that family I saw on that bed is still alive. You two must always get on."

Shortly after, Porter and Cherry were in the car park, thrown out when visitor hours ended.

"That was strange. I do love you, Porter. You know that?"

"Yes, I know that. I love you too."

Cherry's phone rang. She looked up, shocked. "She's gone, Porter. Oh my God - straight after we left."

Porter didn't want to see Ida's corpse. He had an idea of how he might react to a 10-minute-dead body. If the effect was anything like the trolley-corpse two weeks ago, he might undo all the progress he'd made with Cherry. But his protestations came to nothing - she insisted they go in together.

The staff were already thinking about how quickly they could free up the bed space. Ida was bound for the morgue as soon as the siblings said their goodbyes. Porter's head was pounding. He pushed himself flat against the wall. Cherry did something he'd never seen her do before. Cry.

She gestured for Porter to join her, kneeling on the floor, where she was kissing their surrogate mother's hand. Porter hesitated, but the look from Cherry was enough to make him move.

He joined her and was instantly in the pain and distress of the Quincunx world. More experienced, he fought to focus, to find Ida's loop. He heard nothing. To his shock, he saw her instead, a ghostly vision. She stood to the side of him, a younger version of herself, dressed in 1960s clothes. Why not from the Thirties? What a stupid question to ask. She faced forward, and he was unable to catch her eye. When she spoke, it was in his direction, though their eyes could not meet.

"I know what you are. I'm proud of you. You must do more. Don't give up. You don't belong here yet. And, before I forget, the socks were important." And she disappeared.

He emerged from the fog like a horse dragged through a car wash. He shook himself down, looked at his sister, looked at his mother, and knelt forward. He put his head on Ida's chest.

His headache was gone. No loop. Her death had been a good one.

Chapter 50

St Dyfnog Church, Llangenneth, Swansea.
Wednesday, April 5th 2017: 4.20pm

Porter stood over Max Cartwright's grave. Nothing. Complete silence. He lay down on the ground and listened. Still nothing. He wished The Gliss was here. No-one else made any sense of any of this. But silence. Was Max at peace now? Did he have to do anything else?

Porter wiped himself down and made for the gate. There was a movement behind the gravestone to his left. Shielding his eyes in the glare, Porter smiled and said, "Reverend Gossamer. How are you?"

The shifty vicar stood up from his hiding place, knocking blades of grass from his frock. "Mr Norton. How are you? I was just er...er…"

"Hiding? Don't worry I don't have a migraine today." Still smiling, Porter left the Swansea cemetery, for good.

One last stop and then you can head home. At last.

Wood Green Cemetery, London
Thursday, April 6th 2017: 12.50pm

Porter was more anxious about attending Soraya's funeral. It had been more than two weeks since her death. He watched mourners arrive. It didn't help that he could smell that morning's cremations hanging in the air. Airborne particles of the dead. They clung to him like a wetsuit lined with pepper.

When he stepped through the main gate, he walked over to the Garden of Remembrance where relatives scattered ashes. Did ashes hurt like bones? He was pleasantly surprised. In terms of his headache, it was quiet for a cemetery. As he moved back towards the physical graves, the familiar voices ping-ponged in-and-out of his consciousness. Cremations are definitely less painful than burials.

He slipped into the chapel seconds before Soraya's coffin arrived. As it passed his pew, he remembered her at the computer. Memories. Not a fresh vision. There were about 30 mourners in the chapel. Most were clearly aunts and uncles. There were very few young people.

One of the younger crowd asked him how he'd known Soraya.

"Not well. We worked together once."

"Such a shame eh? They've arrested her old next-door neighbour I hear? Dirty old bastard. Such a shame."

Despite his fears, it was the only interrogation Porter faced. Soraya's brother Darren stood at the lectern and read out the beautiful parts of the email. Porter knew not all of it was fit for a public airing. As difficult as it was for Darren, he persisted in reading it out loud for the benefit of his parents. Porter watched with some satisfaction as the mother and father looked at each other and smiled briefly through their pain.

After the service, Porter approached the coffin with bowed head. Nothing. Soraya was as gone as Max and Ida. What about you, Harry? I'm coming.

Aeroplane Cemetery, Ypres
Friday April 7th 2017: 3.48pm

Still bruised and aching, Porter made the lonely journey back to Aeroplane by Eurotunnel and hire car, vowing to also see Karin later.

He'd been living on codeine for days. He initially blamed that pharmaceutically-induced numbness for the silence coming from Harry's grave. He was pleased to see it tidy again. The groundsmen had no doubt blamed vandals for the mess their fight with Pelenot had created.

Around him, he could hear the other soldiers' voices as usual, but Harry's was gone. Porter lay down on the grave. Nothing. He remembered Pelenot's desecration and walked over to where he had been pelted with Harry's remains days before. Some of that dust must still be lying around. Again, no Harry.

While he was thinking it through, a small movement caught his eye. On the ground, next to the gravestone where Karin had fallen, was a mushroom. And it was growing fast. It swelled, and enlarged way past the size of any mushroom Porter had ever seen. It was more plastic than organic. He smiled. It was The Gliss, reforming itself. Soon it was hovering mid-air, restored.

"Miss me?"

"I did actually. But I've got a bone to pick."

"Go on."

"Something Ida said. *The socks are important.*"

"Ah."

"If you didn't exist, if you didn't have a physical form, ever, how did you set fire to my socks? Don't bother explaining. You'll only waffle on about how I have to be self-sufficient or something. But next time I ask you to make the tea…"

The pair stood over Harry's grave for a while.

"I came back here to hear Harry's voice, but it's gone. Pelenot destroyed the remains."

"Harry's remains are still here. It's his voice that's gone."

"Resting in peace?" asked Porter.

"His story's been told."

Porter knelt, patting down some of the earth still bulging from the re-filled grave. "If no-one else ever says it, Harry, I for one think you were one of the bravest men I ever heard of. I'm proud to be your relative."

He pulled a hair from his head and threaded it through a button he drew from his coat.
"I'm leaving a bit of me with you. I will make sure your story is known." He used his thumb to make a hole before inserting the button.

The Gliss, hovering, said, "I'd call this progress."

Porter looked up. "Maybe just enough to start again."

"You've already started again. You didn't know Feng, Namita, Karin, Bob or Cas three weeks ago. They're all new starting points. It's up to you where you walk after this."

"Have I atoned yet?"

"Not by a long chalk."

"I chalked up four though? Max, Harry, Soraya and Ida?"

"It's not like for like. All your relatives who killed themselves affected hundreds of people."

"Hundreds I've got to save now, is that it?"
"We'll see."

The bright afternoon light skimmed the edges of the white tombstones as Porter and The Gliss walked side-by-side back to the car. The tormented voices of other soldiers ricocheted off Porter. He heard them, but he didn't flinch. He was ready.

Porter and The Gliss will return in 2019 trying to solve the cold case of an actress who went missing in London's Soho district in the Sixties.

To sign up to the mailing list, visit **www.desburkinshaw.com**

If you have enjoyed this book, the most wonderful, helpful thing you could do is to leave a review on Amazon, Goodreads etc. The more people who leave reviews for the book, the more other people will hear about it.

Thank you,
Des Burkinshaw
London, 2019

If you have any questions, I will do my best to answer them on the email below.

info@magnificent.tv

Acknowledgements

This novel took more than a year to research and write. You would be surprised how much of it is based on historical fact. All the characters however, are entirely out of my imagination.

It wouldn't have been possible without the love and support of Shazna and Zizi Burkinshaw. They let me get on with it, encouraged me, listened to endless plot discussions, character developments etc.

But I also have to thank lots of other people for either encouraging me or reading and feeding back on various drafts and cover designs. Writing anything is hard - I know, I've earned a living from it since I was 17 - but writing a debut novel...another level entirely. Without support it would be impossible. So, in no particular order, huge thanks must go to the following:

Debi Alper for being my editor, Sofia Ullah Khatun, Amber Hetherington, Jean Franklin, Tim Burkinshaw, Beck Burkinshaw, Chris Burkinshaw, Mark Powley, Michelle Tuft-Smith, Mark Hagen, Gilly Hewer, Vicky Cepel, Melinda Waugh, Bethan Cole, Jonathan Seibre, Tony Hough and Peter Buckman of the Ampersand Agency for valuable feedback.

Printed in Great Britain
by Amazon

84497766R00205